davidhaynes

Harcourt Brace & Company
Milkweed Editions and
New Rivers Press congratulate **David Haynes**

A GRANTA BEST YOUNG AMERICAN NOVELIST

"David Haynes is blessed with a wonderful sense of humor and a perfect ear for dialogue. As soon as his characters open their mouths, you're hooked."
—Jill McCorkle

LIVE AT FIVE from Milkweed Editions:
"Intelligent, charming, and significant."
—*Booklist*

HEATHENS from New Rivers Press:
"A wonderful, wise book from a talented new writer."
—Ron Rindo, author of *Secrets Men Keep*

SOMEBODY ELSE'S MAMA now in paperback from Harvest Books/Harcourt Brace:
"A major new novel from an extraordinarily talented writer."
—*Black Media News*

HARCOURT
BRACE

GRANTA 54, SUMMER 1996

EDITOR Ian Jack
DEPUTY EDITOR Ursula Doyle
MANAGING EDITOR Claire Wrathall
EDITORIAL ASSISTANT Karen Whitfield

CONTRIBUTING EDITORS Neil Belton, Pete de Bolla, Frances Coady, Will Hobson, Liz Jobey, Blake Morrison, Andrew O'Hagan

Granta, 2–3 Hanover Yard, Noel Road, London N1 8BE
Granta US, 250 West 57th Street, Suite 1316, New York, NY 10107, USA
Telephone: (212) 246 1313 Fax: (212) 586 8003
Website: http://www.granta.com E-mail: subscrip@granta.com

US FINANCIAL COMPTROLLER Margarette Devlin, SPECIAL PROJECTS DIRECTOR Rose Marie Morse, PROMOTIONS MANAGER Jenoa Brown, PROMOTIONS ASSOCIATE Abbi Lewis, ADVERTISING MANAGERS Lara Frohlich, Catherine Tice, LIST MANAGER Diane Seltzer, SUBSCRIPTIONS MANAGER Ken Nilsson, PUBLISHING ASSISTANT Dario Stipisic

US PUBLISHER Matt Freidson

PUBLISHER Rea S. Hederman

SUBSCRIPTION DETAILS: a one-year subscription (four issues) costs $32 in the US; $42 in Canada (includes GST); $39 for Mexico and South America; $50 for the rest of the world.

Granta, USPS 000-508, ISSN 0017-3231, is published quarterly for $32 by Granta USA Ltd, a Delaware corporation. Second class postage paid at New York, NY and additional mailing offices. POSTMASTER: send address changes to Granta, 250 West 57th St., Suite 1316, NY, NY 10107.

Available on microfilm and microfiche through UMI, 300 North Zeeb Road, Ann Arbor, MI 48106-1346, USA. Printed in the United States of America. The paper used in this publication meets the minimum requirements of American National Standard for Information Sciences—Permanence of Paper for Printed Library Materials, ANSI Z39.48-1984. ∞

Granta is published by Granta Publications Ltd and distributed in the United Kingdom and Ireland by Bloomsbury, 2 Soho Square, London W1V 5DE; in the US and Canada by Viking Penguin, a division of Penguin Books USA Inc, 375 Hudson Street, New York, NY 10014, USA; Penguin Books Canada Ltd, 10 Alcorn Avenue, Toronto, Ontario, Canada M4V 3B2; and in the rest of the world by Granta UK.

Cover design by The Senate.
ISBN 0-14-014135-9

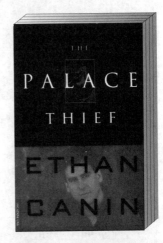

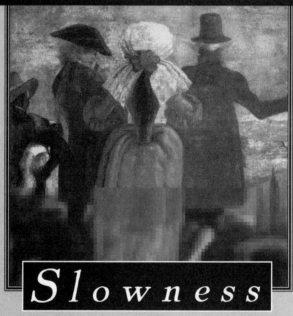

BEST OF YOUNG AMERICAN NOVELISTS

NATIONAL JUDGES

Robert Stone, Anne Tyler, Tobias Wolff, Ian Jack

REGIONAL JUDGES

Richard Bausch, Charles Baxter, Rosellen Brown, Frederick Busch, Stuart Dybek, Maureen Howard, Thom Jones, Beverly Lowry, Leonard Michaels, Howard Frank Mosher, Jayne Anne Phillips, Padgett Powell, Marilynne Robinson, James Welch, Stephen Wright

PROJECT DIRECTOR Rose Marie Morse

From one of Granta's "Best of Young American Novelists."

An unusual romance about a librarian on Cape Cod and the tallest boy in the world, THE GIANT'S HOUSE is a magical first novel from the author of the 1994 ALA Notable collection HERE'S YOUR HAT WHAT'S YOUR HURRY.

"McCracken's attention to the truths of the human heart and her commonsensical literary voice ground even the most fantastic tales in solid quotidian reality...and persuade us that what appears most unlikely is often most illuminating, and frequently most true."

— Francine Prose, *Los Angeles Times*

At Bookstores Now

THE DIAL PRESS

EDITORIAL Ian Jack

One of the important discoveries you make as a judge in a literary competition comes close to the end: the discovery that you may have been spending your time too scrupulously. You have stayed awake in specially chosen uncomfortable chairs to read several dozen novels. You've tried not to skip. You've made notes. None of this can be called hard work. If writing a novel registers 100 on the scale of mental labour and anguish, then reading a novel, even a novel that you may not otherwise have wanted to read, must come in at about .0001. Still, you have taken pains, you have wanted to be fair. You remembered those words of Richard Ford—'Writing even a bad book is hard enough'—and jotted down some thoughts on the theme, the narration, the metaphors that did or didn't work. And then, arguing mildly enough with your fellow judges at the time of judgement, you hear one of them (or perhaps yourself) saying: 'I don't know. Maybe I read it at the wrong time of day. I guess I just didn't like it enough.'

It's worth thinking about this for a moment. Every country in the world with a serious publishing industry has literary prizes. The prizes are important, and in ways other than, say, military medals. Certainly, they reward the valour of the years spent alone with the empty sheets of paper and an immobile cursor on the word processor, the heroism demanded by a twenty-city author tour. But their sheen also reflects the commercial possibilities of the future. Prizes sell books. A prize, or even the citation for a prize, can double, triple, quadruple a publisher's print run. Royalties increase, there may be an author profile in *Vogue*, a man in a fine suit may take the winner to his high office window and say some suitably ironic equivalent of: 'Tonight, my friend, this city belongs to you.' And all this, in every country and with every prize, hangs from a thread: a judge enjoying a book, having read it at the right time of day.

Absurd. Yet I can't think of a better way to do it. Fiction has many purposes and ambitions, but none of them will be brought off unless, in one way or another, the experience of reading it is enjoyable. The word began to be heard a lot in the final judgement of *Granta*'s Best of Young American Novelists campaign. After the arguments about the author's originality, the gap between his or her intention and achievement, Robert Stone or Tobias Wolff would say quietly: 'Well, I enjoyed it a lot,' or 'Yes, I take that point, but it was a very likeable book.' I remember these words partly because of where they were spoken—the library of the Lotos Club in Manhattan underneath a portrait of Andrew Carnegie, a Scotsman born to the Calvinist idea of the novel as a sinful frivolity—and also because it was a shock to hear them. Too many nights spent in an upright chair; fifty-two works of fiction read in a couple of months; it is easy in these circumstances to mislay enjoyment in the pursuit of duty.

Stone, Wolff and *Granta*'s fourth national judge, Anne Tyler, are of course fine American writers of fiction. I am not an American and I have never written a novel (negatives which I like to think have a positive side when it comes to judging young American novelists—they should mean an absence of all the friendships, rivalries and jealousies that get in the way of judicial disinterest). But there we were, Stone, Wolff and I, gathered at the Lotos club on a snowy day last February and discussing our decisions on the phone with Anne Tyler, who was unable to leave her home in Baltimore. The reason for the meeting, if one goes back far enough, was a now-defunct body called the British Book Marketing Council which in 1983 launched the first Best of Young British Novelists campaign, a (then) original stunt whereby the Book Marketing Council appointed judges to choose twenty writers whose new writing was then published in a special issue of *Granta*. It worked well, and the exercise was repeated under *Granta*'s aegis in 1993. Young writers were honoured, books got sold, readers were introduced to writers they might otherwise have ignored. More important, from *Granta*'s point of view, the issues containing their work gave a snapshot of new kinds of writing that were emerging, some from writers who have become Britain's literary establishment. But prescience here is not really the point. We were not, after all, quite so prescient about other names (there is a cruel fascination in the retrospective glance at the lists—whatever became of X, why did Y not prosper?—as there will be some day with this one). What mattered, I believe, was what the selection said about the state of young British fiction at a particular moment: what its most promising practitioners were up to in the business of holding a lamp to our lives, and what they were doing in their next books rather than those already published and noticed (or neglected).

Would the same idea work in the United States? It deserved to, because America is a much bigger country with a much bigger publishing business, and it is both more important and more difficult to know what is going on because so much of it goes on. But these facts about the size and spread of American publishing meant that the old British method couldn't be applied. Under Bill Buford, my predecessor at *Granta*, the submissions and the judging had been informal and private. Publishers were consulted, novels invited, a list was agreed without much fuss. Even if, with ruthlessly corrupt and metropolitan behaviour, this had been possible in America, it didn't seem desirable, so a four-stage process was invented. Stage One: nominations were invited from all kinds of people whose business was books—librarians, booksellers, publishers, agents, authors. The only rule was that the author had to be a US citizen under forty who had published at least one novel or short-story collection by 31 May 1995. Several hundred titles were submitted, which were then divided according to where the author lived into five American regions and sent to the five regional judging panels, each comprising three novelists of distinction (their names are listed on page five). Stage Two: each of the regional judging panels was asked to produce a shortlist. Stage Three: the combined shortlist of fifty-two writers was published, and their books sent to the national judges. Stage Four: we meet and select the twenty finalists.

Around the time of Stage Three in these tiresome (and unBritishly transparent) mechanics, a few unencouraging voices began to be heard in the American press. The campaign was purely a commercial gimmick; it was polluting the literary novel with the cult of celebrity; it was trying to create a new brat pack; it had picked the wrong writers. Quite so, I thought. Every good writer since Dickens—himself well known to go unknown among his readers disguised in a false beard—has cultivated obscurity and the desire to possess no more than a few coins kept in a sock. Celebrity? Tsk tsk, that we pour a little light on to workers struggling in that darkened workshop, the literary novel.

But they were right about the writers. The judges got them wrong, as judges tend to do. Where, for example, was Nicholson Baker? It seemed insane and perverse to me that the judges in his region (the West) had rejected a writer of such striking and wise originality. Robert Stone and Tobias Wolff felt the same, and we wondered for a time if we might not override previous decisions and call in one or two glaring omissions. Like David Foster Wallace, said Stone. Like Richard Powers, said Wolff. But then, how about Donna Tartt? A murmur of agreement. Or William T. Vollmann? Further nods and murmurs. We decided to let the shortlist stay as it was; emendations would need to be wholesale, which would snub the hard work of the fifteen regional judges, turn our exercise into a celebration of the previously celebrated and leave us accused of falling for the hype. In other words, we would have picked another bunch of wrong writers.

All four of us had probably about ten favourites in common. Thereafter it was a question of arguing merits and trading names. All four of us had our disappointments. For myself, I was particularly sorry to lose Chang-rae Lee, Gish Jen and Louis Edwards; heartened to have argued Kaye Gibbons on to the list; disheartened to have another judge successfully argue her off it again.

There were no bad books among the fifty-two, even though there was sometimes unanimity among us in disliking one or two. When I was reading them, I often hoped to come across a book so plainly awful that I could toss it down after three pages and move on to the next. But that happened only once, and after fifty pages rather than three.

What did these books and writers tell us? The most complete and various answer to that is to read the next three hundred pages, but it's tempting to generalize, and I yield to the temptation. As an outsider to the United States, and as someone who has read much more recent English fiction than American, I was struck by the kindness and humanity of most of these authors; their concern to be domestic and geographically specific—regional if you will; their anxiety to write open and spare prose. A lot of new British fiction is altogether wilder and stranger—less interested in clarity, less competent at storytelling. In America, the influence of creative-writing schools and an older generation of writers—Raymond Carver, Richard Ford, Tobias Wolff—is obvious. In most of these books, you know from an early stage who you are among and where—and also *when*, because a new development is a rather English enthusiasm for local history. The when is usually earlier in this century rather than a more distant past, and small-town or rural: a sort of Norman Rockwellization of the novel seems to be going on, though sometimes, in the hands of writers such as David Guterson or Kaye Gibbons, it is beautifully done. Another new development over the past ten years says more about the American present and future. It comes from writers who are not white and often the children of relatively recent migrants—from India, China, Korea and the Caribbean. It may be that there should be more of them in this issue, not out of political rectitude but because they have lived differently and perhaps have more to say.

All this, to me in England, was refreshing. Apart from their other virtues, these writers showed me places and subjects I hadn't seen before. Idaho, North Carolina (frequently), the state of Washington (ditto), on to fishing boats and into orange orchards. In that sense, they had didactic qualities; no bad thing—see what the carefully constructed details of the legal or political professions have done for the popular novel. But the more books I read, the more I began to pick quarrels with them. I longed sometimes to read an embellished sentence. I tired of a couple of categories: the semi-memoir 'coming-of-age narrative' and the family in crisis, 'the family apocalypse'. Where was the satire, the exuberance? Where—perhaps the largest absence—was the novel that took on America full in its political and social face in Wall Street, Washington or South Central LA? Most of our writers seemed in private retreat from that public arena.

Later I wrote to my fellow judges to ask them what they made of our selection and this new generation of novelists, to compare my impressions with theirs. Anne Tyler said that she had found 'lots of energy and vitality and more variety than I had expected'. She was interested to see how often 'a quality of reckless self-wastefulness and/or self-endangerment' was manifested by the characters. She couldn't remember that being so prevalent before. 'And I do love the fact,' she wrote, 'that in so many of these books the American experience is a hyphenated one—Chinese-American, Caribbean-American, etc.'

Stone and Wolff wrote at greater length and had many points in common, but because Stone touched on something which may be the nub of the argument about new American fiction, I shall quote him more fully. In my letter I'd praised the number of 'well-constructed, humane and sympathetic books'—Wolff's phrase was 'well-behaved'—while wondering about the lack of 'deranged ambition'. Stone replied:

> I think the selections reflect a number of things which have taken place in American writing over the past twenty or thirty years. The principal one is probably the resurgence of realism that, during the late sixties, seemed to overcome the postmodernist experiments of writers like John Barth, John Hawkes, Albert Guerard, the Barthelmes etc. This was in large part political.
>
> The resurgent realism was a kind of 'social realism'. It reflected a penitential tone that goes back a very long way in American literature and surfaces periodically, the educated American's alternative to religious revivalism. It also spoke for a vaguely leftist insistence on seriousness, a revulsion for pretentiousness (in the American definition), and that dislike of 'elitism' which often seems so fatuous when viewed from abroad but which burns with a fanatical flame here, embodying much deep, unspoken fear and hatred.
>
> There is an almost obsessive pursuit of 'authenticity', and a *narodnik* romance with land and ordinary people. I grew up in Manhattan, and it never occurred to me that this was a place to write about. 'Authenticity', I was sure, resided just about anywhere else . . . The 'real' America was ever elusive and unavailable yet holy. The young writers of today are suburbanites—simply because the class that produces writers tends to reside in the suburbs. More often than not, they have grown up in the identical suburbs of several different cities. The European-descended writers could be described as post-ethnic and post-regional, in other words beyond the forces that informed much American writing in the past. Aware of this deprivation, they write in pursuit of it.
>
> Much American writing today is self-conscious and defensive, ironic but impelled to conceal its irony. In the right hands this can produce a satisfying subtlety and restraint; it can also be boring. The individual here is notoriously celebrated,

also notoriously suppressed. In a way, some of these modest writers are vastly ambitious. They're looking for Truth, no less, in which they rather believe.

The thing about exuberance, satire and deranged ambition is that they resist consensus. We were after all a committee of many writers, with less of a common literary culture than exists in many countries. Our geography may not allow for the individual hatreds and jealousies that thrive in the literary circles of more homogeneous countries (though we do our best) yet some of us nurture considerable scorn for the literary pretensions of writers who subscribe to different modes than our own. The selections are finally a compromise, and in such a process the 'well-constructed, humane and sympathetic' book has the best shot.

In case anybody is counting by race or gender, the fifty-two shortlisted writers included one Native American, six African-Americans, two Chinese-Americans, one Haitian-American, one Cuban-American, one Jamaican-American, one Korean-American and one Indian-American. There were twenty-five women and twenty-seven men. The final twenty include one Native American, one African-American, one Chinese-American, one Haitian-American. There are seven women to thirteen men. The national judges were three white men and one white woman, unless, of course, you bring into that sum a fifth appointed judge, Henry Louis ('Skip') Gates, Jr, the professor of African-American studies at the University of Harvard. Professor Gates, unfortunately, could not be traced by phone or fax during the judging, and has spoken to no judge since.

I leave the last word to Tobias Wolff, who wrote:

> It seems to me that we could make up another issue of *Granta* entirely of writers who aren't in this one, and lose nothing in quality. The idea of choosing twenty writers to represent a generation makes some sense in your country, but in ours, immense as it is, and teeming with young writers, such a process mainly exposes the biases of the judges, my own included.
>
> Which isn't to say that our list is not a fine one. It is. And on it you will find many writers of eccentric and even visionary gifts . . . We read a great number of good books, and drew attention to some of them, and gave occasion for aficionados to celebrate their own neglected favorites by ridiculing our list. I'm proud of the unsatisfactory, incomplete job we did, and hope that its incompleteness, by stimulating outrage and disbelief, will awaken others to the wonderful range and vitality of the writers now coming into the fullness of their powers. □

GRANTA

SHERMAN ALEXIE
INTEGRATION

Sherman Alexie was born into a Spokane/ Coeur d'Alene Indian family in Spokane, Washington, in 1966. His father held a variety of jobs, including truck driver and logger, for the Spokane tribe; his mother is a social worker. He graduated in American Studies from Washington State University. Since 1992 he has published seven collections of stories and poetry, including *The Lone Ranger and Tonto Fistfight in Heaven* (1993) which was shortlisted for the PEN/Hemingway Award for the Best First Book of Fiction and won the Lila Wallace-*Reader's Digest* Writers' Awards. His first novel, *Reservation Blues*, appeared in 1995. He is married and lives in Seattle.

'Integration' is taken from his second novel, *Indian Killer*, which he is now completing. It will be published by Atlantic Monthly Press.

The sheets are dirty. An Indian Health Service hospital in the early sixties. On this reservation or that reservation. Any reservation, a particular reservation. Antiseptic, cinnamon and danker odors. Anonymous cries up and down the hallways. Linoleum floors swabbed with gray water. Mop smelling like old sex. Walls painted white a decade earlier. Now yellowed and peeling. Old Indian woman in a wheelchair singing traditional songs to herself, tapping a rhythm on her armrest, right index finger tapping, tapping. Pause. Tap, tap. A phone ringing loudly from behind a thin door marked PRIVATE. Twenty beds available, twenty beds occupied. Waiting room where a young Indian man sits on a couch and holds his head in his hands. Nurses' lounge, two doctors' offices and a scorched coffee pot. Old Indian man, his hair bright white and unbraided, pushing his IV bottle down the hallway. He is barefoot and confused, searching for a pair of moccasins he lost when he was twelve years old. Donated newspapers and magazines stacked in bundles, months and years out of date, missing pages. In one of the exam rooms, an Indian family of four, mother, father, son, daughter, all coughing blood quietly into handkerchiefs. The phone still ringing behind the PRIVATE door. A cinder-block building, thick windows that distort the view, pine trees, flagpole. A 1957 Chevy parked haphazardly, back door flung open, engine still running, back seat damp. Empty now.

The Indian woman on the table in the delivery room is very young, just a child herself. She is beautiful, even in the pain of labor, the contractions, the sudden tearing. When John imagines his birth, his mother is sometimes Navajo. Other times she is Lakota. Often she is of the same tribe as the last Indian woman he has seen on television. Her legs tied in stirrups. Loose knots threatening to unravel. The white doctor has his hands inside her. Blood everywhere. The nurses work at mysterious machines. John's mother is tearing her vocal cords with the force of her screams. Years later she still speaks in painful whispers. But during his birth she is so young, barely into her teens, and the sheets are dirty.

The white doctor is twenty-nine years old. He has grown up in Iowa or Illinois, never seeing an Indian in person until he arrives at the reservation. His parents are poor. Having taken a government scholarship to make his way through medical school, he now has to practice medicine on the reservation in exchange for the money. This is the third baby he has delivered here. One white, two Indians. All of the children are beautiful.

John's mother is Navajo or Lakota. She is Apache or Seminole. She is Yakama or Spokane. Her dark skin contrasts sharply with the white sheets, although they are dirty. She pushes when she should be pushing. She stops pushing when they tell her to stop. With clever hands, the doctor turns John's head to the correct position. He is a good doctor.

The doctor has fallen in love with Indians. He thinks them impossibly funny and irreverent. During the hospital staff meetings all of the Indians sit together and whisper behind their hands. There are two white doctors on staff, though only one is on duty at any particular time. There are no Indian doctors, but a few of the nurses and most of the administrative staff are Indian. The doctor often wishes he could sit with the Indians and whisper behind his hand. But he is a good doctor and maintains a personable and professional distance. He misses his parents, who still live in Iowa or Illinois, and often calls them and sends postcards of beautiful, generic landscapes.

The doctor's hands are deep inside John's mother, who is only fourteen and bleeding profusely where they have cut her to make room for John's skull. The sheets were dirty before the blood, but her vagina will heal. She is screaming, of course, because the doctor could not give her painkiller. She had arrived at the hospital too far into labor. The Chevy is still running outside, rear door flung open, back seat damp. The driver is in the waiting room. He holds his head in his hands.

'Are you the father?' a nurse asks the driver.

'No, I'm the driver. She was walking here when I picked her up. She was hitchhiking. I'm just her cousin. I'm just the driver.'

The phone behind the PRIVATE door is still ringing. John's mother pushes one last time, and he slides into the good doctor's hands. Afterbirth. The doctor clears John's mouth. John inhales deeply, exhales, cries. The old Indian woman in the wheelchair stops singing. She hears a baby crying. She stops her tapping to listen. She forgets why she is listening, then returns to her own song and the tapping, tapping. Pause. Tap, tap. The doctor cuts the umbilical cord quickly. A nurse cleans John, washes away the blood, the remains of the placenta, the evidence. His mother is crying.

'I want my baby. Give me my baby. I want to see my baby. Let me hold my baby.'

The doctor moves to comfort John's mother. The nurse swaddles John in blankets, takes him from the delivery room and carries him past the old Indian man who is dragging his IV down the hallway and looking for his long-lost moccasins. John is carried outside. The flag hangs uselessly on its pole. No wind. The smell of pine. Inside the hospital John's mother has fainted. The doctor holds her hand, convinces himself that he loves her. He remembers the family of four coughing blood into handkerchiefs in the exam room. The doctor is afraid of them.

With John in her arms, the nurse stands in the parking lot. She is white or Indian. She watches the horizon. Blue sky, white clouds, bright sun. The slight whine of a helicopter in the distance. Then the violent what-what of the blades as it passes overhead, hovers briefly and lands a hundred feet away. In the waiting room the driver lifts his head from his hands when he hears the helicopter. He wonders if there is a war beginning.

A man in a blue jumpsuit steps from the helicopter. Head ducked and body bent, the man runs toward the nurse. His features are hidden behind the face shield of his helmet. The nurse meets him halfway and hands John over. The jumpsuit man covers John's face completely, protecting him from the dust that the helicopter has kicked up. The sky is very blue. Specific birds hurl away from the flying machine. These birds are indigenous to that reservation, wherever it is. They do not live anywhere else. They have purple-tipped wings and tremendous eyes, or red bellies and small eyes. The nurse waves goodbye as the jumpsuit man runs back to the helicopter. She shuts the rear door of the Chevy, reaches through the driver's open window and turns the ignition key. The engine shudders to a stop. She pauses briefly at the door before she walks back inside the hospital.

The jumpsuit man holds John close to his chest as the helicopter rises. Suddenly, as John imagines it, this is a war. The gunman locks and loads, strafes the reservation with explosive shells. Indians hit the ground, drive their cars off roads, dive under flimsy kitchen tables. A few Indians, two women and one man, continue their slow walk down the reservation road, unperturbed by the gunfire. They have been through much worse. The what-what of the helicopter blades. John is hungry and cries uselessly. He cannot be heard over the roar of the gun, the chopper. He cries anyway. This is all he knows to do. Back at the clinic his mother has been sedated. She sleeps in the delivery room while the doctor holds her hand. The doctor finds he cannot move. He looks down at his hand wrapped around her hand. White fingers, brown fingers. He wonders at their difference. The phone behind the PRIVATE door stops ringing. Gunfire in the distance.

The helicopter flies for hours, it could be days, crosses desert, mountain, freeway. Flies over the city. Seattle. The skyscrapers, the Space Needle, water everywhere. Thin bridges running between islands. John is still crying. The gunner does not fire, but his finger is lightly touching the trigger. He is ready for the worst. John can feel the distance between the helicopter and the ground below. He stops crying. He loves the distance between the helicopter and the ground. He feels he may fall but he somehow loves that fear of falling. He wants to fall. He wants the jumpsuit man to release him and let him fall from the helicopter, down through the clouds, past the skyscrapers and the Space Needle. But the jumpsuit man holds him tightly, and John does not fall. He wonders if he will ever fall.

The helicopter circles downtown Seattle, moves east past Lake Washington and Mercer Island and hovers over Bellevue. The pilot searches for the landing area. Five acres of green, green grass. A large house. Swimming pool. A man and woman waving. Home. The pilot lowers the chopper and sets down gracefully. Blades making a storm of grass particles and hard-shelled insects. The gunner's eyes are wide open, scanning the tree line. He is ready for anything. The jumpsuit man slides the door open with one arm and holds John in the other. Noise, heat. John cries again, louder than before, wanting to be heard. Home. The jumpsuit man steps down and runs across the lawn. The man and woman are still waving. They are white and handsome. He wears a gray suit and colorful tie. She wears a red dress with large black buttons.

John is crying when the jumpsuit man hands him to the white

woman, Olivia Smith. The white man in the gray suit, Daniel Smith, grimaces briefly then smiles. Olivia Smith pulls her shirt and bra down. She has large, pale breasts with pink nipples. John's birth mother has small, brown breasts and brown nipples. John knows there is a difference. He takes the white woman's right nipple in his mouth. He pulls at her breast. It is empty. Daniel Smith wraps his left arm around his wife's shoulders. He grimaces and smiles again. Olivia and Daniel Smith look at the jumpsuit man, who is holding a camera. Flash, flash. Click of the shutter. Whirr of advancing film. All of them wait for the photograph to form, for light to emerge from shadow.

John attended St Francis Catholic School from the very beginning. His shoes always black topsiders polished clean. His black hair very short, nearly a crew-cut, just like every other boy in school. He was the only Indian in the school but he had friends, handsome white boys who were headed off to college. John would never speak to any of them after graduation, besides the one or two he came across in a supermarket, movie theater, restaurant.

'John, buddy,' the white boys always said. 'How you doing? God, what has it been? Five, six years? It's good to see you.'

John could step outside himself during those encounters. At first he listened to himself say the right things, respond in the right way. 'I'm good. Working hard? Nah. Hardly working!' He laughed appropriately. Promised to keep in touch. Shared a nostalgic moment. Commented on the eternal beauty of the Catholic girls from way back when. Occasionally he could not stand to see his friends from high school, and more and more their voices and faces were painful to him. He began to ignore their greetings, act like he had never seen them before and walk past them.

John had danced with a few white girls in high school. Mary, Margaret, Stephanie. He had fumbled with their underwear in the back seats of cars. John knew their smell, a combination of perfume, baby powder, sweat and sex. A clean smell on one level, a darker odor beneath. Their breasts were small and perfect. John was always uncomfortable during his time with the girls and he was never sorry when it was over. He was impatient with them, unsure of their motives and vaguely insulting. The girls expected it. It was high school, and boys were supposed to act that way. Inside, John knew that he was simple, shallow and less than real.

'What are you thinking?' the girls always asked John. But John knew the girls really wanted to tell John what *they* were thinking. John's thoughts were merely starting points for a longer conversation. His thoughts were no longer important when the girls launched into monologues about their daily activities. They talked about mothers and fathers, girlfriends, ex-boyfriends, pets, clothes and a thousand other details. John felt insignificant at those times and retreated into a small place inside of himself until the girls confused his painful silence with rapt interest.

The girls' fathers were always uncomfortable when they first met John and grew more irritated as he continued to date Mary, Margaret or Stephanie. The relationships began and ended quickly. A dance or two, a movie, a hamburger, a few hours in a friend's basement with generic rock music playing softly on the radio, cold fingers on warm skin.

'I just don't think it's working out,' she would say to John, who understood.

He could almost hear the conversations that had taken place.

'Hon,' a father would say to his daughter. 'What was that boy's name?'

'Which boy, Daddy?'

'That dark one.'

'Oh, you mean John. Isn't he cute?'

'Yes, he seems like a very nice young man. You say he's at St Francis? Is he a scholarship student?'

'I don't know. I don't think so. Does it matter?'

'Well, no. I'm just curious, hon. By the way, what is he? I mean, where does he come from?'

'He's Indian, Daddy.'

'From India? He's a foreigner?'

'No, Daddy, he's Indian from here. You know, American Indian. Like bows and arrows and stuff. Except he's not like that. His parents are white.'

'I don't understand.'

'Daddy, he's adopted.'

'Oh. Are you going to see him again?'

'I hope so. Why?'

'Well, you know. I just think. Well, adopted kids have so many problems adjusting to things, you know. I've read about it. They have self-esteem problems. I just think, I mean, don't you think you should find somebody more appropriate?'

The door would click shut audibly. Mary, Margaret or Stephanie would come to school the next day and give John the news. The daughters would never mention their fathers. There were a few white girls who dated John precisely because they wanted to bring home a dark boy to their uptight parents. Through all of it John had repeatedly promised himself that he would never be angry. He didn't want to be angry. He wanted to be a real person. He wanted to control his emotions so he often had to swallow his anger. Once or twice a day he felt the need to run and hide. In the middle of a math class or a history exam he would get a bathroom pass and quickly leave the classroom. His teachers were always willing to give him a little slack. They knew he was adopted, an Indian orphan, and was leading a difficult life.

His teachers gave him every opportunity, and he responded well. If John happened to be a little frail, well, that was perfectly understandable, considering his people's history. All that alcoholism and poverty, the lack of God in their lives. In the bathroom John would lock himself inside a stall and fight against his anger. He'd bite his tongue, his lips, until sometimes they would bleed. His arms, legs and lower back tensed. His eyes closed tightly. He was grinding his teeth. One minute, two, five, and he would be fine. He could flush the toilet to make his visit seem normal, then slowly wash his hands and return to the classroom. His struggles with his anger increased in intensity and frequency until he was requesting a bathroom pass on a daily basis during his senior year. But nobody noticed. In truth, nobody mentioned any strange behavior they may have witnessed. John was a trailblazer, a nice trophy for St Francis, a successfully integrated Indian boy. □

GRANTA

MADISON SMARTT BELL
LOOKING FOR THE GENERAL

Madison Smartt Bell was born in 1957 in Tennessee and raised there. His father was a lawyer and later a judge; his mother worked a farm and ran a riding school. He graduated from Princeton University and Hollins College and published his first novel, *The Washington Square Ensemble*, when he was twenty-five. He has since published seven novels and two collections of stories and contributed fiction and reviews to many anthologies, newspapers and magazines, including *Harper's* and the *New York Times*. Since 1984 he has taught at Goucher College in Maryland, where he and his wife, the poet Elizabeth Spires, are currently writers-in-residence. They live in Baltimore with their daughter.

'Looking for the General' is taken from the second novel in a planned trilogy about the Haitian slave revolution of 1791. The first book in the sequence, *All Souls' Rising*, published by Pantheon in the United States and Granta Books in the UK, was a finalist for the 1995 National Book and PEN/Faulkner awards.

Midday, and the sun thrummed from the height of its arc so that the lizard seemed to cast no shadow. Rather the shadow lay directly beneath it, squarely between its four crooked legs. The lizard was a speckled brown across its back, but the new tail it was growing from the stump of the old was darker, a steely blue. It moved at a right angle and turned its head to the left and froze, the movement itself as quick and undetectable as a water-spider's translation of place. A loose fold of skin at its throat inflated and relaxed. It turned to the left and skittered a few inches forward and came to that same frozen stop. When it turned its head away to the right, the man's left hand shot out like a whiplash and seized the lizard fully around the body. With almost the same movement he was stroking the lizard's underbelly down the length of the broad-bladed cutlass he held in his other hand.

The knife was eighteen inches long, blue-black, with a flat spoon-shaped turning at the tip; its filed edge was brighter, steely, but stained now with lizard blood. The man hooked out the entrails with his thumb and sucked moisture from the lizard's body cavity. He cracked the ribs apart from the spine to open it further and splayed the lizard on a rock to dry. Then he cautiously licked the edge of his knife and sat back and laid the blade across his folded knees.

At his back was the trunk of a small, twisted tree, which bore instead of leaves large club-shaped cactile forms bristling with spines. The man contracted himself within the meager ellipse of shade the tree threw on the dry ground. Sweat ran down his cheeks and pooled in his collarbones and overflowed on to his chest, and his shrunken belly lifted slightly with his breathing, and from time to time he blinked an eye, but he was more still than the lizard had been; he had proved that. After a time he looped his left hand around the lizard's dead legs and picked up the knife in his other hand and began to walk again.

The man was barefoot and wore no clothes except for a strip of grubby cloth bound around his loins; he had no hat and carried nothing but the cane knife and the lizard. His hair was close-cut and shaved in diamond patterns with a razor, and his skin was a deep sweat-glossy black, except for the scar lines which were stony pale. There were straight parallel slash marks on his right shoulder and the right side of his neck and his right jawbone and cheek, and the lobe of his right ear had been cut clean away. On his right forearm and the back of his hand was a series of similar parallel scars that would have matched those on his neck and shoulder if, perhaps, he had raised his hand to wipe sweat from his face, but he did not raise his hand. Along his ribcage and penetrating the muscle of his back the scars were ragged and anarchic. These wounds had healed in greyish lumps of flesh that interrupted the flow of his musculature like snags in the current of a stream.

He was walking north. The knife, swinging lightly with his step, reached a little past the joint of his knee. The country was in low rolling mounds like billows of the sea, dry earth studded with jagged chunks of stone. There were spiny trees like the one where he'd sheltered at midday, but nothing else grew there. He walked along a road of sorts, or track, marked with the ruts of wagon wheels molded in dry mud, sometimes the fossilized prints of mules or oxen. Occasionally the road was scored across by shallow gullies, from flooding during the time of the rains. West of the road the land became more flat, long dry savannah reaching toward a dull haze over the distant sea. In the late afternoon the mountains to the east turned blue with rain, but they were very far away, and it would not rain here where the man was walking.

At evening he came to the bank of a small river, its water brown with mud. He stood and looked at the flow, his throat pulsing. After a certain time he crept cautiously down the bank and lowered his lips to the water to drink. At the height of the bank above the river he sat down and began eating the lizard from the inside out, breaking the frail bones with his teeth and spitting pieces on the ground. He gnawed the half-desiccated flesh from the skin, then chewed the skin itself. What remained in the end was a compact masticated pellet no larger than his thumb; he spat this over the bank into the river.

Dark had come down quickly while he ate. There was no moon, but the sky was clear, stars needle-bright. He scooped out a hollow for his shoulder with the knife point and then another for his hip and lay down on his side and quickly slept. In his dream, long, voracious shadows lunged and thrust into his side, turning and striking him again. He woke with his fingers scrabbling frantically in the dirt, but presently slept once more. Another time he dreamed that someone came and was standing over him, some weapon concealed behind his back. He stirred, and his lips sucked in and out, but he could not fully wake at first; when he did wake he shut his hand around the wooden handle of the knife and held it close for comfort. There was no one near, no one at all, but he lay with his eyes open and never knew he'd slept again until he woke, near dawn.

As daylight gathered, he fidgeted along the riverbank, walking a hundred yards east of the road, then west, trying the water with a foot and then retreating. There was no bridge, and he was ignorant of the ford, but the road began again across the river, beyond the broad flow of brown water. At last he began his crossing there, holding both arms high, the knife well clear of the stream, crooked above his head. His chest tightened as the water rose across his belly; when it reached his clavicle, the current took him off his feet, and he floundered, gasping, to the other bank. He could swim, a little, but it was awkward with the knife to carry in one hand. When he reached the shore he climbed high on the bank and rested and then went down cautiously to scoop up water in his hands to drink. Then he continued on the road.

By midday he could see from the road some buildings of the town of Saint Marc, though it was still miles ahead, and he saw ships riding their moorings in the harbor. He would not come nearer the town because of the white men there, the French. He left the road and went a long skirting way into the plain, looping toward the eastward mountains, over the same low mounds and trees as yesterday. The edge of his knife had dimmed from its wetting, and he found a lump of smoothish stone and honed it till it shone again. Far from the road he saw some goats and one starveling long-horned cow but he knew it was hopeless to catch them so he did not try. There was no water in this place.

When he thought he must have passed Saint Marc he bent his way toward the coast again. Presently he regained the road by walking along a mud dike through some rice paddies. People had returned to the old indigo works in this country and were planting rice in small *carrés*; some squares were ripe for harvest and some were green with new shoots and some were being burned for a fresh planting. When he reached the road itself, there were women spreading rice to dry and winnowing it on that hard surface. It was evening now, and the women were cooking. One of them brought him water in a gourd, and another offered him food; he stayed to eat rice cooked in a stew with small brown peas, with the women and children and the men coming in from the paddies. Some naked children were splashing in a shallow ditch beside the road, and beyond was the rice paddy *lakou,* mudwattled cabins raised an inch or two above the damp on mud foundations.

He might have stayed the night with them but he disliked those windowless mud houses, whose closeness reminded him of barracoons. Also, white men were not so far away. The French had said that slavery was finished, but the man had come to distrust all sayings of white people. He saw no whites or slavemasters now among these people of the rice paddies, but all the same he thanked them and took leave and went on walking into the twilight.

He was as always alone on the road as it grew dark. The stars appeared again, and the road shone whitely before him to help light his way. Presently he came away from the rice country, and now on either side of the road the land was hoed into small squares for planting peas, but no one worked those fields at night, and he saw no houses near, nor any man-made light.

In these lowlands the dark did little to abate the heat, and he kept sweating as he walked; the velvet darkness closed around him viscous as sea water, and the stars lowered around his head to glimmer like the phosphorescence he had seen when he was drowning in the sea. He seemed to feel his side was rent by multiple rows of bright white teeth, and he began running down the road, shouting hoarsely and flailing his knife. Also he was afraid of *loup-garous* or *zombis* or other wicked spirits which *bokors* might have loosed into the night.

In the morning he woke by the roadside with no memory of ever having stopped. The sun had beaten down on him for half the morning, and his tongue was swollen in his head. There was no water. He raised himself and began to walk again.

Now it was bad country either side of him, true desert full of lunatic cacti growing higher than his head. The mountain range away to the east was no nearer than it ever had been. He passed a little donkey standing by the road, its hairy head a tangle of nopal burrs it must have been trying to eat. He would have helped the donkey if he could but when he approached, it found the strength to shy away from him, braying sadly as it cantered from the road. The man walked on. Soon he saw standing water in the flats among the cacti, but when he stooped to taste it, the water was too salt to drink. Presently he began to pass the skulls of cows and other donkeys that had died in this desert place. Somehow he kept on walking. Now there were new mountains ahead of him but for a long time they seemed to come no nearer.

Toward the end of the afternoon he reached a crossroads and stopped there, not knowing how to turn. One fork of the road seemed to bend toward the coast, and the other went ahead into the mountains. *Attibon Legba*, he said in his mind, *vini moin* . . . But for some time the crossroads god did not appear, and the man kept standing on the *kalfou*, fearing to sit lest his strength fail him to rise again.

After a time there was dust on the desert trail behind him, and then a donkey coming at a trot. When it came near he saw it bore a woman, old but still slender and lithe. She rode sideways on the wooden saddle, her forward knee hooked around the wooden triangle in front. The *burro* was so small her other heel almost dragged the ground, as did the long slack straw *macoutes* that were hung to either side of the saddle. She wore a brown calico dress and a hat woven of palm fronds, all brim and no crown.

She stopped her donkey when she reached the *kalfou*. The man asked her a question, and she pointed with the foot-long stick she held in her right hand and told him that the left fork of the road led to the town of Gonaives. She aimed the stick along the right-hand fork and said that in the mountains that way there were soldiers—black soldiers, she told him then, without his having asked the question.

She was toothless, and her mouth had shrunk over the gums, but still he understood her well enough. Her eyes combed over the scars on his neck and shoulder with a look of comprehension, but at the old wounds on his side her look arrested, and she pointed with the stick.

'*Requin*,' the man said.

'*Requin*?' the woman repeated, and then she laughed. '*B'en ouais, requin . . .* ' She laughed some more and waved her stick at the dry expanses all around them. The man smiled back at her, saying nothing. She flicked the donkey's withers with her stick, and they went trotting on the road to Gonaives.

Too late he thought of asking her for water . . . but then those straw panniers had looked slack and empty. Still, he continued walking with fresh heart. These were dry hills he was now entering, mostly treeless, with shelves of bare rock jutting through the meager earth. The road narrowed, reducing to a trail winding ever higher among the pleats of the dry mountains. At evening clouds converged from two directions, and there was a thunderous cloudburst. The man found a place beneath a stone escarpment and filled his mouth and belly with clean run-off from the ledges and let the fresh rainwater wash him down entirely.

The rain continued for less than an hour, and when it was finished the man walked on. Above and below the trail the earth on the slopes was torn by the rain as if by claws. By nightfall he had reached the height of the dry mountains and could look across to greener hills in the next range. In the valley between, a river went winding, and on its shore was a little village—prosperous, for land was fertile by the riverside. After the darkness was complete, he could see fires down by the village and presently he heard drums and voices too, but the trail was too uncertain for him to make his way there in the dark, even if he had wished to. It was cool at last, high in those hills, and he had drunk sufficiently. He scooped holes for his hip and shoulder as before and lay above the trail and slept.

Next morning there was cockcrow all up and down the mountains, and he got up and walked with his mouth watering. The stream he'd seen the night before proved no worse than waist-deep over the wide gravel shoal where he chose to cross. Upstream some women of the village were washing clothes among the reeds. When he had crossed the stream he turned back and stooped and drank from it deeply and then began climbing the green hills with water gurgling in his stomach.

In a little time zig-zag plantings of corn appeared in rough-cut terraces rising toward the greener peaks. He broke from the trail and picked two ears of corn and went on his way pulling off the shucks and gnawing the half-ripened kernels, sucking their pale milk. After he had thrown away the cobs, his stomach began to cramp. He hunched over slightly and kept on walking, pushing up and through the pain till it had ceased. Now there was real jungle above and below the trail, and plantings of banana trees, and mango trees with fruit not ripe enough to eat.

When he had crossed the backbone of this range, he began to see regular rows of coffee trees, the bean pods reddening for harvest. And not much further on were many women gathered by the trail's side, with goods arrayed for a sort of market: ripe mangos and bananas and soursops and green oranges and grapefruit. A woman held a stack of folded flat cassava bread, and another was roasting ears of corn over a small brazier. Also a few men were there, some in soldiers' uniforms of the Spanish army, though all of them were black.

The man crouched over his heels and waited, the knife on the ground near his right hand. The soldiers made their trades and left. They alone seemed to deal in money—among the others all was barter—but the man had nothing to exchange except his knife, and that he would not give up. Still, a woman came and gave him a ripe banana, its brown-flecked skin plump to bursting, and another gave him a cassava bread without asking anything in return. Squatting over his heels he ate the whole banana and perhaps a quarter of the bread, eating slowly that his stomach might not cramp. When he had rested he stood up and followed the way the soldiers had taken, carrying his knife in one hand and the remains of the bread in the other.

The opening of the trail the soldiers used was hidden by an overhang of leaves, but past this it widened and showed signs of constant use. The man crossed over a ridge of the mountain and looked down on terraces planted with more coffee trees. In the valley below was a sizeable plantation with *carrés* of sugar cane and the *grand'case* standing at the center as it would have done in the days of slavery not long since, but all round the big house and the cane fields was encamped an army of black soldiers.

He was not halfway down the hill before he tumbled over sentries posted there. They trained their guns on him at once and took away his knife and the remainder of his bread. They asked his business but did not give him time to answer. They made him put his hands up on his head and chivvied him down the terraces of coffee, prodding him with the points of their bayonets.

In the midst of the encampment some of the black soldiers glanced up to notice his arrival, but most went about their business as if unaware. The sentries urged him into the yard below the gallery of the *grand'case*. A white man in the uniform of a Spanish officer was passing, and the sentries hailed him and saluted. The white man stopped and asked the other why he had come there.

Toussaint, the man said. Toussaint Louverture.

The white officer stared a moment and then turned and sharply saluted a black man, also in Spanish uniform, who was then approaching. The black officer turned and asked the man the same question once more, and the man drew himself up and began to speak. The words did not originally belong to him, but he had repeated them silently in his mind, so many times since he first heard them in his travels. After a while they had begun to repeat themselves.

Brothers and Friends, I am Toussaint Louverture. My name is perhaps not unknown to you—

The black officer cut him off with a slashing movement of his hand, and the man stared back at him, wondering if this could be the person he had sought (as the white officer had seemed to respect him so). But then a silence fell over the camp, like the quiet when birdsong ceases. A large dark stallion walked into the yard, and a black man in general's uniform pulled the horse up and dismounted. His face was no higher than the horse's shoulder when he stood on the ground, and his uniform was thoroughly coated with dust from wherever he'd been traveling.

The two junior officers saluted again, and the black one drew near and spoke softly into the ear of the general. The general nodded and beckoned to the man who had walked into the camp from the mountains, and then the general turned and started toward the *grand'case*. His legs were short and a little bowed, perhaps from constant riding. As he began to mount the *grand'case* steps, he reached across his hip and hitched up the hilt of his long sword so that the scabbard would not knock against the steps as he was climbing. A sentry nudged the man with a bayonet, and he moved forward and went after the black general.

On the open gallery the black general took a seat in a fanbacked rattan armchair and motioned the man to a stool nearby. When the man had sat down, the general asked him to say again those words he had begun before. The man swallowed once and began:

Brothers and Friends, I am Toussaint Louverture. My name is perhaps not unknown to you. I have undertaken to avenge you. I want liberty and equality to reign throughout Saint Domingue. I am working towards that end. Come and join me, brothers, and fight by our side for the same cause.

The general took off his high-plumed hat and placed it on the floor. Beneath it he wore a yellow madras cloth over his head, tied on the back above his short grey pigtail. The cloth was a little sweat-stained at his brows. His lower jaw was long and underslung, with crooked teeth; his forehead was high and smooth, his eyes calm and attentive.

So, he told the man, so you can read.

No, the man replied. It was read to me.

You learned it, then.

Pa'coeur. He placed his hand above his heart.

Toussaint covered his mouth with his hand, as if he hid a smile, a laugh. After a moment he took the hand away.

From the beginning then. Tell me your name.

The white men called me Tarquin, but the slaves called me Guiaou.

Guiaou, then. Why did you come here?

To fight for freedom. With black soldiers. And for vengeance. I came to fight.

You have fought before?

Yes, Guiaou said. In the west. At Croix des Bouquets and in other places.

Tell me, Toussaint said.

Guiaou told that when news came of the slave rising on the

northern plain he had run away from his plantation in the western department of the colony and gone looking for a way to join in the fighting. Other slaves were leaving their plantations in that country, but not so many yet. Then *les gens de couleur* were all gathering at Croix des Bouquets to make an army against the white men. And the *grand blancs* came and made a compact with *les gens de couleur* because they were at war with the *petit blancs* at Port au Prince.

Hanus de Jumecourt, Toussaint said.

Yes, said Guiaou. It was that *grand blanc*.

There were three hundred of them then, Guiaou told, three hundred slaves escaped from surrounding plantations. *Les gens de couleur* made them into a separate division of their army at Croix des Bouquets. They called them the Swiss, Guiaou said.

The Swiss? Toussaint hid his mouth behind his hand.

It was from the King in France, Guiaou said. They told us that was the name of the King's own guard.

And your leader? Toussaint said.

A mulatto. André Rigaud.

Toussaint called over his shoulder into the house, and a short, bald white man with a pointed beard came out, carrying a pen and some paper. The white man sat down in a chair beside them.

Tell me of Rigaud, Toussaint said.

Rigaud, Guiaou said, was the son of a white planter and a pure black woman of Guinée. He was a handsome man of middle height, and proud with the pride of a white man. He always wore a wig of smooth white man's hair, because his own hair was crinkly, from his mother. It was said that he had been in France where he had joined the French Army; it was said that he had fought in the American Revolutionary War, among the French. Rigaud was fond of pleasure and he had the short and sudden temper of a white man, but he was good at planning fights and often won them.

The balding white man scratched across the paper with his pen, while Toussaint stroked his fingers down the length of his jaw and watched Guiaou.

And the fighting, Toussaint said.

There was one fight, Guiaou told. The *petit blancs* attacked us at Croix des Bouquets and, fighting with *les gens de couleur* and the *grand blancs*, we whipped them there. After this fight the two kinds of white men made a peace with each other and with *les gens de couleur,* and they signed the peace on a paper they wrote. Also there were prayers to white men's gods.

And the black people, Toussaint said. The Swiss?

They would not send the Swiss back to their plantations, Guiaou told. The *grand blancs* and mulattos feared the Swiss had learned too much of fighting, that they would make a rising among the other slaves. It was told that the Swiss would be taken out of the country and sent to live in Mexico or Honduras or some other place they had never known. After one day's sailing they were put off on to an empty beach, but when men came there they were English white men.

This was Jamaica, where the Swiss were left. The English of Jamaica were unhappy to see them there, so the Swiss were taken to a prison. Then they were loaded on to another ship to be returned to Saint Domingue. On this second ship they were put in chains and closed up in the hold like slaves again. When the ship reached the French harbor they were not taken off.

Guiaou told how his chains were not well set. During the night he worked free of them, tearing his heels and palms, and then lay quietly, letting no one know that he had freed himself. In the night white men came down through the hatches and began killing the chained men in the hold with knives.

Guiaou showed the old scars matted on his neck. After several blows, he told, he had twisted the knife from the hand of the white man who was cutting him and stabbed him once in the belly and then he had run for the ladders, feet slipping in blood that covered the floor of the hold like the floor of a slaughterhouse. But when he came on deck, the white men began shooting at him so he could only go over the side—Guiaou stopped speaking. His Adam's apple pumped, and he began to sweat.

It's enough, Toussaint said, looking at the tangled scars around Guiaou's ribcage. I understand you.

Guiaou swallowed then, and went on speaking. In the dark water, he said then, the dead or half-dead men were all sinking in their chains, and sharks fed on them while they sank. The sharks attacked Guiaou as well, but he still had the cane knife he had snatched and, though badly bitten, he fended off the sharks and clambered out of that whirlpool of fins and blood and teeth on to one of the little boats the killers had used to come to the ship. He cut the mooring and let the boat go drifting, lying on the floor and feeling his blood run out to mix with the pools of brine in the bilges. When the boat drifted to shore, he climbed into the jungle and hid there until his wounds were healed.

How long since then? Toussaint said.

I didn't count the time, said Guiaou. I was walking all up and down the country until I came to you.

Toussaint looked at the bearded white man, who had some time since stopped writing, and then he called down into the yard. A barefoot black soldier came trotting up the steps on to the gallery.

Take care of him. Toussaint looked at Guiaou.

Coutelas moin, Guiaou said.

And give him back his knife. Toussaint hid his mouth behind his hand.

Guiaou followed the black soldier to a tent on the edge of the cane fields. Here he was given a pair of worn military trousers mended with a waxy thread, and a cartridge box and belt. Another black soldier came and gave him back the cane knife and also returned his piece of cassava, which had not been touched.

Guiaou put on the trousers and rolled the cuffs above his ankles. He put on the belt and box and thrust the blade of his cane knife through the belt to sling it there. The first black soldier handed him a musket from the tent. The gun was old but had been well cared for. There was no trace of rust on the bayonet or the barrel. Guiaou touched the bayonet's edge and point with his thumb. He raised the musket to his shoulder and looked along the barrel and then lowered it and checked the firing pan. He pulled back the hammer to see the spring was tight and lowered it gently with his thumb so that it made no sound.

The other two black soldiers were almost expressionless, yet they seemed to have relaxed a little, seeing Guiaou so familiar with his weapon. Guiaou lowered the musket butt to the ground and looped his fingers loosely around the barrel. He stood, not precisely at attention, but in a state of readiness. □

GRANTA

ETHAN CANIN
ORNO AND MARSHALL

Ethan Canin was born in 1960 in Ann Arbor, Michigan, the son of a professional violinist and an art teacher. He studied English at Stanford and holds a Master's of Fine Arts in creative writing from the University of Iowa and an MD from Harvard Medical School. He published a collection of stories, *The Emperor of Air*, in 1988, followed by a novel, *Blue River* (1991) and four novellas under the title *The Palace Thief* (1994). He is married to a high-school English teacher and lives in San Francisco. When not writing, he works as a doctor.

'Orno and Marshall' is taken from his second novel which he hopes to finish soon.

Orno Pboson met Marshall Gurn on his first afternoon at college, a crystalline September day in New York in 1974, washed by recent rain that sparkled on the car roofs and stone stairwells around Columbia University much the same way it had on the fields of newly harvested wheat, flattened by the reaper, outside of Cook's Grange, Kansas, which Orno had left two days before. He was the first in his family to come east for an education, and his mother and father had made the drive with him and then stayed on a couple of blocks from the university at a hotel with dark, small rooms that were more expensive than they should have been, his father said, simply because stone griffins sat on the front steps. His parents were waiting for him to come downstairs from the dormitory and take a drive downtown with them when Orno ran into Marshall, who was carrying a stereo speaker the size of a door from the stairwell into his room. The speaker was flat, no more than two inches thick and almost as tall as Orno, but when Marshall saw him watching he bent down and heaved it in the air to him.

'My God, what is this thing?' said Orno when he caught it.

'A Tannoy.'

Orno was gleeful. He hoisted the queerly light speaker over his head. 'I thought you must have been on the football team.'

'Not I, my friend,' said Marshall.

'Not I, either, I guess,' said Orno. He had decided with a fair amount of uncertainty not to attend Clarkson College in Miller, Kansas, where most of his relatives had gone, and he was unsure what he would find at Columbia. Most of his parents' friends raised their eyebrows when they heard he was going to New York, or laughed in a knowing way, although their only friend who had actually lived in Manhattan, a disgruntled woman named Helen DuPont, told him that once he lived there he would never come back to Kansas.

Orno found that he'd been assigned a room across the hall from Marshall, in a stone dormitory whose wood-framed windows had been pulled out and replaced with metal ones, their sashes edged with rubber stops that prevented them from opening any more than the width of a hand. When Marshall had put the speakers into his own room he came across the hall to Orno's, where he slid open the glass and pantomimed trying to escape through the narrow gap between the panes. They were both eighteen. He told Orno that the windows had been designed like this to prevent suicides and then he laughed as though this was a joke, although Orno in fact could see no other reason for such a feature. At Clarkson College the windows were huge—paned, wooden rectangles that rotated on pivot hinges and brought in the dusty sunlight and sweeping prairie wind that snapped the flags outside and sent hornets and yellow jackets into the high corners of the rooms. He'd thought hard about staying home to get a degree there. His father had one, his uncles each had one, his sister Clara was there this very moment, a junior studying primary education to become a teacher like their mother. Orno had applied to Columbia without telling his parents.

He went to the window and pushed his own shoulder through the gap, turning his head at an angle that allowed him a view down the narrow passage between two dormitories on to the expanse of the quadrangle, where the sun was throwing a soft, yellowish illumination among the granite steps and Corinthian columns of the campus, and the thrilling, lazy commerce of arriving students appeared and disappeared before him in the narrow trapezoidal shaft of light between two buildings made of stone.

'We're going downtown,' he said to Marshall, 'if you want to come.'

'Who is?'

'My folks.'

Marshall smiled but didn't answer. He was tall and bony, with a prominent skull that Orno could see beneath his face, jutting in his cheeks and pushing at the ridges of his temples, and two winding blue veins on his forehead, as though the blood and bone and muscle inside him had been covered too thinly. He moved his head from side to side to see through the glare in the window out to the quadrangle. His clothes were large for him but they looked carefully chosen in a way Orno had never seen before—although today he'd seen it on three or four of the new dorm-mates he'd met in their hall. It was the New York style, he assumed. Below them in the quadrangle a dark-haired girl in a black skirt and a man's large white T-shirt—these seemed carefully chosen, as well—was moving back and forth across their view carrying duffel bags and small valises, aided by different boys—boxes piled high in their arms—each time she passed.

'Your folks?' Marshall said.

'They came out to settle me in.'

'Out from where?'

Orno took some shirts from a box and began hanging them in the closet. 'We're from the Midwest.'

Again Marshall didn't say anything. He leaned his head out to try to get a view around the corner where the girl's belongings must have been stacked. Orno had expected to be asked further, and he was prepared to say Kansas, or perhaps Eastern Kansas, then Topeka, and stop there; in clear weather, Cook's Grange was an hour from Topeka, but there wasn't any point in saying so unless someone was coming out to visit. 'Anyway,' he said, 'we were going to have lunch downtown. We'd welcome you to come along.'

Marshall smiled at him but again didn't say anything, and Orno went back to setting his shirts on their hangers wondering if he had misunderstood a social convention in New York the way he'd misunderstood, at first, the haphazardness of its fashions; perhaps he wasn't supposed to issue invitations directly. Helen DuPont had told Orno to expect a different kind of person in Manhattan—'friendly and decent underneath,' she'd said, sipping from her tumbler on the Pboson's porch, 'but *way down* underneath.' Later, though, when the shirts were in a row in his closet and he told Marshall his parents were waiting downstairs, Marshall got up from the bed where he'd been lying and came along with him, not having accepted his offer exactly, but not having declined it either. They sauntered down the stairs together outside on to Broadway, where Orno found his parents' Chrysler circling the block, his mother leaning out the window looking up at the dormitory with her hand holding her ribboned hat to her head.

When they were in the back seat, Orno said, 'Mother, Father, this is Marshall Gurn. My parents, Mr and Mrs Pboson.'

'I'm Mister,' said his father.

'You can call me Helen,' said his mother, 'and my husband is Drake.'

Orno looked to see whether Marshall would respond to his

father's humor, which had always had a pointless ramble to it, a small joke or a parry no matter what was said to him. Mr Pboson sold insurance, and his humor was meant to put his clients, many of whom had never been off the farm, at ease. He'd heard Helen DuPont say it was a midwestern habit, but Orno thought it was only his father's.

'I've never been in a private car in New York in my life,' said Marshall.

'Is that right? Where is your family from?' asked Mrs Pboson.

'Upper east side.'

'Who says private?' said Mr Pboson. 'It's a dollar-fifty a mile,' and Orno laughed to let Marshall know this was a joke also.

They spent the afternoon together, Marshall pointing out sights along Broadway, which he pronounced as though it were two words. They parked the car and set off on foot toward a restaurant he knew—quite an expensive one, Orno discovered after they were seated. His father started off the meal by saying, 'Good thing I made some money driving us all down here.' Orno laughed again, for the same reason, and in a moment Marshall did too. At the end of lunch Mr Pboson picked up the tab, and they stayed at the table for quite a while as the plate glass front of the restaurant, which looked out on to a bustling scene of taxicabs, professional men, grocers, panhandlers and traffic policemen, slowly darkened from the sun moving behind the buildings high above them.

Marshall was unlike anyone Orno had ever met before. He was able to converse with Mr and Mrs Pboson as though he was of their own generation. He seemed to know about all the paintings in the Metropolitan Museum, which Mrs Pboson planned to visit in the morning, and about dozens of battles in the Pacific theater of World War Two, in which Mr Pboson had seen action at Corregidor. Marshall's father had been in the service too, he told them, although he'd been in army intelligence and had never left the United States. He was a professor now at Columbia itself—which Marshall seemed to admit with the same kind of trepidation that Orno himself had just suffered explaining Cook's Grange. Vertebrate biology was his field—they spent summers at Woods Hole, Massachusetts, on Cape Cod, where he studied a small, shallow-water crustacean. Marshall's mother, whose last name was not Gurn but Pelham, was an anthropologist, and in the summers, while Professor Gurn and the children stayed in Woods Hole, she did fieldwork in the South Pacific islands.

Orno and Marshall became friends. They found they were in a history class together, a survey course about the Greeks and Romans, among two hundred and fifty other freshmen in black clothing. It was taught by a legendary Professor, Terence Demetrius, who at the podium spoke whole chapters from his own text as though it was open in front of him. Orno sat in the front row and took notes, though he'd bought an underlined copy of the book from a sophomore in their dormitory and read it carefully each night in a carrel downstairs in the library basement. He needed to review things twice; that's how he was, that's how he'd always been. On the first day of class Orno entered the auditorium ahead of Marshall and took a seat in the front row; Marshall looked stricken for a moment but then sat beside him, and a quarter of an hour later when the auditorium had filled, Professor Demetrius entered, walking with a cane and perspiring. He looked down on his way to the podium and smiled at Marshall. Marshall waved back, a small gesture with his hand still in his lap.

Later he explained to Orno that Professor Demetrius knew his father, and after that he tried to persuade Orno that they should sit high up in the auditorium, well back in the rows of thinly cushioned wooden chairs where the desk arms were carved with generations of initials, and the upholstery smelled slightly of lemons—it was said to be flea powder. Orno sat back there for a couple of days. The high seats had a view out the window into the quadrangle where the fall sky—a splendid, darker blue than in Kansas, almost cobalt—set the marble friezes of the academic buildings into an eerily accurate relief that seemed to vibrate in his eyes. Forty yards away he saw pigeons strutting on the cornices. He found his attention wandering from the lectures, which had begun with the Minoans and Mycenaeans and within three days were already moving into the age of Solon. He told Marshall he had a hard time hearing so high in the auditorium and went back to sitting in front.

He didn't know what he would major in, but there was some feeling in his family that he would study either history, like his Uncle Clarence, who was a lawyer in Centerville, Kansas, or one of the physical sciences, so that he could come home and study medicine. Clarence was his father's brother and the only member of the family who kept books in the house; he had a row of lawyer's shelves in his living room, tall cases with glass fronts that slid back on recessed tracks and protected the volumes from dust and moisture. The books gave off a faint smell of oak when they were opened. Orno's father hoped he would become a doctor; it was a noble calling, and Orno would never lack for work. That first semester Orno took history, organic chemistry, freshman composition and, after discussing it with his mother, an introductory course in figure drawing.

Marshall on the other hand didn't know what he was going to major in and liked to say that he wasn't even going to be around for the full four years; his plan was to become a writer. For that, it didn't matter what he studied. Orno never saw him in the library. Most nights when Orno came back from studying he would stop by Marshall's, where the Tannoys, which stood like monoliths against the back wall of the room, were playing the Grateful Dead or Steely Dan, and Marshall was reclining on one of the huge, beaded pillows on the floor. He had taken the mattress off his bed, gotten two more from the supply closet and covered the floor with them; then he covered the mattresses with pillows. His room looked like the den of a Turkish pasha. People left their shoes at the door. Sometimes there were joints in the brass ashtrays among the pillows; sometimes there were bottles of malt liquor or schnapps on the window sill. A whole group of freshmen, mixed with a few upperclassmen, used the room as a meeting place late at night. Orno never felt comfortable with them, exactly—they competed for Marshall's attention, issuing sly remarks for his benefit as they exhaled the dope or debating small points of history with him about old Grateful Dead concerts. Orno had never been to a rock concert and until his third week at Columbia he had never smoked marijuana. He felt the word KANSAS was written on his forehead.

But for some reason Marshall took to him. Orno didn't need a lot of sleep—that's how everyone was where he came from—and it wasn't hard for him to stay late in the night in Marshall's room, picking up a conversation with Marshall after most of the others had gone to bed. Marshall didn't really confide in him, Orno realized later, but he had an ease about him that invited confidences. Orno would come back when the library closed, drop his satchel of books in the hall outside Marshall's door, set his shoes there and go in and take his place amid the ruins of the evening. Sometimes other students were asleep against the wall. The pillows smelled of smoke; beer bottles had worked their way between the mattresses. For as long as Orno was willing to lie there on the pillows, Marshall maintained an intermittent run of conversation, pausing for certain riffs in the music at which he would raise his hands and close his eyes, like a conductor asking for silence. Marshall told Orno he never slept before four a.m. He had a vigilance at night that he lacked during the day, much of which he slept through—he was still asleep, usually, when Orno came back from his morning chemistry class.

In his room at night they talked about the other freshmen in the dorm. Orno enjoyed these conversations, in part because they felt illicit to him; he'd never had any like them before, never really talked about people in the analytic way Marshall did. He had always assumed that people, basically, were good—as had everyone else around him; people worked hard for advancement, certainly, and this advancement was for the good of the family and the community. He couldn't have said this before he came to Columbia, but several times in his first few weeks there he was made to articulate his ideas late at night in the dorm, while their growing group of friends picked apart each theory that was offered. One girl said this was a midwestern outlook, and although she herself was from Chicago, the comment stung Orno. For some reason the easterners had sway at Columbia, and although Orno said inwardly that he did not want to become an easterner himself, he found that he was envious—in a way that shamed him—of their quick words, analytic outlook and dismissive comments.

Marshall subscribed to a theory of personality from a book called *The Enneagram*, the tenets of which he explained to Orno over the course of several late nights. There were nine basic roots of character, and he went through the dormitory systematically, talking about each of the other students as a mixture of two or three of them. One girl, Sarah Lyall, whose full name, Marshall said, was Sarah Morgan Lyall—after her great-great-grandfather J. P. Morgan—fascinated him. At night he usually returned to her after he'd discussed a few other people, granting her special consideration, a complexity that he did not acknowledge in the other students. In Orno's opinion she was shy and polite, simple enough, like a lot of girls he had known at home; but she had a narrow mouth and fine cheekbones that made most people think she was aloof instead, especially after Marshall let it be known who her ancestor was. This seemed a bit cruel to Orno—Marshall's announcing to a group at dinner, which did not include Sarah Lyall herself, that she was the great-granddaughter of one of the wealthiest men in history—but he didn't say anything. He merely asked if Marshall knew the genealogy of everyone in the dorm, and the group laughed out loud. He wondered if Marshall and Sarah would begin seeing each other.

One day in late October, on a still night when the cool had first turned to cold and the leaves on the ground had become brittle, crackling underfoot, Orno came to Marshall's room after spending six hours at the library reviewing the order of monarchy for the Greek and then the Roman emperors. The dormitory heaters had come on, clanking through the night and heating the top-floor rooms to uncomfortable temperatures that the students countered by leaving their doors and windows wide open. When Orno came in, Marshall was pushed back against the wall, legs splayed awkwardly in his own fashion. It was only after Orno had taken his place among a set of pillows across the room that he noticed Sarah Lyall below the window. She was lying quietly with her eyes closed listening to the odd music that was on the stereo, a moody piece that Orno concentrated on as well. It was hard to classify—avant-garde jazz, perhaps, a mixture of strings and lower-register bells that in the cool, autumnal air seemed a perfect manifestation of sadness. It wasn't the kind of thing Marshall usually listened to. They all had midterms in the morning.

Sarah nodded at him.

'Where have you been?' Marshall asked.

'Studying the Greeks and Romans. Hi, Sarah.'

'Ah, the Greeks and Romans,' said Marshall, 'although Terence Demetrius is teaching us all the wrong things from them, company man that he is. Let's see,' he said, rubbing his chin, 'let me see what I remember—"From the division of the Roman Empire into East and West in AD three-ninety-five, until the fifteenth-century conquest of Greece by the Ottoman Turks, Greece shared the fortunes and vicissitudes of the Byzantine empire."'

Orno took the book from his bag and opened it. 'Darn, Marshall, that's word for word.'

Sarah stood and came over next to Orno. 'Try this,' she said, flipping through the pages. 'Page ninety-two.'

'Oh, come on, I can't do that.'

'Try it.'

'What's it start with?'

Sarah held the book up. 'These colonies had a great influence on the history of the Greek mainland—'

'—where the city-states were developing in quarrelsome freedom,' said Marshall.

'Was he right?' said Orno.

'Exactly right. My Lord, that's the most amazing thing I've ever seen.'

'No wonder you don't wake up for class.'

Marshall lifted a bottle of schnapps from the mattress and took a drink. 'It's a gift,' he said, 'I know. But all the Gurns can do it. It's not that big a deal in my family. Not all the Gurns, I guess. My mother and my sister Simone can't. But my father and I can, we all do it, and my father's father could too. He was a civil rights attorney. He used to argue before the Supreme Court and cite the exact holdings on any case in American or British history. In that profession it's a useful gift, but in other ways it's a hindrance.'

'Some hindrance,' said Orno.

'One of my uncles can do it, too. My father's brother, but he has Asperger's Syndrome, which is a kind of autism. He was one of JFK's close advisers. He kept him informed about technology, but he had to wash his hands every time he touched somebody.'

'You don't do that, do you?' said Sarah.

Marshall looked at her. 'So far, nothing like that.' He smiled.

She looked down.

'So how's it a hindrance?' said Orno.

'Weird ways. It's hard to explain. I have to read things to remember them, but then they're just up there with no real importance attached to them. That's the hard part to explain. I can't always get at them when I need them, say in an argument, but I can always do it just like that, the way you just saw me. On the other hand, if I don't see it written down somewhere, I don't remember it. Like I'll forget about a party I went to or somebody I spent three hours talking to, or even a whole vacation. That's not good if you want to be a writer. You need to be able to remember your life. I remember what I read, instead. I have to see it, up close, on a page.'

'Still,' said Sarah.

'You don't have to open a book for the test tomorrow, do you?'

'Not really,' he said, 'except if you mean that yes, I had to read it once.' He took another drink. 'But I've already finished it.'

Sarah eyed him. 'When did you read it, Marshall?'

'What do you mean?'

'I mean, how long ago did you read Professor Demetrius's book?'

'Why do you ask?'

'I think I know the answer,' she said.

He drank again. 'I think I read it in grade school, actually. I think it was on my parents' shelf.'

'That's what I thought.'

'I think I'll go home,' said Orno. 'I think I'll go right back to Kansas. I'll just go to my room and pack.'

'I'll pack, too,' said Sarah. 'I'll go back to Connecticut.'

'That's why I didn't tell you,' said Marshall. 'The thing is, if you could do it yourself, you wouldn't be so impressed. We're amazed at a dog's sense of smell, but the dog isn't.'

'Yeah, but every dog can do it,' said Orno. 'You're not going to have to study at all the whole time you're in college, are you?'

'He's right, isn't he?' said Sarah.

They both looked at him, and after a moment he nodded.

A week later, when the midterms were graded, Orno went with Marshall to pick them up outside of Professor Demetrius's office. Orno had a B, an eighty-three; Marshall had a perfect score. There was an A-plus circled on the front of his blue exam booklet. Professor Demetrius was in the office when they came by, and he gestured to Marshall through the half-opened door. 'Just like the old man, I see, eh Mr Gurn?'

'Yes, sir,' said Marshall, and on the walk home he dropped the test in a trash can.

For Thanksgiving Orno went with Marshall to his family's house on the east side. The morning was brilliant and cold, and they walked all the way down from Columbia, crossing Central Park at Seventy-ninth Street, where the trees had turned but not yet dropped their leaves. Near noon they came out on to the east side, where Fifth Avenue flowed with taxicabs honking their horns, and the sidewalk bustled with walkers in their winter coats; it was like stepping from a forest, Orno felt, into the bright, shining center of the world. The stone buildings gleamed. The mantles and cornices and granite window-wells were of a scale that seemed to come from another time, from an era when artisans rowed in from the ships berthed low in New York Harbor, their dinghies laden with boulders of marble and sheets of Italian alabaster.

Marshall wore his usual black shirt beneath his black wool overcoat, but Orno wore a coat and tie as all his family did for holidays; no doubt Marshall's mother would appreciate the acknowledgement of her efforts. The house was on Sixty-third Street off Lexington Avenue, in a row of brownstones all of the same size and shape but differing exquisitely in their roof lines and friezes and stone staircases that ran up to mid-landings behind wrought-iron newels and rails. When they reached the Gurns', a light-colored house with untrimmed ivy on the front and overgrown hedges inside the gateway, they went in the service entrance, a dark green door set behind a grating a couple of feet below the street; inside was a narrow, basement hallway and an old servants' quarters, now filled with a washing machine and an ironing board and an old upholstered armchair, from which rose an elderly black woman, whom Marshall embraced and then held in his arms, his eyes closed, for quite a while as Orno shuffled behind them in the hall. He was in a world he had never imagined.

Marshall then released her, turned and introduced Orno and, without making any more conversation, set out down the hall with him, talking over his shoulder. She was Olivia, their Caribbean maid, he said, and she was the one who had raised him; she still stayed with the family though she had long ago stopped working in their house. Orno followed, trying to act at ease. In Cook's Grange, he'd occasionally heard of a cleaning woman after a party, but other than that people cleaned their own houses, and they certainly raised their own children. Marshall was too big for the narrow hallway. He seemed suddenly to have led a complicated life.

When they arrived at the staircase, Orno found both of its walls hung with countless framed objects, which he stopped to admire as they climbed up to the main house. His own father had, for safety reasons, always forbidden anything—brooms, shovels, clutter of any sort—to be hung along their stairs in Kansas; on either side of the Gurns', however, hung dozens of small drawings, exotic carved figures of black wood, Lucite boxes containing tiny sea animals pinned on cork mountings. He took his time while Marshall waited at the top. Once upstairs, they had to step among piles of books to make their way to the kitchen, and even there he found bookshelves, stacked with cookbooks and hung heavily with plants. At the far end of the room, underneath the window, was a carved, primitive table that looked to have been cut whole from the trunk of an ebony tree. Marshall's sister, Simone, was standing in the light of the window; she crossed the room to embrace her brother, stepping into and then out of the shaft of sunlight.

At dinner everyone was intent on talking to him. Marshall seemed to have told his family nothing of his life at Columbia, and Orno kept looking over at him to see whether it was all right to tell Mr Gurn, who looked like Marshall in every feature, about what classes Marshall was taking, or Mrs Pelham—Orno remembered to call her this—about the other students who hung out with them at night in Marshall's room. Simone was at the far end of the table; she laughed now and then at what was said but she was not quick to speak herself.

'So you're taking Terence Demetrius's course, are you?' said Mr Gurn after Orno had told them.

Marshall nodded.

Mr Gurn put down his fork.

'Now, take it easy, Walter,' said Mrs Pelham.

'That man is a grifter and a fraud,' said Mr Gurn. He clasped his hands together on the table.

'Walter, leave it alone.'

'The man's name is Irving Dinnerstein,' he said. He turned to Orno. 'Did you know that? His name isn't any Terence Demetrius. He's a Jew from Queens, he's the son of a barrel salesman.'

'I like the class,' said Marshall, spooning cranberries on to his plate.

Orno looked at him.

'Stop it, you two,' said Simone, the first time she had spoken. 'Daddy, Marshall can take what he wants. That was such a long time ago.'

Mr Gurn picked up his fork and took a bite of the turkey. Nobody spoke, and then suddenly the cloud that had been over the table seemed to pass. Mr Gurn reached for the potatoes.

Finally Orno said, 'I was wondering if you'd show me something, Professor Gurn. Marshall says you can all do what he does, the memory thing.'

'Not all of us,' said Simone.

'Almost all of you, I guess.'

'So Marshall showed you? He doesn't usually show people,' said Mrs Pelham. 'He must like you.'

'I don't know if I was the one he was showing it to,' said Orno.

Marshall glanced at him. 'They forced it out of me,' he said.

'Can you do it too, Professor Gurn?'

'Oh, it's nothing, young man.'

'Oh, show him, Walter,' said Mrs Pelham.

Mr Gurn seemed to be composing himself. 'Fair enough,' he said. 'Go get out a book from the shelf.'

'Which shelf?'

'Any one,' said Simone. 'That's the point of him asking you like that.'

Orno rose from the table and retrieved a volume from a set of shelves on the wall of the dining room. It was a novel called *Josephine's Way*, an old hardback with gilded pages.

'Ah,' said Mr Gurn. 'Old Josephine. Now, you might as well learn something from this, Orno. This is called eidetic memory, which is what your pal Marshall and I are fortunate enough to possess. Eidetic memory is to be distinguished from what's thought of—'

'Come on, Dad,' said Simone. 'Just show him.'

'All right then. Where shall we start? At the beginning, say?'

Orno opened to the first page. Marshall stood and went into the kitchen, where Orno heard him rummaging in the cabinets as Professor Gurn began reciting the opening of the novel, every word correct, adding theatrical twists to the sentences and flourishing his hands in the air whenever the prose was overdone. He ended by asking Orno if there was still a stray mark on the page, a black blotch of printer's ink near the signature binding above the title heading.

'Indeed there is,' said Orno.

'It looks like a goose,' called Marshall from the kitchen. 'If you stare at it. Heading away from you with its wings out.'

Professor Gurn closed his eyes for a moment. 'Indeed it does,' he said.

For the rest of dinner, Orno was shy to speak, though the Gurn-Pelhams still prodded him with questions about Marshall's life at school, and though he still answered them as carefully as he could, glancing at Marshall for direction, steering his stories away from what really went on in his room, the dope and late nights and pillows spread along the floor. Marshall had come back from the kitchen with a tall glass of what looked like apple juice and he sipped it as Orno told his parents the edited version of their lives together at college.

Suddenly Simone said, 'All you're doing is asking him about Marshall. I'm sure he'd rather talk about other things, such as his own life, for one. Please excuse us, Orno.'

'That's OK,' said Orno. 'Marshall's fun to talk about, aren't you?'

'Of course he is,' said Mrs Pelham, 'but Simone's right. We can be like that sometimes, although it's only because Marshall won't tell us anything himself. He wouldn't tell us himself if he won the Nobel prize.'

'Well,' said Marshall, 'I haven't.'

'But you'll tell us if you do?' said his mother.

'I promise.'

'Well then, Orno,' said Professor Gurn, 'I understand you're from Kansas.'

'Yes, sir.'

'Marshall says your family knows the DuPonts.'

'Marshall says what?'

'I said he knew someone named Helen DuPont,' said Marshall.

'Oh, Helen DuPont,' said Orno. 'She used to live in New York City. She was the one who encouraged me to come here.'

'I see,' said Professor Gurn. 'Well then, what is Kansas City like? I was there during the war for a time. A broad city, expansive, no high-rises to dilute the sunlight. Dusty air, though. I remember the dusty air. It used to cling to everything, cover everything.'

'I've actually never been to Kansas City,' said Orno. 'Do you know the DuPonts?'

'No, I'm afraid not,' said Mrs Pelham.

'Well then,' said Professor Gurn.

'Come on, Dad,' said Simone, 'that's not all you can come up with, is it? Do you know the DuPonts?' She drank from her wine.

Orno looked down.

'What classes are you taking, Orno?' said Mrs Pelham.

He told them, and then when she asked what he planned to major in, he discussed that too, telling them first that his father thought medicine was a noble and reliable profession, but not going further, about his Uncle Clarence or the law, because he could tell that Professor Gurn wasn't interested. Mrs Pelham asked him about Cook's Grange, and he was even briefer about that, although he wondered how she had known where he was from. At school he'd never said any more than Topeka, even to Marshall. Only Simone seemed to be listening closely, nodding her head as he spoke; she seemed to be three or four years younger than Marshall.

As soon as the meal was done, Marshall told his parents they were due back at the dormitory for a party, and to Orno's surprise the whole family seemed to disappear into different parts of the house while the dishes were still out on the table. Professor

Gurn said he had a meeting to attend and left right away; Mrs Pelham went upstairs to her study; Marshall told Orno he needed to get a few things before they could go, and then he left him in the living room and disappeared.

Alone now suddenly, Orno looked around at the drawings and primitive artifacts and books which lay everywhere in the living room without order, stacked on tables, piled on the mantel, balanced on the edges of couches and chairs. He tried to imagine what it was like to have the knowledge of all these words and pictures stored in one's own brain, accessible whole and unaltered the way Marshall described, but somehow also a hindrance, if he could believe what his friend had explained. He was filled with an exciting envy. His own world seemed shabby, but he also felt at the edge of a new one.

'Be careful of my brother,' said Simone.

'Oh, I didn't see you come in.'

'And don't be too impressed with him.'

'What do you mean?'

'Oh, you seem sweet, that's all. Marshall isn't sweet, and neither is my father, if you hadn't noticed. I apologize for what he said about Professor Demetrius.'

'You don't have to. I was just looking at all the stuff you have here. It's quite amazing.'

'My parents work at being amazing.'

'I think they succeed, don't you?'

'I guess they do,' she said. She sat down in the window seat. 'I've seen both of them hurt people, though—my father and my brother that is. They use people. You seem too sweet for that.'

'I don't think Marshall would use me.'

'Probably not,' she said. 'You're right. But just keep it in mind.'

Then Marshall appeared, emerging from the back of the apartment in a velvet smoking jacket that Orno had never seen before, which he quickly covered with his overcoat. Orno waved goodbye to Simone, who had retreated to the dining room, and all he could do was call out his thank you to Mrs Pelham before Marshall took his arm and they set off again into the cold afternoon, flagging down a cab which Marshall paid for when they arrived at Columbia, pulling a roll of bills from the pocket of the smoking jacket.

That evening Orno wrote Mrs Pelham a thank-you note, and then a letter to his sister Clara at Clarkson, telling her story after story of his time in New York. He was breathless as he wrote, overwhelmed with the sense of a tremendous, brilliant world that none of the Pbosons had ever seen. The whole thing was stupendous to him—the Gurn family, about whom he was already composing in his head a heated, braggardly letter to his parents; the polished stone buildings of Manhattan; the never-ending thrum of buses and taxis outside, all the way through till the morning; the freshmen in black trousers and black shirts; the stereo speakers so light they could have been hollow inside. And they were hollow actually, or nearly so, Orno discovered later that night when Marshall used his roach clip to pry the cover off one of them and hide his new roll of bills there. They had just smoked half of a joint. Orno didn't ask where the money was from. Marshall was affectionate when he was high and he chatted and laughed as he worked the bills into a notch in the narrow cabinet. With the grille removed, the speaker was nothing but a black plastic sheet with a round concavity in the middle, and Orno stared at it with detached fascination, a rubberish, indented diaphragm whose simple vibration produced the stupendous, screaming guitar solos and the low, pounding bass-drum beat that he felt in his bed every night across the hall like a rubber hammer tapping the floor as he drifted off to sleep, the high hat crashing on the off-beat like shattering glass.

That winter Marshall disappeared. He and Sarah Lyall had begun seeing each other—first Orno noticed her in Marshall's room more often, then he saw them walking through the quadrangle or sitting on the campus steps together beside the statue of Alma Mater, never among the larger clumps of students but off by themselves, not talking all the time exactly but sitting close to each other and after a while holding hands, and at the same time Marshall seemed to fall right out of Orno's life. He wasn't in his room when Orno returned from the library; or sometimes he was there, or at least Orno thought he was, but the door was locked. Orno liked Sarah Lyall but he began to resent her, and then he chided himself for this; he decided it was good for him to spend time by himself and resolved to attack his studies more diligently, though he'd certainly been diligent before. Sometimes he had to pass Marshall in the hall, and now and then this was awkward. Orno didn't have other close friends in the dormitory, and by that time there were groups already and he didn't find himself among one particularly. People liked him—they always had—but he had grown used to talking with Marshall, and now that he was gone it seemed like an effort he didn't want to repeat with anyone else. Christmas came, and he was excited to go home.

His grades were good—he had done little but study since his friend had disappeared—and he showed them to his parents on a bitter cold morning in Cook's Grange, a week before Christmas, looking out at the first snow that had covered the rooftops the night before and settled into the crotches of the maple trees, glum that at this juncture, when he should have been able to tell them of his astonishing adventures in New York City, he had only a report card to show them. A fierce wind had come up in the morning and massed the snow into drifts.

'Marshall is dating J. P. Morgan's great-great-granddaughter,' he told them.

His mother was mixing bread dough in a bowl and she paused a moment. 'A nice girl?'

'I don't think it matters.'

She looked up.

'Sorry,' he said. 'She's nice enough.'

'That must be difficult for her, when people find out.'

'Yeah, you're right, but I think Marshall likes people to know about it.'

'That's not a very nice thing to say.'

'I don't know. He comes from this amazing family. They're all either brilliant or have traveled everywhere in the world. There are letters on his wall from John F. Kennedy and Lyndon Johnson. His mother talks on the phone with Margaret Mead. They're friends with writers and artists, and I just kind of got the idea that she was part of it, that it was part of what he liked in her.'

'It's what they call the East Coast establishment,' said his father.

'I can only imagine what they think of *us*,' said Orno.

'And what might that be?' said his father.

'You know,' he said. 'Hicks.'

His mother stiffened.

His father lit his pipe, blew out the smoke and laughed. 'They're the ones who don't know how to drive a car,' he said.

Orno went to the window and looked out; his father probably hadn't read a book in five years, and his mother had carried a camera over her shoulder the entire time she was in New York City. He looked over the acreage that sloped down below the house to the frozen creek bed in the distance. It wasn't beautiful to him, but he tried to imagine Marshall seeing it for the first time: the wind that had blown last night's snow into ice, then blown waves into the ice, like a still, white river. Marshall would have noticed that; it wasn't something you saw in Manhattan. He tried to imagine what he would have thought of his parents. It was strange, but he was embarrassed for them.

He turned and without saying anything went out the door into the field. He didn't have a coat on and he was well aware that you didn't venture far in this weather without protection, even in the daytime, but he couldn't stand being in that room with his mother and father. Walking out in the frosted pasture, his hands pulled up into his sleeves, his arms crossed tight against his chest, he wondered what exactly had changed. It was these easterners who had mistreated him; he knew that perfectly well. They had brought him close and then shunned him, but it was exactly their view—he had always suspected that Marshall and his family thought of him as a bumpkin—that he'd found himself harboring against his own parents, who now sat inside the kitchen a hundred yards up the slope from him, his father smoking his pipe and no doubt still looking at his report card so he could tell Uncle Clarence about it on the telephone, grade by grade, and his mother kneading bread dough in a bowl her own mother had made from clay. □

GRANTA

EDWIDGE DANTICAT
THE REVENANT

Edwidge Danticat was born in Port-au-Prince, Haiti, in 1969 and moved to the United States when she was twelve. Her first published work in English was written two years later for a newspaper circulated in New York City high schools called *New Youth Connections*. She majored in French literature at Barnard College and received a Master's in creative writing from Brown University. Her first novel, *Breath, Eyes, Memory*, was published in 1994, and a collection of stories, *Krik? Krak!*, in 1995. She lives in Brooklyn with her parents and three brothers.

'The Revenant' is taken from her second novel, to be published by Soho Press, which she is still writing. It concerns the massacre of forty thousand Haitians on the border between Haiti and the Dominican Republic in 1937.

Doctor Berto came with a new stethoscope to check Victoria's heart. He was shocked to learn that she had died.

After examining Rafael, the surviving twin, he sat with Señor Pico in the parlor, while Señora Valencia took her infant son upstairs with her for a siesta.

'I don't understand it,' Doctor Berto said as I served them each a cup of coffee. 'She was gaining weight, getting bigger.'

'What about Rafael? How does he seem now?' Señor Pico asked about his son. 'When I look at him, I see a sadness that a child shouldn't have.'

'There is nothing physically wrong with him.'

'I tell you, there is this sadness. I saw it yesterday.'

'Perhaps he misses his sister. They grew in the womb together.'

'Will it go away, his sadness?'

'I don't see the sadness. You're his father, you see it. Perhaps you're right. If he's indeed sad, it will pass. Children are very malleable.'

'Are you certain?'

'I'll wager everything I know about human nature on this.'

'I loved my little girl. Does that surprise you?'

'I think you and I often misjudge each other.'

'I loved her more than I thought I would.'

'Why didn't you send for me sooner?'

'There were no signs of sickness.'

'You should have sent for me after she died.'

'Could you have brought her back to life?'

'If you lose a child, I lose a patient. At least I would have come for the funeral.'

'We buried her quickly, just among us. None of this matters now.'

Señor Pico stroked the sleeves of his uniform. He lit a thick cigar and handed another one, unlit, to his friend.

'You have my deepest condolences,' Doctor Berto said, biting the end of his cigar. 'I would have come yesterday, had I known.'

'That clinic of yours takes a lot of your time.'

'For your family, I would always come.'

'Valencia and I wanted it this way. Father Romero was here.

She had her rites. It's finished now.'

'I am very sorry for both you and Valencia.'

'And how is your clinic?'

'Don't change the subject so quickly.'

'Is your clinic lagging? Is it flourishing? Does that kind of place flourish?'

'Very well,' I heard Doctor Berto sigh, 'if you really want to know, a lot of people have been coming to us in the worst condition. It's like an epidemic: accidents, cuts, beatings.'

'*Los con gozos*?'

I hated that term. It was one of the many phrases Señor Pico liked to use. He called us Haitians *los con gozos*, the ones with joy, like jolly pets or simple-minded imbeciles who knew only how to be happy.

'You've watched the border before,' Doctor Berto said. 'You've patrolled there. You know most of my patients are Haitian. Cane workers, many of them.'

'What are you doing for them?'

'Usually we have ten or twelve to see, with digestive illnesses or malaria. Yesterday we had a hundred and ten. We had to put sheets on the grounds around the clinic to lay them on, to care for them outside, in the open. Most of them have machete wounds. Some of them are missing limbs. They say they were ambushed in the night, attacked by soldiers.'

'That's ridiculous.'

'You wouldn't think so if you saw them. People don't tell lies on their deathbeds.'

'Such accusations are insane,' Señor Pico laughed. 'They're delirious.'

'They're being attacked, and it's purposeful.'

'They've been attacking us for years, slowly invading our culture, tainting it with theirs. In many places it's hard to tell who's Haitian and who isn't,' said Señor Pico.

'You put people close together in a place like this, you can't expect them to stay unchanged. When will you forget the past?'

'I'm not talking about my own experience. I'm talking about the nation, the brutal invasions that darkened the pages of our history. Which side are you on anyhow?'

'I'm not on either side.'

'One day you'll have to choose. What if it comes to dying with the Haitians or living with us?'

'Do you think the people who attack them represent the national will?'

'Maybe the Haitians are simply killing each other. Why are you so quick to accuse others?'

'Because I see the proof. They're running—'

'Good.'

'But the people who are chasing them won't let them escape. They try to kill them first.'

'And when and where do your phantom killers attack?'

'In the hills, at night. Always at night. Some have made it across the border and have died in my clinic. I've buried many of them myself. What's going on Pico?'

'Do you think I'd tell you the state's business?'

'Killing Haitians? Is this state business?'

'I am a soldier.'

'We're friends—'

'I don't know where your loyalty lies. Are you a friend of the nation?'

'Who is the nation, if not you and me?'

'Right now, in this conversation, it's just me.'

'Be careful, Pico. I tell you this as a friend. Tomorrow it may be your head on the guillotine. You remember Gilio Peyna?'

'The poet?'

'He was just found in the mountains, his body in pieces, his nose sliced from his face. His wife was pregnant. They shot her twice, in the stomach.'

'These things only happen to Haitians and the traitors among us,' Señor Pico said.

'You're still very naïve, Pico. The Haitians, who have they betrayed?'

'They've betrayed themselves. They should stay in their own country.'

'A lot of secrets may be kept even from people in your position. Have your orders come down from the top? From the General himself? When I cross the border and I see you, I want you to look at me, then at the dead Haitians and list the crimes that merited such a death.'

'The border is quite long. Maybe we'll never see each other. I'm tired of you always preaching. It only displays your own selfish need to be a saint. Show loyalty for once. Show some loyalty to something you know rather than something you wish you knew.'

'This is something I know. This is my life.'

'You've made it your life. I don't have to follow you along that path. Now please let's talk about something else, something more cheerful. When will you marry? I think you need a wife.'

'There's no place in my life for one.'

'You have to make the space. You should leave behind this madness of helping the Haitians and get married.'

'You've tasted the honey and you want everyone to run to the hive.'

'You never know how much love you can feel until you marry and have children. I know you think you love the Haitians in your clinic, but it's not the same.'

'I know that altruism differs from romance.'

'I wonder if you do. What is it you do to entertain yourself?'

'I read and study. I learn.'

'You make friends with stray communist poets who put their lives and their families in jeopardy. When are you going to enjoy yourself and find a good woman to share your life?'

'Please, no more about my phantom wife. How is Valencia taking the baby's death?'

'She's sad. How would you feel if you were in her place?' Señor Pico put his cigar out in his coffee cup. He got up and gave Doctor Berto an abrupt handshake. 'Keep a very close watch on my son. I will join Valencia now.'

'I'll ask your maid to give me a glass of water and then I'll leave,' Doctor Berto said. 'I'll be back soon to give Rafael his vaccination.'

Doctor Berto watched as Señor Pico walked upstairs.

'You listen to everything that's said in this house, don't you?' he whispered to me in Creole.

'I was only waiting for the coffee cups,' I said.

'Be honest. You have every right to listen. You listen for a reason. You listen for survival.'

'I don't know what you mean.'

'Listen now and please heed my words,' he said, moving closer. 'You must leave this house as soon as possible. If you want, I'll take you. I'll go first, then we'll meet further down the road. I'll drive you across the border.'

'Why?'

'It will soon be very dangerous here.'

'I can't leave now.'

'You heard what I said. They're killing Haitians on the roads at night. They want all of you gone from this side of the island. It's just a matter of time before they come into this valley. Do you think Pico will hesitate to hand you over? That's if he doesn't take you himself.'

'Señora Valencia won't let him.'

'Are you certain?'

'Señor Pico is your friend.'

'In some ways he is, in other ways he's not. You had better know that he's not your friend in any way at all.'

'Who is they anyway who want to kill everyone? Who gives them the right?'

'The National Guard? The government? I don't know. In any case, it's growing into an organized movement, a night campaign to purge this country of people like you.'

I was frantic inside but I did not want him to know it.

'What about the sugar cane?' I asked.

'They're not worried about the sugar cane now,' he said. 'They want all of you out of this territory, back on your own side.'

'And the people who have been here for generations? What will they do with them? What about their children who have never even seen Haiti?'

'I don't know what they'll do with them. I don't know the answers to your questions.'

I wasn't sure what to do. Hearing him and Señor Pico talk had frightened me. But I couldn't leave fifteen years of my life behind because a man I barely knew, a man who had no reason to care for my safety, thought I should.

Besides, I had no one to go back to in Haiti anymore.

'If you come with me,' he said, 'we'll go to my hospital. We would come up with a solution for you there. You could start your life all over again.'

'As what? A beggar on the street?'

In my own country I'd be an outsider. The thought of that was much harder for me to take than being a foreigner elsewhere.

'What do you have here that truly belongs to you?' he asked. 'People start from nothing all the time. You delivered the twins. You could become a midwife. I don't know all the answers. I just know you should leave this place. Things are very serious now. Recently I've been seeing Haitians chopped up with machetes like they were meant to be shredded. Do you walk alone at night?'

'I don't often have reason to.'

'You seem very occupied with the work of this household. They're trying to take all they can from you, like the people who own the sugar plantations where many of my patients work. I have been telling everyone, you need to leave and get out of here.'

He seized my arm and made me look at him.

'Last week, an old woman was brought to me,' he said. 'She had worked in the home of a Dominican colonel for forty-nine years. The colonel had just been to his stable, and one of his horses had been stolen. He made up his mind that the thief was Haitian so he plunged his table knife into the old woman's heart. Is that how you want to end your life?'

'Señor Pico might hear you. Let me be.' I pushed him away.

'That woman died in my arms,' he continued. 'I fought to save her. I asked myself whether I should take out the knife and risk a hemorrhage or leave it in and try to operate. All this by the light of a hurricane lamp while a priest stood over her giving her last rites.'

'You have a terrible job, doctor.'

'I simply observe. I don't have to participate. I am afraid that one day I might find you in my clinic as a patient. I wouldn't want to know you dead before I'd known you alive.'

'I will die only when it's my time,' I said.

'I used to think the same way,' he said.

'And now? Now you'd like to be a saint.'

'It's not polite to repeat the insults of others,' he said. 'Now I have begun to realize you can't let things just sweep over you. You have to take action. In my old truck it takes three hours to reach the border. On foot, crossing the mountains might take you the whole day. If you want to leave now, I'll wait for you.'

'You need not wait, doctor.'

'Remember, I warned you.'

'Thank you.'

After Doctor Berto left, Señora Valencia came into the kitchen with her sketchbook and pencils. Her colors—crimson, mango, amber, pinks and greens—brought the kitchen to life. She attacked the paper, breathing heavily as she drew the outline of a baby girl crouched in the same protective pose that Victoria had assumed after her birth.

'Amabelle, I've been thinking since we buried Victoria, maybe it was my fault that she died.'

'Don't punish yourself that way, Señora.'

'I fed her too much. I nursed her three times as much as her brother. I wanted so much to save her life. I killed her with my desire to see her thrive.'

'That isn't true, Señora. Fate was against you.'

'What fate? My fate? My mother's fate? Maybe it was her name that killed her. I never looked at her once without thinking of my mother. Maybe it was passed on to her, from woman to woman, my grief. It poisoned her. She looked so well the night before and even that morning as I fed her.'

'She was only meant to be with us for a while.'

'Amabelle, I'd like you to be Rafael's godmother. We could not make it obvious in the church. You'd have to watch from a distance, but no one else will stand in the godmother's place. Rafael will be your godson. It seems only fitting, since you and I gave birth to him together. We won't tell Pico, but that's the way it will be. Sharing Rafael with you will make me less sad about Victoria.'

It would be awkward having a godson I couldn't even touch.

'Are you certain you want to do this, Señora?'

'This is the way it will be. Yesterday, when I dressed Victoria for her burial, I saw fingermarks on her body. She still had bruises from where you and I held her to pull the caul from her face and to tie the umbilical cord. I was so surprised. Those marks had not even had time to heal. How can I so easily forget what we owe you?'

Before putting her son to bed, Señora Valencia checked his neck and body for fingermarks, but found none.

I went back to my room, listening to the soft breeze blowing through the trees outside. I had barely closed my eyes when I sensed someone standing over me. I saw that it was a woman dressed in a long, three-tiered ruffled dress inflated like a balloon. She was holding necklaces made of painted coffee beans. Around her face she wore a muzzle, and on her neck there was a collar with a lock dangling from it.

I got up from the floor to see her better. I was a skinny eight-year-old girl and I was naked. I reached down to cover myself. The woman pulled my hand away from my crotch.

'Don't worry,' she said, her voice muffled by the muzzle which hid half her face.

'I am ashamed.' My voice, too, was a shy little girl's.

The woman grabbed her skirt and skipped back and forth on the porch, like an earth-bound bird. She seemed to be dancing a *calenda*. My mother and father had often danced the *calenda* together in the yard behind our house at night.

The woman locked arms with the air, pretending to kiss someone. As she danced, the chains on her ankles made a rattling noise.

'Don't worry.' She stopped, breathless. 'You can be naked. You're still very young and you're dreaming.'

'I am not young,' I told her. 'I'm twenty. What are you doing here, in Miseria?'

'I am visiting you.' She laughed, a metallic laugh which echoed inside the mask.

'You're making fun of me,' I said.

'Yes, I am making fun of you.'

'Why?'

'You think life is hard. Wait until you are dead.'

'I'm afraid to die,' I said.

'I'm insulted. Years after my death I'm forced to walk the earth between the mountains and the cane fields but lately I have grown to like it because I can visit with you.'

'Why do you have that thing on your face?' I asked.

'You mean this?' She tapped her fingers against the muzzle. 'Someone strapped it on me a long time ago so I wouldn't eat their sugar cane while cutting it.'

'Are you a slave? Will you go through eternity with that muzzle on your face?'

When I looked down I was myself again, lying on my mat. I had extended my hand to touch her, but she suddenly disappeared.

I woke up sweating. I lit my castor-oil lamp and drilled three small holes in a bamboo reed with a knife.

When I blew into the stem, the wind that came out of the other end was raw and low like a moan. I tapped the reed against the ground and blew again. I puffed without stopping. The sound peaked, becoming like the shrill cry of a cicada. With low, quick breaths, my mouth forced out the sound of a flash flood washing a row of trees downhill. This I made to honor the memory of Victoria who did not live long enough to either see or feel the rain. □

TOM DRURY
BURNING MARY

Tom Drury was born in Iowa in 1956. His father worked for the Chicago Great Western Railroad and his mother for People's Gas and Electric of Mason City, Iowa. He attended the University of Iowa, worked for five years as a journalist in New England, and then went to Brown University. His first novel, *The End of Vandalism*, was published in 1994. He teaches at Wesleyan University in Connecticut and lives with his wife and five-year-old daughter.

'Burning Mary' is taken from his second novel, which will be published by Houghton Mifflin in spring 1997.

That summer, the summer of 1979, Arthur Fiedler died one day, and Skylab fell on Australia the next, and the economy was miserable, but Paul Emmons was a college student with no money behind him and none in front and so he seemed immune from trouble. He had come to Boston for a research internship that had turned out to be meaningless; no one cared what the results were, and if there were no results, it would not matter. But Paul was twenty-two years old and happy to be living in a city. He had grown up in rural Rhode Island and was between his third and fourth years at a college in rural Quebec. His uncle, a captain in the Boston Police Department, had helped him get the internship.

Paul had sub-let an apartment for the summer in the used-furniture district of Somerville, and while the neighborhood did not seem like a good place to get to know people, the rent was cheap, and Paul had found that cleaning the sink with Lysol kept the cockroaches off guard. He lived above a vegetable market run by a large woman in a wheelchair who liked to tell Paul about a time in Somerville's history when the people did not want railroads and put up barricades to keep out the trains. 'They thought they could stop it,' she said. 'Of course they were wrong. No one could stop the iron horse. But you have to admire the fact that they tried.'

'Good for them,' said Paul.

He worked downtown, at night, on the twenty-seventh floor of a narrow building of burnished silver near Boston Harbor. He would ride the Red Line across the Charles River and into town and come up from the subway stop under South Station carrying a brown paper bag with his supper and a beer inside. The sun would be going down, laying shadows across Summer Street. Yellow cabs and Ryder trucks rattled along Atlantic Avenue. The wind came off the harbor, and on stormy nights the elevator would scrape the shaft sides going up or down.

Paul's job was to enter felony-assault data into a computer. He worked alone in a room full of xeroxed crime records from seven cities in the Greater Boston area. The seven cities had not wanted to make or consolidate these copies but had done so under the terms of a federal grant that they used to buy new guns and undercover disguises. The records were kept in damp cardboard boxes on unstable shelves that would groan and shift when Paul took a box down or put it back. He would read one report, type a summary of it, then read the next. It was absurdly slow work. One box took all night, and there were many more boxes than there would be nights.

The computer was called a Bytek Comrade. In those days the computer industry was open to almost anything, and the makers of the Bytek were not the only pioneering manufacturers who seemed to have drawn their design standards from that old television serial featuring a hero in a flying suit with a bullet-like casing over his head. The console of the Comrade curved toward the user, sheltering Paul's typing fingers as the bandshell on the Esplanade might shelter the Boston Pops Orchestra, but not Arthur Fiedler anymore.

The room Paul worked in was dark at night except for the light from the computer and a green-shaded table lamp and moonlight when there was a moon. The fluorescent lights between the stacks were on timers. The room was hushed and tomb-like so that when Paul opened a beer or whistled or scraped the chair legs against the floor, the sound rose and echoed. He did not know what to make of his work. The only trend he had identified was the tendency of domestic assaults to happen in the kitchen.

A professor of criminology named Leonard Draco came up once or twice a week to make sure Paul was doing something. Draco was a tall man with dark, lively eyes and a mustache. One night in the third week of July the professor opened the opaque-glass door wearing a wine-colored vest and a wide-brimmed leather hat and carrying magazines under his arm. These would be copies of *Hot Rod* and *Motor Trend* and *Automobile Week*, Paul knew, for Leonard Draco was an automobile enthusiast who had restored a Fiat convertible.

'There've been three more kitchen scenes tonight, Professor Draco,' said Paul. 'One with a serving fork.'

Draco removed the hat and sat down at the end of the long table. The hat had left an indent in his hair. 'Don't think about patterns,' he said. 'Don't worry about what room you're in or what weapon is being used. Just concentrate on the data.'

Draco lit a cigarette and opened one of his magazines. He smoked emphatically, with the cigarette jammed down between his index and middle fingers. 'Otherwise you could miss things,' he said. 'You take any two researchers and give them the same material, and the chances are that one will make cool and startling observations, and the other one will end up saying, "Jesus, how did that important trend escape me?" Well, your mind was closed. You got entranced by the anecdotal. And for that reason you can kiss your funding goodbye for next time.'

'Was one of those researchers you?' said Paul.

'Maybe it was; maybe it wasn't,' said Draco.

'The woman in the kitchen's name was Cheryl,' said Paul. 'When the cops arrived, she was standing by the electric range with a fork hanging out of her arm.'

'It is a wicked world,' said the professor.

'It really is,' said Paul.

'I drove the Fiat tonight and I'll tell you what, I think it needs a new head.'

'That'll cost you.'

Leonard Draco got up and went to one of the windows. 'I'm getting this white smoke. It's just a little white smoke. And I don't like to drive the Fiat downtown in the best of conditions. The thing with a convertible is that they can slice through the roof and tear out the radio in a heartbeat. But my wife, Mary, has our station wagon, so I don't know what else I'm supposed to do.'

Paul stared at his terminal, interlaced his fingers, cracked his knuckles. 'You leave it on the street?'

'Parking garage,' said Draco. 'And you're right, you'd think I could relax. But I can't. Because even in a garage someone could go ahead and slash through the roof in a matter of seconds.'

'You must have insurance,' said Paul.

Leonard Draco was quiet for a while but finally said, 'Yeah, I've got insurance.'

'Listen to this one,' said Paul. '*Defendant states that he did not mean to hit complainant in face. Defendant states furthermore that he does not know what gets into him sometimes.*'

Draco came back to the long table. He took out a cigarette lighter and a tin of Ronsonol and began filling the lighter. 'What's your major again?'

'Biology,' said Paul.

'See, this is the problem,' said the professor. 'I don't know why this internship never gets criminology majors. It's not like there aren't any. But year after year they throw in obscure majors like you just because your old man is a big deal down at the cop shop. You know who I had last year? A marine biologist.'

'It's my uncle.'

'Very well, your uncle,' said Draco. 'I mean, it's no wonder you don't know what you're doing. What school did you go to?'

'Montrose University,' said Paul. 'It's in Quebec. I'm sorry if you don't think I'm the one for the job, but it all seems like some kind of joke anyway.'

'Well, that's right,' said Draco. 'It is a joke. But even joke books have a serious chapter.'

'I could type faster if I had a better terminal,' said Paul. 'That's what I mean by joke.'

'They'll never go for that,' said Draco. 'Why Quebec? Are you Canadian?'

Paul shook his head. 'I'm from Rhode Island. Montrose gave me the best deal of the colleges I applied to.'

Leonard Draco slid the yellow-and-blue Ronsonol tin into his vest pocket and said, 'I'll bet that was a spirited competition.'

In the daytime Paul went to Revere Beach, the parks of the Emerald Necklace and Harvard University. He was surprised that the Harvard students looked like students at all. He was surprised that you could just walk into the middle of the campus, that you could just walk into Widener Library, sit down and read a book. He had expected gates that never opened, earthen banks, a difference in elevation. He had expected to get so close and no closer. The forking sidewalks of Harvard Yard seemed to suggest the rich and intricate lives that lay ahead of the Harvard students, and once, when a woman asked Paul for the time as he crossed the campus, he thought that she must have taken him for a Harvard student. Paul considered his own school, Montrose, overlooking Lake Memphremagog. It was a pretty campus, but it was not Harvard.

Paul had a black tin mailbox in the doorway of his apartment building but he rarely got mail. One day as he was leaving for work, however, he encountered the mailman, who took from his bag a long white envelope and said, 'Do you work for the City of Boston?'

'More or less,' said Paul.

'I'd like to know how you swung that,' said the mailman. 'You got to know somebody to get that gig.'

Then he handed Paul the envelope, which contained a letter saying that Professor Leonard Draco had died in an automobile accident on Route 127 near Singing Beach. The funeral service would be held at the Church of Saint Bernadette in Lexington, with burial to follow at Hopp Hill Cemetery.

Paul went to a clothing store on Summer Street to buy a necktie for the funeral. The salesman was an old gentleman with a faint accent from some other country.

'It's for a funeral,' said Paul.

'How sad,' said the salesman. 'Well, I've been to my share of them.' From a display table he picked up a blue tie with small white dots. 'Now, this is a good pattern for a funeral, you could wear it anywhere. Go ahead, feel it. That's one hundred per cent silk.'

'Are you from England?' said Paul.

'I come from a small town in the north of Scotland,' said the salesman. 'It's a beautiful place, but my brother is there, and we don't get along.'

'You came a long way,' said Paul.

'He's not the only reason,' said the salesman. 'But if you met him you would know what I mean.'

Paul got his old green Plymouth Fury out of a storage lot in Somerville and drove to Lexington on the day of the funeral. Saint Bernadette's was a brick church with a shallow peaked roof and six bronze medallions set into the façade, three on each side of the doors. The medallions had been embossed with religious scenes, and Paul examined one while waiting for the funeral to start.

Jesus was on the cross with a cut under the ribs from which a wide ribbon of blood flowed into an urn below his feet. Two deer with fern-like antlers drank from the urn, while in the background a candle burned on one side of the cross, and on the other side a skeleton leaned forward as if discouraged, with finger bones fanned over eye sockets. The image suggested victory over death but had been rendered with a lurid lack of subtlety. As Paul read the inscription—MAN IS THE SPRING OF EVERLASTING LIFE—he heard two women talking on the steps of the church.

'They say there wasn't a mark on him,' said one.

'And the car was a convertible,' said the other.

'It's almost a miracle.'

The church had a black-and-white checkered carpet and a large yellow altar. The casket was open. Paul stood in line, waiting his turn. Leonard Draco looked young and self-conscious and as if his lips had been sealed with glue. Paul thought that dying would be easy compared with lying in a box like this with everyone staring. Then he realized something. He and Leonard Draco were wearing the same tie: dark blue with small white dots.

Later Paul would wonder if this had been an omen, but just then he felt as if he had been caught in some sick practical joke. He made the sign of the cross, hurried from the casket and took a seat in the back of the church, far from Leonard, where no one would be likely to make the connection between their ties.

Some of Leonard's friends got up to talk about his life. They said he liked the art of the Southwest, that he was a gifted mimic and that he had a well-hidden generous side. No one mentioned cars. Paul imagined a speech he could give: 'I did not know Leonard Draco well and yet I say to you that he loved cars and car parts.' Then the priest and his helpers gave communion. Paul knelt at the rail eating the bread and drinking the wine. He did not believe in God, but he believed in communion.

Paul joined the automotive caravan to the cemetery. The other drivers would not admit his car until the end of the line, as if they suspected that he did not care about Professor Draco and had wanted only to see what the funeral would be like. Paul floored it through red lights to keep up. He wrenched the dead man's tie off and jammed it under the seat.

It was a hot and sunny day with wind gusting through the beech and willow trees of the cemetery. Paul stood on the opposite side of the grave from the criminologist's wife. She wore a long-sleeved black dress and a dark veil.

'The harvest is past, the summer is ended, and we are not saved,' said the priest.

The casket was silver-blue and suspended on a motorized lift over the grave.

From the cemetery everyone went to the Draco home in Lexington for supper and drinks. Mourners drifted through the house, past desert paintings, sand-colored and green; past rattlesnake bones and lamps made of smooth stones. Leonard had been a Johnny Mathis fan, evidently, and his wife drank Tom Collinses, spun Mathis records and swayed slightly to the rise and fall of the strings. Her veil hung now on a bleached steer horn, and Paul saw that her hair was golden and that her eyes were round and blue and calm. 'Take my hand,' sang Johnny Mathis. 'I'm a stranger in . . . paradise.'

The wake wound down. Students from Leonard's summer classes sat glumly on wooden chairs near the empty fireplace, and Paul felt no affinity with them. He thought his relationship with Professor Draco had occupied some higher level because he had worked alone in a deserted room and because he and the professor had not liked each other. Yes, he thought sagely, drinking Scotch, emptiness and animosity are the touchstones of adult life.

It was late afternoon, and the sun streamed over the garden and into the windows of the house, and the light was clear and warm. Paul finished his drink and went over to the young widow and kissed the top of her forehead.

'I was one of your husband's students,' he said.

She looked up with tranquil eyes. 'So was I,' she said. 'But that was a while ago.'

'How long have you been married?'

'Three years,' said Mary Draco. 'Would you like to see my wedding dress?'

'Yes.'

'Well, you're looking at it.' She was still wearing the black dress with long sleeves. The cloth looked like crêpe. She lifted her arms. 'Get it? This is my wedding dress.'

'I don't get it,' said Paul.

'Well, it isn't a very good joke,' said Mary. She sighed. 'Why don't you come out to the kitchen with me?'

They left the living room, crossed the kitchen, climbed the back stairs and entered a sky-blue bedroom with clouds painted on the ceiling. Mary walked into a large closet, and Paul examined a row of model horses standing on top of a dresser. Little gold chains hung from the horses' bridles, and the saddles were made of leather.

Mary came out of the closet after a while wearing a white dress. The upper part was embroidered, and the skirt was long and glossy and full and smooth. The neckline was not low but it revealed the curve of her shoulders.

'This is really it,' she said.

'Did you like being married?' said Paul.

'We were getting there,' said Mary. 'We were getting to like it. But you have to understand Len.'

'I don't understand Len,' said Paul. 'I had no idea he collected paintings.'

'Those are mine, really,' said Mary. 'I painted them. I can paint in virtually any style, and the desert scenes are what he wanted.'

While they talked, she looked at him very steadily. He was not used to her gaze and he felt heat rising to his face although he could not tell whether she was looking at him any differently from how she looked at anyone else.

'On our honeymoon we went to Lake Mead,' said Mary. 'That's in Nevada. To me it was very hot and dry, but as for Len, I've never seen him happier.'

Paul did no more work on the study of assaults. There was no more supervision and nothing to supervise. He spent his nights on the twenty-seventh floor reading and drinking. He had switched from beer to wine. This seemed to him like a great leap forward. A glass of red wine spilt, staining the pages of *Looking Backward*, a Utopian novel by Edward Bellamy, in which a doctor falls asleep in Boston and wakes up 113 years later, finding the world much improved. Paul lugged in a television set and watched *The Movie Loft* on Channel 38.

One night he opened a file cabinet and found some cigarettes and car magazines. He brought them back to the long table where he used to work and began reading about the new Corvette. The new Corvette looked so bad compared to the Corvettes of his youth that Paul thought the makers should call off the model before the proud name became a joke. The article asked who could resist the chance to drive around in a bright yellow Corvette, and Paul said aloud, 'I could resist that.' Then he called Mary in Lexington and asked her to come into town for the magazines.

'Can they wait?' she said.

'They could,' he said, 'but I want to see you.'

And so she said she would come.

Paul straightened his work table and took the elevator to the lobby of the building, where rain streamed down the big windows. Mary arrived wearing blue sneakers, white jeans and a yellow slicker, and carrying a white canvas bag. Paul took her up to the room where he worked, and she headed straight for the computer.

She took off her slicker and laid it on the table. Underneath it she wore a yellow ribbed sweater with short sleeves. She leaned over the computer and turned it on. 'You don't see many of these,' she said.

'It is junk,' said Paul.

'I program, you know,' said Mary. 'That's how I make my living.' She began typing. 'This terminal *is* primitive but still it responds to the Basic language. What I'm doing right now is creating an infinite random pattern.'

She stood back, and together they watched as a green helix caromed slowly around the screen. Then Paul took her hands. He kissed her hands and her face and her lips.

'Yes please,' said Mary. She pulled a folded Navajo blanket from the white bag, while Paul locked the door of the room. They made their way between the stacks and spread the blanket on the floor.

Later they pulled their clothes on and sat on a window sill. The rain had stopped. They smoked Leonard's Pall Malls. Mary seemed lost in her thoughts, and ash from her cigarette fell on her sweater. Blue pearls of fire raced up the fabric.

'Do you really think I'm a good painter?' said Mary.

'Mary, you're on fire,' said Paul, and at the same moment a key turned in the lock.

'Jesus Christ Almighty,' said Mary. She slid off the window sill slapping her chest and shoulders.

Paul pulled her close and pressed his hand to her mouth.

They could not be seen from the door. Bitter smoke rose from Mary's sweater. Paul thought that someone from either the college or the police was about to discover that his assault research consisted of watching *The Movie Loft* and making love to the criminologist's widow.

Instead it was two men exchanging money.

'Here,' said one.

'I never held in my hands a hundred and forty thousand dollars,' said the other.

'You mean a hundred and thirty.'

'Didn't we say a hundred and forty, Bud?'

'No, Don, we sure didn't.'

'Well, I don't see how that could be. I told Tim a hundred and forty. That's what Tim's expecting.'

'What you told Tim is between you and Tim.'

'You could fix it,' said Don. 'If you wanted to, you know you could.'

'I don't want to.'

'What's that smell?'

'I don't smell anything.'

'Well I do. It's like a chemistry set.'

'I don't smell anything.'

'What do they do in here?'

'Nothing anymore. They were doing research at night, but the guy died. You know—that professor who rolled his convertible.'

'Maybe it was a chemical experiment.'

'Nah. It was that smoking professor and that creepy scowling intern. They say he was thrown from the car. That always makes me wonder. It sounds like it wouldn't necessarily be so bad, you know? It sounds like you might bounce a couple times and then land on soft grass.'

'They bounce all right.'

'Now, how are we going to do this?' said Bud. 'D'you want the money? Or shall I go back and say, "It now appears that Don, for reasons best known to himself . . . "'

'No, no, no, no. But what you forget is by the time everybody gets their cut, I'm bringing home the minimum wage. Meanwhile the addition to my house keeps fading farther and farther from reality. Do you have any idea where my kids sleep?'

'The basement.'

'Well, that's right. Their room is in the basement.'

'You already told me that once.'

'How would you like to grow up in a room without windows? It wouldn't be much fun, would it? You should hear them. It's enough to break your heart. Oh it really is. On a sunny morning, on a perfectly sunny day, they call up the stairs, "Oh, Daddy, can you tell us if it's raining? Should we wear rain clothes, Daddy?"'

'You kill me, Don. What do I look like, Squirrel Nutkin? Is that what I look like to you?'

'No, Bud. I don't even know what Squirrel Nutkin is.'

Then their voices quieted, and eventually the door clicked, and they were gone. Paul and Mary had been pressed together and still for some time now and they began kissing again.

'What were they talking about?' said Mary. 'Who are those people?'

'Maybe they were cops,' said Paul. 'Do you think I scowl?'

'A little you do, but I wouldn't really call it scowling.'

He helped her out of her pullover. 'You can forget about this sweater,' he said. 'Did you get burned, darling?'

She shook her head, pressed her hands to her ribcage. Her skin was dark against the whiteness of her bra.

Paul's Aunt Jean and Uncle Bernard lived in Arlington, and Paul went over to their house one evening in August. After supper he and Uncle Bernard sat in the living room watching the Red Sox on television. Uncle Bernard was a small man who wore a black beret. He and Paul talked while keeping their eyes on the game.

'I imagine you'll be going back to Montreal soon,' said Uncle Bernard.

'Ten days,' said Paul. 'It's not Montreal though.'

'Montreal is a great town.'

'Where I go is south-east of Montreal.'

'Well, I hope you were able to take something from being an intern. Although it's too bad about your supervisor.'

'It is too bad.'

'They say there wasn't a mark on him,' said Uncle Bernard.

'Hey, you know, that reminds me,' said Paul. Then he explained what he and Mary had overheard on the night her sweater burned. Uncle Bernard listened to the story and sipped beer. He and Paul were drinking from tall glasses with the Anheiser-Busch logo printed on them in red.

'Well, hell, Paul,' Uncle Bernard finally said, 'there's no law against putting an addition on your house.'

'Maybe I haven't explained this very well.'

Uncle Bernard got up, turned off the television and sat back down. 'Let me tell you something that might prove useful. This is something your grandfather said.'

'All right.'

'He said: Very easy to get into trouble; very hard to get out. And the reason he said this was because someone had fallen down the stairs, and I wanted to help him, and he didn't think we should.'

'Who was it that fell?'

'A drunk named Hibby, if you want to know.'

'I'm not aiming to get into trouble,' said Paul. 'It just seemed like I should tell someone.'

'Well, you told the right person,' said Uncle Bernard. 'You know, another thing your grandfather liked to say was this: Be careful what you accept, because that's what you get.'

'What did he mean by that?' said Paul.

'I don't remember the context anymore,' said Uncle Bernard. He pressed the heels of his hands to his forehead and let up. He was a man who spoke almost entirely in aphorisms.

Labor Day was coming. The mornings and evenings had turned cold. Paul packed his car for the trip north and turned in the keys to his apartment. On his way out of town he dropped a letter to Mary into a mailbox in Central Square and then stopped into a tavern called Tommy's for a beer.

He leaned on the bar and tried to remember exactly what he had said in the letter. He had wanted to say that he was all for Mary, and that she would be a good painter, but he hadn't quite got it right. He felt as if he were abandoning her. But letters were tough for him anyway. He always thought the person he was writing to would read between the lines and sit there getting madder and madder. □

GRANTA

TONY EARLEY
BIRTHDAY BOY

Tony Earley was born in 1961 in San Antonio, Texas, where his father was serving with the US Air Force, though he would prefer to have been born in North Carolina like his parents. When he was growing up, his father worked in an office-furniture factory and his mother in a department store. He studied English at Warren Wilson College, North Carolina, and creative writing at the University of Alabama in Tuscaloosa. His stories first appeared in magazines and anthologies, including *Harper's* and *Best American Short Stories 1993*. A collection, *Here We Are in Paradise*, was published by Little, Brown in 1994. He is married and lives in Ambridge, Pennsylvania.

'Birthday Boy' is taken from his first novel which will be published by Little, Brown.

During the night something like a miracle happened: Jim's age grew an extra digit. He was nine when he went to sleep, but ten years old when he woke up. The extra number had weight, like a muscle. Jim hefted it like a prize. The ages of men contained two numbers. Jim's age contained two numbers. He sniffed the morning, his first as a grown man. Wood smoke. Biscuits baking. The cool, river smell of dew. Something not quite daylight looked in his window; something not quite darkness stared back out. A tired cricket sang itself to sleep. The cricket had worked all night; Jim rose to meet the responsibilities held by the day.

'There he is,' Mama said. 'Jim the birthday boy.'

Jim's heart rose up briefly, like a scrap of paper on a breath of wind, and then quickly settled back to the ground. His love for his mother was tethered with a sympathy Jim felt knotted in the dark of his stomach. The death of Jim's father had broken something inside her that had not mended, but Jim knew only that his mother was sad and that he figured somewhere in her sadness.

'Jimmy, Jimmy, Jimmy,' she said. 'How in the world did you get to be ten years old?'

'I don't know, Mama,' Jim said, which was the truth. He was as amazed by the fact as she was. He had been alive for ten years; his father, who had also been named Jim Glass, had been dead ten years.

Mama put the biscuits she pulled from the oven into a straw basket which Jim carried into the dining room. The uncles sat around the long table.

The uncles were tall, skinny men with broad shoulders and big hands. Every morning they ate between them two dozen biscuits and a dozen scrambled eggs and a platter of ham. They washed it all down with a pot of black coffee and glasses of fresh milk.

'Who's that?' Uncle Coran said.

'I don't know,' said Uncle Al.

'He sure is funny-looking, whoever he is,' said Uncle Zeno.

'Y'all know who I am,' said Jim.

'Can't say that we do,' said Uncle Coran.

'I'm Jim.'

'Howdy,' said Uncle Al.

'Y'all stop it,' Jim said.

'Those biscuits you got there, Jim?' said Uncle Zeno.

Jim nodded.

'Better sit down, then.'

In all things Jim strove to be like the uncles. He ate biscuits and eggs until he thought he was going to be sick. When Uncle Zeno finally said, 'You think you got enough to eat, Doc?' Jim dropped his fork as if he had received a pardon.

Uncle Zeno was Jim's oldest uncle. His age was considerable, up in the forties somewhere. Uncle Coran and Uncle Al were twins. Each swore that he did not look like the other, which of course wasn't true. They looked exactly alike, until you knew them, and sometimes even then. Not one of the uncles found it funny that they lived in identical houses. Uncle Al and Uncle Coran had built their houses when they were young men, but, like Uncle Zeno, they never took wives. Most of the rooms in their houses didn't even have furniture; only Uncle Zeno's house had a cook stove.

Jim's mother cooked and cleaned for the uncles. Sometimes she said it was too much, and the uncles hired a woman to help her. Uncle Coran ran the feed store and the cotton gin. Uncle Al managed the farms. Uncle Zeno farmed with Uncle Al and operated the grist mill on Saturday mornings. As the head of the family he kept an eye on everyone else.

Jim patted his stomach. 'That ought to hold me till dinner,' he said.

'You ate a right smart,' Uncle Coran said.

'Well,' said Jim, 'I am ten years old now.'

'My, my,' said Uncle Al.

'I've been thinking it's about time for me to go to work with y'all,' Jim said.

'Hmm,' said Uncle Zeno.

'I thought maybe you could use some help hoeing that corn.'

'We can usually put a good hand to work,' Uncle Zeno said. 'You a good hand?'

'Yep,' said Jim.

'You ain't afraid to work?'

'Nope.'

'What do you say, boys?' Uncle Zeno said.

Uncle Al and Uncle Coran looked at each other. Uncle Coran winked.

'He'll do, I guess,' said Uncle Al.

'Let's get at it, then,' said Uncle Zeno.

After breakfast Uncle Coran went off to open the store. Jim rode in the truck with Uncle Zeno and Uncle Al to the field. He stood on the bed of the truck and looked out over the top of the cab. He held on to his straw hat with one hand, and on to the truck with the other. The world at that early hour seemed newly made, unfinished, the air, still sweet with dew, an invention of that morning. In the low places near the river, stray ghosts of fog still hunted among the trees. The state highway led directly into the rising sun; when the sun pulled itself loose from the road, it suddenly seemed very far away. The sky, in a moment Jim didn't notice until the moment had passed, turned blue, as if it had never tried the color before and wasn't sure anyone would like it.

Five field hands met them at the edge of the river bottom. They were black men who lived in the woods on the hill behind the new school. They walked over without saying much and took hoes out of the bed of the truck. Jim grabbed the newest hoe for himself. Its handle was still shiny and smooth with varnish, its blade not yet darkened by rust. Uncle Zeno shook his head. 'Give that one to Abraham, Jim,' he said. Abraham had white hair and could remember the day a soldier told him he was free. He was the father or grandfather of most of the people who lived on the hill. Jim did not want to give up his hoe.

'I want to use this one,' Jim said.

'I'll use this one here,' Abraham said. He took the last hoe from the truck bed. Its handle was broken off about halfway down. All the other hoes had been taken already.

'That one's for Jim,' Uncle Zeno said. He took the new hoe from Jim's hands. Abraham handed Jim the hoe with the broken handle. Jim knew better than to say anything else.

'Let's get some hoeing done,' said Uncle Zeno.

'By dinner time you'll be glad you've got that hoe,' Abraham said. 'It's nice and light.'

Jim was still angry. 'I'm ten years old,' he said.

'My, my,' said Abraham.

Jim walked with the uncles and the field hands through the wet grass to the far end of the bottom. The grass soaked the legs of his overalls; the cloth was cold against his skin. The men fell out of line one by one and arranged themselves two rows apart. Each man would hoe to the end of one row and then back up the other. Then they would walk to the end of the line and take up two more rows. In this way they would hoe the whole field. Jim took up the two rows beside Uncle Zeno.

The corn was knee-high to the uncles, but almost waist-high to Jim. The field contained thirty acres. It would take several days to hoe it all. Then, after the hoeing was completed, Uncle Al would come back with the mules and the cultivator and plow the middles of the rows. The field would then be free of grass and weeds, and the corn could grow without competition. At the end of the summer there would be more to sell and grind into meal and feed to the mules.

Uncle Zeno stepped into Jim's corn row. Jim's cheeks flushed. He could feel the field hands watching him. 'You do it like this, Jim,' Uncle Zeno said. 'You put the blade of the hoe against the stalk and then pull it toward you. That way you don't hack the corn down.'

'I know how to hoe,' Jim said.

'Show me,' said Uncle Zeno.

Jim chopped at a small clump of grass. The hoe blade bit cleanly into a corn stalk. The corn stalk fell slowly over, like a tree. Jim heard a field hand laugh behind him.

'That's one lick,' Uncle Zeno said. Uncle Zeno had never whipped Jim, but Jim was always afraid that he might. Uncle Zeno kept a running count of the licks he was saving for Jim. He said he had them written down in a book. When Jim did something good, he said he erased a lick or two. Jim figured that most of the time he ran a lick or two short of break-even.

'It's this hoe,' Jim said.

Uncle Zeno got down on one knee and looked Jim in the face. 'Jim,' he said, 'I ain't got time to argue. Do you want to help me, or do you want to go home?'

'I want to help you,' Jim said.

'All right, then,' said Uncle Zeno. 'Watch.' Uncle Zeno dragged his hoe sharply across the clump of grass Jim had missed. The grass came up cleanly, and he scraped it into the middle of the row. 'Now you do it.'

Jim scraped up a small sprig of clover. 'That's good,' Uncle Zeno said. 'That hoe works after all.'

Uncle Zeno stepped back into his own row. The field hands and Uncle Al were already at work. Uncle Al was slightly ahead of the line. None of the uncles liked to be beaten at anything. and Jim didn't like to lose, either. He decided he would beat Abraham to the far end of the field. Then after dinner Uncle Zeno would give the broken hoe to Abraham. Maybe Uncle Zeno would tell Abraham to go home.

Without looking up, Jim carefully scraped the ground clean around the first ten stalks of corn in his row. He piled the weeds and grass up neatly. At the tenth stalk, he ran into a clump of grass that was too tough to dig up with his hoe. He got down on his knees and pulled at it with both hands. It wouldn't budge. He stuck the sharp point of his hoe handle underneath the grass and pried at it. He pulled and pried at the grass until the roots finally came loose with a ripping noise. Jim hoisted the clump of grass into the air like a trophy, or a large fish. Its roots held a clod of dirt as big as a cat. He looked around to see if anyone saw him, but everyone was gone. He couldn't see anyone at all until he stood up. The uncles and the field hands were a hundred yards or more ahead of him, and moving away at a slow walk. Uncle Al was out in front of everyone else. Uncle Zeno and Abraham looked to be tied for second.

Jim turned and stared back at the head of his row. He could spit that far. He looked in the other direction at the end of the row in the distance. The woods along the river seemed as far away as the moon. The uncles, as far ahead of Jim as they were, had hoed less than a third of the way to the end of the field.

Jim didn't see how he could ever make it to the end of his row, much less hoe the one beside it. He had started a journey he knew he could not finish. He felt a sob gather up in his stomach.

That Jim felt like crying made him angry. He attacked the ground with his hoe as if he were killing snakes. He struck almost blindly at the morning glories and grass and clover, but in his fury chopped down another stalk of corn. The sob that had been waiting in his stomach climbed up out of his throat and hung in the air for a second, a small, inconsequential sound, heard only by him.

The uncles and the field hands were still moving away, hoeing as they walked. Jim was afraid he would get into trouble if Uncle Zeno found out he had chopped down another stalk of corn. He could not bear the thought of Uncle Zeno being mad at him. He got down on his knees and dug a small hole with his hands. He stuck the end of the stalk in the hole and filled the hole around it with dirt. Then he patted the dirt around the stalk so that it stood up straight.

Jim picked up his hoe and wiped his nose on the back of his arm. He wiped the back of his arm on the leg of his overalls. He felt calmer. He decided that he would hoe until dinner time. He couldn't think of a way to get home until then, but he knew that Uncle Zeno wouldn't make him come back to the field after dinner if he didn't want to.

Jim threw a rock toward the place he had started work. He often threw rocks as a way of gauging how far away things were. He wanted to know how far he had hoed. The rock, however, was a little flat and light, and curved off short to one side. Jim hunted around until he found a better rock. Good throwing rocks were hard to find in the rich dirt of the river bottom. He threw four or five more rocks until he was satisfied that he had hoed farther than he could throw. This seemed like progress, and he turned his attention again to the weeds growing in the field.

He could smell sweat soaking his overalls. He touched the denim covering his thigh with the palm of his hand. The cloth was hot to the touch. Jim squinted up. The sun was small and white; the sky was devoid of color, empty, even of clouds and birds. Jim tried to figure out what time it was by looking at the sun. He tried without success until he could no longer see. He could not remember ever being as hot as he was right then. There was a bucket of water in the truck, but Jim knew that you weren't supposed to drink from it until you had hoed back to the head of the field. The uncles did not believe in wasting steps. The uncles and the field hands had made the turn and were hoeing back toward Jim. They were still a long way off, but Jim knew they would see him if he went to the truck. Two drops of sweat trickled out from under Jim's hat, and he stood still to see where they went. One drop ran into his eyes, and the other trickled down the back of his neck. A gnat flew into his mouth. Jim spat it out. He took off his hat and waved it around his face but could not make the gnats go away.

'What are you doing down there, Jim?' Uncle Zeno said. Jim jumped. He had not noticed Uncle Zeno's shadow cover the ground where he crouched. 'I'm looking at this praying mantis,' said Jim.

'Did it bite you?'

'No.' Jim had knocked the praying mantis off a corn stalk and chopped it in two with his hoe. He was poking at the two pieces with the sharp point of the handle.

'Praying mantises eat other bugs, Jim,' Uncle Zeno said. 'If you want to kill something, kill a grasshopper. Grasshoppers eat corn.'

'Yes, sir,' Jim said. He covered up the two green halves of the praying mantis with dirt. He wondered if in killing it he had added another lick to Uncle Zeno's list.

'Well,' said Uncle Zeno, 'let's see how you've been doing.' He walked back toward the head of Jim's row, looking at the ground. 'You missed a lot of morning glories through here,' he said, scratching at the ground as he walked. 'They'll take over a field if you don't get 'em before they get up on the corn.' Uncle Zeno came to the corn stalk Jim had chopped down and stuck back in the ground. He stood and looked at it a long time. Then he pulled it up and turned around and looked at Jim. Uncle Zeno was extremely tall. Jim had never noticed before exactly how tall.

'What happened to this one here?' Uncle Zeno said.

'I don't know,' Jim said.

'You don't know,' said Uncle Zeno.

'No,' said Jim.

'You know it won't grow, now.'

Jim nodded.

'Then why did you stick it back in the ground?'

'I don't know,' said Jim.

'You don't know.'

'No.'

Uncle Zeno held the corn stalk up like a scepter, as if seeing it better would help Jim answer his questions. 'Jim, this was just a mistake until you tried to hide it,' he said. 'But when you tried to hide it, you made it a lie.'

Jim looked at the front of his overalls. He felt a tear start down his cheek and hoped that Uncle Zeno hadn't seen it.

Uncle Zeno threw the corn stalk away from him as if it were a dirty thing, something to be ashamed of. 'Do you lie to me a lot, Jim?'

'No,' Jim said.

'Should I worry about believing the things you tell me? I never have before but should I start now?'

Jim shook his head. He wasn't able to say no again.

'What's the matter?' Uncle Zeno said.

'I don't feel good,' said Jim.

'Are you sick?'

Jim shrugged.

'Go on home, then,' Uncle Zeno said.

Jim looked down the row toward the river. He suddenly wanted to finish his work.

Uncle Zeno pointed in the direction of town. 'Go on,' he said. 'If you're sick, you don't need to be out in the sun.'

'I think I can make it till dinner,' Jim said.

'No, you go on home and tell your mama you're sick.'

Jim sent a small whimper out into the air between himself and Uncle Zeno, like a scout in advance of the protest that would follow.

'Go on,' Uncle Zeno said.

From the edge of the road Jim turned around and looked back at the field. Uncle Zeno was hoeing the row Jim had abandoned. The field hands were spread out through the bottom. Uncle Al was still way out in front of everybody else. He was approaching the river for the third time that morning, and working as if he would never stop. □

GRANTA

JEFFREY EUGENIDES
THE SPEED OF SPERM

Jeffrey Eugenides was born in Detroit in 1960 and grew up in the city's suburbs. His father was a mortgage banker; his mother 'a perfect mother'. During college, at University Liggett School, he took a year off to travel and worked briefly at Mother Teresa's Home for the Destitute and Dying in Calcutta. Otherwise his life has been uneventful and mostly spent writing: 'I have never been to Bosnia or taken shrapnel in my thigh or been to rehab or attempted suicide.' He moved to California and worked on a sailing magazine and wrote an unsellable screenplay about born-again Christians. From 1988 he worked for four years at the Academy of American Poets in New York City and there wrote most of his first novel, *The Virgin Suicides* (1993), sometimes on office stationery. He completed it after he was fired. He married a sculptor last year and lives in Brooklyn.

'The Speed of Sperm' is taken from his second novel which is still in progress.

I was born twice: once, as a baby girl, at 4.53 a.m. on a remarkably unpolluted Detroit day in 1960; and then again, as a teenage boy, in the offices of our family physician, Dr Arnold Philobosian, in 1976. Some of you more specialized readers may have come across me in Dr Peter Luce's influential study, 'Gender Identity Among Pseudohermaphrodites with 5 Alpha-reductase Deficiency', published in the *Archives of Sexual Behavior*, volume seventy-three. Or maybe you've seen my photograph in chapter sixteen of the now sadly outdated *Genetics and Heredity*. That's me on page 578, arms akimbo, in unflattering light, standing next to the height chart with a black box covering my face.

My birth certificate lists my name as Calliope Victoria Tatakis. My friends call me Cal or Callie. I'm not a biological freak. I'm a former cheerleader and varsity center, lifelong Henry James enthusiast, long-standing member of the Save-the-Manatee Foundation and currently embattled tenor in the First Presbyterian Church choir. I've had my heart broken three times, twice by women. I've attempted to learn a variety of musical instruments without success. I love my mother, Sophie, mourn my father, Milton, and—unfortunately I have to stress this—have never felt anything other than human.

But now, just past twenty-nine, I feel one more birth coming on. It started a few months ago: my maleness, always iffy, became more so. Next I started getting oracular. I've begun hearing things through the plumbing, for instance. Presences are making themselves known to me, speaking in Greek and broken English. I'm not sure what it is. But after decades of ancestral silence suddenly I find myself in touch with departed great-aunts and uncles, with long-lost great-grandfathers, with unknown fifth cousins, or, in the case of an inbred family like mine, with all those things in one. And so before I transform again I want to get it down for good, this rollercoaster ride of a single gene through time: how it bloomed a century-and-a-half ago on the slopes of Mount Olympus, while the goats bleated and the olives dropped; how it was passed down through sixteen generations, gathering invisibly within the small, polluted pool until the first double-recessive appeared—not me but my precursor—whereupon Providence (in the guise of a massacre) sent the gene flying again, blown like a seed across the sea to America, where it drifted through our industrial rains until it fell to earth in the fertile soil of my mother's own midwestern womb. I'm sorry if I get a little purple sometimes. That's genetic too. It's not the style of choice in the *Journal of Endocrinology*. But it'll have to do.

Three months before I was born, in the aftermath of one of our elaborate Sunday dinners, my grandmother Desdemona ordered my eldest brother to go get her silkworm box. Theo was coming out of our living room, examining a vacuum tube he'd just removed from our Admiral radio, when she collared him. Desdemona was standing in the kitchen doorway, blocking what by the sound of it was a great time going on inside. Behind her all the women in our extended family, from great-aunts to regular aunts right down to girl cousins, were in full voice, talking and laughing. At sixty-eight my grandmother's body was pretty much designed to block doorways from view, and Theo went up on tiptoes to see over her hairnet. But Desdemona reached out and pinched his cheek, bringing him back to earth. While he rubbed his smarting face, she sketched a rectangle in the air and pointed at the ceiling. Then, through her ill-fitting dentures, she enunciated one of her all-purpose English words: 'Go.'

Theo knew what to do. He ran up the formal front staircase, grabbed the stepladder from the closet and positioned it in the middle of the upstairs hallway. Climbing up, he took hold of a thin chain that hung down from the ceiling. With a creak, the trapdoor opened. He unfolded its three sections until they met the floor and then climbed up through the hole into the darkness where my grandparents lived. He moved beneath the twelve birdcages suspended from the rafters. He immersed himself in the sour odor of the parakeets, and in my grandparents' own particular aroma, a mixture of cinnamon, dust, luggage and exile. He negotiated his way past my grandfather's ancient phonograph, his stack of unlabeled bouzouki records and, finally, bumping into the leather ottoman and the circular coffee table made of brass, he found my grandparents' bed. He crawled underneath and searched for the heavy olive-wood box. When he found it, he crawled backwards, dragging the box out. Looking to see that no one was watching, not even the parakeets in their covered cages, he opened the lid. It was too dark to see much. An icy blueness glittered up at him, as though the box were filled with nothing but broken light bulbs. One of the birds squawked, making Theo jump. He closed the box and, risking no further investigation, carried it down the ladder and down the stairs to Desdemona.

She was still waiting in the doorway. She took the silkworm box out of his hands and turned back into the kitchen. At this point Theo was granted a view of the room, where everyone now fell silent, gripping each other, containing themselves. As Desdemona crossed the floor, the circle of women parted to reveal, right in the center of the linoleum, my mother. Sophie Tatakis was seated on one of our chrome-and-yellow-vinyl kitchen chairs with her legs apart. She was still wearing her church clothes. Under her dress was what appeared to be a beach ball. Desdemona handed the silkworm box to her daughter Lucille and opened the lid. She felt around in all the objects Theo hadn't been able to see, and came up at last with a silver spoon. She tied a piece of string to the spoon's handle. Then, stooping forward, she dangled the spoon over my mother's swollen belly. And, by extension, over me.

Up until this point Desdemona had a perfect record: twenty-three correct guesses. She'd known that Aunt Helen was going to be Aunt Helen. She'd predicted the sex of both my brothers and nearly all the Tatakis children except her own, it being bad luck for a mother to stare into the mysteries of her own womb. Fearlessly, however, she stared into my mother's. After some initial hesitation, the spoon swung north to south, which meant that I would be a boy.

Splay-legged in the chair, my mother tried to smile. She didn't want another boy. She had two boys already. She'd been so certain that I'd be a girl, in fact, that she'd only picked out a girl's name for me—Calliope. But when my grandmother shouted in Greek, 'A boy!', the cry went around the room and out into the hall and across the hall into the living room where the men were arguing politics. And my mother, by hearing it repeated so many times, began to believe that it might be true.

As soon as the cry reached my father, however, he marched into the kitchen to tell his mother that, this time at least, her spoon was wrong. 'And how you know so much?' Desdemona asked him. To which he replied what any American of his generation would have: 'It's science, Ma.'

It was no surprise to anyone that Milt and Sophie were hoping for a girl. The sole reason they'd begun to discuss having another kid in the first place (initially just the two of them but then, our family being the hydra it was, the other ninety-eight mouths putting in their opinions) was with the hope of producing a daughter. Theo and Nick were, at that point, nine and five years old, respectively. They'd recently BB-gunned their first squirrel, hanging its corpse from the cherry tree in triumph. They hurled novelty-store rubber vomit across the table during family meals. In such a masculine household Sophie had begun to feel like the odd woman out and, extrapolating this trend, saw herself in five years' time imprisoned in a world of hubcaps and hernias. My mother envisioned a daughter as a counter-insurgent: a fellow lover of lapdogs, a seconder of proposals to attend the Ice Capades. Her situation must have been like that of the last living member of a sect. She had wisdom to impart, about cosmetics, child-rearing, the proper way to steam facial pores, cooking, sewing, stain-removal. In the spring of 1959, when discussions of my fertilization got underway, my mother couldn't foresee that women would soon be burning their brassieres by the thousand. Hers were padded, stiff, fire-retardant. As much as Sophie loved her sons, she knew there were certain things she'd never be able to share with them, things she could only share with a daughter.

My father wanted a daughter too. Driving to work in the mornings, he was visited at stoplights by the vision of a little girl who sat on the seat beside him, directing questions up at his patient, all-knowing ear. My prototype was only a vague conception, a pink doll. She would call him 'Daddy'. She would dance with him at weddings, standing on his shoes. She would grow up and marry someone who could never replace him. So pleasant were these daydreams that my father, a man loaded with initiative, decided to see what he could do to turn his dream into reality.

Thus: for some time now, in the living room where the men discussed politics, they'd also been discussing the speed of sperm.

My great-uncle Pete, the chiropractor, who'd read the Great Books twice, was looked upon as a medical authority. One Sunday, drinking Pepsi to help with his digestion (it got its name from pepsin, the digestive enzyme, he sagely told us), he conducted a seminar on the reproductive timetable. In his wine-dark suit showing a white sail of pocket handkerchief, Uncle Pete explained to the assembled restaurant owners, insurance salesmen and fur finishers that, under the microscope, sperm carrying male chromosomes had been observed to swim faster than those carrying female chromosomes. Peter Aristos didn't lower his voice when he said the word 'sperm' but actually amplified it, there in our nicely painted living room, in accordance with his free-thinking ideals. Some men winced. Others grinned and elbowed each other. My father adopted the pose of his favorite piece of sculpture, 'The Thinker', a miniature of which sat just across the room on his green desk blotter. Chin on fist, he calculated the import of what Uncle Pete was saying. Though the topic had been brought up in the open-forum atmosphere of those post-prandial Sundays, a time of reasoned debate and gentle burping, it was clear that, notwithstanding the impersonal tone of the discussion, the sperm they were talking about were my father's. Uncle Pete made it clear: to have a girl baby, a couple should 'have sexual congress twenty-four hours prior to ovulation'. That way the swift male sperm would rush in and die off. The female sperm, sluggish but more reliable, would arrive just as the egg drops.

My father had trouble persuading my mother to go along with the scheme. Sophie Pappas had been a virgin when she married Milton Tatakis at the age of nineteen. Their long engagement, which coincided roughly with the Second World War, had been a chaste affair. My mother was proud of the way she'd managed to kindle and snuff my father's flame simultaneously, keeping him at a low burn for the duration of a global cataclysm. This didn't seem so difficult, however, seeing as she was in Detroit, while he was on a submarine chaser in the middle of the Pacific. For four long years Sophie lit candles at the Greek church for the safety of her fiancé, while he, Milton, gazed at her many photographs pinned over his bunk. He liked to pose

Sophie in the manner of the movie magazines, standing sideways, one high heel raised on a step, an expanse of black stocking visible, her upper torso twisting toward the camera to offer a frontal view of her laughing, happy face. My mother looks surprisingly pliable in those shots, as though she liked nothing better than to have her man in uniform arrange her against the porches and lamp-posts of their humble neighborhood. My father called her 'Rita' after Rita Hayworth, but most of the similarity came from her hairstyle. Beneath her teased bangs, my mother's face revealed itself as unremittingly Greek, the long nose, the dark deep-set eyes, the handsome, masculine chin. Those pictures always depressed me, not just the ones of my mother but of my other female relatives too, her sisters and cousins, all of them trying to look like Hollywood stars or, failing that, like all-American girls, and looking like neither.

She didn't surrender until after Japan had. Then, from their wedding night onward (according to what Theo told my covered ears), my parents made love regularly and unashamedly whenever they were in the mood or Father Jim blessed them. When it came to having children, however, my mother had her own theory, less scientific and more spiritual. It was her belief that an embryo could sense the amount of love with which it had been created. For this reason, my father's suggestion didn't sit well with her. 'I can't just do it like clockwork, Milt,' she said.

'There's no other way. Uncle Pete explained it to us.'

'Is that what you men talk about in there? Honestly, Milt, my getting pregnant is no one else's business but mine.'

'You've got two kinds of sperm, see, the male sperm and the female. And the male sperms are faster.'

'I don't want to hear it.'

'I thought you wanted a daughter.'

'I do.'

'Well, this is how we can get one.'

Sophie didn't buy the theory. For a number of reasons. The idea struck her as quackery, for one thing. Even though Uncle Pete could quote famous authors, what did he know about having babies? He'd never even been married. He lived alone in a bachelor apartment out in Birmingham. He ate his meals out. He hadn't even had a girlfriend that my mother could remember. He spent all his time with his nose in a book. 'Please,' my mother said, 'if you want to tell me how I can have a daughter, at least ask somebody who knows what's what.'

Her other objection was on religious grounds. It didn't seem right, in fact it seemed a piece of the grossest hubris, to tamper with something as mysterious and miraculous as the birth of a child. Sophie didn't believe you could do it, and, if you could, she didn't believe you should try. 'Father Jim said it's OK,' my father answered. 'We can time the thing any way we want.' Then, authoritatively: 'There's nothing in the Bible against it.' In response to this pretense of biblical scholarship, my mother squinted up her heavily mascara-ed eyes. Her deepest spiritual beliefs were in most cases pre-literate. They'd filtered into her as a child, from breathing the incense at church. Now, in her maturity, she based most of her decisions not on what Father Jim might say but on the far more reliable authority of what she knew to be true in her 'heart of hearts'. The women in my family tend to be Delphic when it comes to religion. Just as the Oracle held her young face over intoxicating sulphur fumes, so my mother and grandmother held their faces over steaming pots of *pilafi*, coming up with answers to the questions of life and death. Sometimes these were mysterious and needed interpretation, as when Desdemona had said on arriving in America, 'A hat never fits the same head twice.' Sometimes they were clear and unmistakable, as in the kitchen that day when my mother said, 'God decides what a baby is. Not us.'

Of course a narrator in my position at the time (pre-fetal) can't be entirely sure about any of this. And I have to admit that, in my experience, my parents weren't exactly keen about discussing sex, their own or anyone else's. I can only explain the scientific mania that overtook my father during that spring of 1959 as a symptom of the belief in progress that was infecting everyone at the time (everyone, that is, except Desdemona, who like an obstinate Vatican still refused to recognize the existence of Turkey or condone the diaphragm). Remember: Sputnik had been launched only two years earlier. Polio, which had kept my parents quarantined indoors during the winters of their childhood, had been conquered by the Salk vaccine. People had no idea that viruses were cleverer than human beings, and thought they'd soon be a thing of the past. In that optimistic, post-war America, which I caught the tail-end of, everybody was the master of her or his own destiny. I think my father got a little Promethean. I think he *liked* the idea of manipulating procreation. Anyway, with this overview in mind, with a rocket trail shimmering in the background, let me conjure my parents for you in the next scene that family history has brought down to me. This happened about two weeks after my father first broached the idea to my mother. In the interim they hadn't spoken of it once. Then one day my father brought home a present.

It was spring, and the plants in our sun room were reviving. My mother had put my brothers to bed. It was nine o'clock, and dark out. My father had been working late. When his car came up the drive, his headlights pierced the window panes, lighting up the family photo on the mantel: mother, father, son, son.

My mother heard the engine quit and went to meet my father at the side door. He came in, smiling, hand behind his back, bouquet-style. After they kissed, he brought the hand out. In it was a jewelry box, gift-wrapped.

'It's not my birthday,' Sophie said.

'Open it.'

'It's not our anniversary.'

'Go on. Open it.'

Sophie removed the wrapping without tearing it. She folded the paper, saving it in the pocket of her housedress. Then she lifted the lid off the box and looked at her present.

It was a thermometer.

'Martinis,' my father said.

He led her by the elbow to one of the matching love seats in our living room. At that time my mother hadn't yet grown skeptical of the presents my father gave her. This was before she found another woman's initials stitched into the lining of a supposedly new mink coat, or the faintly engraved tribute: TO MY LITTLE SLICE, FROM HENRY on the inside of a silver-anniversary ring. So she kept an open mind about the thermometer, which certainly didn't look like your normal, run-of-the-mill thermometer, and she waited for an explanation, smiling. Before giving one, Milton went to the bar to make the drinks.

'Is this real velvet in this case?' my mother asked.

'You bet,' said my father, dropping ice into the cocktail shaker.

'And it works? For real?'

'Sure, it works. I wouldn't give you a thermometer that didn't work, would I?' To punctuate this rhetorical question, Milton added two jiggers of gin and a thimbleful of vermouth to the shaker and shook.

'But Milt,' my mother ventured, still looking down at the thermometer, not ungratefully but mystified nonetheless, 'why are you giving me a thermometer?'

A full, two-handed shake, shoulders rumba-ing back and forth, and then my father lifted the cocktail shaker, undid the cap and poured the first of two martinis. 'We got any olives, hon?'

'Should be some there from yesterday.'

'Are these OK? Don't they go bad?'

'Not in a day.'

'I thought you were supposed to keep olives in the refrigerator.'

'I do keep them in the refrigerator,' my mother said, looking away from the thermometer for the first time. 'But, if I remember, you brought two friends home from work last night, *unexpectedly*. And I had to fix the drinks. And that's when the olives came *out* of the refrigerator. And then I had to go make dinner. And while I was making dinner for you and your friends, I forgot to put the olives *back*.'

'They smell fine,' my father said quickly. 'They're perfect.' To prove this, he ate one, rolling his eyes with pleasure, and then dropped one into each of the drinks.

When he brought hers over, my mother took a sip, closed her eyes and said, 'This is going to go straight to my head.' She put the thermometer into the glass like a swizzle stick. She stabbed the olive with it, brought it to her mouth and ate it.

'Look close,' said my father. 'What's different about this thermometer?' He gave her a second. 'Look on the side, at the markings. I had a helluva time finding one of these. Not because of the velvet. Because of how precise this thing is. Look. It reads the temperature down to *a tenth of a degree*.' Eyebrows raised, he went on: 'Not *two* tenths, like a normal thermometer, a *tenth*. Put it in your mouth.' My mother obeyed. My father sipped his martini. She tried to sip hers too, through the unoccupied corner of her mouth, but he motioned her not to. After about a minute, he took the thermometer out of Sophie's mouth and removed his glasses to study the markings. Then he announced: 'Your temperature, right now, sitting on the living-room sofa, is *ninety-eight-point-seven-and-a-half degrees*. I'm estimating the half.'

Suitably agog, my mother took the thermometer back, shaking her head and letting her mouth fall open. Milton said, 'Your body temperature's changing all the time, Soph. You may not notice it, but it does. You're in constant flux, temperature-wise. Say, for instance,' a little cough, 'you happen to be ovulating. Then your temperature goes up. Six tenths of a degree, in most case scenarios. Now,' my father went on, gaining steam, not noticing that his wife was no longer smiling, 'if we were to implement the system we talked about the other day—just for instance, say—what you'd do is, *first*, establish your *normal base temperature*. It might not be ninety-eight-point-six. Everybody's a little different. That's something I learned from Uncle Pete. Anyway once you've established your *normal base temperature*, then you look for that six-tenth-degree rise. And that's when, if we were to go through with this, we'd know to, you know, *hypothetically*, mix the cocktail.' Handing the thermometer back to my mother, my father raised his glass in a toast.

My mother didn't join him. Instead she put the thermometer, still wet, back into the box, closed it and pushed it across the coffee table.

'OK,' he said, 'fine. Suit yourself. We may get another boy. Number three. But if that's the way you want it, that's the way it'll be.'

'I'm not so sure we're going to have anything at the moment,' replied my mother. And they finished their drinks in silence.

While I (as impatiently as a non-being can) hovered in limbo. Not even a gleam in my father's eye yet (he was staring gloomily into his glass). Now my mother gets up from the inaptly named love seat. She heads for the stairway, holding a hand to her forehead, and the likelihood of my ever coming to be seems more and more remote. Then my father gets up to make his rounds, turning out lights, locking doors. Then, as he climbs the stairway, there's hope for me again. The timing of the thing had to be just so in order for me to become the person I am. Delay the act by an hour and you change the gene selection. My conception was still weeks away, but already my parents had begun their slow collision into each other. In our upstairs hallway, the Acropolis night light is burning, a gift from Uncle Yiannis who owns a souvenir store. My mother is at her vanity when my father enters the bedroom. With two fingers she rubs Noxema into her face, wiping it off with a tissue. My father only had to say an affectionate word, and she would've forgiven him. Not me but somebody like me might have been made that night. An infinite number of possible selves crowded the threshold, me among them but with no guaranteed ticket, the hours moving slowly, the planets in heaven circling at their usual pace, weather coming into it too, because my mother was afraid of thunderstorms and would've cuddled against my father had it rained that night. But no, clear skies held out, as did my parents' stubbornness. The bedroom light went out. They stayed on their own sides of the bed. At last, from my mother, 'Night.' And from my father, 'See you in the morning.' The moments that led up to me fell into place as though decreed. Which is why, I guess, I think about them so much.

The following Sunday my mother took Desdemona and my brothers to church. My father never went, having become an apostate at the age of thirteen over the outrageous price of votive candles. Likewise Desdemona's husband, my *papou* Stavros, preferred to spend his Sundays (as well as Monday, Tuesday and Wednesday nights, not to mention the occasional Friday afternoon) at the casino on Belle Isle where he played the roulette wheel. So, during the two-and-a-half-hour service, with my brothers playing paper, scissors, rock on one side, and Desdemona crossing herself more or less continually on the other, my mother had some time to think. Overhead, way way up past the incense and the lights, the Christ Pantocrator arched over the cathedral's dome. In terms of sheer arresting size, the Christ Pantocrator had an effect akin to a float in the Macy's Thanksgiving Day Parade. And that's not even to mention the added theological or emotional weight the figure conveyed. Our Christ Pantocrator was curved like the dome of heaven, or like space itself. Unlike the suffering, earthbound Christs depicted at eye-level on the church walls (like Santa Clauses at Christmas, one on every corner ringing the same sad bell), our Christ Pantocrator was clearly transcendent, all-powerful, heaven-bestriding. He was reaching down to the apostles done in mosaic above the altar—but also, by extension, reaching down to Sophie—to present the four rolled-up sheepskins of the gospels. My mother's face, looking up for guidance, was lit by oil lamps hanging out of nowhere, their long chains disappearing into the smoke they gave off. Two six-foot candles flamed on either side of the pulpit, and all twelve tiers of the central chandelier blazed. 'I don't know what to do about this thermometer business,' Sophie said silently to the grave, water-stained face above. 'On the one hand, it seems sacrilegious. On the other hand, what's so bad about a husband and wife trying to have a daughter if they love each other? Between you and me I don't think it'll work anyway. Milt's always got some crazy idea. Like the time he tried to raise those chinchillas and they all got out and about a year later we found one in the basement practically starved to death. But I want a daughter. I really do.' So, in my imagination, did my mother pray that day, and—uncap your yellow highlighter—I need to point out that her anxiety about the thermometer was already well-established and was, therefore, already growing into the guilt that would later stand between us when I accused Sophie of believing that my condition was a divine punishment.

At coffee hour after mass Sophie left my brothers by the cookie table while she went to compliment the priest on his sermon. She never failed to compliment the priest on his sermon. He happened to be her brother-in-law. She found Father Jim surrounded by a pack of widows offering him home-baked *koulouri* and bathing in his beatific essence. This essence consisted primarily in Father Jim's perfect contentment at being only five foot four. 'Hello, Sophie,' he said sweetly when she came up and, before she could even respond, declined any more *koulouri* with a wave of his hand. 'Excuse me, ladies,' he said, and led Sophie away. At the other end of the room, he folded his hands and inclined his head, asking in a delicate, confidential voice, 'So, Sophie, how are things at home?' But my mother didn't take the bait. She didn't ask about the legality of plotting a baby's gender. She rebelled at all these people knowing about what she and Milton did in the privacy of their own bedroom. Certain aspects of that activity she didn't even want Milton himself to know and so she was strict about lights. My mother was dressed that day (I'm taking an educated guess) in her cream-colored dress with the scalloped hem that resembled a theater curtain. Two strands of imitation pearls hung around her neck, amid the gold brooches, the lapis lazuli pins, the rather immense Orthodox cross, also gold. Over all this, a short yellow jacket hung, matching her handbag. Just then, however, she turned abruptly away. (This part I have no doubt about.) During the years it was my privilege to observe my mother's startling personal radar, a beacon which issued not from her third eye but a little lower down, from the horizontal wrinkle at the bridge of her nose, I came to take for granted Sophie's ability to find a lost shoe under the couch, or to shut windows five minutes before it rained, or to know what any of us was thinking by merely looking into our eyes. Now, in the church basement, without seeing more than that Theo and Nick were standing on either side of a pretty little girl in a green jumper, my mother already foresaw the oncoming catastrophe enough to cry out, 'Watch, watch!' . . . five seconds before Nick, trying to pull the girl's hair ribbon, succeeded in knocking over the coffee urn. The lid went rattling across the floor. Coffee grounds spilt out. Hot coffee too. As my mother rushed across the basement, she saw coffee splash against the green jumper, and the girl's eyes open wide. Her mouth opened too, but no sound came out. With a gesture as swift as her premonition, my mother gathered the girl up and, fixing Nick with a furious eyebrow, swept into the ladies room.

The girl, whose name no one remembers, didn't belong to any of the regular parishioners. She wasn't even Greek. She appeared at church that one day and was never seen again. Nobody remembers who her parents were. The girl seems to have existed for the sole purpose of changing my mother's mind and, seeing as

I like being alive, I thank her. My mother took her into a toilet stall, lifting her on top of a lowered seat. The jumper had two shoulder straps which buttoned in back. Letting the jumper fall away, my mother pulled the girl out. Her T-shirt steamed a little, like meat from a lobster claw. Underneath, her damp skin was mottled like a lobster's too. She stood very still as my mother pressed cool paper towels over her chest. 'Are you OK, honey? Did you get burned?'

'He's very clumsy, that boy,' the girl said.

'I think we got you out of these clothes just in time. Where's your mother?'

The girl shrugged. Sophie told her to wait right there while she rinsed out the jumper. At the sink, she heard the girl begin singing to herself, alone in the stall, standing on top of the toilet. Sophie held the jumper under the faucet, listening. After a while the girl abruptly stopped. 'It doesn't take that long to rinse out a dress,' she said informatively.

Two weeks later. A humid June, 1959: my parents playing doubles at the Grosse Pointe Country Club. My father, in tennis whites, looks as swarthy as Poncho Gonzales. My mother hits the ball gingerly, protecting her hairdo. Tonight, after the match, my parents are dining with their hosts, Bob and Gerri McKinnon, in the club's stately dining room. Now, on the court, my father grunts, mis-hitting a return. 'Good show!' he shouts, for the hundredth time. McKinnon prepares to serve another. He dips his knees, at the same time tossing the ball into the air. The ball rises over the court, over McKinnon's sandy hair. It rises beyond the golf course, above the trees. At the net, Gerri waits, smiling. Her blonde hair is held back in a pink elastic. The ball descends, McKinnon rising, his racket, lazily dropped over one shoulder, ascending as his arm straightens out. With the easy form he learned at boarding school, perfected in college and has maintained into middle age, he whacks the ball over the net, into the service square, past my father's feet. My father lays his racket down on the court and applauds.

On this day in June my father is about to close a deal with Bob McKinnon's bank. Only a few details remain to be ironed out. After the match, in the locker room, Bob will order drinks. They'll sit in their towels, watching golf on the old television on top of the lockers. Around them, naked, soft-bellied executives will extract one of six combs from the Barbisol and carefully part their hair. They'll talk, they'll sip. 'No sense rushing upstairs just to wait for the girls,' Bob'll say. Over his Manhattan, which he doesn't like but orders from the black, bow-tied waiter because Bob does, my father will move in for the kill. 'Some game today, Bob! You were really firing in those serves! I wish you'd give me a lesson. Now, about that Southland deal, I was just going over some of the numbers . . . '

Behind the court, the sun is falling. The sky is turning pink. There is a pink dot on my mother's hair where hairspray reflects the sunlight. Near the court surface, clay dust blurs everyone's shins, but up above, in the clear late afternoon light, their faces appear distinct, happy, still young. In immaculate socks Bob McKinnon serves out the last game. At the net Gerri smiles, holding her racket like a weapon. One more serve, the sun falling, the sprinkler system kicking on across the immensity of green golf course, and then it'll be time for drinks, for dinner, possibly the suggestion, from Bob, that he'll put Milt and Sophie up for membership. The running around is almost over, and the filet mignon is on the way. But then suddenly my mother calls out, 'Just a minute!' She goes to the bench at the side of the court. She rifles through her bag.

'That a new racket, Bob?' my father asks.

'No, Milt, same one as always.'

'You're really firing them in!' My father checks to see what the hell my mother is doing. She's still bending over the bench. 'Come on, Soph! One more point!' Then to the McKinnons: 'She's just trying to rattle you.'

Now my mother comes back on to the court. But she has something in her mouth, nothing in her hand. 'Sophie, your racket,' my father says, a little impatient.

'Mil,' my mother mutters, barely opening her mouth, 'I'm up two tense.'

'What?'

'My tempacha. Two tense.' She pauses. 'I tinkis time.'

She's talking funny because she has the thermometer in her mouth. This is the first my father has heard of it. She didn't tell him she'd decided to go along.

'Now?' he says. 'Jesus, Sophie, are you sure?'

'No, I'm not sure,' she says, taking the thermometer out and checking it again, squinting in the failing light. 'I don't understand this stuff, Milt. You told me to watch for any rise in my temperature, and I'm telling you I'm up two tenths of a degree. And it's been thirteen days since my last you-know-what.'

'Forty-love,' Bob calls out. He pantomimes a serve. My father looks over the net, at Bob, at the other courts beyond, at the golf course beyond that. He also sees, rising over the country club, in a little golden dream balloon, the little girl of his morning commute. 'Your match, Bob, Gerri,' he calls out. 'Sophie just reminded me. We've got a little family obligation. Nothing serious. We promised the kids we'd take them to a movie.'

At home, half-clad in tennis whites, they accomplish the act. A child's natural decorum makes me refrain from imagining the scene in too much detail. Only this: when they're done, as if hammering in the final nail, my father says, 'That should do it.' It turns out, he's right. In July Sophie learns that she's pregnant, and the waiting begins.

By six weeks, I have eyes and ears. By seven, nostrils, even lips. My genitals begin to form. Fetal hormones, taking chromosomal cues, inhibit this structure, promote that. My twenty-three paired chromosomes have linked up and crossed over, spinning their own roulette wheel, as Stavros puts his hand to my mother's belly and says, 'Lucky three!' Arrayed in their regiments, my genes carry out their orders. All except two, a pair of miscreants, or revolutionaries—depending on your view—hiding out on chromosome number five. Together, they siphon off an enzyme which stops the production of a certain hormone which complicates my life.

In the living room the men have stopped talking about politics and instead lay bets as to whether Milt's new kid will be a boy or a girl. My father is confident. Twenty-four hours after the deed was done, my mother's body temperature rose another four tenths, confirming the moment of ovulation. The male sperm had given up by then, exhausted. The female sperm, like tortoises, win the race. At the time of that last reading, my mother was fresh from a hot bath, but Milton insisted there was no connection. (At which point Sophie handed him the thermometer and told him she never wanted to see it again.)

All this leads up to the day Desdemona dangled a utensil over my mother's belly. The sonogram didn't exist at the time; the spoon was the next best thing. Desdemona crouched. The kitchen grew silent. The older women bit their lower lips. The American girls giggled and pinched themselves in order to stop. It was amazing how mystifying a spoon could be. For the first minute it didn't move at all. Desdemona didn't have the steadiest hand and at one point told Lucille to hold her wrist. The spoon twirled; I kicked; my mother cried out. And then, slowly, moved by a wind no one felt, in that unearthly Ouija-board way, the silver spoon began to move, to swing, at first in a small circle, but each orbit growing more elliptical until it flattened out completely into a straight line pointing from oven to banquette. North to south, in other words. Desdemona cried, '*Koros!*' And the room erupted with shouts of '*koros, koros*'.

That night, my father said, 'Twenty-three in a row means she's bound for a fall. This time, she's wrong. Trust me.'

'I don't mind if it's a boy,' my mother said. 'I really don't. As long as he's healthy, ten fingers, ten toes, that's all I ask.'

'What's this "it"? That's my daughter you're talking about. That's my little Calliope.'

'I hope so, Milt. But either way, I'll be happy.'

Then my mother bled. She thought she was having a miscarriage. My father came home one day to find her sprawled on the couch, weeping. To comfort her, he said, 'Don't worry. We can have another one.'

'I don't want another one!' my mother said. 'I want this one!'

It turned out not to be serious. In fact, my mother took encouragement from the bleeding once it had stopped. Aunt Mathilda said that if a pregnancy differed from those before, it meant that you were carrying a baby of a different sex. My father, who condemned Desdemona's superstitions, supported this one.

On 8 March 1960 I was born. In the waiting room, supplied only with pink-ribboned cigars, my father shouted: 'Bingo!' I was a girl. Nineteen inches long. Seven pounds, four ounces. My discharge weight was three ounces less than my birth weight, a loss which is maybe normal, or indicative of the trauma of entering the world, or both.

One other thing happened at 4:53 a.m., however, and it wasn't good. My grandfather Stavros suffered the first of his thirteen strokes. Awakened by my parents rushing off to the hospital, he'd gotten out of bed and gone downstairs to make himself a cup of coffee. An hour later, Desdemona found him lying stricken on the kitchen floor. His mental faculties remained intact but that morning, as I let out my first cry at Detroit Women's Hospital, Stavros lost the ability to speak. According to Desdemona, who's a fairly unreliable witness, Stavros collapsed right after overturning his coffee cup to read his fortune in the grounds. She saved the saucer, her first clue, maintaining later that the muddy swirl predicted everything.

The following Sunday Uncle Pete wouldn't accept any congratulations. There was no magic involved. 'Besides,' he joked, 'Milt did all the work.' Desdemona took the news a little hard. Her American-born son had been proven right and, with this fresh defeat, the old country, in which she still tried to live despite being five thousand miles and thirty-eight years away, receded one more notch. My arrival marked the end of her baby-guessing, and though the silkworm box reappeared now and then, the spoon was no longer among its treasures.

I was extracted, spanked and hosed off, in that order. They wrapped me in a blanket and put me on display among six other infants, four boys, two girls, all of them, unlike me, correctly tagged. This can't be true but I remember it: sparks slowly filling a dark screen.

Someone had switched on my eyes. □

GRANTA

JONATHAN FRANZEN
HOW HE CAME TO BE NOWHERE

Jonathan Franzen was born in 1959 in Chicago and grew up in St Louis, where his father was a civil engineer. He majored in German at Swarthmore College and from 1983 to 1987 worked part-time as an earthquake analyst for the Department of Earth and Planetary Sciences at Harvard University. After his first novel, *The Twenty-Seventh City*, was published in 1988, he received a Whiting Writers Award. His second novel, *Strong Motion*, appeared in 1992. He is a Guggenheim Fellow and a frequent contributor to the *New Yorker*. He lives in New York City.

'How He Came to be Nowhere' has been taken from a novel in progress.

Room 471, the Federal Building, Eighth Street, Philadelphia: a perfectly square room which for no obvious reason had an eye chart on the southern wall. A leak in the roof two floors up had spread damage across the ceiling and down two other walls—ricotta-like eruptions of plaster, arrested avalanches of softened latex paint. In one corner where the cracks were especially complex, the ceiling was actually sagging. The room gave the impression of a desperate beleaguerment, as if an immense weight of water, that enemy of paper documents and even more so of anything electrical, were bearing down from above. There was a yeasty, incontinent smell of damp plaster, and rustles of official business outside the door.

In the room: two white men. From the fingers and arm and thorax of one of them, Andy Aberant, half a dozen wires in elementary colors stretched down a cheap particle-board table to a partition behind which the other, Special Agent Barry Thewless, was adjusting levels. Aberant looked wired for a virtual-reality experience, but the signals were all outgoing— respiration rate, skin moisture and so forth. Thewless's pants pockets were tumescent with Kleenex, his knobby face a bright pink from his morning shave. Watching over the table was a video camera with the sleek body and long legs of a shore bird.

'You're smiling why,' Thewless said to Aberant.

Aberant, who had indeed begun to smile, said, 'I was remembering the one time I ever had the courage to ask my father why he didn't fight in the Second World War. He was the right age for it, and I always had the feeling he felt like less of a man for not having fought with everybody else. That all his life he didn't feel like he really fit in. So I asked him once, and he said high blood pressure. He said he was late for his physical and he ran up six flights of stairs to the doctor's office. They took his blood pressure and they said he was unfit.'

'This is amusing why,' Thewless said.

'Because it just occurred to me that maybe he was lying. He was a bulldog, healthwise. He took like three sick days in his entire career. He was also uncontrollably honest. When he was dating my mother he told her she wasn't half as pretty as her sister, stuff like that. He couldn't control it.'

Thewless inclined his head to read his watch. 'The point being what.'

'The point being that he didn't tell the doctor that he'd run up those stairs. He didn't ask to be re-tested. So either what he told me wasn't true, or he wasn't completely honest with the doctor. You have to understand, this was a man who never lied. I didn't put it together until this minute.'

Outside the only window, which was closed, the Philadelphia sky hovered proximately. The Ben Franklin Bridge, looking too big for its setting, came to an awkward end among warehouse roofs. On the broad sidewalk below the window, a handful of Catholic pacifists held aloft placards urging an end to the death penalty. There was light residual morning traffic on Eighth Street, the less serious commuters.

'I thought of it because of the blood-pressure thingy here and of course the whole topic of lies,' Aberant said.

'The plethysmograph,' Thewless said affectionately. 'I'm going to pump that up again, if you don't mind, and then we'll do the questions a little differently.' He reached over the partition, gave the rubber bulb a few amorous squeezes and returned to his instruments. 'Your full name as it appears on your passport is what.'

'Andrew Kearns Aberant. Stress on the first syllable of the last name.'

'Your father and mother are alive, yes or no.'

'No.'

'You have three older sisters, excellent though substantially overweight Christian women with many children, all of whom reside in Texas, yes or no.'

'Yes.'

Thewless belonged to the Neutral Phrasing school of polygraph operators, and he read the questions on his clipboard in an unstressed monotone, as though dictating to voice-recognition software. To speak to a machine, one made oneself machine-like. And this, of course, was the point of the poly: that Aberant was a machine, that the organic wiring that instructed his arteries to constrict and his sweat glands to open partook of the same *materia prima* in which his 'higher'-order thoughts held court. There were rumors even now, gnomic whisperings on Wall Street, of new technologies that could patch into this wiring directly and decode, if not thoughts and images, certainly intentions and emotions. The old government-issue poly in Room 471 was Eisenhowerishly sincere and primitive, however, and quite out of its league when it came to reporting on the inside of Aberant.

'You are or have in the past been an anarchist or a member of or affiliated with any Communist or other totalitarian party including any subdivision or affiliate, yes or no,' Thewless said.

'No.'

'You're mentally ill or homosexual, yes or no.'

'No.'

'You're currently sleeping with who.'

'I think you mean whom. Julia Fuller, in Manhattan. I see her on weekends.'

'Who else?' Thewless said, somewhat less robotically.

'The whom here again would be nobody.'

'Prior to your hiring by the Securities & Exchange Commission your position was what.'

'I was a full-time law student at Columbia University.'

'Prior to that you resided where.'

'Bozeman, Montana.'

'Your means of support was what.'

'I had a small inheritance from my parents' death.'

'The cause of their death was what.'

'There was a freak windstorm in Lawrence, Kansas. They were blown off an overpass.'

'At the time of their death you were employed as what.'

'I was a staffer with the Environmental Defense League.'

'At that time you engaged in activities that were in opposition to the United States government or you knowingly associated with individuals engaged in subversive activities, yes or no.'

'No.'

'You're aware that Environmental Defense League literature calls for the establishment of a New Holistic World Order, yes or no.'

'To the best of my knowledge the EDL is a law-abiding group and always has been.'

'Yes or no.'

'No, actually.'

Thewless had no more questions. He released the pressure in the cuff on Aberant's arm and gingerly untaped the other sensors.

Aberant put on his shirt and jacket with the compact, dignified movements of a man whose honesty had been vigorously impugned.

In front of the Federal Building, under the Eakins-like vacancy of the sky, a broad-shouldered, big-chested woman in a thigh-length red T-shirt detached herself from the other Catholic protesters and intercepted Aberant in the no-parking zone where he'd left his car. 'Hey you,' she said. 'What are you doing here?'

'Taking a lie-detector test.'

'No shit. How many times did you lie?'

'Six.'

'So kiss me six times,' she said.

With a laugh he removed the parking ticket that was lodged beneath his wiper blade, tore it in two and dropped it in the gutter.

Although he'd been lying for as long as he could remember, had incorporated deception so thoroughly into his being that it almost seemed as if his entire life had been a preparation for passing with flying colors the final random polygraph test that stood between him and full federal security clearance, Andy Aberant had seldom been pathological about it. He was simply a skilled withholder of pertinent information, a sower of red herrings; an extrapolator, an interpolator. Having visited North Carolina as a child, he saw no harm in claiming, as an adult, that he'd also been to South Carolina. After all, he had no memory of either state.

When he was young there was a mania for science fairs, and for various disreputable reasons he keenly wished to win a regional science fair trophy; the main reason, perhaps, was that his aptitude for science was substantially nil. He went to the university library and combed its holdings in plant physiology, which his class at school was studying, and he found a technical paper on plant growth substances that was both obscure enough and simple enough to be mistaken for the work of a brilliant eighth-grader. It concerned GIBBERELLIC ACID and some mysterious elusive chemical factor named K2, also the name of a mountain. The junior-high biology lab happened to own several grams of GIBBERELLIC ACID, and using some plywood and white paint Andy built a controlled environment in which to grow oat seedlings in test tubes. Once it was all painted and electrified and turning green with young oats, he photographed it with an Instamatic from many angles. Then he ignored it for so long that his mother began to complain about the smell. (At the Aberants' church great stress was placed on Christ's painful crucifixion, but in Andy's own private version of His passion, Christ had been allowed to die of neglect in a terrarium, flowerpot or fishbowl.) To determine the effects of GIBBERELLIC ACID in concert with mysterious, elusive, chemical factor K2, he was now supposed to weigh the oat seedlings, but at this late date they were little more than crusts of dried-out blackish slime. It took him several long afternoons to draw the graph showing the experiment's 'correct' results and then work backwards, fabricating a long list of seedling weights with some artful random variation, and then work forward again to make sure the fictional data produced the correct results, which they did, and he won the three-foot-tall first-place trophy and special commendation from the judges for his photographs.

Afterwards his father took him aside and told him he should smile and thank people who had praised his work; that his self-deprecation looked to them like arrogance, and he hoped that Andy wasn't arrogant about his victory?

Andy said no, he wasn't arrogant about his victory.

So to a house with a fish symbol or a Galilean crowd scene in every room there came a hollow pagan icon—a silver-plated Winged Victory on a faux-walnut base with Andy's name engraved on it incorrectly ('ABERRANT'): SCIENCE VICTORIOUS, presumably, over the forces of darkness and superstition. Whenever he noticed the trophy gathering dust in the family room, what he experienced was not so much guilt (though there was some of that too) as a curious sensation of seeing an artifact from the life of the boy he was supposed to be, the authentic Andrew that he emphatically was not. From here it was a short step to oiling the hinges of the front door and nailing down the loose floorboards of the hallway so that he could silently slip from the house after everyone (including him, with much yawning and stretching of arms) had gone to bed. While the putative Andrew slept, the inconveniently actual Andy drank apple wine with other junior-varsity golfers at the bottom of a gravel pit. And the next morning, so badly hungover that after chewing a bite of toast for a minute or two he determined that swallowing it was not remotely an option, his transgressions were rewarded with special concern from his mother. She put him to bed and brought him liquids and then hurried off to church, because the funny thing about Andy's bouts with stomach flu was that they always seemed to come on Sunday mornings.

The problem was not that he was spoiled, or even, in a household as evangelically correct as the Aberants', particularly over-indulged. The problem was love. The last foamy wave of it, sweet and red as Strawberry Crush, would still be clearing through his gunwales when a fresh wave hit. As the youngest child, the long-wished-for son and little brother, he was inundated, capsized, sunk. There were possibly as few as eight candles on the birthday cake in front of him the first time he found himself, in the glow of their flames and of the expectant smiles that ringed him, feigning pleasure. To the aunts and grandmothers who had remembered his special day he wrote *I love the present and will think of you whenever I use it*, but the truth was that he thought about himself a great deal and about his aunts and grandmothers (who loved him) almost never. He was the best student in his family but he felt stupider than his sisters and parents, who at any given moment had room in their heads for the contemplation of people less fortunate than themselves and for thanking the Lord and for excitement about proms and new curtains for the living room; they were capable of astounding feats of parallel processing, and the only way he could keep up with them, the only way to avoid betraying his unworthiness of their love, was to perfect the art of seeming. He felt like the lone oxygen-breather in a house whose atmosphere of helium made everyone else's voices high-pitched with festivity and optimism. The only place where he could breathe was a private place inside himself, and fortunately his family loved him so much that they didn't notice he was missing.

His father, Gene Aberant, was a home-improvement maven, a traveling agronomist for the state of Kansas and perhaps the most tender-hearted man in the Sunflower State. Wiry and balding, with thick-lensed glasses and big teeth that were forever exposed in his happiness to be alive, he weighed not a whole lot more than half of what his wife did. He loved and was loved by every small child he ever met, which would have included Andy had Andy not been a sour middle-aged French philosopher (this was approximately how alien he looked to himself in hindsight) trapped in the body of a child. For Andy's thirteenth birthday, after his victory at the science fair, Gene unilaterally built him a full-service laboratory bench in the basement, and for many months afterward Andy was so stricken with guilt over the misunderstanding that he spent all the money he earned as a caddie to amass supplies for the lab. He was devoid of scientific curiosity but he genuinely liked the supplies as sensual objects: fresh packages of microscope slides, slabs of paraffin for the microtome that he never figured out how to use, retorts and ring stands and Erlenmeyer flasks, rubber tubes and rubber stoppers, anything related to the deliciously austere word 'reagent', a second-hand microscope with a *rack-and-pinion* focusing mechanism and *knurled* brass knobs; killing jars, agar-agar, vermiculite. He bought a hardbound ledger in which to record his observations, but it remained empty. His concern was simply to appear scientific, and his lab activities were strictly demonstrations—'experiments' that produced smoke or flame or attractive arrangements of glassware or colorful liquids or death to insects.

'We've got a budding young scientist,' Gene announced from time to time.

Only after Gene was dead did Andy become cynical enough himself to suspect the utter absence of cynicism in that household, and to see how he in his young cynicism might have been the most innocent of all of them, because he'd bothered to be a liar, had bothered to try to preserve his family's innocence, had actually *wanted* that stupid trophy and, worst of all, had believed himself to be uniquely deceitful—as if, when the rest of humanity said *I love the present and will think of you whenever I use it*, they actually meant it. He recognized, too late, that innocence is always willful. After all he must have reeked of Boone's Farm Apple

Wine when he was put back to bed on Sunday mornings, and he was often caught in his lies, and his ever-more outrageous second-order lies were swallowed with peculiar readiness. *Why had his mother heard him opening the front door at five in the morning?* He said he'd been stargazing. *How had he used half a tank of gas driving twelve blocks to the university library?* He said he'd heard on the car radio about an interesting partial solar eclipse south of Wichita. *Could that possibly have been Andy whom Mrs Sternhagen had spotted with Alicia Rutting on the eleventh green of the Lakeview Country Club three hours after he'd gone to his bedroom with much yawning and stretching of arms?* He took the opportunity to ask his parents for a birthday gift subscription to *Sky & Telescope*.

If his parents had survived to old age, had lived even just a year or two longer, there would surely have been a correction. Andy would have gotten around to admitting that his post-graduate apartment on West 122nd Street was not 'a few blocks' from Wall Street, that the Environmental Defense League had not been founded by Marlin Perkins, that the woman who sometimes answered his telephone was not his roommate's sister but the girlfriend with whom he was 'cohabiting' (a word which to evangelical Kansans connoted *lewdly fucking*), and that he had majored in astronomy at college because the old gin-smelling chairman of the department would not fail any student who came to his weekly rooftop star parties. Or maybe the correction would have run the other way. Maybe one of Andy's sisters would have found a new God and blown the roof off the house of Aberant, announced to the world that shy, 'honest' Gene had sexually abused each of his three daughters in turn, and that their mother had worn those hideous floral pants suits not because she had bad taste, but because her legs were covered with bruises and burn marks, and that all the piety and cheer, the baking for bake sales and the cherishing of Andy and his pleasures, had in fact been an elaborate quintipartite conspiracy whose aim was the achievement of innocence on Andy's part, because they needed one innocent in their family or they all would have gone crazy. They needed him to believe that he was deceiving them lest he suspect the enormity of their deception of him, because the ravages of Boone's Farm, the moist comforts of Alicia Rutting, the Saturday-afternoon pilgrimage to the Foxxxy Club Cinema in Kansas City, the exhalation of cannabis smoke into the fiberglass insulation between attic rafters in the heart-rendingly naïve belief that no one downstairs could smell it (for Andy had done this too), were all just lilacs and bunny rabbits compared to the sick truths that they were conspiring to keep from him . . .

But there was no correction of any kind. In the year of Big Brother, which was also the year when high-speed monorails rendered the automobile obsolete, which was also the year when Malthusian famines swept the overpopulated planet, his parents took a walk together on a Sunday afternoon, and a wind out of nowhere lifted them off the Harrison Avenue overpass and dropped them on the pavement forty feet below. When Andy flew into Kansas City the next morning, FREAK WIND and KILLER GUST were the lead stories in the two local papers. Apparently the gust, some weird sort of back-door frontal disturbance, had descended full force into a day of perfect calm, like an invisible twister that was everywhere at once, shearing off awnings, denuding billboards and upending mobile homes. According to news reports, a lot of people had believed the wind was the end of the world; it had hit with the uncanny suddenness of a shock wave from a pre-emptive strike on the silos twenty miles west.

During the week he spent at home, it seemed as if everywhere he turned he saw an exact replica of his old science-fair trophy—the identical Winged Victory and fake walnut pedestal. Behind the cash register of the gas station where he filled the tank of the parental Olds: 'Manhattan Kansas Stalk Car Derby, Second Runner Up.' In the richly panelled employee lounge-cum-casket showroom where he shook the soft, pickled-seeming hand of funeral director Ollie Engdahl: 'First Prize, Kiwanis Bwol-AThon, Engdahl Funereal Home Employees.' And in the den of the pastor who led him and his sisters and brothers-in-law in a lengthy private prayer: 'Pilsbury Regional Bake-Off, Daisy Fawcett, Lemin Bars.' The big windows of the Fawcetts' modern split-level were so clean that they lent a painful definition to the late-winter wheatfields and woodlots outside them, the stubble and oak branches blown clean by a sky so starkly blue that there seemed not to be a sun in it anywhere, nor any birds or other life. While the rest of his surviving family went to the Fawcett kitchen and loaded plates with Mrs Fawcett's famous lemon bars, Andy did a thing he later lost sleep regretting. He stole a black Sharpi® from the pastor's desk and defaced the trophy's inscription, changing the 'i' in 'Lemin' to an 'o'. He knew this was a cruel thing to do because he knew that Mrs Fawcett was in midwestern awe of authority and so almost certainly preferred a professional error to an amateur truth.

In later years when people asked him how his parents had died, he generally said 'a highway accident'—which was hardly even a lie—because the true cause of their death seemed ridiculous to anyone who didn't come from Kansas. In Kansas people took the weather seriously; almost everyone had seen a funnel cloud or had slid off a road in a blizzard or knew somebody who'd known somebody incinerated by lightning, usually a golfer. But the sad truth was that even Andy found his parents' deaths ridiculous, and he hoped that they too had been so shocked and amused to find themselves tumbling off that overpass that they hadn't had time for terror before the impact shattered their skulls and a lot of their bones. When he viewed them in their caskets he saw that Ollie Engdahl had been unequal to the task of adjusting their skeletons into restful poses. The bodies lay lumpily in the white satin cushions like battered dolls—crude replicas of two late-middle-aged Kansans who, as far as Andy knew, had done nothing worse in their lives than maybe love him a little too much. He was particularly unimpressed by the smaller doll's pretense of being his father, whom he could not imagine otherwise than as a tiger of lean power. As, for example, when Gene had rushed to get the family's new sprinkler system installed while a summer sky hatched thunderstorms, had sprinted back and forth across the front lawn with undulating lengths of plastic pipe while the sky turned the green and black of spoiled beef and the thunder came from every direction, the muscles in the globes of his shoulders braiding and unbraiding as he tried to shovel all the Kansas clay back in the trenches before the deluge struck, an actual freshet of sweat, not just isolated droplets, coursing from his face. The sky opened before he'd refilled his orderly trenches, and where a different man, a man who had fought in the war, might have shouted curses at the weather, Gene simply grinned and shook his head as a bolt of lightning blew out a nearby utility-pole transformer in a malign experiment of ozone and evil-smelling PCBs, and what basically qualified as a flash flood ripped through the trenches and carried a good part of the Aberant family's topsoil, along with various not-inexpensive pipes and sprinkler-system fittings, down the hill and into the culvert where Andy, then about eight years old, had recently impressed two neighbor girls by cavorting naked. Standing by the caskets sixteen years later, he wept but unfortunately also watched himself weep.

In later years he said 'a highway accident' because he had learned that it was just too wearisome to persuade people of the truth when an easily swallowable half-truth was available. And the weariness became a way of life. He drifted for a decade in a slow curve that eventually landed him in law school, that modern refuge of the aimlessly clever, and from law school he edged by default into public service. The feeling of stupidity from his childhood stayed with him always. He considered himself a person to whom nothing interesting had ever happened. If someone had asked his father if he'd ever been to South Carolina, his father would have said, 'No, but I hear it's a beautiful state,' and then would have listened, beaming and nodding, while the person told him interesting facts and legends of South Carolina, and after ten minutes Gene would have learned a great deal about the state, and the person would have enjoyed talking to him.

Andy, his only son, somehow came into the world needing people to believe that he knew everything, which was another way of saying that he believed he knew nothing about anything but himself; and what he knew about himself, which was that he was very afraid, he dedicated all his energies to concealing. When he told stories, they were usually stories about someone else. In these stories he felt more truly alive than he did in the few he ever told about himself. He had the nagging suspicion that if it had been someone other than himself in the vicinity of whose shattered ulna an orthopedic surgeon had left the cap of a twenty-five-cent Bic pen, someone other than himself who had unwittingly locked himself in an aft lavatory of an L-1011 and spent six hours in a USAir hangar before being rescued by a cleaning-crew member (these were the two most colorful things that had ever happened to him), he might have told the stories with relish. But since it was he to whom these things had happened, he quickly lost interest in them, because they were simply colorful and there were only two of them, and two seemed approximately his allotment as a citizen of a well-ordered republic in which mildly zany or tragic things once in a while befell almost everyone—the freak gust of wind, the massacre at a Wendy's, the six-legged calf, the red bell pepper which when photographed from the proper angle uncannily resembled the head of Richard Nixon. Why bother mentioning one's own few contributions to the general static? There was no truth whatsoever to his stories. They did not begin, 'I met the woman of my life at' or 'I found God when' or 'I decided to join the Revolution because'. He seemed to himself an anti-raconteur. The only thing about himself that felt singular was the degree to which he experienced the shallowness of his personality and the emptiness of words. He had the breadth and depth of knowledge of a card catalog. He was full of data which often proved not very reliable. He was good at taking tests, at causing women to fall in love with him and at escaping from these women with his reputation for kindness intact. Only once had he failed to escape in time; he was living in Bozeman with a girl who was seriously Catholic, and her last words to him were: 'Your soul is dead.'

Had his father deceived the army doctor? He would never know. Had his father deceived *him*? He would never know. By missing the war and then living in a house of women, Gene Aberant had become estranged from the world of men. Andy had simply completed the development and become estranged from the world of everyone. The only rules he believed in were rules of grammar, spelling and punctuation. And now he really did love the present. It was the only place he could bear to live. □

GRANTA

DAVID GUTERSON
APPLES

David Guterson was born in 1956 in Seattle, where his father was a criminal defense attorney and his mother 'a perennial college student'. He attended public schools in Seattle and the city's University of Washington and then taught for ten years in public high school. He has written non-fiction as well as fiction, including *Family Matters: Why Homeschooling Makes Sense* (1992). His novel, *Snow Falling on Cedars* (1994), won the PEN/Faulkner Award. He lives on an island in Puget Sound, Washington State, with his wife and four children.

'Apples' is taken from his new novel, set in Washington's apple country and provisionally titled *East of the Mountains*, which will be published by Harcourt Brace in 1998.

He remembered the new, fresh, orchard country of his youth and the rows of apple trees his father had planted on the east bank of the Columbia River. In those days Ben had made apple boxes out of pine shook and picked ripe apples in season. He'd pulled weeds in the kitchen garden with his brother, Aidan; split apple cordwood for the fireplace; and milked the cows twice a day. In the spring he'd helped his father and Aidan put out the pollinating hives. He helped wrap burlap bands around apple-tree trunks to stop the coddling moths. Midsummer he went out to help thin the fruit; in winter he helped with the pruning. There were rows of water sprouts to be collected and burned in a pile at the orchard's edge. He sorted apples, wrapped and boxed them and nailed shut the box lids. He and Aidan would harness up the horses and cart the apples to the river. They would leave the apples at the railroad siding, then go up the hill for more. In the spring there were windbreak trees to be planted and crab apple pollinating trees. In April and May there were young trees to plant and finished trees to pull out. They put spreader sticks in the yearling trees and strapped the branches back. The sluice-gates in the ditches would clog with weeds, and Ben and Aidan would stand in the water to clear the gates by hand. Ditches would slump, and with his brother and father Ben would dig them out again. He fed chickens and burned piles of dried-out sage after his father plowed new land. In July he helped to prop and strap branches to keep them from cracking with the weight of apples. In frost season he helped light the smudge pots. He mowed between the rows in early summer to keep the mice from the orchards. There was always work for him to do—a life composed of work.

The Givenses' orchards were stately, well-pruned and sheltered from the wind by Lombardy poplars; they lay on thirty acres of gentle river slope halfway between Rock Island and Trinidad. There were thirteen acres of Golden Delicious, eight of Winesaps, two of Rome Beauties and two of peaches and apricots. The rest of the land was given over to experiments—Arkansas Blacks, Spitzenburgs and a few sparse winter bananas. The orchards fell toward the river in a great sweep and were full of irrigation ditches, sharp-bladed quack grass growing between the rows, and branch props leaning against forked limbs. There was a weathered packing shed for making boxes and for wrapping apples in oiled tissue and packing them in season. There was a cow barn loaded with hay to the rafters and a stable for the horses and a chicken house and outhouse and an ice house and a small well pump house. There were shanties for the pickers who came in August and an outhouse for them too. The Givens ranch house sat on a knoll surrounded by shade elms and willows. When the wind came up, the tops of the trees swirled so that with the windows flung open on summer evenings the crash of branches was startlingly loud as the Givenses sat at their dinner table. Even in the house the world smelled of apples and of hay and horses and the wind off the river, and from the front window the setting sun bronzed the land stretching away from them westward.

Where the orchards ended, the world began—buttes, coulees, canyons, sagelands, arid expanses of infinite reach, all sun-drenched, forlorn and lonesome. Ben and Aidan took the dogs into this country in search of quail, chukars and sage grouse, and occasionally got a shot at a jackrabbit. They rode on horseback when they had the chance, their shotguns slung across their backs, their canteens slapping against their saddles. Sometimes they camped in the sage at night where they drew and spitted their birds carefully, stuffed sage sprigs inside the empty bellies and cooked the birds on a twig fire. Then they lay back with their hands behind their heads and ate and watched the heavens. As children they talked about any and all things—their conversation was aimless and leisurely—but as they grew older they spoke quite pointedly about girls, or about the lack of them. They spoke of the girls they saw in town, or at school, or at their church. Aidan was older than Ben by twenty months, stocky, sturdy, even-tempered. He worked with a pine sliver set between his teeth, a sheen of sweat against his collarbones, the front of his shirt sweat-soaked in a line from his chest down to his navel. Generally he wore his hat low on his forehead so that his eyes were heavily shaded by its brim but when somebody spoke to him he canted the brim up and listened, his eyes animated, before he made to answer. Aidan was so agreeable, so amiable. His skin was brown, his eyes blue. He liked to swim in the river at dusk just upstream from the ranch house. There was an eddy there where Ben and Aidan would stand to strip off all of their clothing and then toss their shirts and pants up high against the warm, polished shore rocks. Then they would stretch their backs and bare limbs and run their hands along their bellies and through their hair full of pollen dust or apple litterfall or blossom petals. Finally, brown and naked and grateful, they would wade into the river. They would have worked all day in the apple orchards and they would feel overheated and tired. It was easy for them, at dusk in summer, to fall thankfully into the cool water. It rippled gently across their backs, and in the eddy they would ride the current and swim back against it, while up the hill the orchards glowed in the day's last light. The two of them would feel much better then and sit on their heels against the river rocks that were giving up their warmth to the night.

'Let's go somewhere,' Ben said one evening as they squatted by the river peacefully with the stars deepening overhead. 'I'm tired of doing just chores all the time. I'm ready for something else.'

'All right,' said Aidan. 'What about Sunday? We'll go up bird hunting in the rattler canyon. There's some coyote bones I found up there. A skull and a couple of ribs, by the willows. I'll show 'em to you, if you want.'

'There's too much work to do just now. I don't know when we'll hunt birds.'

'Well I guess there's as much work here as anywhere. No more'n anywhere else.'

'But how would you come to know about that? If you hadn't been other places?'

'You don't have to go off nowhere else to know you're going to have to work.'

'Maybe some places you sit on the beach just waiting for coconuts to fall in your lap. Reading a book and just waiting.'

'Reading's work, I guess, though. Most of it is, anyhow.'

Aidan adjusted his weight a little and hawked spit into the river. 'Well, anyway,' he sighed. 'That's the thing with work. You just pitch right in and do it.'

Ben put his hand on his brother's wrist. 'Listen,' he said conspiratorially. 'What do you think? What about this? Let's just up and do something crazy. Let's ride the horses on out of here and go on up to the Grand Coulee or something, hire on at the dam.'

'I don't know what for, though.'

'I don't know why not.'

'Well it'd be crazy, for one thing. It'd just be downright crazy.'

He stood and stretched languidly beneath the stars. He stepped into his underwear and then picked out a loose shard of table rock to pitch into the river.

'We could go up to see the mountains,' Ben said. 'Take the horses on up to Loomis and run sheep across the Paysaten.'

'What on earth for, anyway?'

'Just to do it,' Ben said.

'There's no future in running sheep. Not like in these orchards.'

'Well it wasn't the future I was thinking of. I was thinking more, right now.'

'Better go on and do it without me. I don't have an interest in no dam or no sheep. And I ain't running off with Dad's horses.'

'Well maybe we ought to build a good raft. We could put it in the river just right here and float on down to Portland.'

'You'd wreck right there at Celilo Falls if you didn't wreck somewhere else first.'

'We could portage and all. At the dangerous places. One way or another, we'd get there.'

'What's in Portland anyway?'

'We can run right on past Portland then, if there isn't anything to hold you there, and out to the ocean or something. Wouldn't you like to see the ocean, Aid? We could hire on as steamer hands and make our way to China.'

Aidan pulled on his shirt, then his pants. 'We could fly on up to the moon too,' he said. 'While we're at it, maybe.'

'You think about things,' Ben answered.

When he was nine Ben went deer hunting for the first time, riding horseback with his father and Aidan. They rode into the hills just after lunch when the snow was on the ground. They crossed the river at Coleman's Landing and followed the Colockum Stagecoach Road, his father with his 270 Weatherby Magnum in a leather saddle holster beside his right hand and a .22 pistol at his belt. Everywhere it was dry-cold and winter-still, and the land lay white and paralyzed. They saw no one else, no hint of travelers and no deer sign in the snow of the road bed. When the stars were thick and brilliant in the sky, they stopped on a bench overlooking the river and sat their horses momentarily while Wright Givens buttoned his canvas coat and then cupped his hands to light a cigarette so that his jaw and mouth and the end of his nose glowed in the flaring match light. 'This'll do,' he said to them, and they stamped the snow down, staked out the tent and hobbled the horses for the night. They started a fire of lodgepole pine slabs on which their father boiled water for coffee, and they ate elk jerky from a leather bag and chewed dried apples and apricots. Wright Givens smoked cigarettes with his coat collar turned up, the brim of his hat turned down. He said that in the morning their chances would be good since deer were always nocturnal in habits, moving at dusk and dawn. As they moved to bed down, deer watched their backtrail and traveled with their noses into the wind, but there was no wind just now to assist them in their caution, and they might well be approached from above. Then their father settled in before the fire, and it was silent while they looked at the stars together—Ben wondered aloud how far they were—and afterward they were silent for another long interlude before Wright Givens tapped a pine ember with his boot and cleared his throat to speak.

He said that in the early days there were hardships along the Colockum Road. Wagons were lowered toward Wenatchee by rope; trees were dragged behind wagon axles to supplement the wheel brakes. He said that in the early days there was a schoolhouse on skids which the Malaga men pulled from farm to farm in order to spread justly from year to year the burden of heating the schoolhouse and of boarding the schoolteacher. Then he spoke of the Rock Island wheat chute where at first the wheat smoldered and burned in the pipe because of its own sliding friction. He said that before the railroad came through there had been a tram between Waterville and Orondo for carrying gunnysacks of wheat to the steamboat landing and for carrying coal back up. The Indians grew squashes and pumpkins in the bottom of Moses Coulee. They moved east when the sheep came in and further east when the tractors came, the tractors fueled by sagebrush and bolts of pine and anything that burned, even greasewood. Ben's father had seen Hutterites up on the plateau who lived in earthen hovels in the ground and boiled their soup on dung fires. They were drywheat farmers who never stopped working, fueled by rye bread and sauerkraut. Wright Givens had been to Soap Lake once where a sanatorium had been built on the muddy shore for sufferers from rheumatism, eczema and gout. He'd been to the Yakima powwow at White Swan and to the Yakima horse races in the huckleberry country up in Indian Heaven. He'd floated logs through the Yakima Canyon on the spring flood waters past Ellensburg and down to the mill near Selah. He said that where his grandfather had lived, just outside Walla Walla, freight was carried toward Hell Gate in Montana on the backs of African camels. There were channeled scablands down that way where rich, kilted Scotsmen ran ten thousand sheep herded by indomitable miniature dogs and by men who spoke only Spanish. Ben's father had traveled by steamboat once all the way to the mouth of the Columbia and seen the Pacific Ocean. He'd been on the railroad to Minneapolis and had seen the Black Hills in South Dakota. He'd passed one summer at a placer mine north of Ketchikan, Alaska. He'd been to Chinatown in San Francisco where he'd eaten raw sliced octopus and squid and baby eels.

Then Wright Givens told of how his grandfather had led west a train of covered wagons in 1879. His grandfather, John Hale Givens, had been a fruit grower and nurseryman in the vicinity of Marion, Indiana, but had grown disquieted and malcontent there and had finally built two wagons as soil beds in which he planted newly grafted fruit trees and bushes to bring across the plains: apple starts, pears, cherries, plums, currants, gooseberries, raspberries and peaches. They were canvased over for protection from weather, but on balmy days the canvases were stripped off, and the traveling gardens bounced sun-drenched across the plains, hauled by teams of oxen. The Indians, Wright's grandfather claimed, had vouchsafed the westering party safe passage on account of a belief that the traveling gardens were protected by the hand of the Great Spirit.

Wright Givens said that the boys' maternal grandfather had been a speculator in water rights in the years before they were born. He had purchased two dozen seedling trees from an itinerant peddler passing through Wenatchee—they turned out to be Golden Reinettes from Virginia—and when the offspring of one of these, sprung from a windfall, eventually produced an extraordinary fruit—huge apples growing mild yellow on each branch—he bought up the propagating rights. Next he built an iron cage around his tree—the boys had seen this in his yard—in order to thwart the theft of budsticks. Finally he named his fruit the Golden Delicious and took to promoting it vigorously: in 1921 the American Pomological Society had presented James Chandler with its Wilder Medal; in 1926 a carload of his apples was shipped to the men of the St Louis Cardinals on the occasion of their World Series triumph. And so their grandfather had come to be wealthy and had traveled by steamer to London and Rome and had seen the likes of Bucharest and Prague and Copenhagen and Stockholm. And that was also why he was rarely seen in these parts anymore.

The embers of the fire went quietly red while Ben Givens considered these things, sitting deep in thought until his father bade him look across the coals, to where Aidan was curled asleep on a log, his mouth fully open. 'Not innerested,' his father said, and shrugged.

'I am,' said Ben. 'Keep going.'

'It's time for sleep,' his father answered.

In the morning they broke their camp in the dark and rode silently up Stray Horse Canyon. Ben watched his breath boil off into the dawn until his father motioned him to draw alongside and pointed out the deep track of a buck, heart-shaped and split down the middle. The buck, said Ben's father, had passed the dark hours at the creek because there was no other running water and now at first light was working up steadily toward the higher elevations. The track made an easy meander in the snow with the dewclaws readily visible, and finally they came across droppings in a pile as if the buck had stopped unalerted. 'This is good,' said Ben's father. A quarter mile further there was an opening in the trees, but Wright Givens held them up just below it in case the buck was espying his backtrack from a higher concealed vantage point, and they turned their horses directly up the slope to keep the track below them.

They made the ridge top in gathering light and rode it northward in slow procession, studying the slopes on either side, in case the buck had crossed ahead of them. They came to a saddle where there were no tracks showing, the morning silent with no hint of breeze, the world as still as if it had been painted, and the snow loading up the boughs of pines in cumbersome white mantles. Wright Givens told his sons to take the horses downslope, tether them in a protected place and return silently to the ridge saddle. They would wait one hour in ambush here to see if the buck would cross going west into Dry Springs Canyon. Their father took his Weatherby from its holster, dismounted, turned up his coat's stained collar and pushed his hat down firmly. 'This is good,' he said again.

Aidan and Ben led the horses downhill and tethered them to a fallen pine tree. They ascended again and slid down beside their father, who asked them to sit with their backs to one another so that all points of the compass were covered. After twenty minutes of sitting without motion Ben heard his father's rifle click as the hammer was brought gently back into full cock, and as he turned his head he saw the buck clearly, in high alert with its gaze turned toward them, seventy yards down the hill in deep snow with its sleek left flank exposed. His father's Weatherby exploded deafeningly, and the buck buckled forward on tenuous forelegs, dropped heavily forward over his hooves and did not move again.

Their father sat for a long moment and then he stood with the rifle in his hands while Ben and Aidan scrabbled up, and they all looked downhill at the fallen deer splayed out motionless against the snow. The echo of his shot had died against the hills, silence had fallen across the canyons, before Wright Givens moved forward. He broke off a four-foot length of stick and approached the deer from behind. He touched the tip of the stick against its eye, but the deer neither blinked nor twitched. Ben's father claimed then to have seen a deer rear up unexpectedly from a similar position while his cousin Thomas sat astraddle its back to cut its throat, and Thomas had been thrown, dashed to the ground, as if he were riding a rodeo bull, and had cut himself with his gutting knife.

Wright Givens knelt for a moment, looking closely, and then he showed them the very place where the bullet had passed through the hide. He said it had splintered first the left shoulder joint and then the spine just below the neck and then the right shoulder too. There was blood on the snow underneath the buck, and his father explained how this was a good thing to drain all the blood away from the meat and to keep it cool against the snow. He showed them, pointing with the tip of his knife, the sticking place low on the buck's soft chest and then with no warning he thrust his knife into it, lifting the handle sharply up until the artery inside was severed. The buck's eyes remained open. More blood colored the snow.

Ben's father stepped back with his blood-stained knife to look down at his sons. He took his hat off, still watching them. He was lean in the face, unshaven and wind-worn, with a head of neat black hair. He propped his gun against a tree carefully, knelt with one hand on the buck's flank and, dropping his head, fell silent. 'Dear Lord,' he said softly after a while, 'our thanks to You for the meat You have granted. Our thanks for Your goodness and Your bounty, Lord. May we live according to Your good laws and by Your design and by Your goodwill in Jesus' name. Amen.'

He stopped, looked up and then motioned to the boys to kneel down beside him. They took their hats off too. They all three laid hands on the buck's warm flank, and their father asked if they wanted to speak, but neither of the boys said anything. 'Forgive us,' said Ben's father now addressing the deer's carcase, 'for killing you here today. We're sorry you had to die this way so our family might have meat. Thank you for nourishing these two boys who are finding their way in the world. Thank you for your meat this winter that my sons might grow to manhood. We thank you for the meat you have given us in Jesus' name. Amen.'

His father stood back and waited a moment, and then he cut the scent glands from the hind legs, severed the testicles and knotted the penis so that no urine would seep out to taint the meat. He explained what he was doing and why he was doing it, and the boys watched gravely and asked solemn questions, and then they brought the horses around, lashed the deer quarters over the saddles and left the hide, the head and the guts where they lay on the stained, snowy ground.

Five minutes later, riding down the ridge, their father halted his horse. There was blood across the front of his coat and on his jaw and nose and hands.

'That's how it's done,' he said to his sons. 'That's just the way you'll want to do it when I ain't around anymore.'

There were no near neighbors to speak of. There were the Fisks upriver a mile and a half growing Bartlett pears and Granny Smiths and some apricots and peaches. The Fisks had three grown sons in the vicinity and two daughters living on their place, but the girls were much older than Ben and Aidan and courted by swains who drove out from Wenatchee in fancy, well-polished Model As, coming along the dust-blown river road sporting bow ties, collared shirts and tautly worn suspenders as they passed the Givens place. Downriver a mile was Hauberk Mitchell, who grew Winesaps and White Winter Pearmains.

Every year the migrant pickers came through around the end of August. They were mostly from Oklahoma and Arkansas, sometimes from Missouri or Texas. Many in truth lived nowhere at all but had the road running stubbornly in their blood and worked crops from San Diego to the Canadian border—oranges, cherries, apples, peas, peaches, lemons and apricots. Single men and drifters, loners and vagabonds—sometimes families with eight or nine children—they made the fruit run in pick-up trucks or hopped freight trains or walked the roads. In April they picked cherries near Lodi or Stockton, then worked northward through plums and pears into the apple country. They arrived at the Givens place sun-darkened and lean-jawed, bedrolls slung from manila twine across their backs, a satchel or small duffel bag in one hand, unshaven under broad-brimmed hats and smoking hand-rolled cigarettes. In the rows of apples, high in their ladders, dropping fruit into canvas bags slung from suspenders and belted at their waists, they regaled Ben and Aidan with tales of a down-and-out life on the road. Dust storms, stabbings, arrests, brawls, cars broken down on lonesome byways, painted women in San Francisco, picking lemons in Florida. Riding the rails in Arizona or crossing into Mexico at El Paso for the whores in Ciudad Juarez. Herding sheep in the Sierra Nevada or riding round-up in Idaho. The impossible wastes of the Cactus Range, the Amargosa Desert, the Funeral

Mountains and the Last Chance Range near Death Valley. A camper built from flattened tin cans nailed to the back of a Model-T pick-up and a crank shank brought into round again with a shim made from a bacon rind. Condensed milk poured into a radiator in order to plug a slow-running leak, and hail falling as large as lemons along the Sacramento River. The itinerant pickers had been everywhere and seen all there was to see. Sometimes they were veterans of the war in Europe who had been to Paris or Milan or Barcelona and now, years later, they could not stop traveling, and the orchards beckoned them. They were hard-bitten, dust-covered nomads whose roof was the sky and sun.

School started right after picking season. There were fifteen children on the Rock Island Road, and their schoolhouse sat on a knoll above the river a half-mile downstream from the Fisk orchards, close to the Palisades junction. It was a small single room built of river stones and heated by apple cordwood. The orchardists up and down the road kept the slope-roofed woodshed filled in winter, and the older children kept the stove going strong by stoking it high when the embers glowed and leaving the draft turned open. The county ran power to the schoolhouse for a string of lights nailed over the desks so the children could see their maps and primers and neatly write their assignments. The place was tidy and smelled of woodsmoke, of ink and of wet woolen clothes.

The teacher, Ruth Dietrich, lived with the Cochranes, an elderly couple whose children were grown and who had an extra room to let. She was a serious woman, large, with thick glasses, and she peered at her charges over wire frames and then down through swimming lenses to read aloud from *Ivanhoe* or *Alice in Wonderland.* Miss Dietrich, at fifty, had a full head of gray hair, worn pinned tightly to her head with pins, perhaps a dozen of them. She wore a shawl of cream-colored lace draped across her broad shoulders and fastened with a brooch at her breast. Her face was coarse, lined and thick, and there were two long hairs sprouting from a mole on the left side of her chin. Her black shoes were sturdy for field walking, for Miss Dietrich was a collector of wampum arrowheads, petrified wood and opals. She knew her medieval history, could recite the chronology of British kings and queens and could render from memory 'Frost at Midnight', 'The Passionate Shepherd to his Love' and 'The Nymph's Reply to the Shepherd'. She was prone to quote poetry at the slightest provocation. She could discourse knowledgeably on the agriculture of Mesopotamia, the habits and mores of the Egyptian pharoahs and the scientific notions of the Greeks. She described in detail the Roman Colosseum and the spectacles one might witness there; and she knew all about the religion of the Incas and the travels of Charles Darwin to the Galapagos, the Boxer Rebellion, the Potala in Lhasa and the invasions of the Mongol Khans. Ben took pleasure in listening to her and read with zeal *Macbeth*, *The Canterbury Tales*, *David Copperfield*, *The Pickwick Papers*, *Heart of Darkness* and *Tess of the D'Urbervilles*—all loaned to him by Miss Dietrich. He learned the periodic table and the primary theorems governing geometry and the Latin names for plants and animals as classified by Linnaeus. He learned about the exploration of the poles, the formation of crystals and of sedimentary rock, the propagation of light. He was interested in all the world, he found, in its every corner and nuance. Miss Dietrich held him after school one day and told him he was her brightest hope in seventeen years on the western plains and a candidate for a good university should he decide on that noble and glorious path—a path she urged him toward greatly. A path he should have no fear about; a path he should walk with confidence. Ben thanked her profusely for this encouragement, then went outside to stand beside his brother, who was waiting sprawled on the ground against his elbows, chewing on a stem of wheatgrass. The January wind was blowing hard off the river, and Aidan had his back turned to it.

'What did she want?'

'She said I should go to college.'

'You going to do it?'

'I don't know.'

'I reckon you're smart enough.'

'Maybe. Maybe not.'

'You're smart enough, Ben. You ought to go.'

While Ben watched him, Aidan pulled his hat brim low in order to protect his eyes from the wind and rose still chewing on his grass stem. 'Come on,' he said. 'Let's get to the ranch. We still got horses to feed.'

'All right,' said Ben. 'Let's go.'

There was a grade-and-pack conference in Yakima where Ben's mother had spoken against lowering standards in 1932. She was dressed in black, and her hair was black, and she was tall and confident and plain speaking. It was her contention that even C-grade apples should not be permitted to go out worm-stung or discolored or pocked by hail. She paused for effect and then insisted that culls sold at three dollars a ton should go directly to vinegar plants because the brokers in Spokane and especially in Portland were flooding the C market with high-grade culls and driving prices down. The price for winter bananas, she added, had fallen to a dollar twenty-five per box and that wouldn't cover picking and packing, not to mention freight and auction. Half the shippers in the industry, she reported, had gone broke after the stock-market crash, and this exposed all orchardists to jeopardy because shipping contracts were the necessary collateral for a bank to cover growing costs. Did everyone understand this? she asked. Did all support the shippers? She favored a lobbying effort made through the shippers to bring the Great Northern into line at a dollar twenty-five per hundred pounds and she insisted that apples could be shipped by sea from rail points on Puget Sound as a counterbalance to the railroads. Otherwise, she said, there would be a lot of orchards out of business within two years. There would be a general tightening of belts for five years no matter what they chose to do, but the belt would hold, and they could mostly endure it, and eventually things would get better. In the meantime, she said, picking wages would have to be set at somewhere near fifteen cents. The fixed wage for the construction of boxes should be no more than seventy-five cents per hundred; to pay more was worse than folly. She encouraged everybody gathered there to take advantage of the Crop Production Loan Office plan for the purchase of spray and fertilizer. She explained how the Agricultural Credit Corporation could do what the banks had once done. She spoke from the floor, not from the podium, after sitting for two hours beside her sons and husband listening to men joust bitterly, and she announced herself as the wife of Wright Givens, whose grandfather had brought the first fruit stock across the plains, and as the daughter of the founder of the Golden Delicious apple, and the gathering was silent while she spoke and even more silent afterward. She sat down again with her eyes turned forward, fanning herself with a Yakima newspaper, and her husband reached calmly across her lap and took her right hand in his.

Once every month she took Ben and Aidan on her business trip to Wenatchee. The avenues were paved with large fir blocks that froze and buckled in the winter months, and the cross streets were done in paving bricks against which the horses had trouble. There was a fountain shop on Kittitas Avenue where they stopped in for a hamburger and ice cream at the counter, and the boys sat on either side of their mother, who ate neatly and slowly. They accompanied her to the bank and the post office and to pay the bill at the utility office. They went to the market for bacon, salt, flour, rice, beans, pepper, corn syrup and sugar. They stopped at the apothecary and the fabric shop on Miller Street and they visited the nickel-and-dime store. When all their errands had been completed they sat in the reading room at the city library combing through magazines and newspapers. The Wenatchee people spoke to their mother about matters pertinent to the growing of apples—progress on the new irrigation pipeline going in on the east side of the river, or her estimates of where prices might fix for Rome Beauties or Stayman Winesaps. Their mother answered in the same way to everyone—with confidence but no trace of arrogance. She had attended a boarding school near Boston as a girl and had learned about decorum, manners and conversation. She had done what she'd wanted with these lessons and had come west with her parents enthusiastically, in the spirit of an adventure. Now she kept the books for the orchards and told her husband when to plow new land or when to pull up trees. After dinner nearly every evening she sat for an hour at her roll-top desk with a ledger book in front of her and her hair falling into her eyes. With one hand she held her hair behind an ear; with the other she scrawled neat figures. As she worked, she liked to listen to the music of string quartets playing on the Victrola. Violins, she told her sons, were in perfect accord with the orchard landscape. She liked to have a half-hour in the evening to sit in an armchair with her needlework and the Victrola softly in the background. The sweet orchard air came softly through the screens, and she would stop and shut her eyes and breathe the world in and sometimes fall asleep in her chair with the violin music still playing.

In the summer she worked with Ben and Aidan in the packing shed, making apple boxes. They bought box shook from the mill at Malaga and ferried it across the river. They bought a hundred-pound wooden keg full of five-and-a-halfpenny nails. The sun filtered in and lit up the pine dust slowly rising on the air. His mother drove her nails with a box hatchet and hummed softly while she worked. She wore her kitchen dress with the sleeves rolled up, wiped sweat from her face with the hem of her apron and could hammer with either hand. His father could make sixty boxes in an hour, but his mother could make sixty-five. She held ten nails in her hand at once as if they were sewing needles. On each box she stenciled the label she'd designed: a border composed of pink apple blossoms enclosing a view of their orchards by the river, hung heavily with ripened fruit. In picking season she wrapped apples in oiled tissue before packing them tightly, nailing down the lids and loading up the wagon.

Ben was seventeen—it was just after Christmas—when he noticed one day, seeing her outside, a yellow cast to her eyes. His mother said she had seen it too when looking closely at herself in the mirror, and that Ben's father had noted it as well and urged her to visit the doctor. Then she had gone to Doctor O'Neil and been told that her jaundice—for it was jaundice she had—was generally difficult to understand and might derive from many sources. For a few days she held out hope that the condition would simply and easily evaporate. Then after New Year's she went again to the doctor and this time he drew blood and collected urine and concurred with her that the yellowing had grown deeper, pervading the skin around her eyes and her cheeks, chin and forehead. By the middle of January her skin was green, and when she cut herself with a paring knife one day—a shallow slice through her index finger—it was difficult to staunch the bleeding. Her blood ran thin and dark. By February she had lost her appetite and grown more gaunt around the eyes, hollow-cheeked and deeply green. She complained of a pain in her side and back that gnawed at her incessantly. She took to bed one afternoon and could not rise to attend to dinner but lay on her side curled up beneath the comforter, apologizing endlessly. Dr O'Neil came the next morning. He listened to her heart, took her pulse and temperature and at last gave her tincture of opium for the pain and prescribed as much food and water as she would take and plenty of quiet and bedrest. After that she lay in bed all day or sat in the armchair wearing her bathrobe, and once a week Dr O'Neil came to dole out more of the tincture of opium and encourage her to eat more of everything before she wasted away. She had, she replied, no appetite. The mere smell of food sometimes sickened her. She sometimes vomited in the early mornings, tasting bile in her mouth. The green hue of her skin was now tinted orange, and she became increasingly feverish. She was hot, then cold, then hot again. She lay with a washrag over her forehead, sweat on her throat and upper lip. In April their father sat Aidan and Ben down and revealed to them the state of things: their mother had cancer in her pancreas, against which medical science was defenseless. She would live for a few months, in pain mostly, and then she would die in bed.

In June she turned forty-two years old, but they did not speak of it in front of her. Blood ran from between her lips, and Dr O'Neil came to the ranch house at one-thirty in the morning. He explained to them how to move her carefully so as not to irritate the bedsores she'd developed and how deftly to change the sheets one side at a time. He rolled up his sleeves, loosened his tie and gave their mother a sponge bath. She was very thin now, green and small, and moaned quietly with each breath. Dr O'Neil increased two-fold her dose of opium. She quieted, and they left her room to sit on the porch and talk. Dr O'Neil explained to them that this was precisely the sort of moment that made him feel the most helpless. He wished there was more that medicine could do; he wished he could somehow reverse matters. He explained to them that he wasn't God but only a man, a simple doctor, with a limited set of tools. Their job, as he saw it, was to make her comfortable, and toward that end he granted them permission to use their discretion with the opium: he would leave them plenty of it. They should use it amply if they saw fit.

Later that week her moaning became constant, and Ben and Aidan, on the doctor's advice, placed shavings of ice on her tongue. Then the moaning became a sort of wheeze, and she curled up like a fist, like a leaf, like a baby in the end, and died at 6.35 in the morning on 28 June 1939. Ben, Aidan and their father were sitting there on kitchen chairs brought into the room, their father with his elbows on his knees, his forehead low, close to hers, and then her wheezing came to a stop and he dropped his cheek to her heart. 'Lenora,' he said, and that was all.

They buried her on a knoll above the river with the Fisks and Miss Dietrich and her own father looking on, and Dr O'Neil and twenty-three Givenses from up and down the river—from Kennewick, Wenatchee, Brewster, Kettle Falls—and that evening there was a thunderstorm, and the rain beat across Ben's mother's grave.

Afterward nothing was the same anymore, and they worked their apples with a hollow feeling until the next winter came. Then Ben left the orchard country behind in order to travel westward across the mountains and take up a place at college in Seattle. He'd stood eagerly at the verge of the road with his entire life in front of him. He'd stood with his thumb out and his duffel bag beside him, while a few dry flakes of incidental snow descended from a sky of no clouds. At noon had come sheets of lightning across the orchard country, and he'd sat beneath an apple tree outside Cashmere until the thunderstorm had quieted and passed. He'd leaned back against his duffel bag with the rain beating the leafless trees and with his canvas coat pulled tightly against his neck and his hat pulled low against his forehead, he'd decided that he would become a doctor because human beings were feeble in this world and suffered and died indecently, and the injustice of it enraged him. He was eighteen, his mother had died and he felt that if he became a doctor he might somehow conquer death. □

GRANTA

DAVID HAYNES
SOMETHING CALLED CRAB DELUXE

David Haynes was born in St Louis, Missouri, in 1955 and had what he describes as a typical American childhood. His father repaired the bodywork of automobiles, while his mother prepared 'a wholesome selection of recipes from the *Betty Crocker Cookbook*'. He attended 'large overcrowded schools where I didn't pay much attention' and, after graduation from Macalester College in St Paul, Minnesota, spent twenty years in similar classrooms as a teacher, mainly of twelve-year-olds. He now works for the National Board for Professional Teaching Standards in Washington, DC, though his home is in St Paul. He has published five novels, including *Somebody Else's Mama* in 1995, and is now working on a series of books for children as well as a new novel and a play.

'Something Called Crab Deluxe' is taken from *All American Dream Dolls* which will be published next year by Milkweed.

What can I tell you? I was in need of fixing, and Oprah and Phil and *The Young and the Restless* were there for me. When you are a woman in her late thirties who has foundered on the sea of love, you'll take the fix wherever you can get it. Here I'd washed ashore in my mother's basement in St Louis. Upstairs she and my twelve-year-old sister had waited a whole week already for the new, improved me to emerge. So on Saturday morning I arose like Venus from the sea.

Go ahead: slap me for the literary allusion. I went to good schools. I majored in English and work with language. Anyway I really did sort of see myself as Venus, a particularly juicy, soft and padded one. Luscious and ripe, I felt, like a peach: soft, pink and sweet. I think I had the same look on my face Vivien Leigh had after she was ravished by Clark Gable.

'Good morning,' I said.

Mama and my sister, Ciara, were sitting at the kitchen table, and I rather floated into the room, swept in with my robe splayed out behind me like Loretta Young's gown in flickery black-and-white memories I have of some old TV show.

'It's afternoon, Deneen,' Mother said.

They were having lunch. Mother picked through a plate of salad greens, while Ciara munched crudités.

Undaunted by my chilly reception I bent and gave each of them a kiss on the tops of their heads. This seemed to annoy them.

I rummaged through the cupboards looking for something to eat.

'Anything in here?' I directed that towards my sister, but it was Mother who answered.

'Plenty to eat. Serve yourself.'

'I'm looking for something good.'

'There's tuna fish and there are Lean Cuisines and there's plenty of soup. There's leftover baked chicken.'

Personally I was hoping for something along the lines of salsa and chips, or a pint of frozen custard. I wanted something tasty and crisp, or chewy and sweet. I wanted a gooey butter cake. Only in St Louis can you get a gooey butter cake. When you ask for gooey butter cake back home in Minnesota, people just look at you funny.

I got out the peanut butter and a box of raisins. I scooped out a mound of brown goo, mashed in a bunch of raisins and licked off the spoon.

My mother and my sister were giving me dirty looks.

'So,' I said to Ciara, 'you and I haven't had a chance to get to know each other.' I didn't say it too clearly because my mouth was glommed with the peanut butter and fruit. She heard me though.

'All you do is sleep and watch TV,' she said, and I thought I saw my mother shoot her some sort of look across the table.

'Well, I'm on vacation,' I told her. 'How's school?'

'It's summer. Only retards go to summer school.'

'Ciara!' Mother warned.

'Summer camp?' I asked. She was a surly one, I could tell. And apparently I was failing the big-sister test.

'Ciara is busy with a lot of her little activities, aren't you, precious?' Mother reached over and patted her on the hand, giving her a look that was both condescending and at the same time fearful. 'You finish up your lunch, sweetie. Come on. Join the clean-plate club.'

'Gotta get ready for skating,' Ciara said. She grabbed a handful of carrots and celery and left the room. Mama looked at her watch and started clearing plates.

'So you're up and about,' she said to me.

'Yeah. I thought I'd pick up some groceries.'

'We don't keep a lot of junk in the house.'

From what I could see they didn't keep any junk in the house. I'd already eaten everything that might reasonably pass for junky.

'I was hoping to borrow your car,' I said, feeling the need to go driving around, to go look at the old neighborhood again.

'You can ride with me when I drop Ciara,' Mama said, and then, as she bent over to place the last dish in the dishwasher, she added, 'You'll be taking a shower, of course.' It was a question, really.

Now, my mother can be as bitchy as the next woman, even with her loved ones, but the way she said this to me betrayed something other than bitchiness. Rather than sniping or admonishment, I heard reluctance, a kind of frightened embarrassment. She spoke to me the way a person might offer to help a homeless person who had fallen in the park. There was a crude mixture of sympathy and reticence in her voice that stung me and started a ripple of shame.

'Of course,' I said, and for some reason I felt worse for her than I did for myself. 'How much time?' I turned up my wrist to look at a watch that wasn't there.

'Hurry,' was all she would say.

There was a small bathroom with a shower in the basement. I went in there, took off my robe and jumped in the stall. I put the water on hot. There was one of those loofah scrubbers hanging from the shower head, and I took it down and loaded it up with the liquid soap my mother keeps in all her bathrooms. I went to work. I had never before used a loofah brush. I am more the kind for a washcloth and a bar of Ivory. But it was there, and there wasn't a washcloth, so I thought, what the hell. I held the hot-pink handle and pulled the brush across my stomach. It was rough, like a cat's tongue, but, lubricated with soap, it crossed my skin in a wake of bubbles leaving a trail of prickles and heat beneath the surface. I twisted my arm behind me and dragged the brush across my back. I squeezed on another layer of soap and ran it up and down my legs and my arms. I was panting, and my breath was coming hard and fast. I gripped tighter, urging the brush deeper into my skin. I ran it between my legs. I collapsed back against the wall of the shower, sank down, rinsing and breathing deep, the pulse of the water drumming against my torso. Does this sound vaguely pornographic to you? Like one of those tapes an old boyfriend of mine, Ron, made us watch, where one of those women with plastic bodies writhes around in the shower to bad disco music? I felt rather that way, actually, partially because this was my first loofah experience. What had happened, I believe, was the confluence between all the sensuality I had ever experienced and the permission I had been given by Oprah and Sally and Maury to enjoy it. That's the real charm of those TV people, you see, or the danger, depending on your perspective. You watch them, and they present some practice or some opinion that may be entirely perverted or completely reprehensible, but they do it in a context that seems as ordinary as white bread. I would say they look just like you and me, but often they are a lot plainer, more banal. Many of them are downright homely. And so these people come on and they talk about things such as men having sex with teenage boys, and women who like to whip men with cats-o'-nine-tails, and Oprah and Ricki nod and shake their heads, and they may get a disgusted look on their faces, but that look—their approbation or condemnation—is really beside the point. The point is, you, the viewer, watch whatever is going on and you think, particularly if you are a person like me with an open mind (crazy), hey, if they're doing it, maybe it's not so bad. Maybe I should try it. As for my open mind, try to imagine something like the opposite of Pandora's box where instead of releasing all the evil into the world, someone had packed away all of my id. For someone like that, someone like me, you can imagine that if you are able to follow the logic of a man who claims to be married to his five daughters, there certainly isn't much of a problem with getting off in the shower with a loofah brush.

So, I was lying there, looking as if I had been cleaned with a Brillo Pad—patches and strips of peeled-looking skin, glowing and pink against my creamed-tea coloring. At this point I had the vague expectation that one of those porno-movie men with the enormous penises would be tearing back the shower curtain, and the disco music would start playing again, and I would be another hour and a half getting dressed. Instead I heard my mother outside the door.

'Deneen! I said hurry!'

If you imagine I was jolted back to my senses, I was not. I was rather more like a puppy who had been playing with a ball and had then been thrown a stick. I thought, 'Oh well, I guess I'll do this for a while.'

I got out of the shower and wiped the steam from the mirror. I looked at my hair, and although it was in the sort of condition that could get me summarily dismissed from MABLE (Minneapolis Association of Black Ladies of Enterprise), I was delighted. It sprung from my head in coils and snakes and wires and whorls. Here and there dreadlocks had formed. I thought of fountains and, for some reason, cruciferous vegetables, such as cauliflower and broccoli.

'Deneen!'

I wrapped a towel around my hair and ran and threw on some clothes.

My mother and my sister were waiting for me in the living room. Mother was spinning her keys and tapping her foot. Ciara had her hands on her hips and was shooting me daggers.

'I'm late,' my sister said.

'Sorry,' I replied. 'I'm ready now.'

She gave my mother the look I always give my boss when he asks me should he buy his wife a birthday present or just take her out to a nice dinner: the is-you-crazy? look. Ciara stomped over to the closet, took out a Cardinal's baseball cap and handed it to me. I took off the towel I was wearing—a festive towel with pale pink roses on a field of yellow—and stuffed my hair into that. As much of it as I could.

They looked at each other, and we got in the car.

In this way I was initiated into the routines that made up the lives of my mother and my sister. Most days were just like this one. At some point we would drive Ciara to a studio or a classroom building or a recreation center. Just like today, a covey of other young women of various complexions, though all them the well-heeled type, would be waiting for her on the parking lot. A few would break off, and they would come and greet her in that breathy and shrill-sounding way of twelve-year-old girls. That first day when we stopped at the skating rink there were only a few girls waiting. One of them looked Korean. 'Where were you?' I heard her shout, and as they scurried away to their lessons, I saw Ciara turn around and point in my direction.

How did I respond? I waved of course. Ciara and me, it was still early in our relationship. We'd get used to each other. Also, I was too fascinated by what these girls were wearing to sense any ill will. They wore these little jumper-and-shorts sets in what I, at their ages, would have thought were juvenile colors—bright primaries and secondaries—combined in stripes and primitive patterning, like bad or imitation Keith Haring. The designers had figured out, since I outgrew the junior department, some way of making shorts look almost chaste. The girls showed plenty of thigh, but it didn't look the least bit provocative. Or at least not to me. I did feel for just the tiniest of moments a tinge of trashy melancholic nostalgia. Ah, to be able to shop in the junior department. Or petites, for that matter.

'To the store,' I said cheerily. My mother put the car in gear and peeled away from the curb like a gangster.

Though in my craziness I had a vague sense that the woman I was with was *my* mother, it would be more true to say that I knew that she was *a* mother. She exuded those motherly vibes, the ones that our built-in mother detectors are designed to pick up. You know how back in the days before optical scanners you would be walking through the Target store and find two identical pieces of merchandise—say, two sweaters—except that one would be marked two dollars higher than the other, and the expensive one wouldn't have any flaws, but the cheaper would have a great big string hanging off it, and you'd say to yourself, I'm gonna just switch these tickets, and you'd start to do it, but you'd stop when a mother walked by? Those are the motherly vibes I'm talking about, and though at the time I liked to think I was fairly immune to my mother's voodoo, I still found myself trying to please her. I tried to behave for the same reason you try to be patient with the elderly man beside you on the airplane: you don't know him and you don't care about his grandkids, but, like your mother said, a little courtesy never hurt anyone. That the particular mother who might have taught me that was sitting right next to me wasn't important.

She took me to Schnuck's Superstore on Manchester, and going in I had the kind of reaction the lions must have had when the Romans opened the gate and they saw all those Christians standing there. Food! I grabbed me one of those talking shopping carts and I took off.

I remember everything I put in the cart because I remember how hard it was to figure out where even to begin. Anything I had ever wanted to eat was in that store. How to decide? I took my cart up and down the aisles.

'Delicious Del Monte green beans. While stocks last, two for eighty-nine cents. Limit four.'

My shopping cart said that. But I didn't want green beans. It also told me about specials on flour and toilet paper and cake mix and Malt-O-Meal. I had selected a cart that was interested only in staple items and was making my way back to the front of the store to exchange it for a companion with more exotic tastes when I got an idea. What if this were my last meal? If I were on death row, what would I ask the guards to bring me just before they pulled the switch, and I fried like a big fat piece of bacon? What did I enjoy most? I thought about egg rolls and shrimp toast and those little *rumaki* things. Oh, and those miniature wieners soaked in barbecue sauce. Hors d'oeuvres. My favorite food was hors d'oeuvres. I headed for the hors d'oeuvres department, but its location was not readily apparent. I typed H-O-R-S on to the keyboard that was attached to the part of the shopping cart that had been doing the talking, but it only told me that horseradish was on aisle two. I should have known that particular cart wouldn't know or care. Through the haze I could hear this voice saying to me, 'Deneen, Deneen. Get real. You have to *make* hors d'oeuvres. You buy all the stuff and you make them yourself.' Occasionally I would hear what I believed was a voice of reason, pushing me along, helping me with the tough decisions. At the time I was comforted by the thought that this was some sort of foothold in the rational world, but looking back I recognize that every time I heard those voices, they were advising me about matters involving food or sex or some marginally ethical behavior. On the voice's recommendation I made for the deli department, and there, to my amazement and delight, I found hors d'oeuvres in many forms, some already prepared and cut up into tempting bite-sized pieces. I selected spinach dip and King's Hawaiian bread, a half-dozen egg rolls, little links and a bottle of Open Pit barbecue sauce, a pound of chopped liver, a half-pound of smoked salmon, a two-inch slice of pâté and something called crab deluxe. To be on the safe side I also got a couple of cups of Kaukauna cheese spread and a box of Ritz crackers.

I found my mother waiting by the greeting cards, riffling through them but not really looking. I saw her before I recognized her. I saw this short, carefully dressed woman with medium brown skin and I noticed that she had had her hair done in the elegant way that many older African-American women with a certain amount of money did. Styled up off the crown of her head, it cascaded in a graceful flip above each of her ears. Rinsed into it were shiny silver highlights. She wore the kind of simple jewelry that wasn't meant to catch your eye, but designed to blend into her outfit—a mannish, tailored pantsuit. (Although one could tell that those bracelets and rings and necklaces were anything but cheap.) I saw this woman standing there and I was admiring how well she put on her make-up, the deep purple and warm gold treatments above her eye, when she spoke to me.

'Deneen?' she said.

I had been standing there admiring this woman. In my one-activity-at-a-time-only-please mode, the acts of admiring her, recognizing her and greeting her had only progressed as far as activity number one.

'Shall we go?' I said.

Wheeling along behind her on the way to the check-out stations I realized that I had no money. Not one cent. I could sort of see my purse sitting on the floor by the bed back in the paneled room in mother's basement.

I placed my purchases on the conveyor belt next to my mother's. The voice told me to do it. 'Deneen, Deneen,' it said. (I can't tell if the voice is a he or a she because it speaks in a husky androgynous whisper.) 'Put your stuff up there with your mother's. Go ahead. She won't mind.' I tossed my treats up there and then I gave my mother a big smile. She hadn't noticed my goodies yet. She dug through her own purse, looking for her bill fold.

'Ninety-seven dollars and seventy-nine cents,' the cashier said.

Mother looked at the cashier, then she looked at the food. A boy was tossing our groceries into thin plastic sacks. Then she looked at me, over the rims of her half-glasses. What a lovely beaded chain, I thought. She removed a card from her wallet, swiped it through a machine and punched in some numbers. She was shaking her head the whole time.

I grabbed two of the sacks and left one for her. The automatic door blasted open in front of me, and a wave of shimmering heat and humidity battered me in the face. I gasped. Rays of sun burned through my baseball cap, and a wet ribbon of sweat rolled from the nape of my neck and into the shelter of the back of my top. My mother arrived behind me at the car and punched the buttons that unlocked the door.

'I told you we don't eat a lot of junk,' she said. Her voice had assumed the edge that she used with recalcitrant sixth graders when their teachers sent them to her office. She had dropped it about a half register; done that trick where it sounds as if she's taking louder but really she's talking more softly; had emphasized, if only minimally, the words 'told' and 'eat' and 'junk'.

Well, you've got your nerve, I thought. In my world, when someone in the audience spoke this way, they could expect a scolding from Ricki or Jenny or Phil. They had a way of picking out certain people like her. If you notice, her kind rarely gets to speak. Phil certainly never allows them to hold the microphone. I mustered my best, non-judgmental, non-shaming Maury-Geraldo-Sally voice.

'Well. You don't have to eat it,' I said.

Mother made one of those noises that people make when their panties ride up on them or when they're trying to pass a large bowel movement.

'Deneen, what on earth is the matter with you?' she asked.

'Me?' I started to ask. Me! I don't believe my voice reaches the octave required to register the indignation I felt. Me?

But I didn't say that. Instead I forgave her. I remembered that what she was, after all, was one of those mothers. Doling out unsolicited nutritional advice was more or less a requirement of her job. □

GRANTA

ALLEN KURZWEIL
SLIPS OF LOVE

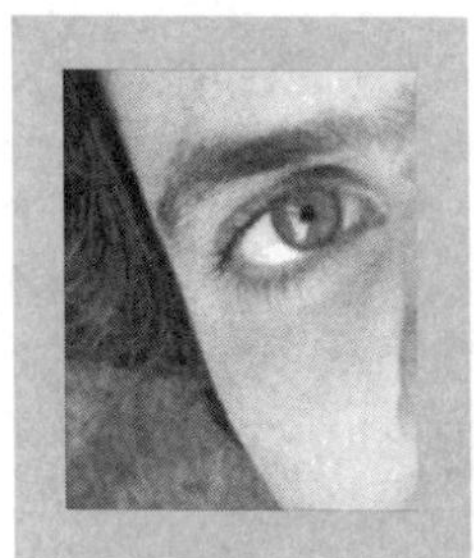

Allen Kurzweil was born in New York City in 1960. He graduated from Yale University and was a Fulbright Fellow in Rome. His jobs have included assisting the foreign desks of two Italian newspapers, shepherding American high-school students on tours of Europe and the Antipodes and teaching fiction at Yale. His first novel, *A Case of Curiosities*, was published in 1992 and won the Premio Grinzane Cavour in Italy. In 1994 he was awarded a Guggenheim Fellowship. He lives in Connecticut with his wife, who is a French anthropologist, and their two-year-old son.

'Slips of Love' is taken from his second novel which he has yet to complete.

I came home from the library and reached my building just as the sun lowered behind the water towers. Lopez, the fruit vendor, was out front in his secondary role of building superintendent. He gripped a paint roller in one hand, a bucket in the other, and was covering the month's graffiti with gray latex. He worked the roller sloppily, running it over the edges of an ancient ceramic sign that read NO LOITERING & NO BALL PLAYING, a wistful reminder of a time when the neighborhood suffered harmless forms of hooliganism.

The tenement in which I live is located in a section of the city that once carried the cozy name Manhattan Valley, but this was before the drug dealers started hanging sneakers over traffic lights to announce they were open for business. Newspaper headlines chronicled what followed. Manhattan Valley became Cocaine Alley, and later, as a natural evolution in product development, Crack Corridor.

A shiny-nosed acquisitions librarian from Parsippanny, New Jersey, a man with whom I once shared a room during the regional meetings (the hotel had overbooked), mailed me a news clipping that included a 'Map of Murder'. My street corner was obliterated by an overlapping cluster of dots marking the sites of violent crime. The oleaginous correspondent scrawled a brief salutation. 'Whoa! You live there!?' His punctuation agitated me as much (probably more) than the insensitivity of the remark. 'Yes!' I wrote back. 'That's where I live!!!!' I posted my answer on the verso of an obsolete catalog card for a novel called *Death in Suburbia* and hoped he'd get the hint.

'Hey Lopez,' I said to the super. 'We should get the owner to change the notice.'

'Eh?'

'Maybe, "No drug dealing. No urinating on mailboxes. No guns. No holding a box cutter to the throat of class-two librarians."'

Lopez said, 'OK, my friend'—which is what Lopez always said, except when I complained about the overheating, or the brown-outs, or the rats sharpening their teeth inside the rotting walls. Then it was, 'Call owner. Call owner.'

I hooked my jacket and book bag over an ornate nub of painted metal that protruded from the wall, a pleasant vestige from the days of gaslight. 'I'm home.'

'Salut'

We could barely hear each other. Nicole had tuned the radio to something adamantly modern. I'm tempted to say Cage, but that's only because I attribute all atonal non-melodic music to him—a personal prejudice, one of many. I took a deep breath and picked my way down the corridor, wading through a tide of paper scraps that had washed out of her studio.

Nic must have anticipated my mood. 'Sorry,' she said pre-emptively. She sat at her drafting table, feet hooked in the rungs of a stool, surrounded by a clutter of paint pots, glue brushes, tongue depressors, bone folders and the rest of the arsenal with which a paper engineer mounts an assault. Taped against the cork board that covered one wall were images of palm trees and beach scenes of lovers variously posed. In the corner, on the floor, was a fresh mound of junk culled during one of her trash-bin expeditions.

I averted my gaze to a more calming view; a shelf of sno-domes, some of which Nic purchased, others of which she made. I waited for a break in the radio transmission and asked, 'What's the project?'

'Golf resort in the Virgin Islands. They want a new brochure.' She waved a bone folder at the cork-board wall. 'The palm trees have to pop up and the couple has to kiss.'

'Thai?' I asked.

'What?' The radio had started up again.

'I said I wanted to know if you wanted to eat Thai.'

Nic flicked off the radio, a concession. 'I have to do this.' She lifted a row of purple bushes (bougainvillea?) between thumb and straight edge and stripped it in next to a beach house. Without looking at me she said, 'I thought we were broken.'

'It's *broke*, Nic. And I have coupons for free satay.'

'That's what I said. *Broken*.'

Nic lowered her head closer to her work, ignoring me.

'Busy?'

'Deadline.' She fiddled with a palm tree.

'Right,' I said. 'I'll just go fix something for myself.'

I carried my spousal resentment to the kitchen, where it was allowed to flourish. The sink, stacked with dishes, reminded me of the overburdened book depository that I emptied after weekend returns. The refrigerator, on the other hand, presented a no less irritating, albeit confusing perspective on Nic's attention to order. Inside, she had composed a still life of fruits worthy of Cézanne. We had discussed this more than once. The top rack was supposed to be reserved for tall objects. Apples, however beautifully they might be arranged, were to go in the FRUIT compartment, which, I discovered, was filled with the high-speed film and the dyes that Nic used in her work.

I broke off a banana and put the fruit bowl one level down, next to a ceramic dish of Normandy butter. Why couldn't Nic put her damn butter in the compartment designed to house it? I lifted the door marked DAIRY and discovered it was packed with the homeopathic medicines her mother mailed in string-tied boxes from Toulouse. A clip of French suppositories with an unpleasantly evocative name—Ammorectal, if I remember correctly—fell on the floor, confirming both Nic's devotion to non-oral medication and her inexplicable need to make unpredictable environments in which routine could so easily have prevailed.

I crammed the foil-wrapped bullets back in DAIRY and angrily sought further confirmation of Nic's illogical urges. She didn't disappoint. The vegetable bin contained a strand of cultured pearls, another cross-Atlantic absurdity. Madame Dufresne had told her daughter always to hide jewelry in the brewing basket of an old percolator. When Nic wrote back that we didn't have an old percolator, my mother-in-law suggested *le frigidaire*, which is how the pearls ended up in VEGETABLES.

MEAT, naturally, contained nothing to satisfy the flesh-eater, accommodating as it did small plastic bags of 'good luck brew' and other expensive botanicals that promised luck or revenge or potency. (Nic insisted I try the last item more than once, but its impact was negligible.) There was also a pack of tarot cards, not the reproduction Besançon deck I purchased for her birthday at almost no discount in the library's gift shop, but a tattered deck she used to chart our futures.

I suspended my reconnaissance and grabbed a mason jar of cereal from an architectural arrangement of grains, then went back for the pitcher of milk. I fixed myself a large bowl, returned the jar, reluctantly, to its assigned spot and carried what passed for dinner back to my cage, hoping to suppress the intensifying swirl of petty thoughts. I couldn't. A catalog started forming: superstition, homeopathy, mess, sexual voracity, junk picked up off the streets . . . How could a woman who spent hours carefully configuring the interior of a refrigerator leave a mountain of dishes in the sink? How could style and chaos coexist so casually? The fact that my silent recriminations emerged while I sat in the cage only made matters worse.

Nic had constructed my little workspace long before shrillness and impatience dominated our lives. It was about six months after she'd moved herself, and all of her stuff, into my apartment. It was a languid weekend afternoon in July, and I was showing her a picture of a seventeenth-century scholar's library highlighted in Witold Sharansky's monumental seminar on Bibliomania.

'You like it, don't you?' Nic said.

I nodded.

'So then? Let's make one.'

'Make one?'

'A scholar's library. We can put it under the loft bed.'

And so for my birthday, Nic did exactly that, unassisted, basing her eight-by-six-foot design on nothing but a fuzzy black-and-white photograph of the Dublin library of Narcissus March. I told her she should economize. 'Use knotted pine,' I said. 'Spray-paint some chicken wire.' She refused. An inveterate scavenger, Nic found, at a downtown demolition site, real brass wire and some planks of oak she dovetailed expertly. (Nic is the only woman I know with a passion for miter boxes and power tools.) She used card-catalog drawers—tossed when the library went on-line—to house my small collection of call slips, hand-lettering reversed Bristol guides to separate my fields of study. She even chained my early editions of the *Dewey Decimal System* and *Hand Book of Tachygraphy* to the wall, though the likelihood of burglars, in our neighborhood, stealing books was remote. Over the door of the cage, Nic stenciled a quote from Leonardo about the virtue of small spaces allowing the mind to soar. A quick gander at the cage made it obvious why. I could reach out from my chair and touch shelves on three sides. But that sense of enclosure only added to my joy, at least in the beginning. Narcissus would have been proud.

The loving carpentry had a goal, one Nic often invoked. The cage was where my catalogs and her graphic talents were going to be wed. She believed that the union of my annotations and her paper engineering was the only way we could rescue ourselves from professional tedium. Books would be our salvation. I would write them; she would make them. That was the plan she spun out, over meals and in late-night conversations when neither of us could sleep. To which I usually said sure, or *d'accord* in my unsteady French. But I knew, early on, these dreams would be hard to fulfill.

I was still brooding when I finished the Nuts 'n Honey. To relieve my mind, I pulled down a sturdy reprint of the *Universal Penman* and studied its annotated calligraphies. I was so engrossed in my analytic deductions, I hadn't noticed Nic open the door of the cage. She was holding the pitcher of milk, which I apparently had left on the kitchen counter. And I thought, as she stood there accusingly, This from a woman who piles plates!

'Sorry,' I said. I had no wish to fight.

Nic sucked her tooth and said, 'You make me a banana.'

I looked down at my empty cereal bowl to hide an uncontrollable smile. Even in anger, I could find her idioms endearing. '*Drive*, Nic. It's, "You *drive* me bananas."'

Nic whipped around and released an oath, perfectly expressed but too crude to warrant repetition. I closed my eyes and listened to her storm down the corridor to the kitchen, where the pitcher clinked as she reconfigured the fridge. Then I heard the studio door slam shut, muffling her modern music.

I opened my girdle book to 'N'. After all, a new Nicolism was a new Nicolism, and I had, from the very start of our relationship, kept a pretty rigorous list of her delicious linguistic slips. 'You make me a banana' would come after 'I thought we were broken.' Before those, I had taken down an accusation leveled at me when I confronted Nic about our bank account, once again overdrawn. She yelled: 'You're so crazy about money, you should go back and see your shrimp.' The comment was meant to wound me, and it did, the humor notwithstanding. My ill-fated foray into therapy was a financial and emotional fiasco, and Nic knew perfectly well I didn't like it brought up.

Shrimp. Banana. Why did so many Nicolisms involve food? This was a question better left unasked, at least right now. Had I tried to approach her, she might have reissued yet another of her idioms, and I had no interest in threats of a 'black-buttered eye'.

Our relationship wasn't always so troubled. Long before I made Nic a banana, I was, to cite the very first 'N' I ever took down, 'the apple of her eyeballs'.

We met while I was still in library school, struggling through the taxonomic inconsistencies of the *Anglo-American Cataloguing Rules*, attending Sharansky's lectures on leather grain and paleography, doing my Melvil Dewey research and holding down a job as a page. Without a degree, my opportunities were limited to ill-paid grunt work. I served as the library's Step 'n Fetch It, and it was in this capacity that I managed to run over Nic's foot with an overloaded book cart. By way of apology, I transgressed the sacred barrier between technical and public services, and asked if I could help with her research. She accepted, explaining in fractured English that she was a graphic artist in need of books on plastic sno-domes. She had been commissioned by a friend of a friend to make some Christmas cards for a ski-apparel company. Her idea: see-through cards that would resemble the effect of *boules de neige*. She said she was having problems getting the tiny plastic gloves and hats to float properly. Tap water had proved unsatisfactory for the kind of flurries she desired.

I pulled up a solid cite easily enough and helped with its translation. The following week she returned to the library, tracked me down and deposited a gift in my hands: a transparent dome containing miniature books and bits of white plastic snow floating in a mixture of glycerin and antifreeze. The flurries were perfect. As I told my colleague Norton later, I shook the gift, and its maker shook me.

Nic's call slips charted my infatuation. After *Sno-Domes: Magic Under Glass*, she requested a biography of Lothar Meggendorfer, a Titan in the world of moveable books. After that: back issues of the *Journal of Stereoscopy*, a publication that included cardboard eyeglasses with one green and one red lens. This was followed by the submission of a call slip asking for a pop-up version of *The Love Teachings of Kama Sutra*, a shockingly explicit work located in the Archive of Material Cultural. The curator, George Speaight, supplied the book personally. After he got a good look at her, and learned we'd become friendly, he pulled me aside and said, 'You're a fool if you don't add her to your holdings.' Speaight had a tendency to talk that way, crudely; it was a by-product of professional activities, a residual effect of the stuff he was sanctioned to collect. He called her many things in the days that followed. Frenchie. *La blonde*. The waif. I told him to restrict such labeling to his books, though secretly I was pleased. The matter of her nationality and hair color was a point of fact. She *was* French; she *was* blonde. But the third Nic-name was also apt. There was a decidedly waifish aspect to her. The address-line of her call slips changed constantly. The first five or so bore an address on the Lower East Side. Then she relocated to Brooklyn Heights, followed by Chelsea, followed soon after by a place below Canal.

Such instability would have taken a toll on me. Not Nic. She was always in good spirits, always beautifully dressed. How she managed that while living out of suitcases, I have no idea. On sunny days she displayed a preference for harem pants and quirky scarves and girlish little shoes, clothing every bit as unconventional as the books she requested and the objects she made. When it rained, she wore bright yellow galoshes with tiny Prussian-blue bows. Often she wrapped her upper body in bolts of vibrant material, or mixed and matched her stockings—one leg blue, the other leg yellow. That was Nic: vibrant, bold, shocking, original, superstitious, sensual.

I spent more than a few coffee breaks with Norton talking about this. He happily added his own descriptors to my growing list. 'She's cuspy,' he said. That was one of the computorial mantras he used to characterize people and things he deemed

attractive. 'Ask her out. How many women like her do you meet? Can't you see she wants more than books?'

'I don't know.'

Speaight, who was with us at the time, shook his head in disbelief. He peered over his mug and said to Norton, 'The man's as spineless as a paperback.'

'Maybe I am,' I replied. 'But she's too attractive and too weird to be interested in someone like me.' My reasoning was feeble, but I didn't have the courage to explain the real source of my timidity. (A pop-up *Kama Sutra* for God's sake!)

Though I'll never be sure, I suspect that Norton or Speaight—one or the other, maybe both—said something. Six call slips after she'd moved to that place below Canal, Nic gave me a second gift: a photo taken surreptitiously while I was posted at Information. The picture would never have won any technical prizes. It was blurred, taken without proper lighting, and showed me standing before the horseshoe with a puzzled look on my face, a look reinforced by the huge neon question mark hovering over my head. On the back of the photo, Nic had magic-markered, *'Je doute, donc je suis.'*

I confessed the inadequacy of my French.

She translated. 'I doubt, therefore I am.'

'Maybe. Then again, maybe not. I'm not sure.'

'Ha ha,' she said. With an inky finger she traced a question mark in the air just above my head, dotted it by touching my mouth and winked.

I wanted to disprove the accusatory credo by asking her on a date. I couldn't. That little tap on the lips struck me dumb and confirmed the appropriateness of the neon question mark. Doubt was indeed an essential part of my life.

Nic persisted despite my sheepish indecision, and we began to spend more time together. Soon after, we confessed our love, if not for each other at least for the interests that brought us together. Books. Each of us had big plans. Nic wanted to create bindings that would unbind ideas. She wanted words to pop off the page, literally and figuratively. Thus the interest in pop-ups and the principles of paper engineering. She referred to her designs as 'mechanicals'. It was impossible to pooh-pooh the term;

her constructions had gears and springs and pendulums and embraced Archimedian laws. They had nothing at all in common with the children's books I occasionally helped repair with rubber glue and tape.

I was unable to reciprocate with revelations of my own—at least not at first. But I did give Nic special tours of the library, calling up my most cherished books (an early edition of *Gulliver's Travels* for instance) and showing off my special spots, many of which became hers. She embraced the culture of the library with a fervor I had already started to lose. She loved the book dummies and the zip tubes and, on a more ideological level, marveled at the access. She was constantly telling me that American libraries were far more democratic than their French counterparts.

'But our stacks are closed,' I said. 'There are some parts of this place that even *I* can't get into. At least not officially.'

She shook her head as if to say, You have no idea how lucky you are. Then she ran through the access procedures at the Bibliothèque Nationale: mandatory letters of recommendation, interrogations, identity cards with mug shots, assigned seats and arcane rules governing the submission of call slips.

Our talks made me feel good, even confident. A little later I confessed my desire to compose lists, explaining that I used the verb 'compose' in the musical sense. I worried Nic might consider the statement pretentious, which it was, but she accepted my hopes wholeheartedly. She ran to the card catalog and pulled a cite for an astronomy text with volvelle cuts that allowed the planets to rotate around the page. 'That's what we will do with the lists you compose, Alexander Short. Make them spin! Make them whirl! We will turn them into music of the spheres!'

The excitement she generated was palpable. How could I not hitch my wagon to hers? And so it was decided: Nic would handle the images, I would handle the words.

As I filed away the slip for the astronomy book I noticed that Nic's address had changed once more. She had relocated to a youth hostel situated smack in the middle of Crack Corridor. My mood darkened.

'You can't move there!' I blurted out.

'What are you talking about?'

I waved the call slip. 'The neighborhood's too dangerous.'

'And how do you know?'

'I live three blocks up.'

'Isn't that a good reason *to* move there?' She adjusted her scarf and winked. (Nic was an inveterate winker.) Two days later she installed herself in my apartment. We were brought together by attraction and, if I can provide a measure of retrospective honesty, that other social mastic of the city: real estate.

The fights started within days of her arrival. I resented her messiness, she resented my resentment. I wanted the butter in the compartment marked DAIRY. She, for her part, insisted on banishing commercial packaging from the dining table and the fridge. Hence the glass pitchers of milk, the mason jars of cereal. In short, I had my quirks, and she had hers. But for all the tussling, we managed to get along. The tussling, if anything, helped. Fights tended to resolve themselves in laughter more often than in tears, at least at first, with the pleasure of resolution overwhelming the anger that precipitated it.

After one skirmish, about what I can't even remember, Nic made a trip to the library and requested a copy of *Knife Throwing as a Modern Sport.* I intercepted the call slip and had Delivery provide her with a copy of the classic *How to Poison a Friend.*

How could we not fall in love?

By the time I finished library school and got a job in Reference, Nic and I were calling up booklets on immigration and naturalization. Nic wasn't even on a G-9 visa, and her status as a tourist carried all sorts of humbling and stressful restrictions, to say nothing of the looming threat of deportation. One hundred and sixty-four call slips after we were brought together by *Sno-Domes: Magic Under Glass*, a solution proposed itself. Actually it was Nic who did the proposing.

She approached me while I was on Desk. She wore a light fleecy wrap tied around her head and shoulders in a manner that can be fairly called angelic. Without saying a word she handed in a request for a Victorian instructional work called *The Perfect Bride*. Then she winked and walked over to Delivery to wait for my response.

Panicked, I retreated through the swing-gate to a supply closet, where for five minutes I hyperventilated privately. I then found Norton and talked through what to do. After an explosion of nervous babbling, I came to a decision.

'How are you going to tell her?'

'I thought a simple Yes might do.'

'Nonsense. You should answer with style. It's *Nic* you're planning to marry.'

By the time I had returned to Delivery, Norton had configured the indicator board to flash the word *Oui.*

The bulbs blinked on and off. OUI . . . OUI . . . OUI.

Dozens of readers looked up, confused by the light show until one of the tube clerks spread the word. The round of applause that followed echoed all the way from the North Hall to the telephone reference booths.

Nic and I were married fifteen call slips later in less dramatic circumstances. We never considered a lavish wedding ceremony. Nic's father, a poster hanger living outside Toulouse, had little to show for his years of work except for forearms made of rock. Nic's mother spent much of her day bagging homeopathic plants she pulled from the fields around her home. My future in-laws didn't have the resources to travel, and my adoptive parents, pension-bound in a North Florida retirement community, were no better off.

When colleagues at the library learned that our relatives wouldn't be attending the marriage, they generously offered assistance. Abramovitz, the curator of Judaica (and unofficial social conscience of the staff), suggested we have a nice little celebration in his department. He even showed us the perfect spot for the *chuppah.* 'You see, we have here a beautiful Torah scroll and right next to it a dictionary of French Catholicism. Perfect, no?'

'No.' I told him neither bride nor bridegroom had any interest in a religious event. I'd never felt especially Jewish; Nic had never felt terribly French, let alone Catholic. Spiritual disaffection had been, in fact, a touchstone.

A week after we had persuaded Abramovitz to suspend his well-intentioned efforts, Speaight started up a campaign of his own. He wanted to throw us a party in *his* little duchy. 'We'll set up a punch table near the French erotica.'

'I'm not sure Nic would welcome the proximity,' I said.

'From what I can tell, she'd love it.'

He was probably right, but the point turned out to be moot. The head librarian scotched the idea as soon as it was raised.

So with no fanfare whatsoever, Nic and I were married in a civil ceremony, or as civil as the Court of New York could muster. A jowly justice of the peace mumbled a few stock phrases and ratified our union by sticking the marriage certificate between the jaws of a punch clock at exactly 12.42 p.m. on a frigid February day. Nic recorded the scene less bureaucratically in one of her sketchbooks. The picture shows us in a room with a ceiling so low that the American eagle on the top of the flagpole pokes up through an acoustic tile. All that remains of the bird is a body and pair of outstretched wings. Nic called the sketch 'Marriage, or Liberty Decapitated'. At the time, we considered it a joke.

With the library itself off-limits, my colleagues took us out to one of those cavernous Cantonese restaurants catering to the drug cartels of Chinatown. After the dim sum carts circled us a few dozen times, and after we had picked at a gelatinous cake of unnaturally green color, Nic and I received his-and-her wedding gifts on behalf of the entire staff. I was given a buckram-bound edition of *Authority Control: the Key to Tomorrow's Catalog.* Nic got a facsimile Meggendorfer.

'Better than matching towels,' Norton said, and he was right. My parents provided us with a two-night stay at a fancy midtown hotel. (A neighbor of theirs had a son-in-law whose brother had a friend who ran a travel agency.) It was in that cell-sized room that Nic and I had our first fight as husband and wife. Nic objected to the reproduction Vermeer staring down off the headboard.

'What's the problem?'

She said she had copied the delicate original in the Louvre as an art student. The oversized silkscreen offended her. *'C'est grotesque,'* she said. I didn't think it was that bad, and the bathroom all but glistened, but Nic was adamant. She refused to make love under the gaze of 'The Lacemaker'.

'What if we drape a sheet over her?'

'Out of the question,' she said in French.

The headboard was bolted to the wall, so I ended up pulling

the mattress on to the floor. More rearranging followed. By the time it came to the conjugal act itself, our heads were positioned six inches away from a stainless-steel toilet bowl, a proximity to which I responded detumescently. Nic insisted we check out early the following day.

More examples of stubbornness followed. When I was helping her fill out the forms for her temporary green card and asked what she wanted to put down under OCCUPATION, she said, 'Bookmaker.'

'I don't think that's going to help our case.' I explained the underworld meaning of the term.

'Perfect. Put it down.'

In retrospect, Nic was right to insist. She was a gambler, and in this situation her bet paid off. The Immigration and Naturalization Service inspector *loved* the occupational title settled upon, and after she presented him with one of her mechanicals (a Statue of Liberty that could raise and lower a baguette), we sailed through the interview. So to the earlier list of adjectives intended to describe my wife, let me add: inventive, obstinate, self-assured, charming and coy.

We'd been married almost a year when Nic asked me, 'First anniversary is paper, no?' I gave her a quizzical look. She persisted. 'According to *Perfect Bride*, the first anniversary is paper.'

'I guess . . . Why?'

She responded by placing a gift in my hand. 'Well then, here.'

I unwrapped it. Nic had secretly rifled the drawer where I saved call slips and copied every single one we had presented to each other. Fastened together by a four-inch carriage bolt was a record of our book-based courtship. Nic called it *Slips of Love* and, on the compendium's tiny title-page, listed us as co-authors. My colleagues loved it and persuaded us to donate the book to the library's permanent collection.

Pleased by this, Nic indicated that *Slips of Love* was to be the first of many efforts that would push the material possibilities of the printed word. 'We will make what we are,' she said. 'A union of image and word.'

What to say to that? I struggled to align my aspirations with hers, and when doubts arose, which happened regularly, I chalked them up to my indecisive temperament, to the debilitating question mark that hovered over so many of my thoughts.

Nic had no such problem, but then again she had no idea that the phrase 'slips of love' could be taken in more ways than one. I felt other kinds of slips almost every day. My only reprieve, apart from the very rare moments of satisfaction at work, came when I turned inward, girdling quietly alone in my cage.

I suppose the references to my girdle book demand clarification. The simplest way to begin is to say I love lists. But that's *too* simple. It does nothing to explain the specific nature of my passion, which, let me state point-blank, satisfies much more than what my 'shrimp' described as (and I quote) 'a need to give order to the shards of a life, offering as it does a buffer against unpleasantness and a means of social survival.'

As if I didn't know *that*. Would he, I wonder, make such bone-stupid assessments about a drug addict or intemperate drinker? The shrimp further argued that my impulse to catalog functioned as a kind of 'belief system', one I maintained 'with an ardor others reserve for their gods'. On that count, maybe he had a point: my annotations seem to do much more than simply temper frustration, fear and unsatisfied hopes. But where do such pronouncements leave us? *Leave me?* Some people, after all, find solace in doodling. Others seek relief in numeric permutation. I know. I see them in the North Hall reading room, counting window panes, calculating shelving capacity, obsessing over split ends or split infinitives, timing their page-turning to the movement of the clock. The notes I keep under 'Readers' Tics' are lengthy and varied. Can I justifiably be lumped together with the fellow who spends whole afternoons writing down sums on the back of bank deposit envelopes? And why shouldn't I take occasional (OK, maybe not so occasional) comfort in my compositions? Lest we forget, that little 'belief system' is one of the things Nic liked about me. *She* was the one who said they should be bound, expressing this opinion in practical terms while I was showing her some star attractions of the Rare Book Room. As I stopped at a Benedictine breviary I greatly admired, she asked about the cord and nubbin of leather trailing off the binding like a tail. I explained that clerics would attach the knob to their robes so that the Word would be with them throughout the day.

'That's perfect for you.'

'Perfect how?'

'We'll make one for your lists.'

And so I received yet another of Nic's offerings, a rubricated ledger with decorative tab cuts and a cover of sturdy leather from an old army boot. (Nic and her dumpster tours!) A shoelace she wove and knotted enabled me to tether the book to the buttonhole of my jacket and carry it about the way the monks had done a half millennium before.

Nic, Norton and Speaight called the gift a great many things in the months that followed. The *vade mecum*, the scribble-scribble and, when my mood began to sour, the *Domesday Book of Alexander Short*. I stuck with my original term. 'Girdle book' connected me to the monastic rigors of the friars, and to a time when words and the Word could be one. That being said, I must admit that my first entries were anything but spiritual. They tended to the inconsequential and falsely aphoristic, observations worthy of the garbage skip. I told this to Nic one night. She scoffed, until I read her what I had written. She quickly agreed to remove the offending pages with a razor blade.

The next day as I went off to work, my girdle book purged of pretense (if only momentarily), I found the third-floor hallway blocked by the gleaming fenders of a late-model Lincoln Town Car, an uncommon sight even for the visually unpredictable domain in which I was forced to live. I decided that auto parts (or more precisely their location) warranted description. I flipped to 'H' and girdled my first Hallway notes. That night the fenders were gone, but I observed, on the steps going to the roof, a colorful mingling of crack vials and prophylactics, a composition betraying an all-too-common barter of goods for services. This I registered too. From then on I had little trouble girdling. Other categories sprouted up in quick succession: Chairs of Distinction, Enclosures, Mechanicals, Nicolisms, Readers' Tics. The list could go on—and it did. Because I knew space would be a problem, I used a tachygraphic shorthand acquired during my devotional study of Dewey's methods. In less than a month I was attached to the girdle book by much more than a shoelace. Girdling turned into a nervous habit, an addiction, an escape. When things were difficult, whether at work or at home, I would girdle. When things were *not* difficult, I would do the same.

Nic very quickly regretted her ingenuity and urged me to abandon it. I refused. She said I clutched the book as if it were a lover. An argument erupted, and as if to substantiate the language of infidelity, albeit one in which the object of my affections was a pocket-sized ledger formed from the upper of an army boot, Nic and I slept apart for the first time since she'd moved in. The frequency of that arrangement increased until separate beds was the norm.

Nic and I fought less and less because we cared less and less. Like so many couples living in cities where housing is in short supply, we resided together in body, but not soul. Neither she nor I could afford to move out.

Slips of Love . . . How to Poison a Friend . . . Marriage, or Liberty Decapitated. Choose whatever title you wish, the relationship was in jeopardy.

The morning after Nic said that I made her a banana, I lowered myself from the loft bed to find her stretched out asleep on the couch, part Madame Recamier, part Jean Seberg. Her hands were stained purple by the dye used to complete the pop-up that rested by her side.

I opened it.

A palm tree and two bathers lifted off the page. I tugged on a pull tab that caused the lips of two lovers to touch. It would have been so easy to duplicate the gesture, but I left Nic alone to her dreams. □

ELIZABETH McCRACKEN
THE GIANT OF CAPE COD

Elizabeth McCracken is the daughter of academics and was born in Boston in 1966. She has degrees in English literature from Boston University, in fiction writing from the University of Iowa and in library science from Drexel University. She worked in libraries on and off from the age of fifteen until last year. She now writes full-time and lives in Somerville, Massachusetts. Her collection of short stories, *Here's Your Hat, What's Your Hurry?*, was an American Library Association Notable Book of 1994. She says that she has not lived a life of particular note and frequently vacations in Des Moines, Iowa.

'The Giant of Cape Cod' is taken from her first novel, *The Giant's House*, which will be published by the Dial Press later this year.

I do not love mankind.

People think they're interesting. That's their first mistake. Every retiree you meet wants to supply you with his life story.

Thirty years ago a woman came into the library; she'd just heard about oral histories and wanted to string one together herself.

'We have so many wonderful old people around,' she said. 'They have such wonderful stories. We could capture them on tape and then maybe transcribe them—don't you think that would make a wonderful record of the area? My father, for instance, is in a nursing home . . . '

Her father, of course. She was not interested in *the* past, but *her* past.

'If I wanted to listen to old people nattering on,' I told her, 'I would ride a Greyhound bus across country. Such things get boring rather quickly, don't they.'

The woman looked at me with the same smile she'd had during the entire conversation. She laughed experimentally.

'Oh Miss Cort,' she said. 'Surely you didn't mean that.'

'I did and I do,' I answered. My reputation even thirty years ago was already so spoiled there was no saving it. 'I really don't see the point in it, do you?'

I felt that if those old people had some essential information they should write it down themselves. A life story can make adequate conversation but bad history.

Still, there you are in a nursing home, bored and lonely, and one day something different happens. Instead of a gang of school kids come to bellow Christmas carols at you, there's this earnest young person with a tape recorder, wanting to know about a flood sixty years ago, or what Main Street was like, or some such nonsense. All the other people in the home are sick to death of hearing your stories, because, let's be honest, you have only a few.

Suddenly there's a microphone in your face. Wham! Just like that, you're no longer a dull conversationalist, you're a natural resource.

Back then I thought, if you go around trying to rescue every fact or turn of phrase, you would never stop, you would eavesdrop until your fingers ached from playing the black keys of your tape recorder, until the batteries gasped their last and the tape came to its end and thunked the machine off, *no more*, and still you would not have made a dent on the small talk of the world. People are always downstairs, talking without you. They gather in front of stores, run into each other at restaurants and talk. They clump together at parties, or couple up at the dinner table. They organize themselves by profession (for instance, waitresses), or by quality of looks, or by hobby, or companion (in the case of dog owners and married people), or by sexual preference, or weight, or social ease, and they talk.

Imagine what there is to collect: every exchange between a customer and a grocery store clerk, wrong numbers, awful baby talk to a puppy on the street, what people yell back at the radio, the sound the teenage boy outside my window makes when he catches the basketball with both his hands and his stomach, every *Oh Lord* said at church or in bed or standing up from a chair. *Thank you, hey watch it, gesundheit, who's a good boy, sweetness, how much? I love your dress.*

An Anthology of Common Conversation. Already I can tell you it will be incomplete. In reference works, as in sin, omission is as bad as willful misbehavior. All those words go around and end up nowhere; your fondest wishes won't save them. No need to be a pack rat of palaver anyhow. Best to stick with recorded history.

Peggy Cort is crazy, anyone will tell you so. That lady who wanted to record the town's elders, the children who visited the library, my co-workers, every last soul in this town. The only person who ever thought I wasn't is dead.

Let me stop. History is chronological, at least this one is. Some women become librarians because they love order; I'm one. Ordinal, cardinal, alphabetical, alpha-numerical, geographical, by subject, by color, by shape, by size. Something logical that people—one hopes—cannot botch, although they will.

This isn't my story. Let me start again.

I do not love mankind, but he was different.

He was a redhead as a child.

You won't hear that from most people. Most people won't care. But he had pretty strawberry-blond hair. If he'd been out in the sun more, it would have been streaked gold.

He first came into my library in the fall of 1950, when he was eleven. Some teacher from the elementary school brought them all trooping in; I was behind the desk, putting a cart of fiction in order. I thought at first he was a second teacher, he was so much taller than the rest, tall even for a grown man. Then I noticed the chinos and white bucks and saw that this was the over-tall boy I'd heard about. Once I realized, I could see my mistake; though he would eventually develop cheekbones and whiskers, now he was pale and slightly baby-faced. He wasn't the tallest man in the world then, just a remarkably tall boy. Doctors had not yet prescribed glasses, and he squinted at faraway objects in a heroic way, as if they were new countries waiting to be discovered.

'This is Miss Cort,' the teacher said, gesturing at me. 'Ask her any question you want. She is here to help you. That is what librarians do.'

She showed them the dusty oak card catalog, the dusty stacks, the circulation desk I spent hours keeping free of dust. In short, she terrified them.

'Fiction is on the third floor,' she said. 'And biography is on the second.' I recognized her; she read Georgette Heyer and biographies of royalty and returned books so saturated with cigarette smoke I imagined she exhaled over each page on purpose. I wanted to stand by the exit, to whisper in every eleven-year-old ear, just come back. Come back by yourself, and we'll forget all about this.

At the end of the visit the tall boy came up to talk. He seemed studious, though that is too often the word we give to quiet, odd people.

'I want a book,' he said, 'about being a magician.'

'What sort of magician?' I said. 'Like Merlin?' Recently a teacher had read aloud from *The Sword and the Stone*, and they all wanted more stories.

'No,' he said. He put his hands on the circulation desk. His fingernails were cleaner than an ordinary eleven-year-old's; his mother was then still alive. 'Just tricks,' he said. 'I want to make things look like they disappear. I looked in the card catalog under magic but I didn't find anything.'

'Try "conjuring",' I told him.

We found only one book, an oversized skinny volume called *Magic for Boys and Girls*. He took it to a table in the front room. He wasn't clumsy, as you might expect, but terribly delicate. His hands were large, out of proportion even with his big body, and he had to use them delicately to accomplish anything at all.

I watched his narrow back as he read the book. After an hour I walked over.

'Is that the sort of thing you wanted?' I asked.

'Yes,' he said, not looking at me. The book was opened flat on the table in front of him, and he worked his hands in the air according to the instructions, without any props. His fingers kept slowly snatching at nothing, as if he had already made dozens of things disappear, rabbits and cards and rubber balls and bouquets of paper flowers, and had done this so brilliantly that even he could not bring them back.

It's been years now, and nearly every day I dream up my hours and meetings with James Carlson Sweatt. I am a librarian, and you cannot stop me from annotating, revising, updating. I like to think that—because I am a librarian—I offer accurate and spurious fact with no judgment, good and bad next to each other on the shelf. But my memories are not books. They are only stories that I have been over so many times in my head that I don't know from one day to the next what's remembered and what's made up. Like when you memorize a poem, and for one small, unimportant part you supply your own words. The meaning's the same, the meter's identical. When you read the actual version you can never get it into your head that it's right and you're wrong.

What I give you is the day's edition. Tomorrow it may be different.

I lived then, as now, in Brewsterville, an unremarkable little town on Cape Cod. Brewsterville lies halfway up the spit curl of the Cape, not close enough to the rest of the world to be convenient nor far enough to be attractively remote. We get tourists who don't know exactly what they've come out to see. These days we have little to show them: a few places that sell home-made jelly, a few guest houses, a small stretch of beach on the bay side. Our zoning laws keep us quaint, but just.

Once we had more. We had James Carlson Sweatt walking the streets. Some people came out specifically to visit James; some came for the ocean and happened upon him, more impressive than the ocean because no philosopher ever wonderingly addressed him, no poet compared him to God or a lover's restless body. Moreover, the ocean does not grant autographs. James did, politely, and then asked how you were enjoying your visit.

Everyone knew him as The Giant. Well, what else could you call him? Brilliant, maybe, and handsome and talented, but mostly doomed to be enormous. A painter, amateur magician, a compulsive letter writer, James Carlson Sweatt spent his life sitting down, hunching over. Hunching partly because that's the way he grew, like a flower; partly to make him seem smaller to others. Five feet tall in kindergarten; six feet two at age eleven. He turned sixteen and hit seven foot five the same week.

The town is talking about building a statue to honor James, but there's a lot of bickering: for instance, what size? Life-sized puts it at about the same height as the statue of the town founder, who's life-and-a-half. Some people claim it'll attract tourists, who even now take pictures in front of the founder. Others maintain that tourists will take a picture of any old thing. 'Who's this behind me?' a lady tourist asks her husband, who is intent on his focusing.

'Pilgrims,' he answers.

For some people, history is simply what your wife looks good standing in front of. It's what's cast in bronze, or framed in sepia tones, or acted out with wax dummies and period furniture. It takes place in glass bubbles filled with water and chunks of plastic snow; it's stamped on oversized pencils and alluded to in reprint newspapers. History nowadays is recorded in memorabilia. If you can't purchase a shopping bag that alludes to something, people won't believe it ever happened.

Librarian (like stewardess, certified public accountant, used-car salesman) is one of those occupations that people assume attract a certain deformed personality. Librarians are supposed to be bitter spinsters, grudging, lonely. And above all stingy: we love collecting fines on overdue books, our silence.

I did not love collecting fines; I forgave much more than I collected. I did not shush people unless they yelled. And though I was, technically, a spinster, I was only bitter insofar as people made me. It isn't that bitter people become librarians; it's that being a librarian may turn the most generous person bitter. We are paid all day to be generous, and no one recognizes our generosity.

As a librarian I longed to be acknowledged, even to be taken for granted. I sat at the desk, brimming with book reviews, information, warnings, all my good schooling, advice. I wanted people constantly callously to approach. But there were days nobody talked to me at all, they just walked to the shelves and grabbed a book and checked out, said, at most, *thank you*, and sometimes only *you're welcome* when I thanked them first. I had gone to school to learn how to help them, but they believed I was simply a clerk who stamped the books.

All it takes is a patron asking. And then asking again. The patron you become fond of will say, *I can't believe you have this book*. Or even better (believe it or not), *you don't own this book—is there a way I can get it?*

Yes.

Even at age eleven, twelve, James asked me how to find things in the catalog. He told me of books he liked, wanting something similar. He recognized me as an expert. Despite popular theories, I believe people fall in love not based on good looks or fate, but knowledge. Either they are amazed by something a beloved knows that they themselves do not know; or they discover common rare knowledge; or they can supply knowledge to someone who's lacking. Hasn't anyone found a strange ignorance in someone beguiling? An earnest question: what day of the week does Thanksgiving fall on this year? Nowadays trendy librarians, wanting to be important, say *Knowledge is power*. I know better. *Knowledge is love*.

People think librarians are unromantic, unimaginative. This is not true. We are people whose dreams run in particular ways. Ask a mountain climber what he feels when he sees a mountain; a lion tamer what goes through his mind when he meets a new lion; a doctor confronted with a beautiful malfunctioning body. The idea of a library full of books, the books full of knowledge, fills me with fear and love and courage and endless wonder. I knew I would be a librarian when I was in college as a student assistant at a reference desk, watching those lovely people at work. 'I don't think there's such a book . . . ' a patron would begin, and then the librarian would hand it to them, that very book.

Unromantic? This is a reference librarian's fantasy.

A patron arrives, says, *Tell me something*. You reach across the desk and pull him toward you, bear hug him a second and then take him into your lap, stroke his forehead, whisper facts in his ear. *The climate of Chad is tropical in the south, desert in the north. Source: 1991 CIA World Factbook. Do you love me? Americans consumed 6.2 gallons of tea per capita in 1989. Source: Statistical Abstract of the United States. Synecdoche is a literary device meaning the part for the whole, as in, the crowned heads of Europe. I love you. I could find you British Parliamentary papers, I could track down a book you only barely remember reading. Do you love me now? We own that book, we subscribe to that journal, Elvis Presley's first movie was called* Love Me Tender.

And then you lift the patron again, take him over the desk and set him down so gently he doesn't feel it, because there's someone else arriving, and she looks, oh, she looks uninformed.

He became a regular after that first school visit, took four books out at a time, returned them, took another four. I let him renew the magic book again and again, even though the rules said one renewal only. Librarians lose reason when it comes to the regulars, the good people, the *readers*. Especially when they're like James: it wasn't that he was lonely or bored; he wasn't dragged into the library by a parent. He didn't have that strange, desperate look that some library-goers develop, even children, the one that says: this is the only place I'm welcome anymore. Even when he didn't want advice he'd approach the desk with notes crumpled up, warm from his palm, his palm gray from the graphite. He'd hold it out until I grabbed the wastebasket by its rim, swung it around and offered it to him; his paper would go thunking in.

James was an eccentric kid, my favorite kind. I never knew how much of this eccentricity was height. He sometimes seemed peculiarly young, since he had the altitude but not the attitude of a man; and yet there was something elderly about him too. He never returned a book without telling me that it was on time, and, every now and then when he returned one late, he was nearly frantic and almost angry; I didn't know whether it was at me for requiring books back at a certain time, or at himself for disregarding the due date.

He'd been coming in for a year when I finally met his mother. I didn't know her by sight: she was an exotic thing, with blonde wavy hair down her back like a teenager, though she was thirty-five, ten years older than me. Her full cotton skirt had some sort of gold-flecked frosting swirled over the print.

'My son needs books,' she said.

'Yes?' I did not like mothers who come in for their children; they are meddlesome. 'Where is he?'

'In the hospital, up in Boston,' she said. A doleful twang pinched her voice. 'He wants books on history.'

'How old is he?'

'Twelve-but-smart,' she said. She wouldn't look me in the eye and trilled her fingertips over the edge of the counter. 'Ummm . . . Robert the Bruce? Is that somebody?'

'Yes,' I said. James and I had been discussing him. 'Is this for James? Are you Mrs Sweatt?'

She bit her lip. I hadn't figured James for the offspring of a lip-biter. 'Do you know Jim?' she asked.

'Of course.'

'Of course,' she repeated, and sighed.

'He's here every week. He's in the hospital? Is there something wrong?'

'Is something wrong?' she said. 'Well, nothing new. He's gone to an endocrinologist.' She pronounced each syllable of this last word like a word itself. 'Maybe they'll operate.'

'For what?' I asked.

'For *what*?' she said. 'For *him*. To slow him down.' She waved her hand above her head, to indicate excessive height. 'They're *alarmed*.'

'Oh. I'm sorry.'

'It's not good for him. I mean, it wouldn't be good for anyone to grow like that.'

'No, of course not.'

He must have known that he was scheduled to go to the hospital, and I was hurt he hadn't mentioned it.

'I was thinking Mark Twain too,' she said. 'For him to read. *Tom Sawyer* or something.'

'Fiction,' I said. 'Third floor. Clemens.'

'Clemens,' she repeated. She loved the taste of other people's words in her mouth.

'Clemens,' I said. 'Mark Twain, Samuel Clemens. That's where we file him.'

Before his mother had come to the library, I hadn't realized that there was anything medically wrong with James. He was tall, certainly, but in the same sweet, gawky way young men are often tall. His bones had great plans, and the rest of him, voice and skin and balance, strained to keep pace. He bumped into things and walked on the sides of his feet, and his hair would not stay in a single configuration for more than fifteen minutes. He was not even a teenager yet; he had not outgrown childhood freckles or enthusiasms.

They didn't operate on James that hospital visit. The diagnosis: tall, very. Chronic congenital height. He came back with more wrong than he left with: an orderly, pushing him down the hall, misjudged a corner and cracked his ankle.

He was twelve years old then and six feet four.

A librarian is bound by many ethics no one else understands. For instance: in the patron file was James's library card application with his address and phone number and mother's signature. It was wrong, I felt, to look up the address of a patron for personal reasons, by which I mean my simple nosiness. Delinquent patrons, yes; a twenty-dollar bill used as a bookmark in a returned novel, certainly. But we must protect the privacy of our patrons, even from ourselves.

I'd remained pure in this respect for a while, but finally pulled out the application. I noted that James had been six when he had gotten his card five years before; I hadn't even seen Brewsterville yet. He had written his name in square, crooked letters—probably he'd held the pen with both hands. But it was a document completed by a child and therefore faulty: he'd written the name of the street, but not the number. If I'd been on duty, such sloppiness would never have passed.

However I could telephone his mother for library purposes. The broken ankle promised to keep him home for a few weeks, so I called up Mrs Sweatt and offered to bring over books.

'I'll pick them up,' she said.

'It's no bother, and I'd like to wish James well.'

'No,' she said. 'Don't trouble yourself.'

'I just said it's no trouble.'

'Listen, Peggy,' she said. That she knew my Christian name surprised me. There was a long pause while I obeyed her and listened. Finally she said, 'I can't do too much for Jim. But I can pick up his books and I intend to.'

So of course I resigned myself to that. I agreed with her; there was little she could do for him. Every Friday—his usual day—I wondered whether James would come in. Instead Mrs Sweatt arrived with her big purse, and I stamped her books with a date three weeks in the future. Mostly she insisted on choosing herself—she seemed determined that James read all of Mark Twain during his convalescence—but she always asked for at least one suggestion. I imagined that it was my books he really read, my choices that came closest to what he wanted. I'd sent *Worlds in Collision* by Immanuel Velikovsky; *Mistress Masham's Repose* by T. H. White; *Hiroshima* by John Hersey. Mrs Sweatt was always saying, 'And something else like this,' waving the book I'd personally picked out the week before.

'How's James?' I asked her.

'Fine.' She examined the bindings of a row of books very closely, her head tilted to a hunched shoulder for support.

'How's the ankle?'

'Coming along.'

'Not healed yet?'

She scratched her chin, then rucked up the back of her skirt like a five-year-old and scratched her leg. 'He's still keeping off it,' she said. 'Ambrose Bierce. Do you have any Ambrose Bierce?'

I looked up the card for the magic book; James had not been in for three months. Surely an ankle would knit back together in that time. Maybe Mrs Sweatt was keeping James from the library, had forbidden him to come. It wouldn't be the first time. A certain sort of mother is terrified by all the library's possibilities.

I was meddlesome myself: I decided to cut off James's supply of interesting books. He was one of my favorite patrons—that is to say, one of my favorite people—and even this early in our friendship, the thought of never seeing him again was more than I could bear.

'This looks difficult,' said Mrs Sweatt, looking at a translation of *Caesar's Wars*.

'Oh,' I said. 'I thought he was bright for his age.'

'Of course.' She tucked the book under her arm. 'Half of it's in Latin,' she said under her breath.

If they ever want me to teach a course entitled 'History: the Dull and the Punishing', I have the reading list all worked out. Bulwer-Lytton, the poems of Edgar Guest, cheap novels whose morals were that war was bad but sometimes resulted in lifelong love between a soldier and his girl. We owned the complete works of a certain nineteenth-century lady author who drew quite a few more morals out of history than that: her books were called things like *A True Friend of Christ* and *Daisy, a Girl of the West*. I chose fiendishly well, and sent the books home with the unfortunate Mrs Sweatt, who brought them back unread.

'This one's close,' she'd say sometimes. 'But not quite. How about the Civil War?'

I gave her *Gone with the Wind*, which I knew James would never be able to stomach.

I won't pretend that I was in love with James right away. He was only a boy, though one I liked quite a bit.

Well, now. Only this far into the story and already I'm lying. In juvenile magazines they feature close-up photographs of things that are, like love, impossible to divine close up for the first time: a rose petal, a butterfly's wing, frost. Once you're told what they are, you can't believe you didn't see it instantly. So yes, I loved James straight off, though I didn't realize it then. I know that sounds terrible, the sort of thing that makes people think I'm crazy or worse.

But there was nothing scandalous about what I felt for

James. I am not a scandalous person. No, that isn't true either. Given half a chance I am scandalous; later facts bear that out. But life afforded me few opportunities in those days. He was not even a teenager and more than half a foot taller than the average American. I was almost twice his age and I already loved him.

There's a joke about that. A forty-year-old man (it's always a man) falls in love with a ten-year-old girl. He's four times her age. He waits five years; now he's forty-five, and she's fifteen and he's only three times her age. Fifteen years later he's sixty, only double her age. How long until she catches up completely?

I love that joke. It reads like a chart, like the grids that were eventually printed in medical journals, describing James's growth, at age ten, age twelve, steady intervals of time and quite nearly as steady in inches. Imagine it: my age on one side of a chart, James's on the other. How long until he catches up?

James and I met at a particular, happy time in his life. He was just six foot two, remarkably tall but not yet automatically noticed on the street. At school, yes: he was eleven, and this was the year that the tallest kids in the classes were girls, and the boys, innocent of adolescence, occupied the front row of class pictures, the far right hand side of gym-class line-ups. James always knew where he belonged in such indexing, but he wasn't strange. Out in the world, he just seemed like a nice, naïve, full-grown man.

In 1950, when I met James Carlson Sweatt, I was twenty-six years old, without any experience of love whatsoever. I don't mean beaux; I'd had those, stupid boys. In college I'd had friends and boyfriends, was invited to parties and asked to the movies. I wasn't objectionable, not then, but neither was I exceptional: after graduation I never heard from a single college chum. In library school I had a few after-class-coffee friends, but that was it.

Then I moved to Brewsterville. Suddenly that part of my life seemed to have ended: I felt quite sure I would never hear an affectionate word from another human being in my life. Most days I spoke only to my library patrons, which is one reason I loved my work—it kept me from being one of those odd women discussed in books about odd people: *her neighbors saw her only as a shadow on the street, then she died, buried beneath newspapers, movie magazines and journals filled with imaginary conversations.*

Even with work I was odd enough. Every morning I walked along the gravel path from my house to the sidewalk, thinking, *is this who I am? A lonely person?* I felt as awkward as a teenager most days, as if Cape Cod were one big high school that I had enrolled in too late to understand any of the running jokes. My life was better in many ways than it had been in high school, I knew that. I worked harder, which was a blessing; my skin had turned up pleasant enough. I had been kissed.

But I still dreamed of kisses that I knew wouldn't be delivered and I grew morose as I waited to be stood up by nobody in particular. I was aware that I didn't know anything about love; every morning I realized it again.

And then I met a tall boy.

If I were a different sort of woman, I would point to fate. I would claim that I understood the course of the rest of my life the minute James walked into my library. But if I were a different sort of woman, I wouldn't have needed to cling to the weekly polite visits of a tall boy, or to wonder what went on in a house with painted flowers on the side, dreaming of the day I might be allowed back in.

That, perhaps, is all you need to know. *I was not a different sort of woman.* Right there you have my life story, because my life is beside the point. Most lives are. Just as *Barlett's* is not interested in the librarian's quotations, *Who's Who* is not interested in the librarian's life. In a big library you will find dozens of biographical dictionaries: South American women writers, Scottish scientists of the eighteenth century, military men and psychologists and business-people; the important citizens of every country.

You will not find a volume marked *Everybody Else.*

You will not find me in any reference source; your finger will slide along index after index, under Cort, under librarians—American, but you won't find the slightest reference to me.

You might be tempted to ask, but I'll tell you: it's a colorless story, one that no one could possibly be interested in. By now it's outdated and probably riddled with lies. If somebody wrote the story of my life before James (and it would be a short book, repetitious and unillustrated) I would not buy it; I would not have it on my shelf. It would be a waste of the budget.

The Giant of Cape Cod

I was a librarian when I met him. That much is important. I had my library, which I loved and despised. All librarians, deep down, loathe their buildings. Something is always wrong—the counter is too high, the shelves too narrow, the delivery entrance too far from the offices. The hallway echoes. The light from the windows bleaches books. In short libraries are constructed by architects, not librarians. Do not trust an architect: he will always try to talk you into an atrium.

Space is the chief problem. Books are a bad family—there are those you love and those you are indifferent to; idiots and mad cousins whom you would banish except others enjoy their company; wrong-headed but fascinating eccentrics and dreamy geniuses; orphaned grandchildren; and endless brothers-in-law simply taking up space whom you wish you could send straight to hell. Except you can't, for the most part. You must house them and make them comfortable and worry about them when they go on trips. And there is never enough room.

My library was no exception. It had started its life in 1880 as a nice, one-room building; almost immediately the collection was crowded. The town started to tack on additions: a skinny hall, a dusty reading room, two stories of stacks with frosted-glass floors. These floors—an invention of the nineteenth century—were composed of panes cloudy as cataracts which only allowed close-up objects to show through. On the second floor you could see the glow of the light bulbs that lit the first floor; on the first floor you could see the outline of people's feet by looking up.

The panes of glass were always cracking and had to be replaced with wood. The shelves went right through the floors, and there were gaps where they met the glass panes, which meant that a man on the first floor could look up the skirt of a woman on the second if he were so inclined, and at least once a month, some man was.

The tiles teared up at a hint of moisture; the slender-throated plumbing choked on the daintiest morsel. The roof leaked. There were staircases that led nowhere.

I came to the job fresh from library science school. Purgatory would have seemed quite an adequate set-up to me then; I would happily have issued cards to the not-quite-condemned and the not-yet-blessed and thought it a vast improvement over the dullness of catalog class. I loved that building when I first met it; I suppose I continued to love it the way a woman will love a husband who sticks around while she silently prays he will leave or die. Indeed until 1950 the library occupied much of my heart and mind. When we were apart, I wondered what wrong-headed thing it would insist upon in my absence (bursting a pipe, inviting birds through broken windows); when we were together, I cursed it and made apologies for its behavior to visitors. Before I met James Carlson Sweatt, the library was my best comfort and company. I was a fool for that library.

We are fools for whoever will have us.

I did see other people. My patrons, for instance. Pharmacists are the same, I guess—you learn the dirty little secrets of what's wrong with your customers and what might possibly cure it: shy men who want to read about wars, any war at all; fading women who need a weekly romance. Plenty of people came in more than once a week. Mr Mackintosh, a widower, fancied himself a writer and wanted me to read his stories. I read one; it was about a stripper. Mrs Carson was on her fourth husband; I wondered when she had the time to read her bestsellers. A nice couple brought in pictures of their dogs, fox terriers, natty dressers—the dogs, I mean, not the couple. My landlord, Gary, a tragic man whose wife had left him eight years before, came to read magazines once a week.

I had my co-workers too, who some days I forget. I see myself alone in the library, alone with the patrons. Pride does this. At the library I worked with two other people: Astoria Peck and Darla Foster, both part-timers. Darla was a twenty-year-old who'd have been better suited to waitressing. I don't know why I hired her, other than the fact she was my sad landlord's daughter. Darla shelved the books, put the daily papers on the forked wooden spines that rested in metal stands, worked the front desk when I was busy. She had a rear end as big as an opened dictionary, and a bad attitude.

Astoria Peck handled most of the library's technical processes—repairing books or sending them out to a bindery, if they could be saved at all; cataloguing; billing. Like me, she was a librarian (that is, she had a master's in library science), and had for many years worked at the elementary school. Once she hit forty, she said, she got tired of the smell of children.

'They smell like bad cookies,' she told me. 'Go ahead, get a good whiff.'

I demurred, which was never enough for Astoria. The next child through the door prompted her to nudge me—'Go ahead.'

Astoria had been told once that she should go to Hollywood; she never did but she also never forgot the suggestion and wore her hair and make-up like a movie star. She was the type of person who relied very much on what other people told her about herself. She'd been informed, variously, that she was a card, an enigma, a heartless woman. Her mood depended on what was last said to her; it prevailed until the next assessment. Her husband told her she had beautiful legs, and she was happy; her niece told her she had big ears, and she was devastated.

'I have big ears,' she told me mournfully. 'I'm a big-eared woman.'

Astoria and I were bound together by our terrible struggles with the library building and the troubles it caused with the town manager, who, when we wanted our book budget increased, said that he'd *been* to the library, and the shelves were *already* full. He'd look at a repair bill and say, 'What did they fix that toilet with, gold?' Between the building, which was falling to pieces, and the town manager, who was solid rock, we were left to setting out buckets for leaks and fixing wobbly tables with books we were going to throw out anyhow, books that had not circulated in thirty years. For some reason, though, a table leg square on a dust jacket seemed to patrons the highest recommendation; they wanted to take those books out, accused us of neglecting great works.

Mrs Sweatt started coming to the library for herself, for romance novels and women's magazines. She nodded at me shyly, sneezed in the dust. You could hear her sneeze in the stacks from anywhere in the library; it sounded like a reproach.

'What is her name?' I asked Astoria. 'She calls me Peggy, but hasn't even told me what her Christian name is.'

'That's it,' Astoria said. 'That's what everyone calls her. I guess when she and her husband got married, they called each other Mister and Missus—you know, like any honeymoon couple—and they just never got out of the habit. Then other people picked up on it.'

'She's not from around here.'

'No,' said Astoria. 'Heavens, no, Midwest, somewhere. Came out on vacation with her parents, met Mr Sweatt, stayed. He could have swept any girl off her feet, that one. Charming, a fast talker. Nobody could figure out what he saw in her.'

'Well,' I said.

'I mean, she was this sort of tragic character—even then she was, I'm not sure why—and Mr Sweatt was a boisterous, friendly guy. A bad guy who made himself seem nice sometimes, or the other way around, you know the type?'

No, I said, I didn't.

'He left. About six years ago, maybe. Just disappeared out west. That's where ex-husbands go, right? There must be whole ranches of ex-husbands out there, leaning on corrals and drinking too much gin.' She laughed. 'And now here's poor Mrs Sweatt. Drinking a little too much herself, actually.'

'Oh.'

'She thinks it's a secret. But listen to her purse when she walks by. Slosh, slosh.'

'I don't listen to purses,' I said. 'Purses are a private matter.'

Shy, sensitive-to-dust Mrs Sweatt. Her arms and legs were plump, as if her heart did not want them to get too far away, and sometimes she seemed to limp. I thought her marriage must never have been happy; I couldn't imagine her enjoying the company of a boisterous man. And if you were boisterous, it would be hard not to torment Mrs Sweatt, who did not have a sense of humor in the way most people do not have a sense of French.

In our town we did not measure time in years but in winters. Summers were debatable daylight; winters were definite, like night. In the dark privacy of winter Brewsterville's citizens were more likely to drink, weep, have affairs, tell off-color jokes, let themselves go.

Then summer came around again, and they ironed their best pants, sewed on buttons popped by eagerness or an extra five pounds and got back to work.

It wasn't that nothing happened during the tourist season, simply that summers were so crowded with quotidian incident as to appear identical to one another. The tourists came in. Every year one had a heart attack in a restaurant; several were accused (rightly or wrongly) of shoplifting a souvenir ashtray from one of the souvenir-ashtray emporiums; dozens tried to seduce coffee-shop waitresses and succeeded or didn't, depending on the coffee shop; and an even hundred tried to get library cards good for one week, despite living in California, despite a remarkable lack of identification. And then the summer ended, and the tourists left, and it was as if the town itself had just returned from a vacation somewhere far off, having never sent a postcard to keep all of us up-to-date on its seasonal goings-on.

There was the winter of 1951, with the bad ice storm (unusual for us) during which, Astoria said, Marie at the post office got stranded and then pregnant with a boyfriend from Hyannis at the only inn open year-round. James was twelve and just under six foot four. The following winter there was barely any snow at all, and the used bookstore closed up when the man who owned it shot himself. Nobody could understand why, with the weather so pleasant for a change. James turned thirteen. Next the winter of 1953. His growth was like weather, some years worse than others: he grew six inches between his thirteenth and fourteenth birthdays, and Brewsterville lost power four times in thunderstorms.

Though I wouldn't have admitted it, what I'd mostly known previously was what everyone did: his height. The tall boy, our town giant. I knew that height well, of course: Astoria had given me the details. When he was a baby, strangers thought he was retarded because he was so slow for his size. The hems on everything he wore were deep as most people's pockets, so they could be let out, and his pockets were twice as deep as his hems.

I'd been captivated by his height, and the heroic way he seemed to bear it. Now I learned he was interesting in many unconnected ways. I could write an encyclopedia on his enthusiasms and how they accumulated, complete with dates and cross-references.

'What's your hobby this week?' I'd ask.

'I'm thinking about model building,' he'd say. 'But not from kits. I want to start from scratch, so I need books on battleships.' Or, 'Gardening.' Or, 'I want to make my own root beer. Are there recipes for things like that?'

He was fond of the sorts of books that I'd loved as a child, huge omnibuses of humor, pranks or science experiments. A serious kid most of the time, he allowed himself to get silly at strange moments.

He came in one day wearing a plastic nose, ordered from the back of a magazine, underscored by the falsest mustache I'd ever seen. (All his life he loved what you could get through the mail. Eventually he had dozens of degrees from correspondence schools and was a mail-order minister several times over.) The nose was beaky and sharp and coming loose at the edges. I said, 'You look like the canary who swallowed the cat,' and he laughed his mustache right off. Every now and then he'd approach the desk with a glass of water filled from the bubbler in the hall and would ask me, in a reasonable tone of voice, to put my hands out or turn my back for a second. I explained to him that I wasn't born yesterday. Astoria, however, was a perfect pigeon, and I more than once had to rescue her: she'd set her hands, palms down, on the circulation desk, and James had balanced a glass filled with water on each, and then whistled his way to the back of the library. James introduced me to my first joy buzzer, and Astoria to her first whoopee cushion. I knew better than to accept candy from him: I knew it would be rubber or bitter or explosive.

Nevertheless I was the town librarian—less a woman than a piece of civic furniture, like a polling machine at the town hall, or a particularly undistinguished mural—and even those years had a sameness to them, uninvolved in gossip as I then was. I have had to consult one of those medical charts to see during which year he grew six inches. James was a library patron then, a cherished one, but when I saw him on the street with his friends, a rare summer sunburn across his nose, or, in the fall, heading toward his house with a bag of groceries, or, in winter, pulling on a knit cap that his mother no doubt insisted on, I was only one of the many people who knew him; everyone knew him.

My own life went on in this way. I woke up, cleaned my apartment, went to work, came home. I almost always had a book in my hand, to shelve or read or consider.

James's life went on too. He grew. That was his life's work. He got the glasses he needed. He acquired a camera and carried it by the neck strap all around town. I saw him making his way down the street clicking pictures. The year-rounders were used to him, but tourists stopped and stared.

Summers made even me feel as if I were becoming famous. That is, people took my picture constantly. That is, I kept accidentally stepping into the frame as a tourist took a picture of something else. These are the two truths of tourists: they walk slowly and they must record their slow progress down the street. I appear in family albums, in slide carousels, sometimes a blur and sometimes a sulky stranger. When I ate my lunch on a bench outside the library, they thought me particularly picturesque and photographed me on purpose.

They loved James, of course, and asked to take his picture, usually alongside a wife. He allowed it as long as they returned the favor. He really was becoming famous; usually they asked his name so they could write it on the back of the snapshot. *Mother, Niagara Falls, 1949. Minna, 1950. James Sweatt, Brewsterville, Cape Cod, 1954.*

He never recorded the names of the tourists; what made one different from another? He read books on developing photographs. He became a boy scout, the world's biggest. He wrote a prize-winning essay on community service. He played basketball, of course, and was always described as the star. By this they meant tall. Any number of the words used to describe James just meant tall.

Certainly things could have continued thus, and I would have completed my life never knowing the lack. Or rather, I would have kept my relationship as it was with James, finding him books and recognizing a lack and counting myself lucky for that. Lacking things was what I did; I might as well lack something interesting. I felt in those days quite set apart from the rest of the human race who regularly got what they wanted and complained anyhow. □

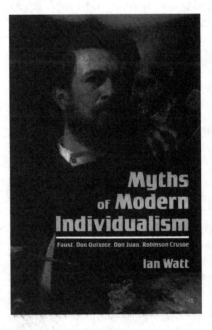

GRANTA

MARION ETTLINGER

PORTRAITS

Opposite: Sherman Alexie. Above: Madison Smartt Bell

Above: Ethan Canin. Opposite: Edwidge Danticat

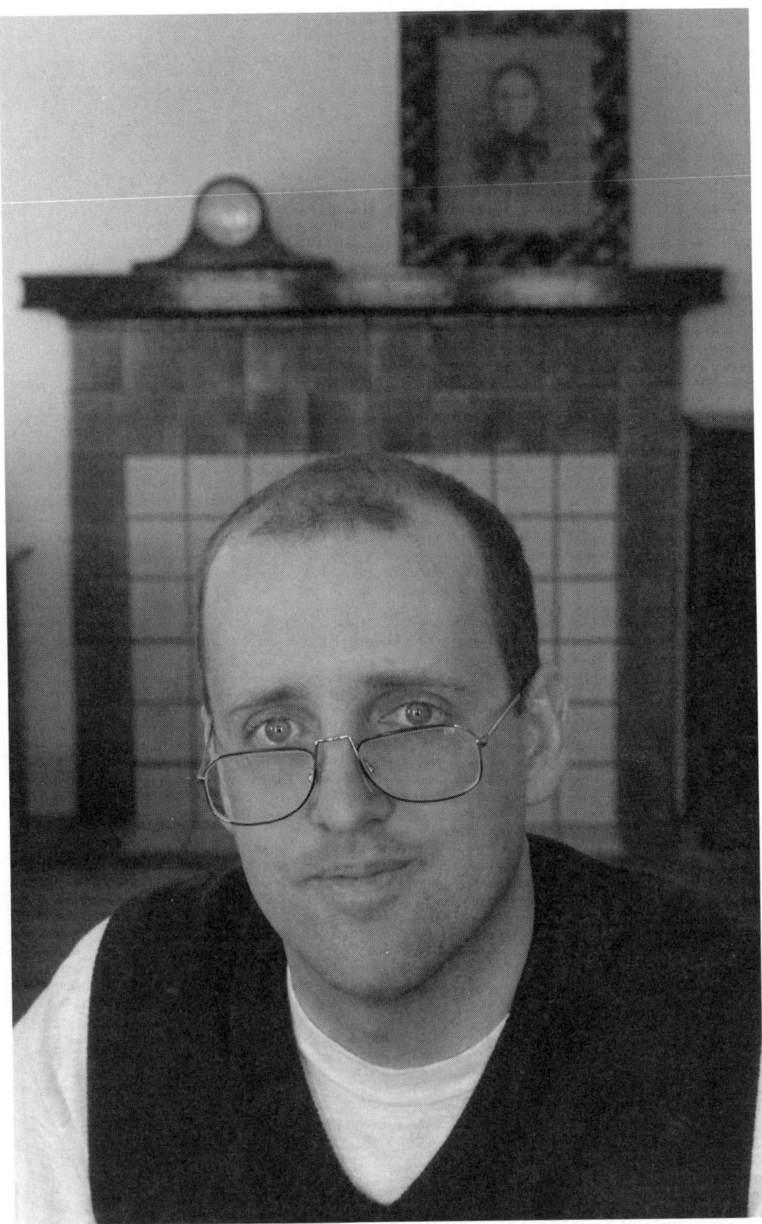

Opposite: Tom Drury. Above: Tony Earley

Jeffrey Eugenides

NO JUEGUES CON TU
1-800-CONTIGO

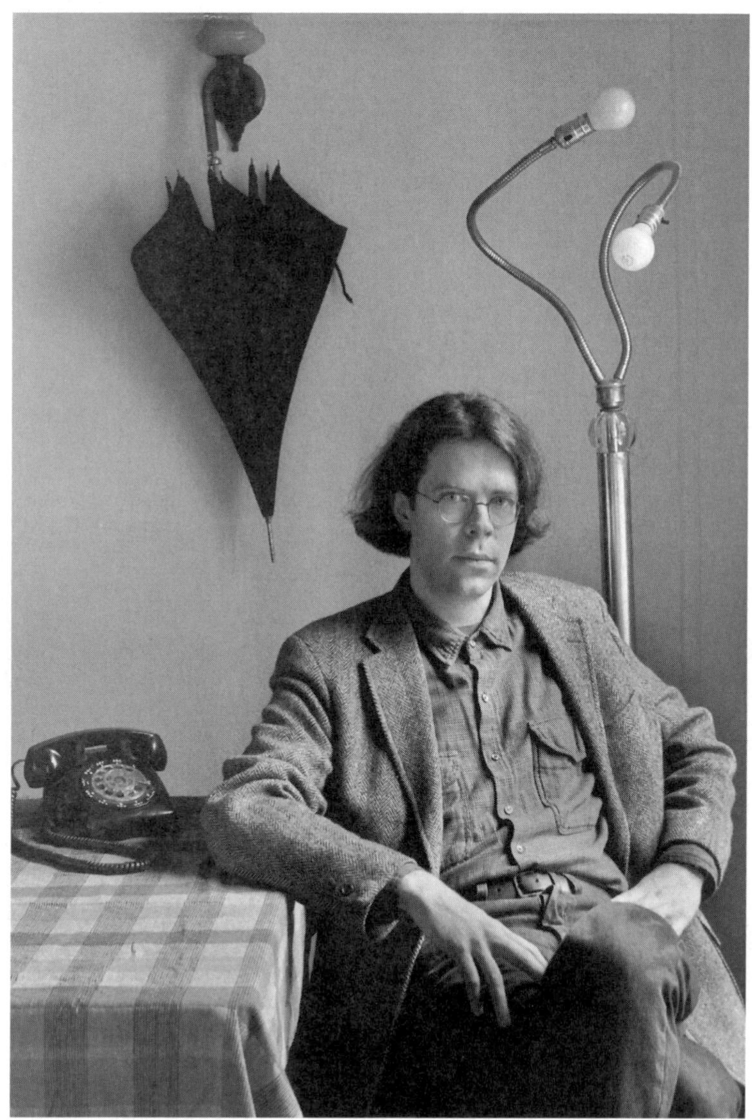

Above: Jonathan Franzen. Opposite: David Haynes

David Guterson

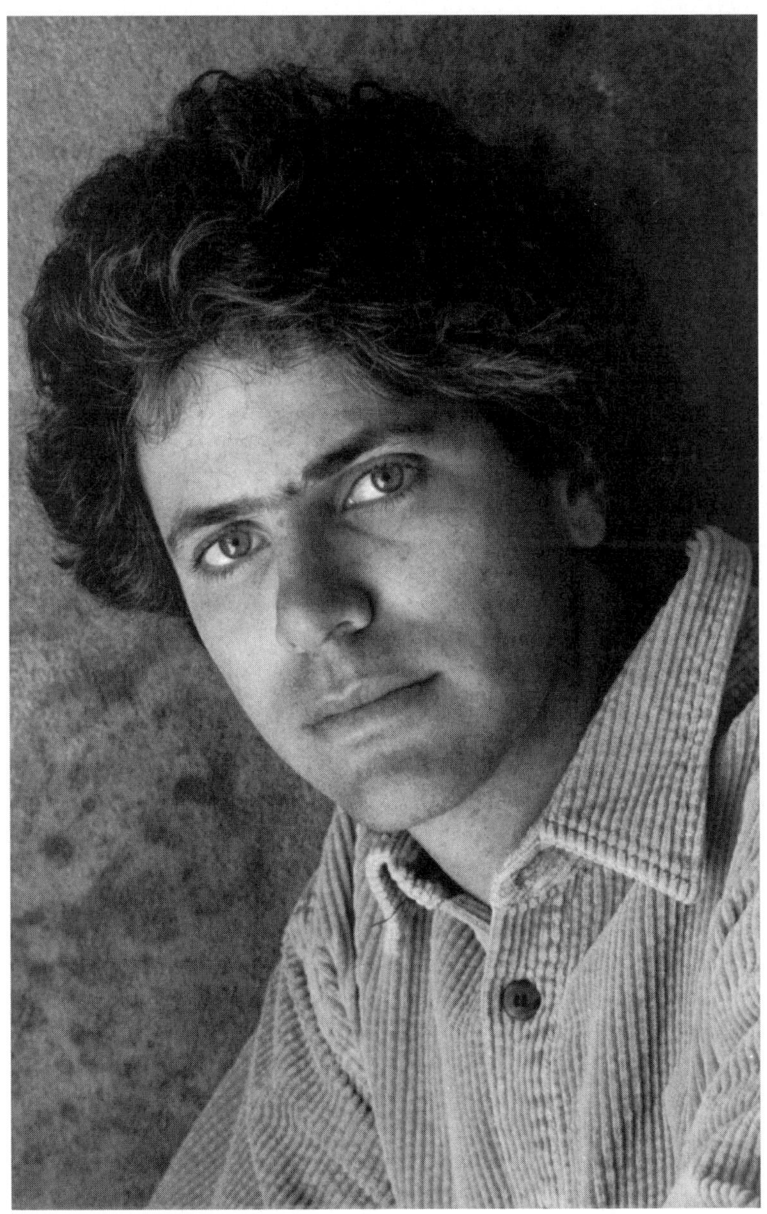

Above: Allen Kurzweil. Opposite: Elizabeth McCracken

Above: Lorrie Moore. Opposite: Fae Myenne Ng

Opposite: Robert O'Connor. Above: Chris Offutt

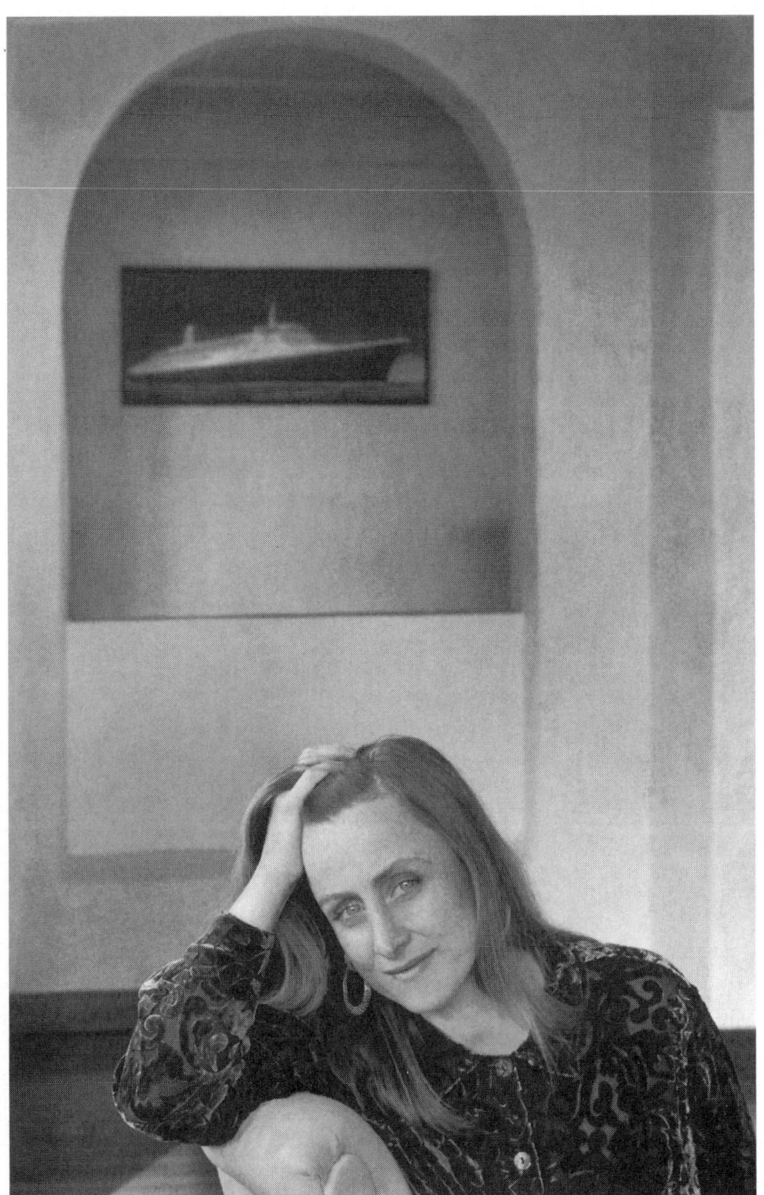

Opposite: Stewart O'Nan. Above: Mona Simpson

Opposite: Melanie Rae Thon. Above: Kate Wheeler

GRANTA

LORRIE MOORE
AGNES OF IOWA

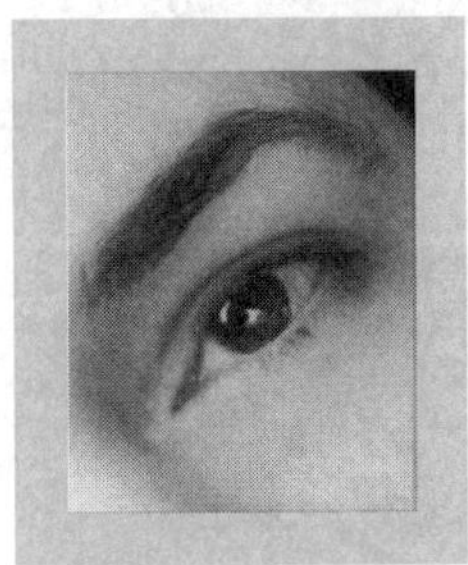

Lorrie Moore was born in Glen Falls, New York, in 1957 and graduated from St Lawrence and Cornell universities. She has published two collections of short stories, *Self-Help* and *Like Life*, and two novels, *Anagrams* and *Who Will Run the Frog Hospital?* (1994). Her stories have also appeared in the *New Yorker* and *Best American Short Stories*. She has received fellowships from several foundations and is currently a professor of English at the University of Wisconsin in Madison, where she lives with her husband and son.

'Agnes of Iowa' will be included in her third collection.

Her mother had given her the name Agnes, believing that a good-looking woman was even more striking when her name was a homely one. Her mother was named Cyrena and was beautiful to match but had always imagined her life would have been more interesting, that she herself would have had a more dramatic, arresting effect on the world and not ended up in Cassell, Iowa, if she had been named Enid or Hagar or Maude. And so she named her first daughter Agnes, and when Agnes turned out not to be attractive at all but puffy and prone to a rash between her eyebrows, her hair a flat and bilious hue, her mother back-pedaled and named her second daughter Linnea Elise (who turned out to be a lovely, sleepy child with excellent bones, a sweet, full mouth and a rubbery mole above her lip which later in life could be removed without difficulty, everyone was sure).

Agnes herself had always been a bit at odds with her name. There was a brief period in her life, in her mid-twenties, when she had tried to pass it off as French—she had put in the *accent grave* and encouraged people to call her 'On-yez'. This was when she was living in New York City and often getting together with her cousin, a painter who took her to parties in TriBeCa lofts or at beach houses or at mansions on lakes upstate. She would meet a lot of not very bright rich people who found the pronunciation of her name intriguing. It was the rest of her they were unclear on. 'On-yez, where are you from, dear?' asked a black-slacked, frosted-haired woman whose skin was papery and melanomic with suntan. 'Originally.' She eyed Agnes's outfit as if it might be what in fact it was: a couple of blue things purchased in a department store in Cedar Rapids.

'Where am I from?' Agnes said it softly. 'Iowa.' She had a tendency not to speak up.

'Where?' the woman scowled, bewildered.

'Iowa.' Agnes repeated loudly.

The woman in black touched Agnes's wrist and leaned in confidentially. She moved her mouth in a concerned and exaggerated way, like an exercise. 'No, dear,' she said. '*Here* we say *O-hi-o*.'

That had been in Agnes's mishmash decade, after college. She had lived improvisationally then, getting this job or that, in restaurants or offices, taking a class or two, not thinking too far ahead, negotiating the precariousness and subway flus and scrimping for an occasional facial or a play. Such a life required much expendable self-esteem. It engaged gross quantities of hope and despair and set them wildly side by side, like a Third World country of the heart. Her days grew messy with contradictions. When she went for walks, for her health, cinders would spot her cheeks, and soot would settle in the furled leaf of each ear. Her shoes became unspeakable. Her blouses darkened in a breeze, and a blast of bus exhaust might linger in her hair for hours. Finally her old asthma returned and, with a hacking, incessant cough, she gave up. 'I feel like I've got five years to live,' she told people, 'so I'm moving back to Iowa so that it'll feel like fifty.'

When she packed up to leave she knew she was saying goodbye to something important, which was not that bad in a way because it meant that at least you had said hello to it to begin with, which most people in Cassell, Iowa could not claim to have done.

A year later she married a boyish man twelve years her senior, a Cassell realtor named Joe, and together they bought a house on a little street called Birch Court. She taught a night class at the Arts Hall and did volunteer work on the Transportation Commission in town. It was life like a glass of water: half-full, half-empty, half-full; oops, half-empty. Over the next six years she and Joe tried to have a baby, but one night at dinner, looking at each other in a lonely way over the meat loaf, they realized with a shock that they probably never would. Nonetheless they still tried, vandalizing what romance was left in their marriage.

'Honey,' she would whisper at night when he was reading under the reading lamp, and she had already put her book away and curled toward him, wanting to place the red scarf over the lampshade but knowing it would annoy him and so not doing it. 'Do you want to make love? It would be a good time of month.'

And Joe would groan. Or he would yawn. Or he would already be asleep. Once, after a long hard day, he said, 'I'm sorry, Agnes. I'm just not in the mood.'

She grew exasperated. 'You think *I'm* in the mood?' she said. 'I don't want to do this any more than you do.' He looked at her in a disgusted way, and it was two weeks after that they had the identical sad dawning over the meat loaf.

At the Arts Hall, formerly the Grange Hall, Agnes taught the Great Books class but taught it loosely, with cookies. She let her students turn in poems and plays and stories that they themselves had written; she let them use the class as their own little time to be creative. Someone once even brought in a sculpture: an electric one with blinking lights.

After class she sometimes met with students individually. She recommended things for them to write about or read or consider in their next project. She smiled and asked if things were going well in their lives. She took an interest.

'You should be stricter,' said Willard Stauffbacher, the head of the Instruction Department. He was a short, balding musician who taped to his door pictures of famous people he thought he looked like. Every third Monday he conducted the monthly departmental meeting—aptly named, Agnes liked to joke, since she did indeed depart mental. 'Just because it's a night course doesn't mean you shouldn't impart standards,' Stauffbacher said in a scolding way. 'If it's piffle, use the word *piffle*. It's meaningless? Write *meaningless* at the top of every page.' He had once taught at an elementary school and once at a prison. 'I feel like I do all the real work around here,' he added. He had posted near his office a sign that read:

RULES FOR THE MUSIC ROOM

I WILL STAY IN MY SEAT UNLESS [*sic*] PERMISSION TO MOVE

I WILL SIT UP STRAIGHT

I WILL LISTEN TO DIRECTIONS

I WILL NOT BOTHER MY NEIGHBOR

I WILL NOT TALK WHEN MR STAUFFBACHER IS TALKING

I WILL BE POLITE TO OTHERS

I WILL SING AS WELL AS I CAN

Agnes stayed after one night with Christa, the only black student in her class. She liked Christa a lot—Christa was smart and funny, and Agnes would sometimes stay late with her to chat. Tonight Agnes had decided to talk Christa out of writing about vampires all the time.

'Why don't you write about that thing you told me about that time?' Agnes suggested.

Christa looked at her skeptically. 'What thing?'

'The time in your childhood, during the Chicago riots, walking with your mother through the police barricades.'

'Man, I lived that. Why should I want to write about it?'

Agnes sighed. Maybe Christa had a point. 'It's just I'm no help to you with this vampire stuff,' Agnes said. 'It's formulaic genre fiction.'

'You would be of more help to me with my *childhood*?'

'Well, with more serious stories, yes.'

Christa stood up, perturbed. She grabbed her paperback. 'You with all your Alice Walker and Zora Hurston. I'm not interested in that anymore. I've done that already. I read those books years ago.'

'Christa, please don't be annoyed.' *Please do not talk when Mr Stauffbacher is talking.*

'You've got this agenda for me.'

'Really, I don't at all,' said Agnes. 'It's just that—you know what it is? It's that I'm sick of these vampires. They're so roaming and repeating.'

'If you were black, what you're saying might have a different spin. But the fact is you're not,' Christa said, and picked up her coat and strode out—though ten seconds later she gamely stuck her head back in and said, 'See you next week.'

'We need a visiting writer who's black,' Agnes said in the next depart mental meeting. 'We've never had one.'

They were looking at their budget, and the readings this year were pitted against Dance Instruction, a program headed up by a redhead named Evergreen.

'The Joffrey is just so much central casting,' said Evergreen, apropos of nothing. As a vacuum cleaner can start to pull up the actual thread of a carpet, her brains had been sucked dry by too much yoga. No one paid much attention to her.

'Perhaps we can get Harold Raferson in Chicago,' Agnes suggested.

'We've already got somebody for the visiting writer slot,' said

Stauffbacher coyly. 'An Afrikaner from Johannesburg.'

'What?' said Agnes. Was he serious? Even Evergreen barked out a laugh.

'W. S. Beyerbach. The university's bringing him in. We pay our four hundred dollars and we get him out here for a day and a half.'

'Who?' asked Evergreen.

'This has already been decided?' asked Agnes.

'Yup.' Stauffbacher looked accusingly at Agnes. 'I've done a lot of work to arrange for this. *I've* done all the work!'

'Do less,' said Evergreen.

When Agnes had first met Joe, they'd fallen madly upon each other. They'd kissed in restaurants; they'd groped under coats at the movies. At his little house they'd made love on the porch, or the landing of the staircase, against the wall in the hall, by the door to the attic, filled with too much desire to make their way to a real room.

Now they struggled self-consciously for atmosphere, something they'd never needed before. She prepared the bedroom carefully. She played quiet music and concentrated. She lit candles—as if she were in church praying for the deceased. She donned a filmy gown. She took hot baths and entered the bedroom in nothing but a towel, a wild fish-like creature of moist, perfumed heat. In the nightstand drawer she still kept the charts a doctor once told her to keep, still placed an X on any date she and Joe actually had sex. But she could never show these to her doctor, not now. It pained Agnes to see them. She and Joe looked like worse than bad shots. She and Joe looked like idiots. She and Joe looked dead.

Frantic candlelight flickered on the ceiling like a puppet show. While she waited for Joe to come out of the bathroom, Agnes lay back on the bed and thought about her week, the stupid politics of it—the Arts Hall, the Transportation Commission, all those loud, smacking collisions of public good and private power. She was not very good at politics. Once, before he was elected, she had gone to a rally for Bill Clinton, but when he was late and had kept the crowd waiting for over an hour, and when the sun got hot and bees began landing on people's heads, when everyone's feet hurt, and tiny children began to cry, and a state assemblyman stepped forward to announce that Clinton had stopped at a Dairy Queen in Des Moines and that was why he was late—Dairy Queen!—she had grown angry and resentful and apolitical in her own sweet-starved thirst and she'd joined in with some other people who had started to chant, 'Do us a favor, tell us the flavor.'

Through college she had been a feminist—more or less. She shaved her legs, *but just not often enough*, she liked to say. She signed day-care petitions and petitions for Planned Parenthood. And although she had never been very socially aggressive with men, she felt strongly that she knew the difference between feminism and Sadie Hawkins Day—which some people, she believed, did not.

'Agnes, are we out of toothpaste or is this it?—Oh, OK, I see.'

And once, in New York, she had quixotically organized the ladies'-room line at the Brooks Atkinson Theater. Because the play was going to start any minute, and the line was still twenty women long, she had got six women to walk across the lobby with her to the men's room. 'Everybody out of there?' she'd called in timidly, allowing the men to finish up first, which took a while, especially with other men coming up impatiently and cutting ahead in line. Later at intermission, she saw how it should have been done. Two elderly black women, with greater expertise in civil rights, stepped very confidently into the men's room and called out, 'Don't mind us, boys. We're coming on in. Don't mind us.'

'Are you OK?' asked Joe, smiling. He was already beside her. He smelled sweet, of soap and minty teeth, like a child.

'I think so,' she said and turned toward him in the bordello light of their room. He had never acquired the look of maturity-anchored-in-sorrow that burnished so many men's faces. His own sadnesses in life—a childhood of beatings, a dying mother—were like quicksand, and he had to stay away from them entirely. He permitted no unhappy memories spoken aloud. He stuck with the same mild cheerfulness he'd honed successfully as a boy, and it made him seem fatuous—even, she knew, to himself. Probably it hurt his business a little.

'Your mind's wandering,' he said, letting his own eyes close.

'I know.' She yawned, moved her legs on to his for warmth, and in this way, with the candles burning into their tins, she and Joe fell asleep.

Spring arrived, cool and humid. Bulbs cracked and sprouted, shot up their green periscopes, and on 1 April the Arts Hall offered a joke lecture by T. S. Eliot, visiting scholar. 'The Cruelest Month', it was called. 'You don't find it funny?' asked Stauffbacher.

April fourth was the reception for W. S. Beyerbach. There was to be a dinner afterward, and then Beyerbach was to visit Agnes's Great Books class. She had assigned his second collection of sonnets, which were spare and elegant, with sighing and diaphanous politics. The next afternoon there was to be a reading.

Agnes had not been invited to the dinner, and when she asked about this, in a mildly forlorn way, Stauffbacher shrugged as if it were totally out of his hands. 'I'm a *published poet*,' Agnes wanted to say. She had had a poem published once—in the *Gizzard Review*, but still!

'It was Edie Canterton's list,' Stauffbacher said. 'I had nothing to do with it.'

She went to the reception anyway, annoyed, and when she planted herself like a splayed and storm-torn tree near the cheese, she could feel the crackers she was eating forming a bad paste in her mouth and she became afraid to smile. When she finally introduced herself to W. S. Beyerbach, she stumbled on her own name and actually pronounced it 'On-yez'.

'On-yez,' repeated Beyerbach in a quiet Englishy voice. Condescending, she thought. His hair was blond and white, like a palomino, and his eyes were blue and scornful as mints. She could see he was a withheld man; although some might say *shy*, she decided it was *withheld*: a lack of generosity. Passive-aggressive. It was causing the people around him to squirm and nervously improvise remarks. He would simply nod, the smile on his face faint and vaguely pharmaceutical. Everything about him was tight and coiled as a doorspring. From living in *that country*, thought Agnes. How could he live in that country?

Stauffbacher was trying to talk heartily about the mayor. Something about his old progressive ideas and the forthcoming convention center. Agnes thought of her own meetings on the Transportation Commission, of the mayor's leash law for cats, of his new squadron of meter maids and bicycle police, of a councilman the mayor once slugged in a bar. 'Now, of course, the mayor's become a fascist,' said Agnes in a voice that sounded strangely loud, bright with anger.

Silence fell in the room. Edie Canterton stopped stirring the punch. Agnes looked around. 'Oh,' she said. 'Are we not supposed to used *that word* in this room?' Beyerbach's expression went blank. Agnes's face burned in confusion.

Stauffbacher looked pained, then stricken. 'More cheese, anyone?' he asked, holding up the silver tray.

After everyone left for dinner, she went by herself to the Dunk 'N Dine across the street. She ordered a California BLT and a cup of coffee, and looked over Beyerbach's work again: dozens of images of broken, rotten bodies, of the body's mutinies and betrayals, of the body's strange housekeeping and illicit pets. At the front of the book was a dedication—*To D.F.B. (1970-1989)*. Who could that be? A political activist maybe, 'a woman who had thrown aside the unseasonal dress of hope' only to look for it again 'in the blood-blooming shrubs'. Perhaps if Agnes got a chance, she would ask him. Why not? A book was a public thing, and its dedication was part of it. If it was too personal a question for him, tough. She would find the right time, she decided, paying the check and putting on her jacket, crossing the street to the Hall. She would wait for the moment, then seize it.

He was already at the front door when she arrived. He greeted her with a stiff smile and a soft 'Hello, On-yez.' His accent made her own voice ring coarse and country-western.

She smiled and then blurted, 'I have a question to ask you.' Her voice sounded like Johnny Cash's.

Beyerbach said nothing, only held the door open for her and then followed her into the building.

She continued as they stepped slowly up the stairs. 'May I ask you who your book is dedicated to?'

At the top of the stairs they turned left down the long

corridor. She could feel his steely reserve, his lip biting, his shyness no doubt garbed and rationalized with snobbery, but so much snobbery to handle all that shyness that he could not possibly be a meaningful critic of his country. She was angry with him. *How can you live in that country?* she wanted again to say, although she remembered when someone once said that to her—a Danish man, on Agnes's senior trip abroad to Copenhagen. It was during the Vietnam War, and the man had stared meanly, righteously. 'The United States: how can you live in that country?' the man had asked. Agnes had shrugged. 'A lot of my stuff is there,' she said, and it was only then that she first felt all the dark love and shame that came from the pure accident of home, the deep and arbitrary place that happened to be yours.

'It's dedicated to my son,' Beyerbach said finally.

He would not look at her, but stared straight ahead along the corridor floor. Now Agnes's shoes sounded very loud.

'You lost a son,' she said.

'Yes,' he said. He looked away, at the passing wall, past Stauffbacher's bulletin board, past the men's room, the women's room, some sternness in him broken, and when he turned back she could see his eyes filling with water, his face reddened with unbearable pressure.

'I'm so sorry,' Agnes said.

They walked side by side, their footsteps echoing down the corridor toward her classroom. All the anxieties she felt with this mournfully quiet man now mimicked the anxieties of love. What should she say? It must be the most unendurable thing to lose a child. Shouldn't he say something of this? It was his turn to say something.

But he would not. And when they finally reached the classroom, she turned to him in the doorway and, taking a package from her purse, said simply, in a reassuring way, 'We always have cookies in class.'

Now he beamed at her with such relief that she knew she had for once said the right thing. It filled her with affection for him—perhaps, she thought, that's where affection begins: in an unlikely phrase, in a moment of someone's having unexpectedly but at last said the right thing. *We always have cookies in class.*

She introduced him with a bit of flourish and biography. Positions held, universities attended. The students raised their hands and asked him about apartheid, about shanty towns and homelands, and he answered succinctly, after long sniffs and pauses, only once referring to a question as 'unanswerably fey', causing the student to squirm and fish around in her purse for something, nothing, Kleenex perhaps. Beyerbach did not seem to notice. He went on, speaking of censorship: how a person must work hard not to internalize a government's program of censorship, since what a government would like best is for you to do it yourself; how he himself was not sure he had not succumbed. Afterward, a few students stayed and shook his hand, formally, awkwardly, then left. Christa was the last. She too shook his hand and then started chatting amiably. They knew someone in common—Harold Raferson in Chicago!—and as Agnes quickly wiped the seminar table to clear it of cookie crumbs, she tried to listen but couldn't really hear. She made a small pile of crumbs and swept them into one hand.

'Goodnight,' sang out Christa when she left.

'Goodnight, Christa,' said Agnes, brushing the crumbs off her hand and into the wastebasket.

She straightened and stood with Beyerbach in the empty classroom. 'Thank you so much,' she said, finally, in a hushed way. 'I'm sure they all got quite a lot out of that. I'm very sure they did.'

He said nothing but smiled at her gently.

She shifted her weight from one leg to the other. 'Would you like to go somewhere and get a drink?' she asked. She was standing close to him, looking up into his face. He was tall, she saw now. His shoulders weren't broad, but he had a youthful straightness to his carriage. She briefly touched his sleeve. His suit coat was corduroy and bore a faint odor of clove. This was the first time in her life that she had ever asked a man out for a drink.

He made no move to step away from her; he actually seemed to lean toward her a bit. She could feel his dry breath, see up close the variously hued spokes of his irises, the grays and yellows in the blue. There was a sprinkling of small freckles near his hairline. He smiled, then looked at the clock on the wall. 'I would love to, really, but I have to get back to the hotel to make a phone call at ten-fifteen.' He looked a little disappointed—not a lot, thought Agnes, but certainly a *little*. She would have bet money on it.

'Oh, well,' she said. She flicked off the lights, and in the dark he carefully helped her on with her jacket. They stepped out of the room and walked together in silence, back down the corridor to the front entrance of the Hall. Outside on the steps the night was balmy and scented with rain. 'Will you be all right walking back to your hotel?' she asked. 'Or—'

'Oh, yes, thank you. It's just around the corner.'

'Right. That's right. Well, my car's parked way over there. So, I guess I'll see you tomorrow afternoon at your reading.'

'Yes,' he said. 'I shall look forward to that.'

'Yes,' she said. 'So shall I.'

The reading was in the large meeting room at the Arts Hall and was from the sonnet book she had already read, but it was nice to hear the poems again in his hushed, pained tenor. She sat in the back row, her green raincoat sprawled beneath her on the seat like a large leaf. She leaned forward on to the seat ahead of her, her back an angled stem, her chin on double fists, and she listened like that for some time. At one point she closed her eyes, but the image of him before her, standing straight as a compass needle, remained caught there beneath her lids, like a burn or a speck or a message from the mind.

Afterward, moving away from the lectern, Beyerbach spotted her and waved, but Stauffbacher, like a tugboat with a task, took his arm and steered him elsewhere, over toward the side table with the little plastic cups and warm Pepsi. *We are both men*, the gesture seemed to say. *We both have* bach *in our names*. Agnes put on her green coat. She went over toward the Pepsi table and stood. She drank a warm Pepsi, then placed the empty cup back on the table. Beyerbach finally turned toward her and smiled familiarly. She thrust out her hand. 'It was a wonderful reading,' she said. 'I'm very glad I got the chance to meet you.' She gripped his long, slender palm and locked thumbs. She could feel the bones in him.

'Thank you,' he said. He looked at her coat in a worried way. 'You're leaving?'

She looked down at her coat. 'I'm afraid I have to get going home.' She wasn't sure whether she really had to or not. But she'd put on her coat, and it now seemed an awkward thing to take it off.

'Oh,' he murmured, gazing at her intently. 'Well, all best wishes to you, On-yez.'

'Excuse me?' There was some clattering near the lectern.

'All best to you,' he said, something retreating in his expression.

Stauffbacher suddenly appeared at her side, scowling at her green coat, as if it were incomprehensible.

'Yes,' said Agnes, stepping backward, then forward again to shake Beyerbach's hand once more; it was a beautiful hand, like an old and expensive piece of wood. 'Same to you,' she said. Then she turned and fled.

For several nights she did not sleep well. She placed her face directly into her pillow, then turned it for some air, then flipped over to her back and opened her eyes, staring past the stark angle of the door frame at the far end of the room toward the tiny light from the bathroom which illuminated the hallway, faintly, as if someone had just been there.

For several days she thought perhaps he might have left her a note with the secretary, or that he might send her one from an airport somewhere. She thought that the inadequacy of their goodbye would haunt him too, and that he might send her a postcard as elaboration.

But he did not. Briefly she thought about writing him a letter, on Arts Hall stationery, which for money reasons was no longer the stationery but photocopies of the stationery. She knew he had flown to the West Coast, then off to Tokyo, then Sydney, then back to Johannesburg, and if she posted it now, perhaps he would receive it when he arrived. She could tell him once more how interesting it had been to meet him. She could enclose her poem from the *Gizzard Review*. She had read in the newspaper an article about bereavement—and if she were her own mother she would have sent him that too.

Thank God, thank God, she was not her mother.

May settled firmly into Cassell with a spate of thunder showers. The perennials—the myrtle and grape hyacinths—blossomed around the town in a kind of civic blue, and the warming air brought forth an occasional mosquito or fly. The Transportation Commission meetings were dreary and long, too often held during the dinner hour, and when Agnes got home she would replay them for Joe, weeping about the photo radar and the widening interstate.

When her mother called, Agnes got off the phone fast. When her sister, Linnea, now in Minneapolis, called about their mother, Agnes got off the phone even faster. Joe rubbed her shoulders and spoke to her of carports, of curb appeal, of mortgage rates and asbestos-wrapped pipes.

At the Arts Hall she taught and fretted and continued to receive the usual memos from the secretary, written on the usual scrap paper—except that the scrap paper, for a while, consisted of the extra posters for the Beyerbach reading. She would get a long disquisition on policies and procedures concerning summer registration and she would turn it over, and there would be his face—sad and pompous in the photograph. She would get a simple phone message—'Your husband called. Please call him at the office'—and on the back would be the ripped center of Beyerbach's nose, one minty eye, an elbowish chin. Eventually there were no more, and the scrap paper moved on to old contest announcements, grant deadlines, Easter concert notices.

At night she and Joe did yoga to a yoga show on TV. It was part of their effort not to become their parents, though marriage, they knew, held that hazard. The functional disenchantment, the sweet habit of each other, had begun to put lines around her mouth, lines that looked like quotation marks—as if everything she said had already been said before. Sometimes their old cat, Madeline, a fat and pampered calico reaping the benefits of life with a childless couple during their childbearing years, came and plopped herself down with them, between them. She was accustomed to much nestling and appreciation and drips from the faucet, though sometimes she would vanish outside, and they would not see her for days, only to spy her later, in the yard, dirty and matted, chomping a vole or eating old snow.

Agnes of Iowa

For Memorial Day weekend Agnes flew with Joe to New York, to show him the city for the first time. 'A place,' she said, 'where if you're not white or not born there, it's no big deal. You're not automatically a story.' She had grown annoyed with Iowa, the pathetic, third-hand manner in which the large issues and conversations of the world were encountered there. The oblique and tired way history obligingly insinuated itself. If ever. She longed to be a citizen of the globe!

They roller-skated in Central Park. They looked in the Lord & Taylor windows. They went to the Joffrey. They went to a hair salon on Fifty-seventh Street, and there she had her hair dyed a vibrant red. They sat in the window booth of a coffee shop and got coffee refills and ate pie.

'So much seems the same,' she said to Joe. 'When I lived here, everyone was hustling for money. The rich were. The poor were. But everyone tried hard to be funny. Everywhere you went—a store, a facial place—someone was telling a joke. A good one.' She remembered it had made any given day seem bearable, that impulse toward a joke. It had been a determined sort of humor, an intensity mirroring the intensity of the city, and it seemed to embrace and alleviate the hard sadness of people using each other and marring the earth the way they did. 'It was like brains having sex. It was like every brain was a sex maniac.' She looked down at her pie. 'People really worked at it, the laughing,' she said. 'People need to laugh.'

'They do,' said Joe. He took a swig of coffee, his lips out over the cup in a fleshy flower. He was afraid she might cry—she was getting that look again—and if she did, he would feel guilty and lost and sorry for her that her life was not here anymore but in a far and boring place with him. He set the cup down and tried to smile. 'They sure do,' he said. And he looked out the window at the rickety taxis, the oystery garbage and tubercular air, seven pounds of chicken giblets dumped on the curb in front of the coffee shop where they were. He turned back to her and made the face of a clown.

'What are you doing?' she asked.

'It's a clown face.'

'What do you mean, a clown face?' Someone behind her was

singing 'I Love New York', and for the first time she noticed the strange irresolution of the tune.

'A regular clown face is what I mean.'

'It didn't look like that.'

'No? What did it look like?'

'You want me to do the face?'

'Yeah, do the face.'

She looked at Joe. Every arrangement in life carried with it the sadness, the sentimental shadow, of its not being something else but only itself. She attempted the face—a look of such monstrous emptiness and stupidity that Joe burst into a howling sort of laughter, like a dog, and then so did she, air exploding through her nose in a snort, her head thrown forward, then back, then forward again, setting loose a fit of coughing.

'Are you OK?' asked Joe, and she nodded. Out of politeness he looked away, outside, where it had suddenly started to rain. Across the street two people had planted themselves under the window ledge of a Gap store, trying to stay dry, waiting out the downpour, their figures dark and scarecrowish against the lit window display. When he turned back to his wife—oh, his sad, young wife—to point this out to her, to show her what was funny to a man firmly in the grip of middle age, she was still bent sideways in her seat so that her face fell below the line of the table, and he could only see the curve of her heaving back, the fuzzy penumbra of her thin spring sweater, and the garish top of her bright, new and terrible hair. □

GRANTA

FAE MYENNE NG
FAREWELL

Fae Myenne Ng was born in 1956 in San Francisco and grew up there. Her father was a merchant seaman and her mother a seamstress in the sweatshops of Chinatown. She wrote her first stories in Chinese at Cumberland Presbyterian Chinese School. An early influence was 'listening to old-timers in Portsmouth Square reciting classical poetry in Cantonese'. Her stories have appeared in several magazines, including *Harper's* and *Bostonia*. She now lives in New York,

'Farewell' is taken from her novel, *Bone*, which was published by Hyperion in 1993.

If Grandpa Leong had been a family man, there might have been real tears, a grieving wife draped in muslin, the fabric weaving around her like burned skin. The wife might have wailed, chanting the lament songs. Other women, older aunts, might have had to support her at the elbows, ready to pull her back if she tried to throw herself on the coffin. Brothers and cousins and in-laws might have all come, everybody weak, everybody woeful. They would have argued about which was the luckiest burial plot. Facing east? Facing west! Over the years they would have spied on each other—who visited the grave on the Ghost Festival? How much grave food was offered? How much paper money was burned? They would have counted each other's oranges. Hopefully—and there was hope if there were children—when his children were grown and making their own money, they'd dig up his bones, pack them in a clay pot, send them—no, accompany them—back to the home village for a proper burial.

The funeral house where Grandpa Leong was prepared was as makeshift as his coffin. Its storefront windows faced Portsmouth Square, and the heavy sheets that were hung to shut out the light looked like the old rubber mats they used on the floor of fish stores. There were a few quickly nailed-together benches, and in one corner, stacks of boxes with odd bits of bright, leafy debris. I remember that there was a certain coolness in the room, a lack of scent. Later someone told me this was the poor man's funeral house; it didn't even have a name; men with families went to Cathay House on Powell or to the Green Street Mortuary.

I learned later that the funeral parlor doubled as Shing Kee Grocery's warehouse, and that they only leased it out for funerals. The space went on to house other things: Everybody's Bookstore, Master Kung's Northern-style Martial Arts Club and the Chinese Educational Services.

At Grandpa Leong's funeral I sat with my sisters, Ona and Nina, on the front bench, watching an old woman tend the ritual burning by the coffin. The smoke hurt our eyes. Ona leaned over and whispered that Grandpa Leong's coffin looked cheap. I agreed that the splintery boards balanced on two stools made a wobbly-looking thing.

We watched the old men file slowly up to the coffin. Each old man approached the coffin alone, bowing to both ends of the box. The Newspaper Man from the corner of Grant and Washington tucked something into the coffin. The man from the Grandview Theatre bowed from the waist like a movie star. I recognized a chess player, the herbalist, a butcher from Hop Sing's, a waiter from the Universal Café. They all went straight up to the coffin, bowed and then came to tell Mah they had to leave and go back to work.

When there were enough people seated, Cousin stood up and walked to the front of the coffin and gave a speech about Grandpa Leong's life. He told about how Grandpa Leong came first to mine gold and then settled into farm work around the Valley. He named all our names. He apologized for not having more to tell, but he said he only knew Grandpa Leong through our stepfather Leon's stories. Nina squirmed; Ona swung her legs under the wooden bench; I gave them both a look that meant, Stop it! Mah hissed at us.

Mah, Nina, Ona and I went up to Grandpa Leong and bowed our last goodbyes. I saw his powdery beard and his borrowed blue suit; I read the words HELL BANK NOTES on the fake money that was scattered across his chest.

We stood in front of the door, and old men filed past; some touched our heads, most mumbled in Chinese. They nodded at Mah, who handed each of them coins wrapped in red and white envelopes. We got them too. We pocketed the red ones. Ona leaned over and whispered the amount to us. We knew the quarter was for buying candy to bring the sweetness back into our lives. We ripped open the white ones and threw the mourning paper immediately on to the ground in the deliberate gesture Mah had taught us the night before. (White is the color of mourning, she said; throw it away from you.) The butterscotch Lifesaver inside had a cellophane wrapping that was colorless, but to be safe, I trashed it too. I popped the Lifesaver into my mouth, not expecting to like it, but knowing I couldn't refuse funeral candy. The Lifesaver took a long time to dissolve but when the rich, buttery taste filled my mouth, I felt better.

We walked outside into the alley, and the sun hit hard,

hurting so much I wanted to go back into the parlour.

Mah carried Nina. Ona clung to her other hand. I leaned my face into Mah's dress and smelled the scorchy trace of just-pressed linen. It's easy to burn linen because high heat and a heavy hand are needed to get the deep wrinkles out. I still love how linen breathes, how, after many washings, the weave softens, supple as skin.

But the day of Grandpa Leong's funeral, Mah's new linen dress scratched my cheeks, burned my nostrils and made my eyes sting. All I could think of was the dozens of hotly ironed dresses hanging in the airless factory where Mah worked.

Cousin, Croney Kam, Jimmy Lowe and the Newspaper Man had a hard time getting the large coffin out the narrow, angled doorway. It became a noisy affair. The men jostled the long box back and then pushed it forward, rocking it out. Then they argued about how to get the coffin on to the van. Jimmy Lowe climbed up on to the van and tugged. The men lifted and heaved, pushing and grunting; and then with a scrape and a bump the long box was in. Tommie Hom slapped the sawdust off his pants, jumped down and slammed the doors shut.

A row of dark suits lined the alley. The old men stood with their canes hooked over their elbows, their hats in their hands. The van started up with a burst. One old man said, 'Too sad. No trumpets.'

Mah, Nina, Ona and I made a small and slow and quiet procession behind the van. Ona and I threw the long strips of funeral papers into the air, then we turned back to see them littering the alley.

'Wave!' Mah said.

The van turned on to Sacramento Street and then picked up speed. We stood at the mouth of the alley watching it move toward the direction of the three big roads: the bay, the bridge and the freeway. We waved until we couldn't see the boxy shape anymore.

Later we went to visit Grandpa Leong's grave during the Ghost Festival. We wore matching pale pink linen dresses Mah had made for the occasion. The cemetery was full—three generations in every cluster—grandparents and parents talking loud, kids playing chase games. It was more crowded than Portsmouth Square, and I had the odd feeling that this was like a school field trip—the hot sun, the wide sky and especially the minty eucalyptus smell, all so different from Chinatown.

Mah stacked oranges and laid out the grave food: a dried fish, a whole chicken and some steamed sticky cakes. Leon started a fire in a large tin canister, slipping paper money into the weak flames. When the wind snatched the dollars up, we ran to catch back the half-singed hell notes. Leon posed us in front of Grandpa Leong's grave and took pictures with a new camera he'd bought in Japan. But he didn't know how to use it, and we stood in the hot sun so long I felt like I was wearing a metal helmet. I squinted at Leon to hurry; Nina stamped her foot and started to cry.

We were disappointed when the pictures came back, a whole thirty-six exposure roll of film, and only one picture came out. It was of Ona. She's standing alone in front of the wooden grave-marker, holding a big orange in her hand. □

GRANTA

ROBERT O'CONNOR
MAXIMUM SECURITY

Robert O'Connor was born in 1959 in Manhattan, and more precisely at St Vincent's Hospital, where his father, a doctor, had met his mother, a nurse, and where both continued to work. He grew up in Eastchester, a New York suburb, and took degrees from New York State and Syracuse universities. He teaches literature and creative writing at Oswego College, State University of New York, and lives with his wife, also a writer, and their three children in the town of Liverpool, NY. His first novel, *Buffalo Soldiers*, was named a Notable Book of 1993 by the *New York Times*.

'Maximum Security' is drawn from his experience at the Auburn Correctional Facility, a prison in upstate New York, where for five years he taught writing and literature. It is part of a 'non-fiction novel' which he hopes to finish soon.

Robert O'Connor

Reality check

Graduation Day at Auburn Correctional. Hot and hopeful under the May sun, air crinkling above the highway. Except my Ford Escort didn't care for the heat and flatlined a few hundred yards from home. My son James on his way to daycare looked at me doubtfully.

'Dad,' he said. I strained at the key and pumped the accelerator, as if at any moment the Ford would give in to reason. 'Dad,' he said again gently, as if adults had to have things explained slowly and clearly. 'I don't think we're going anywhere.'

And so we walked the rest of the way down Morgan Road, James on the padded shoulders of my one suit. I'd bought the suit to get married in, and it now saw service on special occasions: weddings, funerals, job interviews. This was its first prison graduation. As we walked, James's leaky thermos christened my suit with orange juice, ruining the solid-citizen image, such as it was.

At daycare I got through to Pete, whose class I was taking over. He was leaving for a better job, a step up in the world.

'You still want to come?' Pete asked, giving me an out. I hesitated. There was a sound in his voice I didn't like, as if he'd been expecting my call. Problem was, part of me was glad for the excuse.

'Yeah, sure,' I said, trying to sound upbeat.

'I'll be right there.'

Let me just say I've seen a lot of prison movies. In prison movies things were dark and dingy. Guards were sadistic and brutal, inmates worse. The lights dimmed every time they held an execution. One spent one's time trying to escape. In this endeavor one could arrange one's pillows properly to pretend to be asleep while actually slipping through tunnels hollowed through solid rock. The wrongly convicted innocent man might become embittered at first. But through reflection, he would begin to see his essential humanity and even the humanity of others. Suffering brought redemption, the no-frills Christian remedy.

But once we got there, well, the first thing that struck me

about the outside of the prison was that it was kind of tasteful. Lawns nicely clipped, bushes pruned, American flag snapping in the wind. There was even an inmate outside with a hand clipper giving the lawn a serious trim—was somebody keeping an eye on this guy? Even the bars were inconspicuous—interlocking metal circles by the entrance: incarceration by art deco.

The line of friends and relatives of the graduates snaked out the door of the entrance, people sweating under the May sun. Pete introduced me to Rick Steplinger, the director of the Auburn Program for Syracuse University. He was a little guy with a thick beard and combover. He looked nervous, more like an anxious parent than an administrator.

'This is the guy you'll be working for,' Pete said.

'Nice suit,' Rick said, squinting at me. I looked down. The orange juice had dried into a shape resembling the state of Florida.

'See you inside,' Rick said, and walked to the front of the line to escort guests into the prison. The door slid behind them, not with a clang, like in the movies: 'Every time the bars close, a chill runs through me,' I remembered a character in nearly every prison movie saying. No, it was like a well-oiled garage door sliding along its track, that familiar and comforting rumble.

While being searched I set off the airport-style metal detector. I paused guiltily, but the guard waved me through and passed a metal wand over me. I buzzed at my zipper, but after a quick glance at my solid-citizen status the guard printed my left hand with invisible ink which reappeared when passed under a special light. This was to prevent a prisoner from taking my place, which was, I later discovered, the most common form of escape: just walking out disguised as a visitor, or with the change of guard shift. No hollowing through cement for these guys; the modern criminal got out on the clock.

Next we went up and down stairs, through blind turns and doors, then outside again before entering the chapel: nicely appointed with oak pews and wood paneling. A grand piano stood to the side. Presently a man in Rastafarian dreadlocks appeared. He sat down and began playing 'Pomp and Circumstance'. Not bad either, although the piano needed a tune.

As the graduates entered, guards ringed the chapel like heavily armed ushers, their clubs swinging from holsters. They clasped their hands behind them, as if expecting trouble. There were twelve graduates, all dressed in traditional caps and gowns, brushing their tassels from their eyes self-consciously as they waved to people in the audience. They were better behaved than seniors at main campus graduations. They sat down, and the usual run of speeches got underway. The little guy with the combover—what was his name, Rick—leaned enthusiastically into the lectern and said that in the Middle Ages 'universities were made, not of bricks and mortar, but of men,' although there seemed to be enough bricks and mortar to go around. Then a woman stepped to the podium. She was dressed in what I remembered from Catholic school as nun semi-formal, no F-16 sized wimple, but bareheaded in a simple pastel blue dress.

'Who's that?' I asked Pete.

'Sister Mary Frances,' he said. 'Our commencement speaker.'

Sister Mary Frances was a Franciscan nun who had found her calling in convict education, establishing programs in Attica, Sing-Sing and a number of other places I would soon become familiar with. She praised Syracuse University for having started its own program in 1976. Things were going pretty well, the standard commencement 'you are the future and you have to go out and make things happen' spiel, although it occurred to me that going out and making things happen had been what got these guys into trouble in the first place, but then leaps of faith headed over the seven-foot mark as she told the men to consider themselves lucky they'd been sent to prison. Otherwise, she said, they would never have gone to college. Some of the graduates looked back and forth at each other.

Just as Sister Mary Frances was finishing, a dozen walkie-talkies began speaking at once, and most of the guards double-timed out of the chapel.

The inmate in front of us leaned over to the man next to him. 'Reality check,' he said, but the music from the out-of-tune piano weighed in, almost but not quite drowning out the footsteps of the running corrections officers as they scuttled down the hallway, doors slamming behind them.

Outward bound

On the drive back, Pete said, 'So what did you think?'

'Different,' I said. At the end of the graduation lunch, which was held in the prison library, a place where the books instead of the men were symbolically behind bars, the inmates had stood up and ringed the walls, smoking cigarette after cigarette as they stared at us.

'How come you're quitting?' I asked.

'I got a job with Outward Bound,' he said. Pete and I had started graduate school together—me in the Ph.D Program, he in the Poetry Workshop. The Ph.D Program had not gone well, and so I'd bailed and was now a nomad composition teacher at a number of schools. With the prison course, I'd be up to six courses per semester. It was what I did instead of having a life.

'It's a permanent position,' he said, as if admitting to a character flaw. 'Time to grow up, be a citizen. Get on with the old life.'

'I don't know if I want to grow up that way,' I said.

'You'll have to tell me about having a choice,' he said.

We drove for awhile in silence. I wondered what hybrid teacher/prison movie I was entering. *To Sir, Or Else. Goodbye, Mr Chips, You Motherfucker.*

'Did you ever feel that no matter what your life was like,one day you would end up inside?' I asked.

Pete kept his eyes fixed on the road. 'You're going to do just fine,' he said.

Convictions are no longer optional

'See the space on the back here,' the guard who was taking us through the paperwork said. 'Under where it says, List Convictions?'

I located it on my sheet. 'Got it,' I said. Craig, the new art instructor, moved his thumb down the sheet until he found it too. He used his free hand to shift his ponytail out of the way. I'd come dressed in my suit again, to get my photograph taken with a tie and a smile, but Craig had gone in the other direction: dirty dungarees which puffed clouds of dust when he patted himself for matches.

'Under List Convictions it says Optional.'

'Yep,' I said.

'It's no longer optional,' the guard said.

'Just felonies, right?' Craig asked. 'No misdemeanors?'

'That's affirmative,' the guard said.

'You got extra paper?' Craig asked.

'How many arrests we talking?' the guard asked, and another sheet of paper was brought Craig's way. As he bent his head, a good student facing a tough exam, I noticed a long razor scar that ran uninterrupted from his temple down to the corner of his jaw. Even the faculty here is tough, I thought, as Craig slaved away at his arrest record.

On the way to get our pictures taken, I made the mistake of standing under an open window. I felt a sudden sting and brushed my shoulder. When I looked down, I saw a lit cigarette, the smoke circling gently upward. An inmate had dropped it from above.

When I got home I showed my wife, Donna, the hole in my suit. 'This doesn't seem like a good sign,' she said.

AKA Diaz

'This is it,' Rick said, a note of giddy cheer in his voice. Through the windows of the classroom I could see the men. They were not in their seats; instead, they were circling the room restlessly, like lions in a cage.

'Is there going to be a guard in the room while I teach?' I asked. I realized that this was something that should have been straightened out earlier.

Rick looked at me with deep concern. 'I'll come by a bit later, see that you're OK,' he said.

I walked through the door into the classroom. My students barely looked human. The desks were arranged in no discernible order, except that some of the men had clustered in racial groups. Many of them were smoking, and under the glare of the lights I could see their tattoos: elaborate scrawls of suggestive menace. One man with a Fu Manchu beard and a long mane of black hair circled behind me and around the other side of the desk. He was easily the tensest man I'd ever seen. I thought of telling him to sit down but wondered what I would do if he refused so kept the suggestion to myself. I placed my leather bag on the desk and faced the class. Nobody paid any attention to me. If anything, the conversation grew louder. I had the urge to cut and run. I had volunteered for this?

Every teacher has these moments of panic. We worry about rebellion: our moral authority lost, the students taking over. I had a teacher in high school, a Miss Hutchinson, who after taking roll would turn toward the board and be followed by an avalanche of paper airplanes and spitballs, sometimes even the bodies of students flying forward, an impromptu riot.

I unpacked my bag and began the roll. A few names down, I called out, 'Diaz.'

No answer. 'Diaz,' I said again.

'Ain't my name,' a man in the front row with a sparse beard volunteered.

'Why did you answer?' I asked.

'I'm here under another name,' he said. 'An alias. I could tell you my real name, but then I'd have to kill you.'

'We'll count that as a "Present",' I said. Several members of the class snickered: at least that had the effect of slowing down the conversations. I finished the roll and then handed out the syllabus for the class. I read it aloud and when I got to the end I looked up. 'So, any questions?' I asked. The paper trembled in my hand.

'Yeah, I got a question.' AKA Diaz raised his hand. 'I want to know what the fuck it means.'

The trouble with felons

'So, first impressions?' Rick Steplinger asked. Craig and I were walking down the street toward the restaurant where we were going to have lunch.

'The biggest son-of-a-bitch I've ever seen was in my class,' Craig said. 'He must be six foot fucking eight.'

'That would be Gregory,' Rick said. 'Yes, Gregory takes a bit of getting used to.'

'Some of them seemed a little resistant,' Craig said. 'Would you say that, Bob?'

'Some,' I said. After the syllabus débâcle I'd assigned a free writing assignment which had nearly started a rebellion. I had looked about for the fight buzzer, which was supposed to be somewhere in the room. It had panicked me somewhat that I'd been unable to find it. In the end they had settled down and begun writing, although AKA Diaz had repeated over and over that the assignment was bullshit. I decided not to tell this to Rick.

'Bob, have you met Hector yet?' Rick asked.

'Which one is he?' I asked.

'Rosario,' Rick said. 'He's the karate expert. Really muscular.' I thought of the man with the mane of black hair and Fu Manchu beard. When I'd collected the assignments, he had refused to turn his in. I was too intimidated to insist, so I had pretended not to notice.

'I hate to ask what he's in for,' I said.

'Twenty-five to life. Killed somebody with his bare hands,' Rick said.

'We haven't really spoken,' I said.

'He may mention something about Pete,' Rick said. 'He and Pete had a little problem at the end of the summer and, well, the fact of the matter is Hector threatened to kill Pete.'

Pete had somehow neglected to mention this. What made it all the more worrisome was that Pete was about the easiest going human being on the planet. If he hadn't gotten along with Hector, what chance did I have?

'So, what else?' Rick asked.

After the writing assignment, we had worked on William Carlos Williams's poem 'The Red Wheelbarrow'. One of the men, nicknamed 'Deadeye' by the others, confessed he did not know what a wheelbarrow was. The others had jeered him. 'How the fuck do I know wheelbarrows?' he shouted, rising from his seat. 'I grew up in the goddamn City. Where the fuck did you grow up?'

'I stole a wheelbarrow once,' another man said. 'A construction site. Thing takes forever to goddamn push.'

'Go fuck yourself,' Deadeye had said. 'Go fuck all a youse assholes.'

I had been unprepared for the outbursts, the free-flowing insults, and I wanted to ask Rick about this. 'I know this sounds hopelessly naïve, but I hadn't thought the men would be so rude to each other.'

Rick paused. The look on his face reminded me of Pete's look in the car. 'That's the trouble with felons,' he said, finally. 'No manners.'

The Thin Blue Line

The next class I decided to show the Errol Morris documentary, *The Thin Blue Line*. The movie concerned Randall Dale Adams, a wrongfully convicted cop killer who had barely escaped execution in Texas. The men would write newspaper articles and editorials explaining the events they witnessed.

While I was setting up the TV and VCR, Hector Rosario was at the front of the room, talking with another man. They were discussing religion, and Hector's voice began to rise. The other man, Robert Rinaldo, began to retreat as I noticed Hector leaning toward him, the veins on his neck beginning to bulge, his enormous Popeye forearms cording muscle. I finished what I was doing and said mildly, 'Let's get started,' but Hector was now shouting at the top of his lungs. He suddenly looked up, as if surprised at all the noise, and then quietly walked to his seat.

I had decided that I might as well start trying to break up the racial groupings, so I organized the men into a semi-circle and sat between Tyrone, a black man, and Hector, although Hector, I noticed, had pulled his chair slightly out of the circle in some mysterious gesture of protest.

He must have felt me staring, because he suddenly turned and glared at me.

'Did you know the previous instructor for this class?' he asked, in precise, clipped tones. 'I will not mention his name.'

'Sure,' I said. 'He's my friend.'

'You should choose your friends more carefully,' Hector said.

'What was the problem with Pete?' I asked.

'He was the kind of individual,' Hector said, his voice

beginning to rise, 'who did not keep his word. I do not want to speak of him again.'

The movie started, and Hector turned toward his notes. His note-taking did not proceed in the normal fashion, from the left to the right of the page, but formed a circle, as if his writing described a hurricane.

As we watched the movie, there was a part early on where the doomed Patrolman Robert Woods approached the car. The chant started low, then began to fill the room: 'Kill him,' the class chanted. Patrolman Woods bent toward the driver's window. 'Kill him!' The chant picked up speed. 'Kill Him! Kill Him!' The driver lifted his gun. 'Kill him. Kill Him! KILL HIM!' When the shots rang out, the men fell silent, as if their words had brought it into being.

State eyes

Deadeye approached me while the students were working on their papers in groups. I was mesmerized by his blind eye, the eyelid fluttering over the blank interior.

'Look what they wrote on my paper,' he said, talking about the others in his group. On his paper, in big bold letters: THIS IS A PIECE OF SHIT. The peer groups, I realized, were going to require a bit of work.

'I got something else I need to ask,' Deadeye said.

'Sure.'

'You know about Jack Abbott, right?' he asked.

'I read his book,' I said. Abbott's book, *In the Belly of the Beast*, described his years in prison. He'd been incarcerated nearly his whole adult life, first for property crimes, then for killing another inmate.

'He's here,' Deadeye said. Abbott's book had been a bestseller, and he had eventually been released from prison. After getting out, he killed a restaurant manager in a street fight. There'd been a nationwide manhunt; Abbott had been caught, convicted and sent to prison. He was the nightmare version of a convict, a man who could not be tamed.

'We play Scrabble every day,' Deadeye said. 'I told him about your class. He said he'd like to audit.'

'Sure,' I said. I told him I'd have to check it out with Rick, but that I was for it.

A guard opened the door. 'Medical call-out,' he said.

Deadeye looked up. 'I'd go with you, but I'm on the Medical call-out sheet,' he said. I'd quickly learned that call-outs were constantly going on, even during class. Medical call-outs, Legal call-outs, Visitors, Commissary, even Haircut call-outs. A guard would simply open the door of the class, say, 'Haircut,' and three or four men would pack up their books and exit. The prison ran on its own schedule, independent of anything else.

'Just a second,' Deadeye said. 'Make sure I got everything.' He reached into his pocket and dug around, pulling out a piece of plastic. It was a prosthesis. It was covered with lint, which he blew off, afterwards wiping it with a vastly soiled handkerchief. I realized he was enjoying my evident discomfort. Finally he inserted the prosthesis. It bulged under his eyelid, as if trying to escape. I felt my knees weaken.

'State eye, you know,' Deadeye said. 'You never get the one that fits.'

More movies

Rick was in his office when I went to ask about Abbott. Joey G., the Mob boss who had graduated from SU and was now the head clerk, looked up as I came in. He excused himself, as if he already knew the answer to everything. As I explained what I was proposing, panic crossed Rick's face. 'You don't know what you're asking,' Rick said. 'If I say yes, fifteen minutes after the word was out, I'd get a call from the Dep Super of Programs asking me if I'd lost my mind.' He explained that Abbott was a high-profile prisoner, treated differently from everybody else. He did no work, went to no programs, could not, under any circumstances, attend college. He sat. Most likely—and this was his opinion—the State was waiting for someone to kill him. Someone whose movie meant making a name for himself, like the kids charging after Gregory Peck in *The Gunfighter*. If word ever got out that Abbott had been given yet another chance, it could mean the end of the program. 'It's a very political place,' he said.

'I can see that,' I said.

'Do you understand what I'm saying?' he asked.

I said that I did.

The moral of the story

AKA Diaz was turning out to be the best writer in the class. He argued all the time, not necessarily because he believed what he was saying, but because he wanted the battle of wills.

I'd assigned an inductive essay, in which students were to tell a story and, at the end, draw a moral from it. Diaz's story went like this:

A guy named Bill entered a bar. A small man, he sat down to drink. Fred, a big guy (size differential was always carefully recorded in prison essays) walked in and sat next to him. Bill and Fred, as it turned out, were friends. They began buying rounds, leaving their change on the bar. At one point, when it was his turn, Fred ran out of money, and reached over into Bill's change, taking a quarter.

'What the fuck you doing?' Bill asked. 'You stole my quarter.'

'Ain't your quarter,' Fred said.

'The hell it ain't,' Bill said.

The essay went on matter-of-factly to note that Bill and Fred began fighting, whereupon Bill pulled out his piece which he happened to have handy, shot Fred to death and received a sentence of twenty-five to life. It was, Diaz mentioned, a true story, Bill being a pseudonym for his brother-in-law, now serving time at another state prison.

Now came the moral. The moral of the story, Diaz wrote, was 'You shouldn't take what isn't yours.'

'Don't you think this is an unusual moral?' I asked.

AKA Diaz looked at his paper. 'I think this pretty well covers it.'

'You might also conclude that Bill traded twenty-five years for twenty-five cents.'

Diaz shook his head, as if disappointed at my obtuseness. 'Fred took his money,' he said. 'No way Bill could let him get away with that.'

'Bill had options,' I said. 'He could've quit drinking with him. Shooting a man for twenty-five cents is a bit outsized.'

'Let's say I break into your house,' Diaz said. 'You gonna say, "Help yourself to the living room, I'll stay in the kitchen."?'

'It's a matter of perspective,' I said. 'I'm talking twenty-five cents, you're talking breaking into a house.'

'Look,' Diaz said. 'Let Guy read it. A tie-breaker.' Guy Pastorelli was waiting for the next conference. A big, sly fellow, he often walked with Rick, Craig and me as we crossed the Yard. 'Maybe I'll just keep going,' he'd say, slowing as we arrived at the gate. He'd stop there, just touching the boundary, the guard at the gate keeping a nervous eye on him.

Guy read it carefully, then handed back the paper. 'Man shouldn't take what isn't his,' Guy concluded.

'I'm talking about perspective,' I said.

'You want perspective?' Diaz said. 'I'll give you perspective. Just yesterday, I'm walking with my friend in the Yard, and he got a letter, bad news, from home. I ask him what's the matter, he goes, "Suck my dick." Now, I tell you somethin', by rights, me and him should've gone at it right there. But I didn't, 'cause I knew he was hurting, and he was my friend.'

For the first time, I understood perspective. In prison, Diaz was saying, the thresholds were set high. Once one took the first backward step, one would never take another forward.

'What do you say to that, O'Connor?' Diaz asked.

'I'd say you deserve an A.'

Diaz laughed and looked at Guy Pastorelli. 'There's hope for you yet,' he said.

A little bit of drawing and quartering

Hector still had not met with me in conference, whereas I had talked to most of the inmates twice already about their papers. During the break I summoned up my courage and walked over to him.

'I've been waiting for you,' Hector said. 'I just had my journal returned.'

'What happened to it?' I asked.

'Stolen,' Hector said. 'But I knew who took it. I had not completely trusted him. He was always hanging over me, but now I know him.' He paused. 'I want you to know something else.'

'Yes,' I said.

'I did not do anything to him.' Hector paused. 'This is new for me.'

'That's good,' I said. 'I'm glad for you.'

'You don't know some of the people in here,' Hector said. 'You think you do, but you see only one side.'

'I'm sure that's true,' I said.

'They are soulless,' Hector said. 'That is why I sit separate. When they leave this class and go out to the Yard they do not speak to each other—they do not know each other. They are anathema to me.'

'But they talk to each other in here,' I said.

'Some of them should be drawn and quartered,' Hector said.

'What I'm saying is that this is a start. Once you leave here—and I don't mean in the Yard—I mean when you go back outside, there's going to be people you want to kill, but you learn to let them live. That's all I'm saying,' I said.

'O'Connor,' Hector said. He picked up his notebook and handed it to me. 'I'm trusting you.'

The court system

The inmate who frightened me the most was a twenty-three-year-old black named Steve Roosevelt. He resembled Mike Tyson, except Steve was a bit larger and in for twenty-five to life , one of the heavy lifting crimes. He seemed professionally angry, belonging to the Five Percenters, one of the prison gangs, which in Auburn were called 'courts'.

A word on the courts: they were actual physical courts situated in the east yard. Each prison gang occupied a certain amount of space, apportioned according to size and ferocity. Like a parody of suburban developments, the courts were divided racially and by occupation. There was the Mob court (the nicest one supposedly because it was in the lee of one of the cell blocks and so kept the men out of the wind); the Dominicans; the Ricans (these were their terms); the Marielitos (from the Cuban boat lift—this court was small but notoriously violent); the Zulus (a black court); the Black African Nation (Muslim); a biker court; and two Five Percenter courts, one of which Steve belonged to. The term 'Five Percenter' came from the idea that five per cent of all blacks either explicitly or implicitly endorsed the idea of exterminating the white ruling class. A struggle to the death. Their hatred was certainly genuine: it rolled off Steve like heat. One of the things that prevented the great struggle from occurring was that the two Five Percenter courts were constantly at odds, rendering each other ineffective.

We were on a break, and I was conferencing with another inmate when the dispute erupted. Steve Roosevelt had been sitting in his chair, quietly smoking. Bubba Kingsley, an older inmate who had been down twenty-two years and had been in Attica for the riots, decided he couldn't take the smoke anymore, so he opened a window. That got Steve cold, and so he stood up to close the window. Bubba protested. I looked up, suddenly spotting them facing off by the window. They were straining against each other: Bubba holding the window open, Steve pushing it back down.

I jumped up and walked over. 'I have an idea,' I said. 'I'll open a window.'

They stepped back, disengaging for a moment before returning to their seats.

The left-handed Sweeney

The first time Hector saw somebody killed in prison, he wrote in his journal, the hitter approached his victim from behind. It was a contract hit, and the hitter, a man already with a fifty-to-life sentence, began rhythmically stabbing his victim. The other men immediately put their backs to the wall to prevent anyone from taking advantage of the confusion by putting a knife where they'd always wanted. When he was done, and the man was dead, the hitter walked over to the guard who was calling for help and handed him the knife. What Hector remembered most, he wrote, was that everyone immediately pulled out cigarettes and began smoking, as if they had all just enjoyed great sex.

I started reading Hector's journal at ten on a Saturday night. Six hours later, at four o'clock in the morning, I was still reading.

The journal was over two hundred pages long and recorded Hector's upbringing in a Catholic orphanage, and his life in karate as a teenager (it's likely that Hector and I had passed each other at New York City karate tournaments). He recorded how once working as a messenger, he had met Robert Redford; and how, while lifting weights, he had stopped to watch a monarch butterfly rest its wings on the chin-up bar. He didn't allow himself to watch television, he wrote, because he was afraid to become too involved in a show and fail to notice someone creeping up to stab him. He couldn't allow himself not to remember for a moment where he was. He was caught in a reality so fierce that it could not tolerate fantasy.

The journal was addressed to me, a long document expressly meant for my education. He had missed my name in the early going, but knew I was Irish and left-handed, and so the early entries were addressed to 'the Left-Handed Sweeney'. Despite being Hispanic he was a member of the biker court due to his fighting prowess. This was unusual because the rest of the biker court was composed of white racists. He'd been brought in by a big, Irish biker, and he wrote that I reminded him of that man.

'Are you coming to bed?' Donna called from upstairs.

'In a while,' I said.

Escalation

It still had not been settled between Steve Roosevelt and Bubba Kingsley. Because I had intervened, Bubba had lost face. At the break, I was conferencing with yet another student. Steve had gotten up from his chair (he favored a large green swivel chair that allowed him to spin during odd moments of class) and then returned to sit down. As he descended, Bubba, who had been innocently standing by, pulled the chair out from under him. Steve was a large man and he went down with such force that he actually broke the chair with his arm. The class laughed nervously, but Steve muttered how he would get Bubba, in his own good time.

Vacation

I needed a week off and so I called in sick at the prison and volunteered to drive my mother-in-law down to New York City. I stayed with my parents and I read books that I'd been meaning to catch up on for the whole semester.

On the drive back I thought of the things I'd learned. It was the small things, in certain ways, that were most terrible. For instance, there was a bank of phones at one edge of the Yard that the prisoners could use to make collect calls home. It turned out, according to Hector, all of the phones were owned.

'How do you own a phone?' I had asked.

'Easy, and not so easy,' he said. 'You go up and say, "I own this phone."'

'What if someone else owns that phone?' I asked.

'Someone else always owns it,' Hector said. 'That's the not-so-easy part.'

Betrayal

As soon as I came in, Hector reproved me. 'You were not here,' he said.

'I had to go out of town,' I said.

'I hope whatever you had to do was more important than coming here,' Hector said.

'I had to go,' I said weakly. The odd thing was how most of the men behaved—as if I had broken faith with them, deserted them, as in fact I had.

On the way back from lunch I saw Jack Abbott in the Yard. He was coming out of the Control building. I stepped aside to let him pass and then realized it was Abbott. He was taller than I expected, over six feet, thin and ascetic looking. His back was absolutely rigid, and his small glasses gave him the look of an accountant.

'There's Abbott,' I said to Rick, who turned, but Abbott had already passed, his figure blending in with the crowd, already indistinguishable from the others.

Germ warfare

The battle continued between Bubba and Steve. This week Steve came in with the flu. Seated three seats away from Bubba, Steve sneezed toward him, the cloud of phlegm advancing on Bubba's position. Bubba's feet scurried under the table, trying to get away, but the cloud kept overtaking him, drenching him.

'Flu season's a bitch,' Steve said, when I asked him to stop.

I mentioned it to Rick, who told me that I shouldn't concern myself. Steve and Bubba were friends. 'They get a lot of mileage out of their little feuds,' he said.

A visit from Marisa

'What's up?' I asked Hector, who had been uncharacteristically quiet the past couple of weeks.

'In the journal,' he said. 'Do you remember Marisa?'

'Yes,' I said. In the journal, she had been Hector's common-law wife.

'She came up to visit,' Hector said.

'It must have been nice,' I said. If married, the men were allowed conjugal visits in a small trailer park set inside the prison. 'She asked me to kill someone,' Hector said.

'Why?'

'When I was sent to Riker's, she went back to drugs. This man gave her drugs, used her and raped her. Now he's here in Auburn. He is scum. I have been watching him. It would be an easy thing.'

'What are you going to do?'

'Marisa was my mate, my life,' Hector said. 'She begged me,

said I should avenge her.'

'Hector,' I said.

'I told her I would not,' he said.

'You chose the right thing,' I said.

'You don't understand, O'Connor,' Hector said. 'This means I am alone now. There is nobody for me.'

The show rolls on

Steve and Bubba, being friends, decided to settle their differences amicably. Steve started peace negotiations by walking past Bubba and throwing a right cross into his bicep to make it cramp. Each time I told him to stop.

'Not your business, O'Connor,' Steve said. 'Stay out of it.' And he walked on.

At the break they decided to arm wrestle, but a full-scale fight nearly broke out over which arm to use, despite the fact that they were both right-handed. The other men drew back, knowing what was going on, not wanting to be involved. This was the ironclad rule of prison, unalterable as the walls: you were ultimately alone. The fight was going to happen soon, and there was nothing I could think of to stop it.

Serious Scrabble

Deadeye and I were going over his paper. He was writing about Alice Walker, claiming to have the inside scoop because he, like her, had only one eye.

'By the way,' I said, 'I'm sorry about what happened with Abbott. I think he would've been a good addition to the class.'

Deadeye snorted. 'Abbott,' he said. 'That guy is one crazy motherfucker. You don't want him in class. No fucking way. I don't even talk to that motherfucker no more. Not after what happened.'

'What happened?'

'Couple weeks ago, we're playing Scrabble. I never beat him, not even once, but this time I'm pounding him, just piling up points. So I start saying things like "You're getting old, Jack," and "Looks like you're losing it, man." Crazy motherfucker, he picks up the Scrabble board, throws it in my face and reaches into his back pocket like he's going for his gun.' (The men called home-made knives 'guns' in prison.) 'So, I jump up, pretending to reach for my gun, but I don't got one. It's a bluff. I don't go out strapped. There we are, circling the Scrabble board, both of us ready to go. I'll tell you, you writers take your Scrabble very seriously.'

'Well, why did you ask me to let him into the class?' I asked.

'He asked me, man,' Deadeye said. 'You let him in, that's your lookout.'

Class participation

'I'm gonna get you in the Yard,' Steve shouted. 'Spread your black cheeks, put a knife up your ass.'

Steve stalked around the classroom, ready to swoop in again. 'I got my little black book—everything you say goes down, you dead motherfucker.'

The class continued to start and stop, Steve interrupting Bubba, threatening him, saying the kinds of things answerable only by violence. There was no class anymore; there were simply bits of teaching between the hate.

At the break, I approached Steve. 'You see where this is going, Steve,' I said. 'Stop it now before it's too late.'

Steve rolled his shoulders and hunkered down at his desk. He seemed poised to strike. 'You always take his side,' he said. 'How come you're never on my side?'

'I am on your side,' I said. 'You don't want what's going to happen.'

'Fuck you,' Steve said deliberately, and I was afraid he had come to a decision. 'You do what you got to do, I'll do what I got to do.'

I could see no options. When we came back from the break, there would be a fight, Bubba would be severely beaten or killed, and I could do nothing.

'You have to understand, Steve,' I said, absolutely desperate.

'This will affect your class participation grade.'

I expected him to ask exactly which planet I had just parachuted from. I expected him to say, 'OK, so I kill Bubba, but what does that get—ten per cent off?' And here was the kicker: it worked.

Blood Simple

The blood rippled on the floor, pushed by the man with the mop. I hadn't seen it happen, but there had been a mass of confusion, a sudden accordion-like tightening and spreading of men as they struggled to get out of the way. Hector, who was walking in front of me, pushed me back into the classroom, putting his own body between mine and the attack, although we were far enough away that I was not in any danger.

How I know the rest was because AKA Diaz told his story to Joey G., our Mob head clerk. He wanted Rick Steplinger and me to know what the circumstances were, and that he had done his best to avoid what was going to happen.

AKA Diaz and the other man, a Rastafarian named Raoul, had met at Riker's, where they had been involved in what officials term 'an incident'. What the fight was about, no one knew, not even Joey G., who knew everything.

Once Raoul was transferred to Auburn, AKA Diaz recognized him. He approached Raoul and asked if there was still a problem between them. Raoul said no, their problem had happened three years ago, water under the bridge.

Nevertheless, AKA Diaz began to notice Raoul was shadowing him. AKA Diaz would be watching TV in the Yard and feel somebody getting close. He would turn, and there would be Raoul. Walking in the Yard, out of the corner of his eye, he'd catch Raoul sidling by. Wherever he'd go, Raoul. Raoul had even gotten a job as a janitor in the school building. Raoul, AKA Diaz concluded, was stalking him, checking out his friends and affiliates, deciding when to make his play.

The day Raoul cut off his dreadlocks, AKA Diaz knew he didn't have much time. Raoul was stripping down to the essentials, preparing to go into battle. AKA Diaz chose his moment on the Go-Back, when the men were called back from the classroom. The guard post was unoccupied. He called Raoul over, and when Raoul came, AKA Diaz stabbed him, 'running the gears' on him, which meant that after stabbing, he moved the knife around inside Raoul's chest to ensure maximum damage.

AKA Diaz hadn't sat in class that day. Instead he'd gone to Joey G. to explain himself, so that we would understand. Then he waited in an empty classroom, considering thresholds and what necessarily was to come.

Go back

I dismissed the class early to talk to a number of students about their final papers, due the following week. The guards had called the Go-Back, stricter now since the stabbing, and I'd seen the men shuffle off.

I packed my books and checked the classroom one last time. Someone had left his jacket and books in the back. They looked to be Hector's things, and I worried about someone taking them. I folded the jacket neatly and picked up the books, intending to take them to the office. Just as I turned, I saw Hector running at top speed down the hallway. For a moment I was afraid he might accuse me of stealing, but when he turned the corner I saw something else: relief on his face—someone else out there looking out for him, not so alone anymore.

'Thanks O'Connor,' he said, taking his jacket and books and then running from the class back to his cell.

'Are you coming back, O'Connor?' they had asked. 'What are you going to teach in the spring?'

Outside the trees were leafless, and I could taste the cold. Winter would be here soon but it would pass. And when it did, I would be back. □

GRANTA

CHRIS OFFUTT
MOSCOW, IDAHO

Chris Offutt was born in 1958 and grew up in the Appalachian Mountains in Haldeman, Kentucky, a former mining community of two hundred people. After public school, he took a degree in theater at Morehead State University and, ten years later, a Master's degree in English from the University of Iowa. His writing and his travels throughout the United States have been supported by more than fifty jobs, all of them part-time, as well as by various grants, including a Guggenheim fellowship. Today he lives with his wife and two sons aged six and three in Albuquerque, New Mexico, where his wife works as stage manager for the Southwest Opera Company. He has published a collection of short stories, *Kentucky Straight* (1992), and a memoir, and is now completing a novel which Simon & Schuster will publish next year.

'Moscow, Idaho' is a new short story.

Tilden stopped digging and wiped his sleeve across his forehead, leaving a brown smear on his skin. The afternoon sunlight shimmered in the air. He jabbed the shovel into the ground. His arms were sore, and his back hurt, but anything was better than prison, even moving graves in Idaho.

The cemetery sat on a rise outside of town, surrounded by wheat fields that were ready for harvest. The grain rose high and golden, swaying in the wind. Tilden and a fellow ex-con named Baker had spent the last few weeks unearthing coffins. Next spring the state was building a highway through the cemetery. They had been hired to replace a mini-backhoe that damaged the caskets, sometimes cutting them in half. A separate work crew hauled them to the other side of Moscow for reburial.

September still had some hard heat, and the two men moved to the lacy shade of a tamarack. Sweat evaporated from their skin. Baker reached into his shirt pocket for a cigarette without removing the pack. Tilden recognized the prison habit and wondered about his own.

'You know,' Baker said, 'back in Minnesota they got the biggest mall in the world.'

Tilden nodded. Baker liked to talk and needed periodic proof that someone was paying attention.

'There's six bars in that mall,' Baker said, 'and nothing but rent-a-cops. You can get drunk and walk from one bar to another and nobody fucks with you. Not bad, huh?'

Tilden nodded.

'I ever tell you the best thing about getting locked up in St Paul?' Baker said.

'The view.'

'That's right, partner. The river was right there. You could watch boats all day from my cell. Bet you didn't have no view in Kentucky, did you?'

Tilden had been among the first prisoners assigned to a new facility in Morgan County. The inmates called it the Pink Palace due to the pastel color of its outer walls. The prison was surrounded by hills. Sometimes heavy fog prevented the men from going into the yard because the sharpshooter in the tower couldn't see well enough. On clear mornings each tree leaf was clearly visible in the mountain light. Their presence was a daily tease, like a friend's wife who liked to flirt.

Tilden wondered if a view of the river made men sadder or gave them hope. He figured the prison psychologist would like it, since he favored anything that was different, even a new coat of paint. Tilden had learned to give the shrink what he wanted, which was mainly the impression that you wouldn't shank the first son of a bitch who looked at you mad-dog. Getting through the joint took the ability to make everyone think you were crazy enough to be dangerous. Getting out took the opposite. Tilden wasn't sure what it took to stay out.

Heat was on him like water, pressing against his sunburned face. He and Baker took a break on the shadowed side of a stand of pine. The oldest tombstones were pale with black stains, the lettering nearly worn away. Faded plastic flowers surrounded the newer stones, their gray surfaces polished slick. Beyond them lay fresh earth waiting for the dead.

'You know something,' Baker said. 'I ain't spent a whole lot of time in a graveyard.'

'Reckon not.'

'I was just a kid last time, for my grandmaw's funeral. I ever tell you about her?'

'No.'

'She died.'

'I guessed that.'

'Hung herself from a clothes pole in a closet. Knocked her own wheelchair out from under her. The only suicide the nursing home said they ever had, but you can't trust them bastards.'

'You got that right.'

'They ought to close that home down. A little blue-haired lady with no legs hanging in a closet like an old dress.'

'No legs?'

'She had diabetes,' Baker said. 'Know what they did so nobody else would do it?'

'Threw them in the hole.'

'No, man. They took away the clothes pole in every closet. They can't hang nothing no more. All them old folks wearing wrinkly clothes. Just like Deer Lodge. We had a man shoot somebody in the belly with a staple gun he'd re-rigged to fire a homemade bullet. He'd stole it from Art, and they shut down Art tight as a fucking drum. It was my best class. I made pictures of the ocean. Ever see the ocean?'

'No.'

'Me neither. That's why I made them pictures. Anyhow, my grandmaw got her gravesite picked out and paid for about a hundred years ago. It was waiting on her, but coffins got big over the years, and there wasn't enough room. They had to dig up a whole row of my family to get her in there.'

'Guess those others died too soon.'

'Or her too late.'

'I ain't knocking your grandmaw,' Tilden said, 'but I can't figure the use of owning a burial plot. It's the same as having your own cell in case you get put away.'

'Hell, if I owned a grave, I'd have hocked it on jump street.'

They laughed together, the sound fading in the still air. Tilden ate an apple while Baker smoked. Each tombstone threw a narrow shadow that lay over the adjacent grave like a puddle. According to the dates, many people buried here had been dead for a longer period than they had lived. Tilden knew men who'd spent more years inside than out, and it occurred to him that time didn't move forward as he'd always thought. People moved through time instead.

'Ever miss the joint?' Baker said.

'No.'

'I do. The dope especially. I had good connections inside, man. Out here, I don't know nobody.'

'Well, you best watch, or that mandatory sentencing will eat you up. I celled with a guy did two murders and he was on the street before the dopers.'

'I like that mandatory law.'

'Do you?'

'You bet. Fill them cells up with hopheads, and they ain't got room for you and me.'

'They don't need room for me.'

'You know why they called me Storebought inside?' Baker said.

Tilden nodded.

'My first beef. They popped me on some over-the-counter caffeine pills. I kept telling them it was storebought dope, but you can't tell the law nothing.'

'I hear that.'

'Tell you what else I miss,' Baker said. 'All the different guys you meet. I thought it would be like high school, and you went to whatever prison was close. I met guys inside nothing like home. They were from all over the country. Sometimes I miss those guys. I miss them calling me Storebought too.'

'I know what you mean.'

'What I don't like about being out, I never had to hang in a graveyard before.'

A black squirrel with no tail watched the men. Tilden didn't miss anything about prison but he could understand Baker's desire for routine. They ate lunch under the same ponderosa pines every day, and after work they went to the same bar. Baker was like a bee, needing to do the same thing over and over. Prison was his hive.

'Eight years in the can,' Baker said. 'TV was the biggest thing that changed.'

'Some.'

'I seen a guy on it saying you shouldn't eat eggs because raising chickens was slavery.'

'Talking out his neck, ain't he.'

'Only thing good are these true cop shows. They think they're bragging how great the police are, but all they really show is how the chumps get caught. A guy can learn something.'

'Not exactly.'

'I guess you're Square Johning on me.'

'Aim to.'

'Shouldn't be kicking it with me then.'

'Way I see it,' Tilden said, 'maybe I'm a good influence on you.'

'Best influence I ever had was inside. A fence told me what not to move, and a paperhanger said what to look for on funny money. Hell, even the government's doing me good with the gun laws. TV says they got people walking in off the street and giving their guns up. I, for one, am all for it. That's one less bullet to hit me on a job. Citizens are a bunch of idjits. The government figured that out a million years ago.'

'I never thought about it that way.'

'Well, if you watched TV, you'd know something.'

Gravestones rose like teeth from the earth. Tilden wondered how many people buried here had been killed by a bullet. Baker would no more blame a gun for somebody getting shot than he'd scapegoat a shovel for the graveyard. Laws would never slow him down. He didn't think far enough ahead, and getting caught would never happen. There were thousands like him. Tilden wondered if he was lumping himself in with that group. He didn't think so but he was an ex-con, working a job that no one else would take.

He threw a piece of apple to the squirrel. He preferred to feed the birds, but since the squirrels got it first, he went ahead and fed them. He considered it a lesson from prison—not trying to force what he wanted. Still, Tilden knew how the birds felt, compromised right out of the deal.

'You get anything else from being down?' he said.

'Muscles,' Baker said. 'I worked out every day. And my tats.'

One forearm said FTW, and the other showed the number thirteen and a half. He unbuttoned his shirt and slid the collar over one shoulder to reveal a blurred tattoo. Two crudely drawn dice had snake eyes showing. Below them, in block letters, was the phrase BORN TO LOSE.

'No,' Tilden said. 'I mean anything worth keeping in your head.'

'You talk like a shrink.'

'Come on, man.'

Baker cracked his knuckles one by one. He stretched his legs until his boots reached the last lip of shade. He stared into space, and Tilden decided that he'd forgotten the question, led somewhere private by the skipping of his thoughts. He'd noticed that prison often made stupid men turn smart, and smart men become dumb. He wondered which he was.

Baker lay on his back and spoke.

'Biggest is how to make people leave me alone. Next is how to sleep. I never slept good before but now I can sleep fourteen hours.'

'Nothing else?'

'I damn sure know I like girls.'

Passing clouds pushed patterns of shade along the ground. A breeze carried the scent of wheat mixing with the smell of fresh-turned earth. It occurred to Tilden that people always buried their dead on hilltops, often the highest around. Tilden liked the silence. Prison was filled with noise—the crash of steel gates, howls of rage and pain, blaring radios. The only quiet time came after a homicide. Tilden had never seen murder until he got put away and he'd been amazed at how fast it could happen.

Now he sat surrounded by dead that went back a hundred years. He wondered how far into the earth he'd have to dig before he'd stop hitting bone. It seemed to him that the planet was a skin of grass that covered acres of bone, like a skeleton for the earth. Dirt was sinew. Rock was muscle.

After the break they walked to a grave that had been tough to work. They'd dug two days, cutting through roots that veered around the coffin, sometimes holding it tight as if the earth wanted to keep the bones. Tilden remembered an old con who'd been cut loose. He'd done a twenty-five-year flat bit for a bank robbery that had earned him high status in prison. Outside he was an old man no one cared about. Nine days into freedom he held up a bar, set his pistol on a stool and called the police. He returned to prison smiling, glad to be home. A week later he was stabbed three times with a knife made from the instep support of a crippled con's shoe.

Footsteps pounded in the lane behind Tilden, and he turned to the noise. A man was running toward him. He wore green jogging tights and a spandex shirt. Mirror shades covered his eyes, and an antenna bobbed above yellow headphones.

Baker lifted his shovel like a baseball bat. Tilden wanted to shout a warning to leave the man alone, but it went against yard ethics. The jogger came abreast, and Baker fell in step behind him.

'Run!' he yelled. 'Crank it up, punk.'

The man doubled his pace, puffs of dust rising from his feet. He veered around a bend and disappeared among the pines. Baker grinned. There was a wild expression on his face that Tilden had only seen in prison.

'If I was in that big a hurry,' Baker said, 'I'd by God get me a car. See me doing that, you can drop me in a sack. Know what I'm saying?'

'I'll pass on that.'

'I know you're standup, Til. But if I didn't, I might wonder what you were afraid of.'

'I'm chicken of one thing.'

'What's that?'

'Myself.'

'You bet. I wouldn't mess with me if I was me.'

'That ain't exactly what I meant.'

Tilden began moving earth, thinking of the last time he'd seen that look on someone's face. Two men had circled each other in the rec room, slashing with weapons made from a razor blade embedded in a toothbrush handle. Each man wore magazines strapped to his torso by strips of sheet. They bled from the arms, but the crude armor protected their bodies. The crowd drew guards, who beat both men unconscious. Tilden had still been a new fish, so scared he couldn't sleep, stunned by the savagery of the guards. The look in their eyes had matched Baker's.

In the slanting red light of late afternoon Tilden and Baker carried their tools to the storage building. Ripe wheat gleamed as though the surface of the earth had caught fire. Nine cars were parked in the gravel lot reserved for a funeral party.

Tilden heard the neigh of a horse, and he and Baker followed the sound to a rise overlooking the cemetery's edge. A line of people followed a horse-drawn buckboard that held a coffin. Two of the men wore ill-fitting suits, but most were dressed in work clothes, boots and hats. A few women wore black. Four children walked close together. The horse stopped beside a fresh hole, and the men used straps to lift the coffin from the wagon and ease it into the grave.

'What the fuck,' Baker said. 'Guess they don't know about

the highway coming through.'

'Maybe they already got the grave paid off.'

'Long time since I was at a funeral,' Baker said. 'They wouldn't let me out when my mother died.'

'That's tough.'

'I never even seen her grave.'

At the bottom of the hill a man was removing shovels from the wagon. He passed them to each mourner as if handing out weapons. Tilden realized that in the morning he'd be moving the fresh earth, and it would be easy to dig.

'Hey, man,' Baker said, 'I ever tell you about my cellie who was on a firing squad in Utah.'

'No.'

'He said it was just a job, but I think he was fucked up. I mean, who'd want to live in Utah?'

'Not me,' Tilden said.

'Anyhow, you heard how one rifle is loaded with a blank, so each man can think he wasn't the killer. Well, that's bullshit. There's no recoil from a blank, so you know if you shot it. He said to make up for it, everybody aims away from the heart. Sometimes all five guys miss, and the shot man flops around awhile. The day before, he gets to watch any video he wants.'

The people in the funeral party began to fill the grave with dirt. They worked slowly, as if reluctant to finish. A woman rested, leaning on the handle of her shovel.

'They could use some help,' Baker said.

'I don't know about that.'

'Why not?'

'If it was some stranger wanting to bury my family, I might think it was funny.'

'What's funny is that damn horse. Think they're Amish or something?'

'They don't have them out here.'

'They don't have a lot,' Baker said. 'You like it?'

'What, Idaho?'

'All of it, man. The whole West.'

'Yeah, I like it.'

'I don't. All this empty space, you know, makes me feel lonely.'

'That's why I like it,' Tilden said.

A small boy knelt beside the grave and began pushing dirt in the hole. He worked steadily, using his arms to move the soil.

Tears drained down Baker's cheeks into his mustache. His chest rose and fell as he began to pant, and Tilden realized that Baker had lost the mechanics of how to cry. The tears made clean lines in the dirt on his face.

Tilden turned away and began walking down the hill to the storage building. The boss would arrive around dark to drive them back to Moscow. He drank from a spigot and cleaned the shovels.

Baker joined him, chewing gum while keeping a toothpick in his mouth. He walked with the gait of a mainline con, moving slowly from the hips down, his shoulders swaying in a swagger. Tilden knew he had to be careful. Baker was dangerous now that he had seen him weak.

'I'm done, man,' Baker said.

'What?'

'I can't work that grave.'

'That's all right,' Tilden said. 'I will.'

'No, man. I'm done with all of it.'

'You quitting?'

'I didn't bury my own mother and here I am digging up strangers.'

Baker ducked along the row of cars until he found one with the keys in it. He eased the door open and checked the lights, the gas gauge and the turn signals.

'Tell me if the brake lights work,' he called. 'I got to hurry. They'll be here in a minute.'

Tilden nodded as Baker searched the car, talking fast.

'I tell you about my first juvie beef? Stole a car that ran out of gas. There was a bag of dope under the seat. I'm glad they closed that file at eighteen, man. Nobody knows how stupid I used to be.'

He pulled a pair of work gloves from the back seat.

'You want these?' he said. 'Too small for me.'

'This ain't worth it.'

'What is, man?'

Baker dropped the gloves on the ground and opened the trunk.

'Got a spare and a jack?' he said. 'My lucky day, right. Too bad they didn't leave a purse.'

'You can still walk away.'

'I want to see the ocean. Let's go, man. We can road-dog it out of here.'

'No way.' Tilden used his yard voice, low and quick. 'I'm never going back inside.'

'Me neither, man. I been down twice. I'll kill everybody before they put me back in the walls. Everybody.'

Tilden looked over the car's roof to the wheat field in the east. He couldn't find the seam where earth and sky blended together. The world was blurred by dusk.

'Don't keep this rig too long,' Tilden said.

'I won't, man. Radio ain't got but AM anyhow.'

'Later, Storebought.'

Baker eased the clutch and drove along the dusty lane. Tilden left the cemetery quickly before the funeral party returned to the lot. He knew what Baker was up to and where he was headed. He was on a run, like riding a motorcycle wide open until he crashed. The state called it recidivism, but as the old cons said, Baker was doing life on the installment plan.

Tilden crossed the road and lay on his back beside the wheat. He spread his arms. Wind blew loose dirt over his body. The ground was soft, and the air was warm. In prison he had figured out that laws were made to protect the people who made the laws. He had always thought that staying out of trouble meant following those laws, but now he knew there was more. The secret was to act like the people who wanted the laws in the first place. They didn't even think about it. They just lived. Tilden wondered if he'd ever find a woman, a job he liked or a town he wanted to live in. Above him the Milky Way made a blizzard of stars in the sky. There was not a fence or wall in sight. □

GRANTA

STEWART O'NAN
A FAN LETTER

Stewart O'Nan was born in 1961 in Pittsburgh. His father was an engineer; his mother an economics professor. He studied aerospace engineering at Boston University and worked for five years as a test engineer at Grumman Aerospace, Long Island. Subsequently he took a master's degree in fiction at Cornell University and since 1990 he has taught creative writing, currently at Trinity College in Hartford, Connecticut. His three published novels include *Snow Angels* (1994). He lives with his wife and two children in Avon, Connecticut, where he is working on various stages of further novels and on a screenplay based on the life of Edgar Allan Poe.

'A Fan Letter' is taken from his fourth novel, whose title is the subject of a legal dispute. It will be be published by Doubleday next year.

Stewart O'Nan

Testing, one, two, three

I hope you don't mind but I wrote this first part out, so I'll just read it now and get it over with. Mr Jefferies helped me with it. I hope that's OK.

OK, let me just read it.

Before I begin I'd like to say that I'll try to remember everything as best I can, though sometimes I know it won't be right. What you want to know about happened eight years ago, before I found the Lord. I was a different person then, a person I don't completely understand even now. That's not an excuse, nor are the drugs. I take full responsibility for the things that I did do—no more, no less. I maintain my innocence and consider my sentence unjust. I also think it's important for the public to know that legally I oppose capital punishment of any sort, not just in my own case.

Was that OK? You don't have to use it if you don't want to. Mr Jefferies said we might put it right at the front of the book. He said you might want to 'cause it makes it more real—based on a true story, like. I don't know anything about writing a book, so anything like that is up to you. Mr Jefferies said I should just do it to avoid any legal problems.

It's a novel, right? So it's supposed to be all made up. It should have a thing at the beginning like at the end of a movie—everybody in this isn't supposed to be alive or dead—even though everyone knows that's not true. I bet everybody asks you about Jack in *The Shining* and whether that's supposed to be you. You say no, I bet, or maybe he's just a little part of you. This'll be more like *Dolores Claiborne*, but still. As long as you say it's fiction and put that thing in, you're OK, you don't really have to answer that. But Mr Jefferies said that that based-on-a-true-story thing is tricky, so I said, sure, let's do it, let's put it in.

You probably already read Natalie's book. Let me just say here that very little of it's true, and none of the big things. I know why she said what she did, but it's not true. That's one reason I wanted you to do the book. After people read yours, no one'll believe hers.

Thank you for all the money. It's all going to go to Gainey when he's old enough. My mom won't see a penny of it, Mr Jefferies said he'd see to it.

I like Mr Jefferies. He's the only one who's done anything for me in this whole thing. I know he feels bad that we lost. I know he feels that *he* lost, but that's not true. We did the right thing, pleading not guilty. I *am* not guilty. He didn't know the judge was going to be so tough. You should have seen him right after we lost—he gave me this little hug anyway, but I could tell he thought it was his fault. And how can you tell someone it's not?

My mom says she would've paid for someone better. This is after the fact, of course. She's always generous when it's too late.

That part about being against the death penalty was Mr Jefferies's idea. He's against it. Personally, I'm for it—which is funny, 'cause I wasn't when I came in here. You meet people in here there's just nothing else to do with. It's like the Psalm says: *Preserve thou the righteous and let vengeance take the wicked.* And there is wickedness in the world, there are evil people, men and women both. But Mr Jefferies, he's been working so hard for me I figure I owe it to him. It doesn't mean that much to me one way or the other.

Anyway, it's important for me to say all this before I begin. Mr Jefferies said he'll listen to the tapes before he sends them to you, in case I say something illegal. He'll make one copy for you and one for Gainey when he's eighteen and keep this one for his records.

Legally Mr Lonergan and the staff are supposed to listen to these. I've got nothing against Mr Lonergan, he's always been fair with my privileges, but this is private business. I know that legally you own these, but I'd appreciate it if you kept them to yourself. You can use it for your book because it's fiction, but not for anything else. I know this is strange asking you this, since if things go the way they're going you can't really answer me, but if you could write to Mr Jefferies with your answer I'd appreciate it.

I think that's it. Like you asked me, I didn't look at the questions ahead of time. There's a lot of them. I'll try to answer them as best I can before midnight. Janille is here, but no one else, so there's no reason for me to be anything but honest. Sometimes I might not say what you want me to, but I'm just going to be honest. You can make up whatever story you want. I just want you to know the real one first.

1

Why did I kill them?

I didn't kill them. It's not even a question.

You think you'd start with something like my mom or dad or what I was like when I was a kid. Show me riding my tricycle out behind the chicken house, my hair in pigtails, buck teeth, something cute like that. Then you could say, she was a normal gal and look what happened to her. And you'd figure it out. You'd go back and look at everything that happened and say, look, it could happen to anyone.

But I'm glad it's you. When Mr Jefferies said you bought the rights, I didn't believe him. I was over on the Row then. Darcy next door said, 'No!'

'Yep,' I said, 'it's true.'

'No,' she said.

I just nodded.

'What about Lamont?' she said, and I said you'd probably have to talk to his folks.

I'm sorry they didn't give you permission. Lamont would have wanted to be in the book. He liked your books. It's kind of a shame you'll have to change our names. It's dumb; everyone'll know it's us.

Why did I kill them?

I didn't kill them. I was there, but I didn't kill anyone.

I know exactly what happened though. It's pretty boring, actually. It's pretty normal. I don't think people will be that interested. But if anyone can make it interesting, you can. You'll make it funny too, which is right. Sometimes it was really funny. Even now some of it's funny.

I've read all your books. I know that sounds like Annie

Wilkes in *Misery*, but it's true, really. I liked *Misery*. James Caan was really good in it. *Brian's Song* was on the other night. Janille rolled the set over so I could watch.

Janille's all right—right, Janille?

Janille and me get along all right except for *Oprah*. Janille can't stand that Oprah lost all that weight. Janille thinks she looked fine before the diet; I think she holds it against her. I think Oprah's someone who tried to change herself and succeeded and I respect that in a person. We fight about this all the time. We could both stand to lose a few pounds. It's all that junk from the vending machines. We'll take a break—that's what Janille calls it—and have some Funyuns and an RC, or split a Payday when we're being really bad. This is usually around *All My Kids* or *One Life to Live*. Definitely before *Oprah*.

I kind of rely on TV in here, that and the Bible. Tonight they say I can watch as much as I want. I can order anything I want to eat. I can pretty much do anything I want.

They say I can have a sedative about four hours before. The last gal they did here took it—the famous one, Connie Something, the gal who cut up all those truckers. By midnight she was just a mess, all crying and her feet going all over the place. They had to carry her in.

Janille doesn't know, but Darcy slipped me three white crosses before they moved me over here. I've been saving them for tonight. I figure what the heck, I've got to do this thing for you. I'm going to do them right after dinner. I'll tell you when they kick in. You'll probably be able to tell anyway.

That was my nickname in the papers—the Speed Queen. I've always moved a little faster than the rest of the world. That's why I'm here, I guess. I don't always stop to think, I just want to go. Lamont used to say I was built for speed. It's true; the world's always seemed a little slow to me. It's chemical, I think. Everything I used to do just fed into that. When I was using, I didn't have to eat or sleep or anything, just get in that Roadrunner and go. Now I've got a few things that calm me down. My relationship with Jesus, obviously. Gainey. Knowing I've only got so much time left. I think I always knew I'd hit some kind of wall. It's like that movie *Vanishing Point*, the guy out there in the desert in that big old Challenger, just hauling around with Cleavon Little on the radio. In the end he hits the blade of this bulldozer, and the car just rips into flames, little pieces of sheet metal falling in slow motion like snow. That's the kind of life I wanted back then. I guess I got it, huh?

I've been over here twice before. The Death House. Actually it's kind of nice. The mattresses are new, and the walls don't sweat like the old ones. Two-tone—light grey over dark grey, the line right at neck level. Steel john, steel mirror. The only bad thing is there's no windows. It drives Janille crazy.

Last time I got my stay early in the morning, the time before that around dinnertime. My dinner was already here, so they let me have it anyway—barbecue from Leo's, the ribs crusty, sliding right off the bone. Say what you like about Oklahoma, but the barbecue is amazing here. That, and the gas is cheap.

They use lethal injection here. It's kind of disappointing. New Mexico used to use the chair but then they changed to injection too. Mr Jefferies made sure we came here; he thought the publicity would kill us in New Mexico.

Kill us—it's a joke.

Remember Foghorn Leghorn? *That's a joke, son.* I never thought he was funny until Lamont and me did some bong hits in bed one morning and he turned on the cartoons. He smelt good in bed, that's what I always remember about Lamont. He was always good to me that way. He used to kiss me right on my heart.

Lamont taught me a lot. Some of it was good. I won't pretend like it wasn't.

I wish it was the chair. The chair makes me think of heaven. It's like a throne.

It's not the needles I mind. My veins are better than they've been since high school, thick as worms. Everyone says it's supposed to be like going to sleep. It's not going to be like that. I don't know what it's going to be like. Last night I pictured it was like flushing your radiator and putting in new antifreeze. They say the gal who killed those truckers broke one of the straps—and those are new straps. But it sounds good to most people, sleep.

Sister Perpetua said there were four stages I had to go through. She wrote them down for me—denial, anger, grief, acceptance. She was right, kind of. Since I've been here I've been through all of them. The problem is, one stage doesn't just end and then the next one kicks in. They get all mixed up with each other. They're all going at the same time.

Why did I kill them is something I'd expect from Barbara Walters or someone. You're not going to start there, are you? I'd think you'd start at the beginning—not with me as a little girl but maybe when I hooked up with Lamont. Because we had a year or so there before Natalie came along. Good times. We were both working, and Lamont bought that Hemi Roadrunner. We used to cruise down around the Whataburger, just lying back in those bucket seats with the Ramones grinding out a wall of sound, jumbo cherry slushes in the cupholder saddled over the hump. You could start there and show how much we were in love and how normal we were, and then how everything went wrong. That's what I'd do.

2

Lamont used the gun first because he had to. It was an old Colt he got from a dealer in Midwest City. He traded him a patched-up gas tank from a '70 Barracuda and a leather jacket he found in the back of a 280Z. It had an eight-round clip and the kind of safety on the back of the grip you have to press down with the meat of your thumb. It kicked so hard the first time I fired it that the hammer put a dent in my forehead.

You can get all of that from the police reports. You're probably just testing me, like the questions at the beginning of a lie-detector test. I've done some of those and I'll tell you, they don't all work.

I think what I'm going to do is answer the questions in order and then maybe when I'm all done try to put them in the order I think they should go in. 'Cause right now this is backwards. The important thing isn't whether I killed them or how, it's everything. My whole life really. That's what you paid for, isn't it?

Lamont used the gun first, and then Natalie used the knife. I don't really see the difference. I didn't use either of them anyway.

And it's a dumb question. How could *I* use the knife first?

There were five of them and one of me, and back then I weighed like a pound.

Not that it was self-defense at that point. Mr Jefferies said it was going to be murder, even though I didn't do it. The question was, was it second-degree or first, and how many counts of each? That's not even including the Closes and all of that.

But that should go later. First I think you'd want to talk about me growing up in the country. In the newspaper no one ever mentions I'm from the country, and I think it's interesting.

My family was my mom, my dad and me, and our dog, Jody-Jo. He was a basset hound the color of a Fudgesicle except where he'd turned white. He was old and had bad dandruff and farted a lot. He didn't like to play with you. He'd just lie under the glider, and when you wanted to rock, he'd get up and say something before he walked off. His back legs moved kind of sideways. He was my mom's dog from before she got married, and my dad refused to clean up after him. My mom had a shovel around the side of the garage, and a trash bag.

The house though. Did you ever see *Bonnie and Clyde*? It was just like that. The next house was a mile down the road on each side. This was right on Route 66, the real one. All day I'd sit on the glider and watch the cars come by; my dad taught me all the names—Chieftain and Starfire, Rocket 88. The nearest town was Depew. In back we had an old chicken house and back behind that a pond the dirt turned red. The house was yellow and had two floors. I don't remember any of the furniture except a piano that was always broken. You'd hit a key, and nothing happened.

The wind was the big thing there. It really did come sweeping down the plain. I don't know if you've ever been out here, but don't forget to put that in the book. Make it windy like every other day. You could say it's windy tonight, that all those protesters outside the gate are getting their signs and coffee cups blown around. Or say I can hear it whistling around the Death House like a ghost. Something like that, just get it in, you know how to do it.

Out there the big worry was tornadoes. April and May was the season. If you saw one, you were supposed to call the police in Depew, then open your windows a crack and wait in the basement. We had an old mattress down there, and when the warning came on the radio, my mom would take me and Jody-Jo down, and we'd sit on the mattress and eat Ritz crackers with peanut butter until the radio said it was OK. Depew had a siren, but even on a calm day you could barely hear it. All I remember is every few days the wind would take one of my mom's sheets off the line and dip it in the pond, and she'd fish it out, cursing like you never heard.

There weren't any chickens left in the chicken house, just dust from the feathers that made you sneeze, and a smell like ammonia. Behind the house was a little hill I'd ride my tricycle down. I'd pedal as fast as I could and then when the pedals were going too fast to catch up with I'd hold my feet out and let the pedals go crazy. I used to fall off a lot. When I went inside, my mother would slap the dirt off my dress. It was kind of like a spanking. 'What have you been doing?' she'd say. 'Haven't I told you a million times not to do that? What's wrong with you?'

My tricycle had plastic tassels that came out of the hand grips. You could hang on to them like reins. You couldn't steer so good with them, but that made it more exciting.

When I was four I broke my wrist. I was riding down the hill when the front wheel hit this dip. The wheel turned, and I went over the handlebars, and the trike came down on top of me. I thought I was fine. I was used to that kind of thing. I got up and tried to pick the trike up, but my hand wouldn't do what I was telling it. I went inside and told my mom.

'What did I tell you?' she said. 'I told you, but you wouldn't listen to me, would you? Now do you see what happens?'

And I *didn't* listen to her. They put a cast on my wrist that my fingers stuck out of, and when I came back I got right back on my tricycle. A few days later I had the exact same accident again, except this time the cast hit me in the side of the head and completely knocked me out. I woke up a little later and went inside. I didn't tell anyone, but in bed that night I could hear like a radio in my head, just soft so you couldn't make out what they were saying.

I know what you're thinking, but it's not true. I was better the next day. I've never heard any other voices. If you want to do something with that, then fine, but that's not my story, that's yours.

If you do, you might say it was the spirit of a Pawnee squaw.

A few years ago some people from the university dug up a whole ditch full of bones near Depew. They think it was a massacre that got covered up. So you might say it was the sole survivor's ghost coming back to find her husband and babies. (You could do it in parentheses or *italics* so we'd know it was a voice in her head, like in *Pet Sematary*.)

We lived on Route 66 until I was five, when my dad got a job at Remington Park and we moved closer to Oklahoma City. I was excited about moving, but sad too, leaving the pond and the chicken house, the little hill.

I guess I should take this time to apologize to the Close family. Lamont and me are honestly sorry for causing them all such pain, and I wish I could undo what's done. I can't. I hope my death will be some comfort to their family. I'd like them to know that we had nothing against Marla and Terry Close, and that they were not involved with the drug business or anything illegal, like the newspapers say. They just happened to be living in that house at that time. As a Christian I pray they've found their reward, just as I hope to find mine tonight.

That was one thing I noticed when we were there that last time—the piano was gone. I thought something that heavy would never move, I don't know why. It was a shock. I remember saying something to Lamont when we were tying them up.

'What?' he said, because the kerosene was splashing.

'The piano,' I said, 'it's gone.'

And he stopped what he was doing and asked where it used to be.

'Right here,' I said, and made the shape of it with my hands.

Lamont put his arm around me, and we stood there looking at where it should have been. There was a bookcase there with pictures of the Closes. They were on a beach somewhere with a sunset lighting up the sky, drinking those little drinks with umbrellas. Behind us Mrs Close was whimpering inside the trash bag. Mr Close's hand was still flipping like a fish.

'What the heck,' I said, 'the thing never worked anyway,' and we went back to work.

We sat on the couch and watched them a little bit, then got on the road. When we passed Depew, the siren was going wild.

3

I'm not going to say anything about the number of times. You can get that from the newspapers. I'm sorry about that now, but after the fifth or sixth time they probably didn't feel anything. That's not what I will or won't be forgiven for anyway. That was Natalie.

I understand you need all these details to tell the story right, that people are interested in that kind of thing. I don't know why we did it. Everybody asks me that. All I can tell you is that sometimes you just go off, you don't know when to stop. Later you come back to yourself, but sometimes you just go off to this other place.

I'm not explaining it right.

I remember doing it. It's not like I wasn't there or that I wasn't the one doing it, it's like nothing else existed except me. Does that make sense? I was the only one that counted. They were there just to please me, to make me count more. The more I did it, the bigger I got. Gigantic. It's a drug by itself, the size you get.

I'll try to answer that better later on. It's a hard one.

We moved from outside Depew to Kickingbird Circle in Edmond. It was a new development then, the houses were brand new, with just dirt for yards, stakes with strings between them. The city was still building the street lights; the gutters were filled with nuts and bolts. It was like a play where they're still building the set.

My dad was an assistant trainer at Remington Park, and my mom worked at the local post office. That's right, the one where the guy barricaded the doors and shot everyone. I figured you'd like that. Maybe you could make her the only survivor who has these bad dreams or tells me about hiding in a canvas cart. But she'd quit by then. By then she'd made her pension and stayed home all day reading mysteries and listening to the radio.

She doesn't read your books. She likes the ones where you get the same woman detective except they're working on a different case. It's like a TV series, you get the same characters over and over. Like *Cheers*—you know everybody. She goes through two or three a week. She gets them from the library.

When she heard you were going to do the book, she said, 'Anyone but him.'

I said, 'Mom, what do you want, he's the biggest writer in America.'

'He'll do a job on you,' she says. 'He'll make you look bad.'

So just for me, make me look OK, all right?

Anyway we lived on Kickingbird Circle, and I went to school at Northern Hills Elementary. My mom gave me a key so I could get in after school, and she'd always leave me cookies or grapes or a note that said there were popsicles in the freezer, and I could have one if I took it outside. I'd watch *Speed Racer* and maybe *Gilligan's Island*, or go over to Clara Davies's house and play Barbies or Mystery Date or whatever. Then around five-thirty my mom would pull her Tornado into the drive, and ten minutes later my dad would roll up in his Continental, and I'd help make dinner.

It was normal. I had friends. I liked school, especially geography. I belonged to the Glee Club. In gym I was the best at the softball throw. You can check up on all of this, and everyone'll tell you it's true. It wasn't like *Carrie* at all. My shoes were new; no one laughed at my clothes.

The only strange thing about my childhood is that we didn't go to church. Not once. I don't know why that was, maybe because Sunday was a big day at the track. My dad would get up like any other work day and back the Continental out and take off while the rest of Kickingbird Circle was still asleep. Later my mom would make pancakes, and we'd read the paper together at the kitchen table. We read everything, even the stupid cartoons in *Parade* magazine. Our fingers turned gray.

I can hear you thinking it was too normal, it was weird normal. Not true. No one said it was perfect. We wanted to believe that, I think—the kids—but we knew it wasn't true. Darryl Marshall ran over Tallulah, the Underwoods' Siamese. It was mysterious, I guess, because we all crowded around, but I wasn't the one who picked it up with a stick, and that night I didn't worry about it. Before bed I looked out my window at the far-off lights of the city and up at the stars and made the same wish I always did—that my life would always be like this.

4

This is better.

I met Lamont Standiford for the first time ever on Friday, 26 October 1984. I was working the swing shift at the Conoco on the Broadway Extension. I was drinking then. Every night I drank a fifth of vodka. As long as you smoked, they couldn't smell it on you. It was a good job for an alcoholic. All I had to do was punch buttons and accept money. I'd been working there a month and I'd already gotten a dollar raise.

He was driving a firemist red 442 convertible with a black top. I'd seen the car cruising Broadway; there wasn't much to do but look out the window. He pulled up to pump seven, and the light on my board came on. He waved at me to turn the pump on. I hit the button. It was like being a lab rat; the light comes on, you hit the button. Sometimes the customers get angry when you're slow. Not him. He waved to say thank you, and I gave him a smile. He was smoking right next to the NO SMOKING sign. He was slim in black cigarette-leg jeans, and his hair was all over the place, like he'd been riding with the top down. He bent over to fit the nozzle in. I was drunk and I'd just broken up with Rico and I thought it might be nice to have somebody again.

I had a customer to take care of, so I put down my cigarette and made change for him, and then somebody else. When I was done I sat back on my stool and took a drag. I couldn't see him. I thought he'd flipped down his license plate to fill up, but I couldn't see him. I stood up for a better look and saw that he didn't have a license plate, and right then he pulled out and across traffic and was lost in the stream of tail lights.

For every drive-off you had to fill out a form. The more you had, the harder the manager looked at your receipts. Each one made you remember what a crummy job you had. I hit the reset for seven and started filling it out. I hated seeing my handwriting going all over the place. By then I was tired of being a drunk, but there wasn't anything else I could do. I got down to Description of Vehicle and thought how easy it would be to find a car like that, and I started to put down the wrong car. I'd only seen him for a minute but I started to put down a Buick Skylark.

And right when I'm finishing the description, the 442 pulls in again. It's got the grabber hood with rally stripes, raised white letter tires, spinner hubs—nothing fancy, just very tasteful. It pulls right up in front of my window, and out he gets. He swings his hair back out of his eyes and bends down to the hole in the plexiglas, and his pupils are huge. He has these teeth that are almost fangs. I like his eyebrows, the way they bend down at the ends.

'I forget what number I was on,' he says, and slides a twenty into the trough.

'Lucky seven,' I say.

'Yeah,' he says, surprised I know, and looks at me.

I can still bring back that look—his eyes like an eclipse, the way his hair blew around his face, how he hooked a piece out of his mouth with a pinky.

'Nice ride,' I said, and I think we knew. Sometimes love doesn't take much. You just have to be there when it shows up.

My dad wanted to be a jockey but he was too big. He was just over five feet, but by the time I knew him he was heavy. He wore a different-colored windbreaker to work every day, all with his name over his heart—Phil. I never called him anything except Dad, but my friends would say, 'How's old Phil doing?' or 'When's Phil getting home?'

He used to pick me up and swing me by the ankles. I'd ask him all the time. 'Swing me,' I'd say, 'swing me.' He stood in the middle of the living room, spinning to keep up with me. One time he must have gotten dizzy, because my head went right into the side of the TV console. I went right out and when I came to I was on the couch with a towel under my head. My dad had ice in a washcloth. There was blood on it, watered down. He didn't seem worried. He'd probably done this a lot at work.

He was saying my name, but I could barely hear him. Something was humming. The ice came down like he was going to put it in my eye.

'Margie,' he said. 'Margie.'

Every time I could hear it a little better, like the humming was melting away.

My mom came in from the garden; she had dirty gloves on. 'What happened?' she asked, and my father told her. He showed her the washcloth.

She came over and looked down at me. I tried to smile.

'She'll be all right,' she said.

At dinner I fell asleep in my chair. My dad said I just fell right off it. At the hospital the doctor said I had a fractured skull.

On the way home I sat between them in the front seat. My dad was too upset to drive, and my mom kept reaching over me to stroke the back of his neck.

'It's just a hairline,' she said. 'Phil, she'll be fine.'

5

My mom didn't think anything about Lamont. When I met him I was living with two of my girlfriends—Garlyn and Joy—in a bungalow behind the library in Edmond. This was after Rico and me broke up. My mom wasn't talking to me then, for a lot of reasons.

Garlyn and Joy made a place for me. We were all drinking and going through a lot of jobs. But the place was clean, that was one thing we were careful about. Most of our furniture was plants, because Joy had a talent for them. We'd all get up around noon and zombie around the house, cleaning up in slow motion. Garlyn had a crate of old blues records, and we'd get stoned and eat cereal on the couch and listen to Lightnin' Hopkins and Sonny and Brownie.

It's funny, half the songs were these guys in prison for murder. They'd be hooting and hollering stuff like: *I done killed my woman/Don't you know she done me wrong*. They weren't sorry exactly; it sounded like they'd learned something from it, like they wouldn't make the same mistake again. We'd make up our own verses. *I done paid that electric bill/I done just paid it yesterday*. Joy would sing into a beer bottle like it was a microphone and do Janis Joplin or put on a pair of shades for John Belushi. She could do all these dead people. We respected people like that, who'd killed themselves having a big time. We were like them except we weren't famous yet, or dead.

That was the best part of the day then, before we had to get ready for work. We'd sit there drinking and singing until someone said, 'It's that time.' That might be a good place for some wind—when we leave the house in our uniforms. We all had to wear one. Joy worked the drive-in window at Taco Mayo; Garlyn had just moved to Crockett's Smoke House. I'd been at the Conoco only a month or so and I knew that wasn't going to last because I'd already started stealing.

I'd steal cartons of Marlboros and sixes of 3.2 beer. In the beginning it was mostly for myself. Later, when I knew I was going to quit, I'd fill up a trash bag and toss it in the dumpster for Lamont to pick up. Another thing I took was gum. We always had lots of gum—Bubble Yum, Bubblicious, Wrigley's, Carefree. I'd bring it home in my purse. It was good, because I felt like I was doing my part for the house. We all needed it, especially on the job.

That's how Lamont got to know me; he'd take me home after my shift. The first time he offered, I knew he was going to because he'd cruised through the lot twice. He came in around ten to eleven and parked by the air pump. By then I'd finished my bottle and I was feeling all right. At home I had another pint in the freezer, hidden in a box of frozen peas. It was a good time of the night.

He waited until Mister Fred Fred, the graveyard guy, came in. You'd love Mister Fred Fred, he's a whole book in himself. They hired him as part of this outpatient placement thing the state was doing. He was basically nuts. He had this notebook he was filling up with scientific formulas to prove something about the planets. He showed me the diagram once. All the planets were lined up right in line with Oklahoma City—really with Mister Fred Fred. In a circle in a corner there was a smaller diagram showing this lightning bolt going through his head. He was trying to prove the planets were doing something to him, that they were against him somehow. I don't know what he thought anyone was going to do about it if he actually proved it.

I gave Mister Fred Fred his name. Really he gave it to himself, I was just there when he did it. Some counselor guy brought him over from Nancy Daniels, this group home. All he had to do to get the job was fill out an application. Stan the manager brought him in the back of the booth to do it. His hair wasn't completely combed, it was kind of fluffed up in back like he'd been sleeping on it. The counselor guy was saying everyone thought Fred was ready for this big step and how generous it was of us and everything, and meanwhile Fred is filling out the form all by himself. I go in back to get a box of Milky Ways and on my way out I look over his shoulder. The only thing he's filled out is his name. He's circled MR. First name: Fred; last name: Fred. The rest is blank.

That first night Lamont drove me home, Mister Fred Fred came in with his notebook. All he ever said was hello; after that it was like you weren't there. I always said a little extra, thinking it might trigger something.

So I close out my register and sign the tape and slip it into the safe. Mister Fred Fred is already ringing people up. 'Goodnight,' I say real loud, and go outside and wait for Garlyn to pick me up.

But I'm not really waiting for her, I'm waiting for Lamont to come over and offer me a ride. I like that he doesn't right away. The 442 has tinted glass; under the lights the purple turns black, you can't see a thing.

Then he starts the car. It's like an animal, it makes my heart jump. The lights shine right on me. It's silly—I already want him—but it's sweet.

He pops the clutch, and the 442 leaves a streak. It lunges and then stops right in front of me, the exhaust popping. I still can't see anything through the windows.

The passenger door swings open, letting out some vintage MC5. It's like high school, I'm thinking, but so what?

I look around one last time for Garlyn, then get in.

His eyes are the same as the other night, just sucking me in. He smiles and gives me those fangs of his.

'So,' he says. 'Where you want to go?'

I forgot to tell you about Jody-Jo. He didn't make it to Edmond with us. One day he laid down under the glider and died. Nobody noticed until after supper. Usually he'd clean up under the table by licking the rug. It was disgusting. My mom called him, but he didn't come. She found him under the glider and thought he was asleep. She stuck her foot under and pushed his shoulder. She did it again and then knelt down.

'Get your father,' she said.

My dad came out and put one hand on Jody-Jo's neck, like he was trying to take his pulse.

'It doesn't look good,' he said.

My mom was hugging herself, holding her elbows like she was cold. I remember that because she did the same thing at my trial.

My dad got up and held her. 'He lived a long life,' he said, like it was an accomplishment for a dog. He squeezed her and then turned her toward the door, an arm over her shoulder, and I could see he wanted us all to go inside.

My mom went in to finish the dishes while I watched TV. This was way before cable, and out near Depew there wasn't much of a choice of stations. Outside, the glider clanked and screeched. There was some nature show on—animals eating each other—and I went to the front window to see if I could see my dad.

He was wearing my mom's gardening gloves. He had a big trash bag he was trying to stuff Jody-Jo into. He had the twist tie in his teeth. Jody-Jo's back legs kept flopping out. My dad lifted the bag off the floor to get him all in, then closed the mouth, spun it around and fastened the tie. The bag held air like a balloon. When he set it down it toppled over. He threw the gloves on the glider and lit a cigarette, then after a few hits tossed it into the yard. He grabbed the stem of the bag and dragged it across the floorboards. Before he made it to the stairs, it ripped, and one of Jody-Jo's legs fell out.

My dad saw it but didn't stop. He bumped the bag down the stairs and hauled it across the yard all the way to the road, where he leaned it against some other bags. Then he came back and put the glider back where it was supposed to go and brought my mother's gloves inside.

That morning the county garbage truck woke me up, the back of it grinding. I went to my window and watched its lights blinking. The two guys riding the back had sweatshirts with hoods on. They threw the bags in and climbed on again, and the truck pulled away.

At breakfast my mom said Jody-Jo was buried behind the chicken house. Later we took some flowers out. My mom stuck them in the turned dirt like they might grow.

'Dad put him in the trash,' I said. 'The garbage truck squished him.'

'How many times do I have to tell you?' she said. 'If you keep making up stories, no one's going to believe anything you say.'

6

No, I hadn't done that many drugs before I met Lamont. I was pretty conservative. I smoked weed all through high school, but everyone does that. Drank beer, a little vodka, just on the weekends. It was pretty tame. I used to do downs when I could get them—Percodan and Percocet, bootleg Quaaludes. Percocet and gin used to be my favorite. I could watch TV for hours that way. Saturdays we'd go over to Mary Alice Tompkins's house and watch the Sooners destroy somebody. By half-time it didn't even matter. But that was just fun stuff, things kids do.

I did a little acid, maybe five or ten trips in all. It was mostly speed, I think. You'd sweat something terrible, and your fingers would go cold. You'd drop before homeroom and cut the rest of the day and when you got home you'd still be going and you'd have to force yourself to eat. I remember spreading my food around on my plate to make it look like I did. I'm sure my mom thought I was anorexic. Getting up the next day was always tough.

So no, not really. I was pretty straight.

I drank a lot. No one ever says anything about that. It's the Speed Queen thing. It started when I was living by myself. I was going to the university during the day and working at Mister Swiss nights.

Mister Swiss was an old Tastee-Freez made up to look like a chalet. You had to dress up like a milkmaid. All the burgers were named after the Alps; the double-decker was the Matterhorn. The big thing was the sundaes, which they called avalanches. The manager made you say these things. You couldn't say, 'Double cheeseburger,' you had to say, 'Matterhorn.' It was on a speaker so everyone in the place could hear you. Everything they made was fried—burgers, rings, chicken and shrimp baskets. Every other day you had to drain the Fry-o-lator and take the bucket of grease to a special dumpster out back. There was a big grease spot on the parking lot, and when it rained you didn't dare step on it. After your shift you felt like you'd been dipped in oil.

I got home around midnight and I'd take a cold beer into the shower with me. It was my reward for making it through the day. I'd have another while I dried my hair, and then one watching Letterman, and pretty soon I was sleeping in and missing class.

I got put on probation, and my mom said she wouldn't help me pay for classes unless I started doing better, but the next semester was worse. I took some summer classes and did all right, but that fall I got sick and fell behind and just stopped going. I forgot to withdraw, so I got all Fs. My mom said that was it, my dad, who was dead by now, wouldn't have wanted her to throw any more money away. It didn't really matter that much to me; I was only going because he'd wanted me to. It was easier not to. Now all I had to do was go to work.

You might say I was going to school to be an artist or a writer or something. That might be interesting. I never really declared a major, so technically it wouldn't be untrue. All I took were some business courses—statistics and economics, boring stuff. You could make me a painter, and I'd paint weird, runny pictures of my dad, or the house near Depew, or Jody-Jo, or my tricycle out behind the chicken house. I'd meet this other painter from New York City or Paris, and we'd have this unbreakable bond. All we'd do is drink wine and make love by candlelight, and then he'd be killed somehow or die of some rare disease, and I'd start drinking more wine and painting him over and over until I couldn't stand it. I could break a mirror with a bottle and I'd look just like one of my paintings, all runny and weird. Then I'd burn all my paintings and quit Mister Swiss and go work at the drive-thru at Schlotzky's and meet Rico.

Another thing about Jody-Jo is that he had a house. It was under the one tree in the front yard and had actual shingles on the roof. After he was dead I'd sit in it and spy on the cars driving by. You could still smell Jody-Jo; there was a dark ball of hair in one corner. Sometimes I'd close my eyes and pretend I was him. My mom said that he'd gone to heaven, and I wanted to go there too. I couldn't picture what it looked like, I could only see Jody-Jo walking this white path surrounded by cotton-ball clouds. Then I'd see the trash bag and his legs going into the cruncher and I had to open my eyes.

My mom wanted another dog, but my dad said no. It got to be a kind of joke between them, like when she saw a puppy on TV, but they were both serious. When my dad died, my mom went down to the Animal Rescue League and got Stormy. It's funny, she never said my dad went to heaven.

Where am I going to go? I know you'll ask that later. But in case I don't make it there, let me say now that I'm going to heaven. I'm a prayer warrior, and I've had to fight my own evil heart to get there. If Jody-Jo and my dad are there, I'll give them both a big hug. But I don't want to live with them again. I'd like to have a place with Lamont if that's possible, and if for whatever reason it isn't, then I'd like a place of my own.

Hang on, Janille wants something.

Yeah?

Double on the hot links, double on the beans. And sauce, lots of sauce. The hot.

Hold the Texas Toast, or you can have it.

Gimme the regular. I think it's too late for the diet.

Sorry. That was Leo's double-checking my order. Last time they forgot the brisket, and Janille let them hear about it. You like barbecue? You should come out here. I could take you some places.

The Last Supper, right? I'm sure you can do something with that. I'll have to stop the machine for that. You've got to concentrate on good barbecue.

I think I saw an 'Outer Limits' where this guy who's going to the chair asks for this impossible last meal. He just keeps ordering, and the cooks keep bringing the food, and he's eating and eating and getting bigger and bigger until he's too big for the cell, and the bars bend and the concrete cracks and he breaks out. He's as big as Godzilla, and the guards in the towers are shooting at him, but he kicks right through the wall. In the end it's all a dream he's having while he's in the chair. You see him jerking. Rod Serling or whoever is talking about how a man finally becomes free, and they zoom in on the guards unbuckling the straps. When they do that to me, I'll have hot sauce under my nails.

7

What do you mean by evaluated? I was tested in New Mexico when they caught me, but I was never committed or anything. Mr Jefferies said everybody gets those tests. He said we wouldn't use it as a defense because of the judge.

There are some people here who think I'm crazy, and there are some people here who think I did all of it. A lot of them are the same people. I can see why they'd think that, the way they were all cut up. I heard that Sonic took all their ads off the air right after that.

I'm not saying that wasn't me, just that I wasn't the only one. I wasn't the one who started it and I wasn't the one who planned it in the first place; I was just there. When you're there, and it's happening, you don't say, 'Wait, this is crazy.' It's different just sitting somewhere and thinking about it; you think you'd never do it. Then you're there and you do, and there's nothing at all crazy about it.

Those tests are like lie detectors—you can't trust them. They're easy to trick; you just pretend you're someone else.

When I was a kid I used to think I was crazy. I thought I was the only one who could talk inside my head. I'd sit inside Jody-Jo's house and talk to myself.

'Dad put him in a bag,' my inside voice said.

'Mom said he buried him,' I said. It was like two people talking.

'Dig him up and see.'

'With what?' I said.

Sometimes my inside voice would surprise me and say things I didn't know—like the guy in *The Waste Lands*. It would say things I know *I* didn't think.

'With the pitchfork,' it said. 'With Mom's garden shears.'

'It was just a story,' I said.

'With your hands.'

'Dad wouldn't do that.'

'You're just afraid to find out.'

But everybody does that. It's not like voices, it's just the way people think. I used to think it made me crazy. No one told me different, and I wasn't going to ask.

In eighth grade they gave me a test to see what I was best at, one of those ones where you're supposed to describe yourself. You'd say what you'd do if this or that happened to you, like *You find out your friend Mary has been spreading lies about you. What do you do? a) Confront her. b) Say nothing*, and other stuff like that. They wanted to see if you'd be a good waitress or something. I was stoned, so I just filled in all the As.

The next week I got called down to Mrs Drake, the school counselor. She had posters on her walls of seagulls with poetry on them, and ivy plants spilling over her desk. She took her glasses off to talk to me.

'Marjorie,' she said, 'I was looking over the scores, and yours jumped right out at me.'

'I just wrote down all the As,' I said.

'Now why did you do that?'

'I don't know,' I said.

'Have you ever had a problem with anger or aggression?'

Mrs Drake wanted me to retake the test and a bunch of other ones, and I did. I did fine. They were easy. The big one said I would enjoy a career helping other people.

8

I have no idea what my IQ is. In grade school I got Bs and Cs, and then Cs and Ds in high school. I didn't like high school; the teachers made me feel stupid. I didn't see the point. I learned more from watching TV and reading books. My dad had really wanted me to go to college, so I did. Lamont used to call me his college girl. I liked that at first.

I've gotten smarter since I've been here. That's one good thing, it gives you time to think. In the morning one of the trustees rolls the book cart around, and you get to pick one. They've got all of yours, but they're always out. The last one I read was an old one—*Cujo*, I think. I liked it, how the rabies made this regular dog into a monster. At first I thought it would be stupid—I mean, who's really afraid of a dog?—but it was good. You could almost believe something like that could happen.

The cart's got everything: Danielle Steel, Mary Higgins Clark—all the good ones. Sometimes the good pieces are missing, like when you cut coupons out of the newspaper, but I like filling things in on my own.

You're allowed two books of your own here, and one has to be religious. Besides the Bible, I have my road atlas. *Discover America!* the cover says. I lie on my bunk and drive all across the country. I just pick a road and go.

I read the Bible every day. Not much, just a page or so. When Sister Perpetua comes, we talk about it. She's a good teacher, she knows what it's like to lose yourself. She's an orphan. Darcy said her family was on vacation in New Mexico when they were in an accident, and only Sister Perpetua lived. Sometimes I picture it on Route 14, the Turquoise Trail. Maybe they're driving a station wagon, and her dad tries to pass this gravel truck on a blind rise. When she tucks her hair back, her one ear looks like melted wax. Sometimes I come up with things she hasn't thought about, and she nods like she's thinking and says we'll talk about it next time.

She treats me nice, her and Mr Jefferies. Over the years they've never left me like everyone else did. Gainey's still with me. So that's three. If it weren't for them, I don't think I'd be OK now.

So no, I don't know what my IQ is. A hundred something, I guess. I'm not a moron, if that's what you mean. I know what's happening to me.

When they electrocute you, they put this leather helmet on your head. On the top is this bronze knob. It connects to this copper screen inside with a sponge on it. That's the top electrode. They shave your head so it sits right on your skin. The other one's part of the chair; in most states, it's attached to the left leg, sometimes your spine. It's bronze too. They cut the back of your pant leg so it's right against your calf. The straps on the back and the arms they make such a big deal of on TV don't do anything except hold you down.

It's simple. The electricity needs to go from the electrode in the cap to the electrode in the ankle. You're like the piece of wire in a light.

The usual dose is two thousand volts. They do that twice, in some states four times. What's supposed to happen is the current goes through you and stops your heart. What you do is go stiff. All your muscles tense up at once. It doesn't always work like it's supposed to. Back around the turn of the century, one guy went so stiff he ripped the legs off the chair and they had to hold his feet down with concrete blocks. The second jolt made him kick those over. They were going to try a third time, but he'd already died from third-degree burns.

In Florida five years ago they did this guy named Jesse Tafero; when they threw the switch, flames a foot high shot out of his head. Sparks were flying everywhere. The whole place was filled with smoke. When the guards unstrapped him, his skin fell off his bones like boiled chicken. This other guy in Virginia, they got the voltage wrong on him, and the steam built up inside his head until his eyeballs popped and ran down his cheeks. The book I read had all these horror stories. If you made it the chair, you'd be able to use them.

9

I consider myself sane. So does the State of Oklahoma. It's the only thing we agree on.

There's a joke in here, 'I'm as sane as the next person.' Which over on the Row would be Darcy. She's in for running over her stepdaughter with her car. She didn't just run her over once; she got her caught between the bumper and the garage door and kept ramming her till the door broke. She lived a week. Darcy told me the whole story. Her boyfriend was sleeping with both of them and decided to go with the younger one. You might use that for Natalie and me, I don't know.

When I was first in, I might have been insane. Lamont was gone, Natalie was still in the hospital, and I was coming down after a month of just going. I couldn't think of anything. I'd look at the bolt holding the flange of the bunk on the wall, and it would be fascinating but it didn't mean anything. Nothing did. Everything was made of cardboard. The first time Mr Jefferies came to see me, I could see the wires in his head, the gears that made his mouth go. He wanted to steal my secret numbers, so I put my hands over my eyes. I held my breath so I wouldn't hear him. He talked like a recording on the phone; none of the words went together.

'Well,' he said, 'that's all I've got,' and got up to go.

The guard started to take me away, but Mr Jefferies was still looking at me.

'I know what you are,' I said. 'I saw you in the movie of angels. My dad is watching us on TV. He'll get you.'

A few years ago he played that tape for me. I recognized my voice, but it wasn't me. Not that that's any excuse.

People say it was all Lamont's fault, that he was the crazy one and we just did what he told us. I don't think that's true. It's easy to think that now. Like I said, it's different when you're there.

When the detectives cleared out our apartment, I asked them to send me any pictures of Lamont they could find. There were a few envelopes from the Motophoto. I sat down on my bunk to look through them, and there we were sitting on the balcony at Mia Casa, kissing Gainey on each cheek. We were so young. There I was in my bikini, posing like a centerfold on the hood of the Roadrunner. There was even a bunch taken at a barbecue in the courtyard with all our neighbors. It looked like everyone was having a fine time. Even though I knew Natalie had to have taken some of them, Lamont looked happy with me, his arm over my shoulder, his cap pushed back. There was chicken and coleslaw, and everyone had a can of beer, but I couldn't remember when they were taken, what day, what the weather was like. The girl in the pictures was skinny, with long hair, and smiled all the time. It was like looking at a good friend, someone who meant a lot to you once but that you hadn't seen in a long time.

How do you tell if you're insane? I still talk to myself. I remember things that never happened and forget ones that did. Some days I pretend I'm cruising Meridian with Lamont and Gainey in his car seat. This is before Natalie, before any of that. We slide into Coney Island and park under the awning and take turns feeding Gainey fries. We both have the chili-cheese footlong with double onions, and Lamont has to finish mine. Later we roll over to Arcadia Lake and watch the sun set over the water and then go home, and when I'm almost asleep, when I'm lying here with Janille there going through the newspaper, I feel him reach for me. Is that insane?

10

I dream every night. Normal dreams, I think. No more nightmares than anyone else. I don't see the Closes coming to get me, if that's what you mean. I don't see Lamont or the knives or the fire. I'm not afraid to sleep.

I dream of driving across the desert with a cold grape soda. I dream of sleeping beside Gainey on top of the covers. I dream of being out of here.

It's funny how sometimes your dreams don't change even when your life does. I still dream that the Conoco's going to blow up. I'm working swing, waiting for Mister Fred Fred to relieve me, and this car wobbles in. It's muddy like it just came from the bottom of a lake, and its wheels are falling off. It's just like the beginning of *The Stand*—I'm sure that's where I got it from. The guy behind the wheel is drunk or falling asleep or something, and the car just rolls into the pumps. One of the hoses splits open, and the gas pours down on the roof. It's a blue Malibu, the gas washes some of the mud off. In my booth I can see the muffler chugging out exhaust, and the gas streaking down the fender for it. There's no way I can get out from behind the counter. The zodiac scroll dispenser is in the way, and the Slush Puppy machine, all the lighters and ChapSticks and beef jerky; it's like I'm buried. I look up on the monitor, and the Malibu's on fire. The guy's forehead is on the wheel; the horn's going non-stop. There's a sticker by the pump controls that says: IN CASE OF EMERGENCY, FOLLOW CONTINGENCY PLAN, but I can't remember what the plan is.

I never get to the end of the dream, to the explosions I know are coming. I started having the dream the week I started working there. It hasn't stopped since. There really was a sticker that said that. It was a joke; the manager never told us what the plan was. It didn't matter. Back then I was too drunk to be any help anyway. I would have stood there and burned.

I dreamed about my dad for a long time after he died. Saturday mornings he'd bring me to the track and let me watch the stable boys run their workouts. There was hardly anyone else there; you could sit wherever you wanted. In my dream he was sitting high up in the grandstand, and I was climbing the stairs. The stairs had numbers stenciled on them, but the numbers weren't in any order. I kept climbing and climbing, and the sun was hot over the grandstand. He was still sitting there with his hat on, far across the rows. And then the PA would come on—not a voice, just this humming—and I knew I was going to fall against the concrete and I'd feel it against my skin forever.

I still have this dream once in a while, but right after he died I had it every night. And others too. There was one where he was driving his Continental around and around the block, and another where he came home from work and gave me all the change in his pockets. He used to do that in real life, but in the dream all the money was from another country; the coins were square and had holes in them and pictures of birds. Once we were talking, and my mom woke me up. I was mad at her all day.

It wasn't just dreams then. Sometimes I'd see him walking down the street. I'd think it was him from the hair, or his hat. Any short, fat man who walked by. It got so I couldn't go to the mall. The gal who helped Natalie write her book made a big deal of this, like it proved I was crazy. Sister Perpetua said it's absolutely normal, so whatever you want to do with it is fine. I loved my dad and I still miss him. He was a regular guy and doesn't have anything to do with what happened.

11

I don't have many fears for myself anymore. My biggest fear is that Gainey won't know who his parents were. That's one reason I'm making this tape. I don't want him reading Natalie's book and thinking it's the truth.

Honey, I love you and I'm always looking over you, and so's your daddy. I know this won't answer everything. We were young and mixed up. Don't you be that way; you see what it leads to.

That's about it for fears. After a while you understand they're a waste of time. There's only so much you control.

I used to be afraid of the weather. Out near Depew you could see it coming a hundred miles away. You were supposed to get hail right before a tornado. It would get dark, and then you'd hear it dinging off the hood of our car. My mom loved it. 'Look,' she said as it hopped in the grass. 'How big around would you say those are?' She put a slicker on and a pot on her head and ran outside to put the car in the garage. On the way back she filled her apron with hailstones, saving the bigger pieces for the freezer. Jody-Jo stayed under the dining-room table, resting his head on the carpet. I turned the TV on to see which counties were getting hit. The weathermen were on all the channels. Pea-sized, they said, marble-sized—golf-ball, baseball, softball. Outside it was like nighttime. My mom went out on the porch.

'Come see the lightning,' she said.

I'd only go to the door. Leaves flew in around my shins. The glider was going all by itself; the yard looked like it was covered with mothballs. I knew at work my dad would have to calm the horses down. I was afraid one would kick him in the head like they did in the movies. I was afraid he'd be trying to get home, driving with his windshield wipers on high. He'd have to lie in a ditch when the tornado came. His car could roll over on him, or the wind might pick him up, and then there were the wires still shooting sparks, the poles falling like trees.

In the west lightning branched down the sky.

'Marjorie, look!' my mom said. 'Isn't it beautiful?'

Of all the ways they kill people, the only one I'm afraid of is the firing squad. Here's why. It's made up of five people, usually guards. They stand behind this screen with a slit in it, and you sit in a chair with a cloth target over your heart. If they like you, they don't want to be the one to kill you. So what the state does is put a blank in one of the guns. Anyone who's fired a rifle knows a blank doesn't have a recoil like the real thing. It's not like the electric chair, where there's two switches and one's a fake. The same thing goes for lethal injection; there are two buttons that press the plungers. With the firing squad, you know who's doing it.

What happens sometimes is everyone on the squad likes the person, and they all fire away from the heart. It's happened a bunch of times in this country and even more during war. Everyone hits you in the right side of the chest, and you bleed to death while they're reloading. So it's better if they don't like you. When they killed Gary Gilmore, the four shots overlapped at the heart of the target—like a four-leaf clover, the book said.

You asked me about dreams. There's this great dream in *Monty Python* where this guy's about to be shot. The firing squad's locked and loaded on him, and all of a sudden he wakes up in this chaise longue in his backyard. His mom's there, and he says, 'Oh, Mom, thank heavens, it was all a dream.' And his mom says, 'No, dear, this is the dream,' and he wakes up in front of the firing squad again. That's what it's like sometimes, especially this last week.

The firing squad's not very popular any more. Only Utah and Idaho use it. It's worse in foreign countries and during wars. They'll shoot you anywhere. □

GRANTA

MONA SIMPSON
THE DRIVING CHILD

Mona Simpson was born in Green Bay, Wisconsin, in 1957. Her father was a professor of political science and her mother a speech therapist. She attended the University of California, Berkeley, and Columbia. She has published two novels, *Anywhere But Here* (1986) and *The Lost Father* (1992), and her short stories have appeared in *Harper's*, *Granta*, the *Paris Review* and *Ploughshares*. She is a winner of the Whiting Prize and the Lila Wallace award. She was the Hodder Fellow at Princeton University and is now a fellow at Bard College. She lives with her husband and two-year-old son and is working on a collection of short stories and a fourth novel.

'The Driving Child' is taken from her third novel, *A Regular Guy*, which will be published by Knopf later this year.

Jane was born in Gray Star, a settlement in remote Eastern Oregon, where her cries were lost in miles and miles of orchards stilled by a constant rain. One of the people who lived in the commune drove to town to wire her mother Mary's message to Tom Owens. Eight days later she'd heard nothing. Staring out at the endless gray, Mary wrote a letter to her mother and told her she'd named the baby Jane, the name she'd years ago given her only doll.

Mary and Jane had moved many times in the decade since, always because of a man. First there was the one who repaired string instruments and lived with nine cats. He gave Mary a guitar and made a high chair where he allowed Jane to eat with her hands. Then, for a long time, there was the man who constantly traveled, following the greatest band on earth; he left them a truck after he'd only begun to teach Mary chords. Then came their months in Seattle with the man who almost eclipsed Owens because he was beautiful, although he wanted to see them only on weekends and said goodbye every Sunday by noon. Though he professed little aptitude for children, he taught Jane to read because he couldn't stand the garbled language of toddlers and wanted to rush her to the age of conversation. It was this man who first showed them Owens's picture in the newspaper. With the small photograph, composed of dots, Mary tried to prove to Jane that Owens was her father.

The city man's weekends shrunk. When his visits began at midnight on Saturday, Mary and Jane moved again. But by then Tom Owens seemed to them the most famous man in the world.

They moved to a mountain town where they lived in a wooden cabin at a camp once operated, during the warm months, by the park service. There, around a campfire, Jane told a group of children her father was rich.

'And I'm heir to the crown of Curaçao,' a boy replied. Actually it wasn't unusual for the children Jane met in communes and ashrams to claim lineage so distant it would be impossible ever to trace while they lived in trailers and trucks on bare mattresses.

Jane understood that no place they had ever lived was where they were from. Auburn was the name of that place, and although she'd never seen it she knew it from her mother's stories. She drew the one wide Main Street blue with yellow lanterns and ended it in a pink square where there was a newspaper-and-tobacco shop and a movie palace. She rimmed the town with stunted peach groves and palms full of dates and set houses in every direction, each with its own yard and fruit-bearing tree. At night she imagined the town sighing as the sky turned pink, then slowly dark. Jane had seen Auburn on only one old postcard they'd found in a dusty drugstore, showing horses and carriages instead of cars.

Unlike most towns, Auburn had been started by one person who'd had an idea. He had stopped there not because the place was beautiful or different. In fact it so exactly resembled land he'd already covered that only the collapse of his young wife made him stop. She had been called Auburn for the color of her hair. Once she was buried there, he would never leave. Others in his party noticed the kindness of the evening, a faint sweet smell emanating from pink-white flowers in the dark. The man envisioned a clean town, no saloons, where ordinary people could grow their living. A self-instructed engineer, he divided the land into lots of equal size and directed water to the highest spot in each parcel with a cement pipe. Over the next decades more immigrants arrived, wealthy New Englanders from the long sail around the Horn, midwesterners in covered wagons, off the overland route and eventually on Pullman coaches, with modest expectations for the smell of fruit trees wafting through their afternoon rest. By then Auburn had become an apricot town.

Mary sometimes ached, missing the soft blurry start and end to the days in Auburn.

But when Jane asked when they'd return, she replied, 'That cow town? What do you want to go there for?'

Mary di Natale had grown up on an old road in the part of town where overland settlers had built small brick houses like those they'd left, matchboxes on big yards with ancient trees.

Mary's mother supported herself with her husband's small bakery. She became famous as far away as Fresno for her wedding cakes that gave a mysterious happiness, caused by a secret ingredient that only Mary knew was wild flowers broken into the batter.

Although she'd never been there, Jane felt she would recognize the dead-end road near the train tracks where prim brides of all ages stood in line. As a girl, her mother played in white ruffled dresses with a bow in her hair. These came from Browns' catalogue, the same as other children's, but Jane's grandmother favored the less durable styles.

When Jane heard her mother's stories, she wanted that white dress with the white bow. Her clothes, like the other children's, were muddy colors from being collectively washed.

'Can't you write to her and ask if I can have it?'

Mary sighed. 'Someday we'll go back. I don't want you wearing dresses anyway.' This was an idea she'd heard once from a man and kept because her own childhood dresses had no pockets, and she couldn't collect things except in her skirt, and then her underpants showed.

'By the time we go back, they won't fit anymore.'

'I'm sure she saved a few. Like the communion dress. That she'll have.'

Jane's grandmother had delivered eighteen intricate cakes with small beans in their pale-bellied centers so that Mary could have her first communion wearing a silk dress and Jane's own wedding veil, cut down. Wax orange blossoms held the lace on her head.

'You look just like a little bride,' Phil the milkman had whispered.

It was windy that day, and Mary felt so light from fasting, having eaten only a paper-thin wafer, that when the old nun led them up a hill by a rope that had loops for their hands, she believed it was to keep them tethered, to prevent them, in their white dresses, from billowing away.

'Why don't I get to have a first communion?' Jane asked.

'Because the Pope's a liar,' her mother said.

Jane's grandmother silently conducted 284 weddings in Auburn. She baked the brides' cakes, wired mortified bees and pressed butterflies into attendants' bouquets and took the festal photographs. She'd thought about her own daughter's wedding since the day Mary was born and every year, on her birthday, presented her with a silver knife, fork or spoon to contribute to an eventual nuptial set. When Mary announced that she was moving out to live with Owens, her mother immediately disowned her. She had never liked Owens, not then, nor later when he appeared on the covers of magazines, because he didn't know decent manners.

By then Mary had become slovenly and lank-haired, a disgrace to her mother, who tried to maintain the standards of a Frenchwoman in Auburn, wearing a permanent bun so no one could have the slightest apprehension of finding a strand of hair in their cake.

'She says she's from France,' Mary heard them say, behind her mother's back, 'but we all know she's a Belgian.'

Owens and Mary lived together for one summer. In September he went to Harvard. Mary sent him a twelve-inch chiffon nasturtium cake in the mail but received no letter of thanks.

By Christmas, when Owens returned, he had renounced all food but rice and beans and the smallest increment of green vegetables. He rented a cheap house near Auburn's only highway, splitting it with Mary and his friend Frank.

In the house that shook with the rumble of trucks, this was a period of giggling love, repeated chases that ended with her caught on the soft bed, and pancakes for dinner at midnight. But at her job at the dimestore cash register Mary sometimes cried because she and Owens hadn't known each other as children.

She wanted to get him off alone, somewhere simple and small. Her dreams at that time were always dreams of closure. And he did sometimes say, 'Well, maybe if this thing doesn't work, I'll just go and live on an apple farm. In the mountains somewhere.'

Owens wanted to establish a business where everyone was young. He had already proven himself unable to work with bosses. He and Frank both had the nightshift now at the company that employed half the valley. The nightshift was where they put misfits and Mexicans.

Mary got pregnant accidentally, and from the day she told him, he made it clear that her condition held no enchantment.

Every day he was up and out of the house by noon. At that time Owens and Frank were inventing the business that would later make them famous and put their drowsy valley town on the map of the world.

The last day of her life in Auburn Mary did the unthinkable and burst in on him at work. She had never been to the place where he and Frank planned their empire because it was the basement of Owens's parents' house. She'd expected test tubes, Bunsen burners, petri dishes, chemicals, wires, smoke and possibly a conveyor belt, but instead she found Frank whistling 'I've Been Working on the Railroad', while Owens stirred his beans and rice on a hotplate. The only evidence of scientific activity was an open ruled notebook with pencilled equations. The rest of the basement seemed to be a woodshop.

'Owens,' she said, 'we've got to decide what to do.'

He lifted his hands to a loose position of prayer, while Frank climbed the stairs.

'You can stay, Frank,' Owens called, but the whistling became fainter, and then they heard the door bang.

'I can't have a baby now, Mary.' With one cupped hand he touched her hair. Mary closed her eyes and basked. Her neck weakened, and the weight of her head fell to him. It had been a very long time since he was kind to her. But it occurred to her that she would have to choose between him and his child.

'I've just started something,' he whispered. 'It's brand new. I've got to give it time. It's young.'

'What about me? I'm starting something too.'

'I didn't ever ask you to get pregnant.'

'But now it's happened, and we have to deal.'

Their fight escalated until he threw the beans at her. He noticed, as she walked away with the mess on her shirt, that her breasts had become large. The only vanity he'd ever suspected in her was the tendency to wear T-shirts back-to-front. Some girls in high school said she did it to show off her figure, but he knew now that was a lie. Mary was guileless.

Mary had been pregnant at nineteen. She had gone with her predicament and asked strangers for advice, as if carrying the small globe of her life and offering it to them. This made a mission of a youth that had previously lacked direction. Mary kept asking until she found someone to say yes.

She had her tea leaves read by an old woman near the

railroad tracks who told her that life is a long time, and good-for-nothing young men are always abundant, plenty to pick from, like weed flowers. The milkman's daughters, who went to church every Sunday, their heads covered by the thinnest veils of spider webs, whispered the ingredients of remedies to flush out the mistake.

Only one person offered a different solution: a Buddhist priest who lived on a high ridge of the coastal range, eclipsed half the day and all the night in fog. He had not mastered English and he said only, 'Child is a miracle.' But that was enough to start Mary on the journey that led her to seek refuge on a communal apple farm in Eastern Oregon, where everyone was responsible for cleaning up, and every meal included apples.

For ever after Jane's mother blamed the Buddhists because the priest never sent the smallest check to help.

Owens visited them once in the mountain camp. He came at night, while Jane was asleep, and she remembered the visit afterwards as in a silver dream. She'd heard the racket of a car and felt the milky heat of headlights, but then she rolled over and fell into an embracing sleep like swimming into a spot of kinder water in a lake.

He and Mary hauled Jane up, opening her from a curled position. He spread her across his outstretched legs, measuring. Mary tilted down to the floor with a candle. Mary had always believed her daughter was a rare beauty.

Owens put his fingers on Jane's knee, through a hole in her green stretch pants.

'She has your forehead,' Mary said, pulling back her daughter's bangs to show him.

They did that all night, isolating a part of her anatomy and saying it belonged to one or the other. And they both looked at her with wonder, because she was a physical marvel—the only thing they had in common now and could agree on.

They played a game on the floor, drawing a grid with their fingers in the dust.

'I'm five ahead of you and eight ahead of Mom,' Jane said, grabbing her feet and rocking her small body. Jane competed avidly, sucking her hair for inspiration, rocking, shrieking when she won. The score finally finished with him first, Jane second, her mother far behind. And that seemed to settle them all.

The next morning the floor was swept, and there was no trace of him, except the stack of new, unbent money on the kitchen table.

Jane couldn't remember what he looked like.

There was another man now, Mack Soto, who had two boys of his own and a fat, short wife who had once been petite.

Mack drove to the winter camp one night, while his wife had her book club. His coming made a party. They lit candles and drank brandy. In the deep middle of the night they sent Jane outside to walk.

'We're lucky he has no girl,' Mary had said. 'He always wanted a girl. She did too, I suppose.' The fat, short wife who had once been petite took to her bed when her second son was born. She got up again two months later wanting no more children and refusing to let him touch her, except to rub her head.

Jane and Mary were always like this, knowing intricate stories about other people, while the other people knew nothing about them, not even that they were alive. Jane wondered if her father understood how they ran out of money and worried about what they would eat.

Jane walked the long road, her shoes so soft the bottoms of her feet felt pine needles. Stars touched the tops of her hands like bites, and trees on both sides drew up tall, tilting. She pulled the caps off acorns with her fingernails and chewed the bitter, green meal.

She was drunk too. Her mother didn't like to leave her out, and Jane craved the taste of liquor, like harsh dissolved candy. She fingered uncurled pine cones in her jacket pocket to steady herself under the close, stinging stars.

She ended up shivering and vomited, heaved out like an animal, then cold, curled up by the side of the dirt road. Her mother came later, searching the ground with a flashlight, her slippers whispering, and the red wool plaid robe itchy when she gathered Jane in her arms.

'Look,' she said, turning Jane to the millions of small stars, which seemed to fleck the sky with chalk. 'Do you believe in God?'

'Yes,' Jane said cautiously, as if she'd guessed the right answer but didn't know why.

Mack's feet hung blunt off the edge of the bed, pointed stiff, like a butcher animal's. She had touched the hoof of a hanging cow once—it was dry like that.

The next morning the liquor woke them hard and early. Mack was gone, and there was no money on the table, only white rings where glasses ate the wood near bulbous candle wax.

'I give up, you win,' Mary said, not to Jane.

All day they never left the cabin's one room. But the outside lured Jane. Bright-colored insects ticked against the screens, high pines slowly waved.

'Can we get something to eat? I'm hungry.

'Do you want me to bring you a glass of water?

'Mom, when are you going to get up?'

There was never any answer, only the breathing, the snagging torn breath that seemed to fill not only the space of the small cabin, but time itself.

Jane watched the day, tempting, effervescent, behind the screen. But she couldn't live without her mother.

It seemed hours they lay there, turning on the sour sheets. The busy optimism of the world passed—they heard the habits of civilization roll and clank by, rushing the highway, delivering food and milk to apartment dwellers on patios in distant cities, to the whistles and confetti shouts of children outside.

Mary and Jane had always been different anyway. They never read the newspaper or heard radio—they couldn't keep the daily habits when they tried and often were slow and late.

As the noises outside leapt and grew, Jane discovered the suspended pleasure of resignation.

Her mother woke, rubbing her own head. 'I can't anymore,' she said, smiling down haplessly, the way Mack had said to her, on his hands and knees when their affair was young, 'I can't help it,' and the same way he had said, the night before, 'She knows everything and she's forgiven me.'

Sunday, Mary stayed in bed, and a pink cup of coffee floated before her. They hadn't eaten anything for days now. Jane stood in the cool air like a statue, holding the cup. Clouds outside meant evening. Mary sat up on the bed and sipped, then began to move.

They drove out to Tastee Freeze, half an hour away. They sat at a table on the tar lot, cluttered with dry spills and autumn flies. The highway spread serene, lavender, the land quieting, tall grass blurry at the top. They ate hamburgers, warm grease darkening their yellow wrappers, and drank malteds, thick and hard to suck through flimsy straws. Jane stuck her fingers in and licked off the sweetness. She never used knives and forks, and Mary blamed the long-ago violin-maker who'd let her eat with her hands.

Time returned to Jane's body, drop by drop, through the straw. Tomorrow would be school again, the bus. She put one hand between her rump and the metal bench. Her mother would write a note. The teacher would nod once and take the scrap of paper without reading it, put it in her left top drawer. The teacher was used to children from the camp; most of them fared poorly in school and, like Jane, came for the chocolate milk they gave out free. Even as long as she'd been gone, ten days, going back didn't frighten Jane. They did the same things in school each day anyway. The minutes passed slowly, as if they were sorting sand into its constituent elements: granite, crystal, lava.

When her hand fell asleep, she blew on it.

Mary watched her daughter with exhausted relief. Jane was not a sensitive child. She was mainly this—eating with her fingers, slowly, after twenty hours of dizzy hunger, without regular days or school. This was the way she knew happiness, her foot on the bench, the other heel kicking metal, the bite of wet gold-brown meat against the cold.

Mary's own childhood had been all rules, napkins at table, a dessert served on flowered china with her glass of milk. She'd wanted anything but the sameness of that house, though she missed it sometimes now.

A wind slipped in her sleeves and touched her ribs, making her shiver. They both wore old soft clothes. 'Honey, I'm going to send you to your dad,' she said. 'I'd take you myself, but I can't. I just don't think I can.'

Her daughter knew when not to say anything. But she pulled her knee closer, blew on it, softening a scab with her tongue. 'I don't even know him,' she finally said.

Her mother's round face looked out into the distance. 'You met him that once.'

'Was at night. I don't remember.'

'He's got a house and all now. And a lotta lotta money. He's an important man down there. He might even be governor someday. Governor. Wouldn't you like to be the governor's daughter?'

'No.'

'Yes you would. Later you would.' Mary sighed. She unclasped her purse and gave Jane money for two swirled ice-cream sundaes with nuts. 'I'm going to teach you to drive.'

The only car they had was a truck, and it was old. Jane herself was nine.

Teaching Jane to drive took a long time. She stopped going to school. As the fall progressed, they absorbed themselves in the nesting of the truck. Mary fitted pillows to the seat, sewing telephone books in between padding and stitching on a slipcover, so Jane sat fifteen inches above the regular cracked vinyl. They had to strap wood blocks to the brake and gas and clutch pedals so Jane's feet could reach. But the blocks slid, and they couldn't trust the straps and finally borrowed a drill from the Shell station and attached the wood with deep barnum screws. Never once did Mary call Mack, although his long letters arrived every day, small forlorn script in blue ink on yellow lined paper.

'They're probably having some bad times,' Mary said, 'but little moments of contentment too, I suppose.' They both waited a moment, reverent to the idea of marriage, the two boys, Mack and the fat, displeased wife sitting down to supper around one table.

'He says she's on a diet,' Mary read from the letter. Mack used to tell them stories about his wife's weight. When I married her she was a wisp of a thing, he'd said softly.

'Remember the time she ate the big zucchini,' Jane said. Once he'd made a week's worth of stuffed zucchini, a huge oversized squash as big as an arm, and she'd come in after her book group and scarfed it all down.

'She tries to diet and then gets mad at herself,' Mary pondered. 'She should just accept that's the way she is.'

The fixing of the seat took six days, sewing, adjusting the padding so the phone books wouldn't slip and the sides rose up to enclose Jane. Fortunately, the truck's long stick shift was easy for her to reach. Mary taught a little every day and tested Jane. Where is the choke? OK, do it. Lights, brights, wipers, emergency brake. They fixed the broken back window with tape and a piece of cardboard. Mary sealed the seams with clear nail polish.

Then the real lessons started. They went on an old road, columns of trees on both sides, straight as far as they could see. They practiced starting, the gradual relay of clutch and gas. Jane found the brake again and again until it was easy. When the car sputtered and died on the late afternoon road, no one knew.

Clouds bagged huge and magnificent.

In the rosy, cricket-loud dusk, Jane shifted and pedaled, as naturally as a woman they'd seen once playing the organ in an empty church.

Mary made her do it all again with her eyes closed, which was like swimming in rain.

On Thanksgiving Jane sat on the end of the mattress while her mother brushed her hair straight up from her head, pulling it tight, then braided it into a basket around her ears. She dressed Jane warmly, with two pairs of socks in her new shoes.

Mary rolled down the top of the grocery bag, with Jane's four twinkies, fig newtons, an apple and a banana.

Then everything was done. Jane's braids were tight, and her scalp still felt as if someone were pulling her up by the hair. She sat on the bed, hands clutching under the mattress.

Her mother knelt on the floor. She took off Jane's left shoe and rolled down the double sock.

'Now, I'm giving you money,' she said without smiling. 'That's twenty, forty, sixty, seventy. And one, two, three, four, five ones. That's a lot of money, do you hear?'

Jane noticed that her mother kept no dollars for herself, and this frightened her.

'Now, don't, whatever you do, let anyone see you when you take that out.' Her mother folded each bill into a small triangle, like a flag, and put them in the bottom of the sock. She pushed the shoe on over Jane's heel, tied the laces and patted it finished.

'Now don't take it out when you don't need to, do you understand? Because it was hard to save that. And here.' She pulled the special undershirt over Jane's chest. She'd sewn in a pocket to hide her ring—as proof. Years ago Owens had given her the ring hidden inside a cherry pie. She'd sent him pictures of Jane every season, but he had never acknowledged them, so they couldn't be sure.

They watched the sky change, waiting. Finally stars glittered against black, and Mary clapped a hat on Jane's head. With the hat and the height of the telephone books, no one would see Jane was a child.

Mary fixed a glass of coffee the slow way and fed it to Jane with a spoon, as she had when Jane was a much younger child. From the first taste Jane knew her mother had used the last sugar.

'Now I don't want you to go.' Mary laughed a little.

'I don't want to go either,' Jane said, her hands lifted, soft on her mother's shoulders.

'But it'll be better for you there. Really. It's the best thing, my little paw. He'll have a house, and you'll get your own bedroom. He'll probably buy you your own bike.'

For a moment Jane lapsed to imagine. She'd seen a television show once where children ran around an obstacle course hammering bells, winning a prize with each ding. But in less than a minute Jane went from being someone who'd always wanted many things to someone for whom prizes, if they rained on her now, came too late. 'I won't have a mother,' she said plainly, as they walked under the high, cloudless sky.

In a tree above the truck, Jane saw an owl. She pressed closer to her mother, listened to her heart like the far sound inside a shell and felt the pull of an empty immensity, the attraction of wind, the deep anonymous happiness of sleep. 'I want to stay with you.'

'No,' her mother said, separating their bodies, the way a lover might.

Through the window, her mother pulled on the truck's lights, illuminating the invisible before them, and Jane had the sensation of being pushed, as she had been years earlier, trying to learn to ride a bike. In no time at all she was down the road, the cabin contracting in the small rounded mirror. She stopped the truck, leaned out the window and cried, 'Mama!'

Her mother's choked voice echoed back through trees. 'Go on ahead, Jane. Go now.'

Jane drove.

Her mother had taught her patiently and well, at dusk while others ate their supper. Jane saw her own leg, long for a ten-year-old, reaching the wooden block pedal, and she thought of her mother and the man who was her father marveling over her parts and understood, for the first time, *this is why*. The world seemed for a moment to have become clear, and remarkable uses for her brow, arms, cheekbones and widow's peak would soon become apparent: she could use them to cross mountains, to collapse distance and to fly back in time.

She rounded a curve and felt herself flying already—sitting so high in the truck, she could feel the velocity and whistling air—but her hands steered the wheels back into chronological time without her, and she drove down a long simple road. Her mother's pencil-drawn map lay on the seat next to her. She was traveling west, with an old sense of which way west was.

Jane understood she was driving at night so shadows would conceal her childhood. Her mother had put her to bed six afternoons, waking her late and leading her on stumbling walks outside, to prepare her dreams for daylight and accustom her eyes to the dark.

There was no heat or radio in the truck, there never had been, and the sounds that entered through cracks were sounds of the world repairing itself in its sleep. Animals moved in the distance; water seeped somewhere invisible. Jane listened to the sounds people almost never hear and forgot about driving and then snapped erect at attention when she caught herself swinging hammock-like into the lurching swoon of sleep. She opened the window and drove rigid, eating the air.

No one passed but twice mile-long semis, and then it was clutching the wheel hard through an arc like an amusement park ride, the noise so whole it took you up in it. And it wasn't up to her if it let you down again or not. But it did, and she was still there, her teeth chattering loose, the truck wobbling on the plain, dark road.

For the rest of her life, moments from that night would rise into Jane's memory to haunt and enchant her, though the sequence of the drive itself remained as much a mystery to her as to those she told the story, so that finally she could claim only what her great-grandmother had once said after lifting a Ford off the junkyard ground to save her child's back: 'I don't know how I did it. I couldn't do it again now if you paid me.'

Jane wanted to stop and lay down in the seat but she was afraid of the day. What if she couldn't make herself wake up? She had the clock, she could put it by her ear or inside her shirt on her chest. She decided to pull over and eat just one fig newton. That would help. But it tasted dry and strong; she didn't really like them without milk. Water from the round canteen tasted metallic, sticking to the back of her teeth. She finally let herself sleep, holding the clock against her chest, then woke with a start after only a quarter-hour. On her knee she had a scab. She picked it off and ate it, liking the tough opening taste of blood.

Her mother had warned her not to let the gas go down to empty. She had painted a red line on the glass gauge with nail polish. But now the needle was hovering below, and there was no filling station. When Jane felt frightened, she pulled on the wheel and made herself sit up straight. 'I will always sit up straight from now on,' she told herself.

She made numerous promises to any God that night. By the end she'd promised her whole life away to goodness.

Later the road widened, and she stopped at a gas station, got her money out and put her hat back on. She was trembling, and her knee jumped when the man came out to help her. He was an old man and small.

'Fill 'er up?'

She handed him one of the twenties.

'Okie dokie.'

She picked a scab from her elbow, watching. When he put the hose back in its slot, she drove away. That was done.

At one point Jane began singing all the songs she knew, the night everywhere around dimensionless and still beginning, and she came to understand that she knew very few songs, and of those she remembered only one verse and a scattered mess of words with spaces between. Most were from camp meetings, and she despised them. After 'The Farmer in the Dell', she tried the Beatles songs her mother liked to hum.

She tried to do numbers then—picturing them, the line, the-carry-the-one—and for a while she named the things she knew. Capitals lasted nine states, history was little better, and she remembered only the first two lines of a poem she'd once had to memorize: '*By the shore of Gitchee Gumee, By the Shining Big-Sea-Water* . . . ' She now understood the point of memorizing. Rhymes and numbers and state capitals and presidents could keep you awake at a time like this. All Jane knew was what she hated.

But she had been doing other things while her classmates chanted their multiplication tables. Jane stored things outside. In the tree hollow she had taken seven acorns, unfitted their hats and sprinkled each with salt: that was for Mack to come back to her mother. She'd made offerings too for weather and the end of weather. She didn't plan. Each commandment came complete, sometimes in school, and she had to obey. One time she took a nest down and put in the three broken parts of her mother's sparkly pin. These were her small duties that guaranteed nothing. But if she did not do them, it could be worse.

She drove that night in a straight line, through a storm, the crack of lightning, trees of white, sheets of water dividing, spray on both sides, and it came to her that she had passed into the other world where her mother was dead. Jane felt sure her mother was going to die because that was the only reason she could imagine they had to be apart. Her mother so pretty and, everyone always said, so young. 'Yeah?' Mary questioned, with a strange expression, whenever Jane reported a compliment. Mary didn't trust people talking about them. She felt always alert to the possibility that they were making fun of her.

Jane had never had a death yet. Mary had told how she'd leaned down and kissed her mother in the coffin. And Jane had the picture now of her mother dead. She would be dead the same way she had been a thousand times on the bed, sleeping, the way her face went, lying down, everything draped from her nose. Jane started crying for herself because she didn't even get to kiss her mother.

In the beginning, more things were alive: plants felt, something commanded, creatures lived in the sky. The morning after her trip to her father, she work up in a hole of dirt, her mouth full of stones, her hands smelling of gasoline.

The most terrible and wondrous experience in Jane di Natale's life was over by the time she was ten, before she'd truly mastered the art of riding a bicycle.

Dawn began long before light. The air tasted now like something you could drink. Dark weeds by the side of the road swayed, as tall as men. Sooner than she expected, the first turn came.

She thought again of her acorns and what she'd forgotten. She was supposed to glue the caps back on over the salt, but they had no glue. This was to be sure the man found her mother in time. Last night this lapse made her wince, but now it seemed nothing, a breath on air. She understood she would never believe in her childish powers again.

The sky was lightening in thick bands of color. Highway signs worked. She would find his house today. And she would discover the town she had been promised since she was born. She would use signs and numbers and songs of outside now. But she would have to learn them, system by system, in a new school.

For the first time Jane wondered who built the roads, and if there was one person sprawled somewhere, like she had on the floor with her crayons when she had drawn the whole world, plotting the highways, wondering how one person got the men to build them, and where the money came from, and was that person God when he made the lakes and the dry land or was it the president? They were still building new highways all the time. That was what those striped mixing trucks were that you sometimes got stuck in back of. One of them had dropped glop on the road where she went to school, and kids ran up to write their names with sticks and put their hand prints forever in the sidewalk.

There in the mountains was an uneven corner with the imprint of Jane's small hand.

When she finally saw the town, it was alive with order. A flock of children walked in sunlight to their everyday school. Men sat outside a tobacco shop, reading newspapers. It had all been going on without her and her mother.

After her drive, when she became a passenger again, she always buckled her seat belt without being asked. Danger had little allure for her, no music. In fact she seemed to retain almost no desire for her earlier life, the whisper of a dawn wind, the cold promise of an autumn moon over the high sierras, when all the tourists have gone home and woodsmoke spikes the air and the ones who are left are those you will know your childhood with. Her only remnant of nostalgia seemed to rise with inclement weather. Storms reminded her of the years when she inhabited a larger region. Less than a forest but in every way different from a home.

Then she would find herself—no coat, no umbrella, soaked shoes—running across roads, darting and slanting, daring cars, gauging the density and smear of headlights. She yearned to live unsheltered again and to recognize: this rain is the voice of the world. When teeth chatter, and the body shivers beyond control, this is the real cold, the real hunger.

In the mountains she had eaten her scabs. It was a habit she could never quit.

Here she vowed she would become normal. She would walk right up to her father's door and knock. □

GRANTA

MELANIE RAE THON
XMAS, JAMAICA PLAIN

Melanie Rae Thon was born in 1957 in Kalispell, Montana, where her father was an architect. She graduated from the universities of Michigan and Boston, and has also lived in Arizona and New York, where she taught in the graduate creative writing program at Syracuse University.

She has published two novels, *Meteors in August* (1990) and *Iona Moon* (1993), and a collection of stories, *Girls In the Grass* (1991). Her work has appeared in the *Hudson Review*, the *Ontario Review* and the *Threepenny Review*. This summer she moves to Colombus, Ohio, to take up a teaching appointment at Ohio State University.

'Xmas, Jamaica Plain' is taken from a second collection of stories, *First Body*, which will be published next year by Houghton Mifflin.

I'm your worst fear.

But not the worst thing than can happen.

I lived in your house half the night. I'm the broken window in your little boy's bedroom. I'm the flooded tiles in the bathroom where the water flowed and flowed.

I'm the tattoo in the hollow of Emile's pelvis, five butterflies spreading blue wings to rise out of his scar.

I'm dark hands slipping through all your pale woman underthings; dirty fingers fondling a strand of pearls, your throat, a white bird carved of stone. I'm the body you feel wearing your fox coat.

I think I had a sister once. She keeps talking in my head. She won't let go. My sister Clare said: *Take the jewelry; it's yours.*

My heart's in my hands: what I touch, I love; what I love, I own.

Snow that night, and nobody seemed surprised so I figured it must be winter. Later I remembered it was Christmas, or it had been, the day before. I was with Emile who wanted to be Emilia. We'd started downtown, Boston. Now it was Jamaica Plain, three miles south. *Home for the holidays*, Emile said, some private joke. He'd been working the block around the Greyhound Station all night wearing nothing but a white scarf and black turtleneck, tight jeans. *Man wants to see before he buys*, Emile said. He meant the ones in long cars cruising, looking for fragile boys with female faces.

Emile was sixteen, he thought.

Getting old.

He'd made sixty-four dollars: three tricks with cash, plus some pills—a bonus for good work, blues and greens—he didn't know what. Nobody'd offered to take him home, which is all he wanted, a warm bed, some sleep, eggs in the morning, the smell of butter, hunks of bread torn off the loaf.

Crashing, both of us, ragged from days of speed and crack, no substitute for the smooth high of pure cocaine, but all we could afford. Now, enough cash between us at last. I had another twenty-five from the man who said he was in the circus once, who called himself the Jungle Creep—on top of me he made that sound. Before he unlocked the door, he'd said: *Are you a real girl?* I looked at his plates, New Jersey—that's why he didn't know the lines, didn't know the boys as girls stay away from the Zone unless they want their faces crushed. He wanted me to prove it first. Some bad luck once, I guess. I said: *It's fucking freezing. I'm real. Open the frigging door or go.*

Now it was too late to score, too cold, nobody on the street but Emile and me, the wind, so we walked, we kept walking. I had a green parka, somebody else's empty wallet in the pocket—I couldn't remember who or where—the coat stolen weeks ago and still mine, a miracle out here. We shared, trading it off. I loved Emile. I mean, it hurt my skin to see his cold.

Emile had a plan. It had to be Jamaica Plain, *home*—enough hands as dark as mine, enough faces as brown as Emile's—not like Brookline where we'd have to turn ourselves inside out. Jamaica Plain where there were pretty painted houses next to shacks, where the sound of bursting glass wouldn't be that loud.

Listen, we needed to sleep, to eat, that's all. So thirsty even my veins felt dry, flattened out. Hungry somewhere in my head, but my stomach shrunken to a knot so small I thought it might be gone. I remembered the man, maybe last week, before the snow, leaning against the statue of starved horses, twisted metal at the edge of the Common. He had a knife, long enough for gutting fish. Dressed in camouflage but not hiding. He stared at his thumb, licked it clean and cut deep to watch the bright blood bubble out. He stuck it in his mouth to drink, hungry, and I swore I'd never get that low. But nights later I dreamed him beside me. Raw and dizzy, I woke, offering my whole hand, begging him to cut it off.

We walked around your block three times. We were patient now. Numb. No car up your drive, and your porch light blazing, left to burn all night, we thought. Your house glowed, yellow even in the dark, paint so shiny it looked wet, and Emile said he lived somewhere like this once, when he was still a boy all the time, hair cropped short, before lipstick and mascara, when his cheeks weren't blushed, before his mother caught him, and his father locked him out.

In this house Emile found your red dress, your silk stockings. He was happy, I swear.

So why did he end up on the floor?

I'm not going to tell you; I don't know.

First, the rock wrapped in Emile's scarf, glass splintering in the cold, and we climbed into the safe body of your house. Later we saw this was a child's room, your only one. We found the tiny cowboy boots in the closet, black like Emile's, but small, so small. I tried the little bed. It was soft enough but too short. In every room your blue-eyed boy floated on the wall. Emile wanted to take him down. Emile said: *He scares me.* Emile said your little boy's too pretty, his blond curls too long. Emile said: *Some night the wrong person's going to take him home.*

Emile's not saying anything now, but if you touched his mouth you'd know. Like a blind person reading lips, you'd feel everything he needed to tell.

We stood in the cold light of the open refrigerator, drinking milk from the carton, eating pecan pie with our hands, squirting whipped cream into our mouths. You don't know how it hurt us to eat this way, our shriveled stomachs stretching; you don't know why we couldn't stop. We took the praline ice cream to your bed, one of those tiny containers, sweet and sickening, bits of candy frozen hard. We fell asleep, and it melted, so we drank it, thick with your brandy, watching bodies writhe on the TV, no sound: flames and ambulances all night; children leaping; a girl in mud under a car, eight men lifting; a skier crashing into a wall—we never knew who was saved and who was not. Talking heads spit the news again and again—there was no reason to listen—tomorrow exactly the same things would happen, and still everyone would forget.

There were other houses after yours, places I went alone, but there were none before and none like this. When I want to feel love I remember the dark thrill of it, the bright sound of glass, the sudden size and weight of my own heart in my own chest, how I knew it now, how it was real to me in my body, separate from lungs and liver and ribs, how it made the color of my blood surge against the back of my eyes, how nothing mattered anymore because I believed in this, my own heart, its will to live.

No lights, no alarm. We waited outside. Fifteen seconds. Years collapsed. We were scared of you, who you might be inside, terrified lady with a gun, some fool with bad aim and dumb luck.

The boost to the window, Emile lifting me, then I was there, in you, I swear, the smell that particular, that strong, almost a taste in your boy's room, his sweet milky breath under my tongue. Heat left low, but to us warm as a body, humid, hot.

My skin's cracked now, hands that cold, but I think of them plunged deep in your drawer, down in all your soft underbelly underclothes, slipping through all your jumbled silky womanthings.

I pulled them out and out.

I'm your worst fear. I touched everything in your house: all the presents just unwrapped: cashmere sweater, rocking horse, velvet pouch. I lay on your bed, smoking cigarettes, wrapped in your fur coat. How many foxes? I tried to count.

But it was Emile who wore the red dress, who left it crumpled on the floor.

Thin as he is, he couldn't zip the back—he's a boy, after all—he has those shoulders, those soon-to-be-a-man bones. He swore trying to squash his boy feet into the matching heels; then he sobbed. I had to tell him he had lovely feet, and he did, elegant, long—those golden toes. I found him a pair of stockings, one size fits all.

I wore your husband's pinstriped jacket. I pretended all the gifts were mine to offer. I pulled the pearls from their violet pouch.

We danced.

We slid across the polished wooden floor of your living room, spun in the white lights of the twinkling tree. And again, I tell you, I swear I felt the exact size and shape of things inside me, heart and kidney, my sweet left lung. All the angels hanging from the branches opened their glass mouths, stunned.

He was more woman than you, his thick hair wound tight and pinned. *Watch this*, he said, *chignon*.

I'm not lying. He transformed himself in front of your mirror, gold eyeshadow, faint blush. He was beautiful. He could have fooled anyone. Your husband would have paid a hundred dollars to feel Emile's mouth kiss all the places you won't touch.

Later the red dress lay like a wet rag on the floor. Later the stockings snagged, the strand of pearls snapped, and the beads rolled. Later Emile was all boy naked on the bathroom floor.

I'm the one who got away, the one you don't know; I'm the

long hairs you find under your pillow, nested in your drain, tangled in your brush. You think I might come back. You dream me dark always. I could be any dirty girl on the street, or the one on the bus, black lips, just-shaved head. You see her through mud-spattered glass, quick, blurred. You want me dead—it's come to this—killed, but not by your clean hands. You pray for accidents instead, me high and spacy, stepping off the curb, a car that comes too fast. You dream some twisted night road and me walking, some poor drunk weaving his way home. He won't even know what he's struck. In the morning he'll touch the headlight I smashed, the fender I splattered, dirt or blood. In the light he'll see my body rising, half-remembered, snow that whirls to a shape then blows apart. Only you will know for sure, the morning news, another unidentified girl dead, hit and run, her killer never found.

I wonder if you'll rest then, or if every sound will be glass, every pair of hands, mine, reaching for your sleeping son.

How can I explain?

We didn't come for him.

I'm your worst fear. Slivers of window embedded in carpet. Sharp and invisible. You can follow my muddy footprints through your house, but if you follow them backward they always lead here: to this room, to his bed.

If you could see my hands, not the ones you imagine, but my real hands, they'd be reaching for Emile's body. If you looked at Emile's feet, if you touched them you could feel us dancing.

This is all I want.

After we danced, we lay so close on your bed I dreamed we were twins, joined forever this way, two arms, three legs, two heads.

But I woke in my body alone.

Outside snow fell like pieces of broken light.

I already knew what had happened. But I didn't want to know.

I heard him in the bathroom.

I mean, I heard the water flow and flow.

I told myself he was washing you away, your perfume, your lavender oil scent. Becoming himself. Tomorrow we'd go.

I tried to watch the TV, the silent man in front of the map, the endless night news. But there it was, my heart again, throbbing in my fingertips.

I couldn't stand it—the snow outside; the sound of water; your little boy's head propped on the dresser, drifting on the wall; the man in the corner of the room, trapped in the flickering box: his silent mouth wouldn't stop.

I pounded on the bathroom door. I said: *Goddamn it, Emile—you're clean enough.* I said I had a bad feeling about this place. I said I felt you coming home.

But Emile, he didn't say a word. There was only water, that one sound, and I saw it seeping under the door, leaking into the white carpet. Still, I told lies to myself. I said: *Shit, Emile—what's going on*? I pushed the door. I had to shove hard, squeeze inside, because Emile was there, you know, exactly where you found him, face down on the floor. I turned him over, saw the lips smeared red, felt the water flow.

I breathed into him, beat his chest. It was too late, God, I know, his face pressed to the floor all this time, his face in the water, Emile dead even before he drowned, your bottle of Valium empty in the sink, the foil of your cold capsules punched through, two dozen gone—this is what did it: your brandy, your Valium, your safe little pills bought in a store. After all the shit we've done—smack popped under the skin, speed laced with strychnine, monkey dust—it comes to this. After all the nights on the streets, all the knives, all the pissed-off johns, all the fag-hating bullies prowling the Fenway with their bats, luring boys like Emile into the bushes with promises of sex. After all that, this is where it ends: on your clean wet floor.

Above the thunder of the water, Clare said: *He doesn't want to live.*

Clare stayed very calm. She said: *Turn off the water, go.*

I kept breathing into him. I watched the butterflies between his bones. No flutter of wings, and Clare said: *Look at him. He's dead.* Clare said she should know.

She told me what to take and where it was: sapphire ring, ivory elephant, snakeskin belt. She told me what to leave, what was too heavy, the carved bird, white stone. She reminded me: *Take off that ridiculous coat.*

I knew Clare was right; I thought, Yes, everyone is dead: the silent heads in the TV, the boy on the floor, my father who can't be known. I thought even you might be dead—your husband asleep at the wheel, your little boy asleep in the back, only you awake to see the car split the guard rail and soar.

I saw a snow-filled ravine, your car rolling toward the river of thin ice.

I thought, You never had a chance.

But I felt you.

I believed in you. Your family. I heard you going room to room, saying: *Who's been sleeping in my bed?*

It took all my will.

I wanted to love you. I wanted you to come home. I wanted you to find me kneeling on your floor. I wanted the wings on Emile's hips to lift him through the skylight. I wanted him to scatter: ash, snow. I wanted the floor dry, the window whole.

I swear, you gave me hope.

Clare knew I was going to do something stupid. Try to clean this up. Call the police to come for Emile. Not get out. She had to tell me everything. She said again: *Turn the water off.*

In the living room the tree still twinkled, the angels still hung. I remember how amazed I was they hadn't thrown themselves to the floor.

I remember running, the immaculate cold, the air in me, my lungs hard.

I remember thinking: I'm alive, a miracle anyone was. I wondered who had chosen me.

I remember trying to list all the decent things I'd ever done.

I remember walking till it was light, knowing if I slept, I'd freeze. I never wanted so much not to die.

I made promises, I suppose.

In the morning I walked across a bridge, saw a river frozen along the edges, scrambled down. I glided out on it; I walked on water. The snowflakes kept getting bigger and bigger, butterflies that fell apart when they hit the ground, but the sky was mostly clear, and there was sun.

Later, the cold again, wind and clouds. Snow shrank to ice. Small, hard. I saw a car idling, a child in the back, the driver standing on a porch, knocking at a door. Clare said: *It's open*. She meant the car. She said: *Think how fast you can go*. She told me I could ditch the baby down the road.

I didn't do it.

Later I stole lots of things, slashed sofas, pissed on floors.

But that day, I passed one thing by; I let one thing go.

When I think about this, the child safe and warm, the mother not wailing, not beating her head on the wall to make herself stop, when I think about the snow that day, wings in the bright sky, I forgive myself for everything else. □

GRANTA

KATE WHEELER
FUTURE SHOCK

Kate Wheeler was born in Oklahoma in 1955 and grew up in several countries in South America, where her father worked as a geologist exploring for petroleum; both her grandfathers had done the same thing before him. She graduated from Rice University and Stanford's creative writing program and has traveled widely in Europe, Asia and Australia. She quit the *Miami Herald* as a reporter because she found that she could not stick to facts. In 1988 she was ordained a Buddhist nun in Burma. Her collection of stories, *Not Where I Started From*, was published by Houghton Mifflin in 1993 and shortlisted for the PEN/Faulkner Award. She lives with her dog five minutes' walk from Harvard University. She writes travel journalism as well as fiction and also occasionally teaches meditation.

'Future Shock' is taken from her first novel, *When Mountains Walked*, which she is now working on with support from the National Endowment for the Arts.

Ingrid and her grandmother Althea were alone in Althea's bedroom. The day nurse was reading last April's *Glamour* in the sunroom at the end of the hall, where Althea kept her dead husband's fossil collection. The rest of the family—Ingrid's parents, Julia and Calvin; her older brother, David; and David's wife, Lisa—had gone to an exhibition of Peruvian gold. Ingrid had seen many of the pieces in Peru when she was there five years ago. Now she was cramming in extra time on duty with Grandma because she planned to leave Friday, two days before the others; she'd been happy to have a reason to send them all off.

Althea's neck strained. Her black, small eyes shifted swiftly, blinked, then fixed evilly on Ingrid.

'Get me a drink,' she commanded. 'A martini. A Pisco sour. Jackal urine. I don't care.'

Ingrid said, 'You know they say you shouldn't drink on painkillers. Would you like some orange juice, or milk?'

'No!'

'How about some water, then?' Ingrid lifted the half-full pitcher on her grandmother's night table.

Althea's chin pulled up toward her nose.

Ingrid stood, emptied the pitcher into a potted *dracaena*. 'It was getting old,' she said, in self-justification. She came and sat down again.

'Old,' Althea said. She pronounced it *aw-wulld*: it was an accusation.

Deep in the basement, metal clunked, and the heating came on, forcing hot air through the floor grates. It sounded exactly like the river rapid that had run behind a house where Ingrid had once lived in Nepal. Ingrid's father said Althea's house must be worth half a million. This price was astonishing to Ingrid: the house was not enormous, though its neighborhood, between Harvard and the river, had once been populated by loyalists to the British Crown.

Since arriving here a week ago from Bolivia, Ingrid had hardly gone outside. After six months in South America on a Catholic Charities contract, advising on nutrition and sanitation for pregnant and nursing mothers, her blood was tropic-thin, too thin for New England in March, and the raw light cut her as sharply as the icy, gritty air did. The back of her nose felt clogged with enormous molecules, dead skin covered up with an old-lady smell of rotting talcum. In fact, she thought, Althea was doing pretty well for it to be only this bad; the sickroom architecture suggested far worse possibilities, the walker's chrome bones, the blue kidney pan, the toilet on its frame, a tray holding a half-gnawed chop. Things utterly out of whack with all the other objects that had furnished her grandmother's life, things of wood, bone, stone, straw, cloth, clay.

'I could make coffee,' Ingrid offered now.

Althea's windy whisper gathered steam, became a voice that rose above the sounds of the heating system. 'You ought to know better. I'd never get to sleep tonight. Sun's over the yardarm: it's time to name your poison. Ah. Poison. That's what I really want. An asp.' In her dry mouth the pointed tongue clicked, protruded.

Althea had broken her right hip two weeks before, driving her blue Ford forty miles an hour through an intersection. Braking, skidding, she collided with the side of an elephantine white recycling truck. She claimed the driver had backed out of a store car park without looking. The truck driver, along with his helper and everyone else in the world, knew that Althea's license should have been revoked long ago. Althea's family all could testify to her capacity for carving her half of the road out of the middle; and they all knew that no amount of reasoning or pleading could stop her from taking the car out whenever she felt like it.

She'd never do it again.

'Elevated mortality rate,' the doctor said, 'within the year.'

Ingrid's mother faxed her in Bolivia offering the round-trip airfare. Better to come now, when Althea was as lucid and energetic as she'd ever be again, than to wait for a funeral.

Ingrid had always wondered how Althea could have submitted to her husband, Johnny Baines. Johnny had dragged his wife to the eighteen farthest corners of the earth, where he had abandoned her in cottages for months on end while he went off into the bush to gather data for a massive theory to predict earthquakes. Ahead of his time, the charitable said. Johnny's career was a simple index of his capacity for whim and obsession.

As his wife, Althea had been a rather shy woman, a plain dresser, not sweet at all: rather, she'd seemed stubbornly subdued, a use of stubbornness Ingrid disapproved of. Ingrid had always wanted better examples from her family than she received. Now it was going to be too late for grand reconciliations and gifts, a family scene illumined in surrounding darkness. Althea was slipping into a senility, or some kind of grand uncaring, as blithe as it was sinister. Today she'd called for poison; yesterday she was ranting about white slavers surrounding the house, ready to kidnap her and cart her off to the casbah. Her daughter, Julia, couldn't stand Althea's helplessness and kept correcting her: 'Mo*therr*!' Ingrid didn't like to see that, either. At least, she thought, Althea's lurid fantasies did not seem to indicate any readiness to die.

She reached for her grandmother's knuckly hand. 'Wish I could bring you what you want, Grandma.'

'You can't.' Althea jerked the hand back, slithered it under the mess of sheets, crumpled towels, newspapers, detritus that littered the bed. 'Leave me alone. I got to prepare to meet my goddamn Maker.'

'You're not dying.'

'Oh, shut up, of course I am. This is the end. Look.' Althea tossed back the top half of the blanket, opened both legs so that the knees fell sideways, exposing her inner thighs. The left thigh was silver-skinned, a fine fresh salmon; the right one looked small and dead, with banana bruises around the knee. An edge of gauze dressing peeked out below the Christ-like diaper taped across Althea's belly.

She was wearing her husband's socks and pajama top, these ten years after his death: one sock had a hole in the toe; the shirt was faded Black Watch flannel, missing one button, another fastened wrongly. Half of Althea's chest was visible. Like her left leg, the inside edge of her breast looked young, shapely, almost girlish.

'It's too cold in here,' Ingrid said, leaning forward to get the blanket off the floor. The thermostat was set at sixty-five degrees, the maximum Althea allowed.

'I'm not cold,' Althea said. 'I want you to see my legs.'

'I see.' Ingrid did see: humiliation, finality and the lack of any good reason for this and any other human damage. And if I cannot look at all that, Ingrid thought, my own fate will be harder to bear. 'And I'm very sorry.'

'Good,' said Althea, almost gently. 'I kept them out of the sun for nothing all these years. You, you're young. Might as well give up now. Make it easy on yourself. The only good thing about old age is that nobody cares, including you. You can do anything you want.'

'You had a husband,' Ingrid suggested. 'And a child. Doesn't it give you satisfaction, to look back on that?' She was afraid that this conversation might become morbid and unmanageable.

'Everything is a mistake,' said Althea extravagantly. 'Johnny was useless, and you see what Julia came to. Trying to see her face in the dinnerware. And that husband she pretends to adore. Calvin. My God! He's rigid as a plank. He's worse than Johnny. If my daughter had any gumption she'd have an affair.'

'Julia's my mother,' Ingrid said. 'Those are my parents.'

'Sorry,' said Althea. 'I thought you'd agree with me.'

Ingrid almost did, except that it didn't feel quite right not to suppress such feelings. Obviously Althea was no longer into suppression. Perhaps she was facing such an enormous compromise that any smaller ones seemed unnecessary. She'd become a famous bad patient. Outraged to find herself in a nursing home, she had made her feelings abundantly clear and secured her own release only four days after hip surgery. Here, at home, she had nurses day and night, and a physical therapist who came three times a week to force her to put weight on the leg. She was cordial enough to the family, but didn't make life easy for the staff; one of the day nurses claimed she was going to write a book about Althea. Her demands to be dressed in tennis whites or evening clothes for the visits of the physical therapist. Her complaints of abuse, including accusations that the caretakers were stealing painkillers in order to drug their children for perverted sex. 'Such a character,' they had begun to say of her.

'You're my favorite granddaughter, you know,' Althea now remarked. 'I certainly want you to know that.'

'I'm your only granddaughter,' Ingrid said.

'Don't get on your high horse because of it.'

'I wouldn't dream of it,' said Ingrid.

'You take after me,' Althea reflected. 'You've got my high

forehead. I see you running all over the world. That's good. You're opening new roads. Your mother's always been a frightened person, deep down. Julia. She's afraid to be a nigger. Afraid to be herself. Every day she wishes her face weren't so round.' This was probably true: Julia had often praised Ingrid as a child, saying what a pretty, heart-shaped face she had.

'Sssh!' Ingrid said. The nurse, in a room fifteen feet away, was black-Vietnamese. 'Please don't use racist terms.'

Althea shut her eyes. 'Nigger-nigger-nigger.' But she was whispering.

'Stop it, Grandma. I don't care how old you are.'

'I'll say it, I'm the only one who can. You didn't have to exist, you know. According to most people, you shouldn't.'

'If I didn't exist, I wouldn't care,' said Ingrid.

'Don't think it bothers me,' said Althea, 'but I'm very glad you're here.'

'I'm so glad you appreciate it. I came a long way. I'm leaving Friday.'

'I wish you'd stay,' Althea said. 'You're the only one who listens. You're much better than Julia, I'll say it again, right out: Julia's mad at me. She loves to see me like this.'

Ingrid wished there were some water left in the pitcher so that she could pour it over Althea.

'Grandma,' she said. 'If there's anybody home, if you're still in there, your daughter does love you. She may not be perfect, but neither are you and I. And personally I wouldn't mind being a member of another race. In fact, sometimes I wish I were.'

'Whatever Julia is, you are at least half as much of one,' Althea said. 'Any children you have will receive one quarter of the blood. She just heard too many rumors, people saying I slept with an Indian. I don't mean an Indian, I mean an Indian Indian. Don't believe Julia, poor thing, when she talks about me and that priest. I never did sleep with him and I never will. He was not the red kind of Indian, he was brown. Or yellow, or gold. Slant eyes. A beautiful, lovely man. In a way he was my real friend. He gave me himself. Oh, Father, Father. If I could have him again, just one night. Johnny's great-grandmother was a Cherokee, thank God! But you're not Johnny's anyway.'

'Mom never says anything about a priest. I guess I don't understand you, Grandma,' Ingrid said. She had heard about Althea staying in convents while Johnny went on his long field trips, but that was all.

'Don't lie, of course you do. You've got my soul. You could have done the same thing I did. You and I, chased all over the world by the same old devil.' Here Althea paused, and looked up at Ingrid, who just stared at her. 'In fact, I'm going to leave you my house. You can sell it, if you want. Never meant a thing to me. I had all the luck but never knew it. There, that's my last will and testament. Bring my lawyer,' she called past Ingrid's shoulder.

Turning, Ingrid saw the day nurse who had come to the bedroom door with her bag of things to wave goodbye.

'You!' Althea cried. 'Can't you hear me? Too much hair over your ears? Get a haircut!'

The nurse was a tall, glamorous young woman with a flipped, straightened, Barbie-doll perm; she rolled her eyes theatrically at Ingrid, and said, as if Althea did not exist, 'Olena is coming in twenty minutes, mind if I leave?'

'Fine. Thanks. Bye,' said Ingrid, while her grandmother glared in silence.

The woman disappeared from sight. Ingrid could not remember her name. Really, she thought, it was terrible that they'd all be abandoning Grandma here in this condition. Althea had friends, even one old fellow who seemed to be an admirer, but they were all too old to prevail against the slackness of these agency nurses. And Althea's maunderings and imprecations would tax the most loyal person; Ingrid understood how the nurses would, finally, just ignore her, not try to decipher what she really needed. She'd seen it many times. No matter where in the world you were sick, you needed family to take care of you and feed you properly.

'The nurse is gone. I'll get you a drink,' Ingrid said, taking the pitcher off the bedside table.

'After all, I don't have to drive anywhere,' Althea said.

Ingrid had forgotten about the martinis, the jackal urine; she'd been planning to bring water only. The conversation had put her in a strange mood. She wanted to let go of everything, and simultaneously to celebrate. Althea's constitution was still powerful; it wouldn't kill her to have a drink. Probably just soothe her a little, make her more amusing.

She went down the basement steps, found a bottle of Clos de Vougeot. It was a 1986, and Calvin would probably miss it, but it was one of the few names she recognized.

When she came back up with the open bottle and two tumblers on a tray, her grandmother was staring out the window. White afternoon light slanted in through the shredded damask curtains.

They held their glasses to the light. 'Ruby, pink, brown,' said Ingrid. 'Black, gold and purple,' Althea said.

They drank together in silence, one glass and then a second. Ingrid began looking forward to what Althea might say after glass number two. It wasn't the truth she was telling, that was for sure.

'I see Johnny's face,' Althea said sadly. 'I didn't tell my story right. But I was trying. I hope you will stay with me for the rest of your life. I mean my life. It would be the happiest day. Already is. It won't be long now. I haven't told them, but it's hurting me to breathe. The only good thing about old age is nobody cares about you any more. So you can say and do exactly as you please. That's the ticket. You'll all find out. You'll all forgive me, one day.'

The front door opened, letting in the wet, ripping sound of tires on the street. Boots stamped at the entry. Althea's knees began to tremble; her heels fluttered against the mattress. 'What's that?' It was a stage whisper.

'It's just Olena,' Ingrid said. She pulled the blanket over her grandmother's legs. 'Don't worry.' But the legs still shook.

'Olena?'

'That night nurse. The one who gives massage.'

'Oh yes. The fat one. Olena. What kind of a name is that?'

Ingrid put one hand on Althea's jacking knee. 'It's Russian. She gave it to herself. Are you all right?' She squeezed the kneecap, hoping to warm it into submission.

'I can't remember if I like her. Some of these gals, I think they're coming to drag me straight to hell.'

'She's OK, I guess.'

'Olena. Margarina. If you say so,' Althea said. Her leg

relaxed, but quivered again as soon as Ingrid lifted her hand. 'She ought to pick something less greasy. If I were someone's mother, I'd never name her after a petroleum product.'

'It's her grandmother's name, Grandma. Her mother named her Susan.' Sometime last week, Olena had had to be reimbursed for a bag of groceries, and had asked Calvin to write the check to 'Susan Witz'. 'Olena wanted to honor her female ancestors. She told Calvin she'd had five names in this life, if her two marriages counted.'

'Ha. Well I've had two, myself,' Althea said.

'Right. Wait here, I'll be back in a second.' Ingrid grabbed the wine bottle and ran on tiptoe toward the upstairs bathroom. Passing the stairs, she could see the back hem of Olena's denim skirt bobbing as Olena replaced her snow boots with apostolic sandals. Olena would notice boozy breath; she made all of them feel discredited, defensive.

Ingrid bit off a dab of toothpaste and stashed the Clos de Vougeot under the sink behind some dried-up sponges, where it took on the appearance of a poison. Four inches left, ten dollars' worth; and she hadn't yet focused on its nuances, which she might need to describe to Calvin, should he notice the theft. Olena was lumbering up the stairs. She was fifty, but with her fine transparent skin, round red cheeks and unworried forehead, she looked miraculously preserved, at least until her smile revealed small, brownish teeth.

'Hello!' Olena said. 'It's snowing out! The sidewalks are terrible! How's everything in here? It's so nice and cozy!'

Althea called from her bedroom in a parrot's querulous, lost voice. 'Hello?'

'Olena's here!' said Ingrid. And to Olena: 'Everything's fine, though she was anxious a minute ago. Thanks for coming.'

Together they walked into the bedroom, saw Althea, a murky shape, struggling to raise herself. The room seemed much darker than when Ingrid had left it.

'What do you two want?' Althea said.

'Hello, it's me, Mrs Baines!' Olena said, brushing past Ingrid. 'Sorry I'm so late. Were you sleeping? Why are you lying here in the dark?'

She flicked on the bedside lamp, fixed pillows, ran her hand under the blanket. 'Your feet are blocks of ice. Would you like some water? How are you today?'

'Fine, and yes, and no, and please and thank you,' Althea said. 'Oh, I'm very well, as you see, just living the life of Riley.' She cleared her throat and glared around the room.

Olena laughed. 'We're feisty today.'

Althea settled back against the pillows and assumed an expression verging on meekness. 'You'll give me my rub?'

'Certainly.'

'I've got pins and needles in both feet. And I'm feeling very nervous. I get the heebie-jeebs lying on my back all day. But you'll fix that. Won't you? You'll make me relax?' Althea was breathing through her mouth. Panting, almost; she had bright red, allergic-looking maps on her cheeks. Ingrid regretted giving her the wine. It seemed to have increased Althea's frailty, so that her tough talk no longer seemed the sign of a strong mind, but rather of a cornered desperation. Maybe this was an effect of Olena's presence. 'Certainly,' Olena said. 'Have you taken your anticoagulant?'

'I've eaten nothing but pills since dawn.'

Ingrid leaned on the door jamb, not volunteering to refill the empty water pitcher Olena set at her elbow, on top of the chest of drawers. Instead she watched her grandmother blinking with heron-like dignity while the nurse refolded the newspaper, closed the curtains, stacked the lunch tray with an assortment of dirty dishes and debris.

'How about rolling on to your stomach.' Olena pumped a gob of cream into her palm.

'Yes, yes, yes,' Althea said.

Snow was falling slowly past the tall windows, big flat flakes like shreds of ash. Some flakes were traveling upward. Inside and out, all distinctions were vanishing into pewter-colored flatness. Ingrid went into the living room to finish the bottle of wine. The small front garden was strafed with shafts of near-daylight, which was making the snow glow with a weird, extraneous brilliance. She curled into a pink wing chair that smelled faintly of cat. One of the good things about her grandmother was that there were sixteen possible ways that this upholstery could have acquired its aroma, including that Althea might have picked the armchair off the sidewalk on trash day, enamored of its claw feet. Althea had never had a cat, but she'd lived close to the bone for most of her life; her husband had not exactly been an economic miracle.

Ingrid rolled the blood-thick liquid on her tongue. Leather, velvet, smoke, rose petals. At the end a quick, unpleasant catch. Red wine always affected her: it made her want to gnash and weep and bleed. The same with cello music; or those Indian sunsets where you looked across the darkling plain at serried domes and palms and mounds diminishing into dusty earth tones, and it always seemed so clear that birth and death had been going on for much too long without any tangible result. No benefit to anyone.

But in India futility became transcendent. Here it was just grim, horrifying, so cold outside, her grandmother helpless upstairs in a house that now, in the dark, filled with ghosts of those who had died here. Clearly Althea would never inhabit any other home. Johnny had suffered his first headaches here, the early signs of the brain tumor that killed him, which Ingrid thought of as a coagulated obsession.

How could Althea have stayed with him?

Grandpa Johnny, in his scientist's costume, black-framed eyeglasses, stained khaki trousers. He had frightened Ingrid as far back as she could remember. His barking laugh. Incessant, excessive opinionating. As soon as she was old enough, Ingrid had begun to wonder why, and how, Grandma Althea could put up with him. Talking in portents, never listening; then leaving her alone for months and months, without money, in places where she did not speak the language.

According to Julia, Althea had funded Johnny's megalomanic career, using up most of a small inheritance from her family in Philadelphia. So Julia had complained, though infrequently and discreetly. 'Ingrid, you and David would have a little if she hadn't spent so much on your grandfather.'

Whenever Althea and Johnny came to visit their daughter's family—and they'd come often, too, wherever Calvin and Julia and David and Ingrid had been living, Ecuador or Singapore or Holland—they'd arrived in a welter of psychological noise, bearing many heavy bags full of Johnny's instruments and books and blasting caps. However long they stayed, for days or weeks or months, Althea would take over the kitchen and servants in supposed compensation for her and Johnny's impositions. Once, she had induced a Malay gardener to cut down the gardenia tree, hoping for a view of the ocean, she said. She would produce, either herself or through the medium of a cook, strange foods: rings of aspic; homemade sauerkraut; beef stewed with canned peaches, cooked inside a pumpkin, which she would serve with a flourish, claiming first that it was 'a gaucho dish from the Argentine', next, 'a Nicaraguan feast, a cane cutters' party dish'.

At the last minute Althea and Johnny's existence had risen above this peripatetic eking out: Johnny got the first, and last, steady, salaried job of his life as an associate professor of seismology at Harvard, on the strength of his only concrete achievement, having measured the tensions in stable rocks and found them to be greater than anyone expected. He and Althea bought a house in Cambridge, this house, where they lived for five years, until Johnny died.

After his death, however, his predictions had come true: an enormous earthquake in Chile, an underwater tremor in the Ryukuyus or some such archipelago. These had been based on some kind of global intuition, an assemblage or compilation of too many factors ever to make sense on paper. Johnny's theories remained unfinished, inscrutable. An officeful of spiral notebooks, each one crammed with notations in tiny, tiny handwriting, had been willed to Harvard, where they sat in boxes in a moldy basement, waiting for the right disciple to decipher them and proclaim Johnny's genius.

Upstairs, Althea's massage was an intensity of silence. The snow was falling thicker now, accumulating in ridges on the top of the chain-link fence and on the branches of the rhododendrons. And Calvin's enormous white rental car was urging itself up the driveway, wipers full blast.

Ingrid turned on the light. It had been dark for an hour.

Calvin, Julia, David, Lisa blew in with a doorful of snow, their arms full of crisp, white takeout bags. They boasted cheerfully about how they'd overcome the snow, the rush-hour traffic.

Except Julia, whose face was implacable. 'How was Grandma today?' she asked.

'Fine,' Ingrid said, 'we had a nice long talk.'

But Julia had started up the stairs without listening for the answer. Calvin went up behind her.

'She's asleep,' Ingrid cried, then stood staring after her parents, trying not to burst into tears. She should never have finished that bottle of wine.

Her older brother touched her shoulder from behind. 'Mom's freaked. You understand. It's her mother. It's a big deal to her.'

'It's a big deal to me, too,' Ingrid said, following David and Lisa into the kitchen, where they unbagged half a dozen oblong plastic containers.

'Well, well, Miss Purple Tongue,' said David. 'What have you been doing all afternoon?'

'I had a bit of wine. But I had a long talk with Althea too,' Ingrid said. 'Boy, was she wild. Did you ever hear about her affair with a priest?'

'What? No way.'

'She kept denying it, and then sort of saying there had been rumors about Mom being illegitimate.' The enormity of what Althea had been suggesting hit Ingrid all of a sudden, and she began to laugh. 'Complete wish fulfillment.'

'Don't tell Mom!'

'Well, if it had been me, I might have done it,' Ingrid said.

'Me too, I think,' said Lisa.

'What?' David said in mock alarm.

'You don't leave me alone for months on end,' Lisa said.

Slowly the real heft and weight and proportion of Althea's life were becoming apparent to Ingrid. One day Ingrid's life too would be seen from the point of view of its completion: it would have assumed a form. After dinner, when Calvin and Julia had gone to their hotel, and David and Lisa had retired to the downstairs bedroom, she'd have to ask Althea if she had been in love with Johnny for her whole life or for only part of it. And whether she felt it had all been worthwhile. Surely her grandmother was lucid enough to answer questions like that.

Surely those were exactly the kinds of topics she had, in her garbled way, been trying to discuss.

Julia and Calvin came back down to the feast now spread out on the dining-room table.

'Your grandmother's asleep,' Calvin reported. 'Ingrid, do you think she'll get better?'

'I don't know too much about old people, or long-term care,' said Ingrid. 'But I don't see why not. She's certainly got an outrageous spirit.'

Julia said, 'There are some wonderful places round Boston where it's semi-independent. Like having your own apartment. Calvin and I are going to visit a few of them tomorrow.'

'Althea won't like that idea,' Ingrid said.

'What do you know about Althea?' Julia said. 'Just because you've spent an afternoon with her. What else do you think we're going to do?'

'Wouldn't these nurses cost the same? She could just stay home.'

'The insurance covers them short-term. She'd need to sell her house to pay for them. It's a Catch-22,' said Calvin.

'What about a companion?' David said. 'When she can walk, when she gets a little better. Some Salvadoran person. They wouldn't need qualifications. I'm sure Althea would get along fine.'

'I'm looking into it, believe me,' Calvin said.

This is a dream from which I must awaken, Ingrid thought. She felt four years old. 'Excuse me,' she said, and went up the stairs. Olena was knitting in the sunroom, her hands focused under a cone of light. She dropped half her work carefully into her lap, put one finger to her lips. Ingrid nodded, but defied her and ducked into Althea's darkened room. 'Grandma,' she said, but there was no answer.

The skin of Althea's hand was the texture of vinyl, like simulated skin. If Ingrid was not mistaken, it was beginning to drop down to room temperature. She turned on the lights, saw the lips set hard into an expression of final disapproval: proof that Althea was no longer there. □